Rise of the W

Book 1 of the 'Reaper' saga

By Dougal Reed

ISBN # 979-8-5161-9710-9

Dedications

This book is dedicated to:

The mighty Kaz, my love and my world, who has stuck by me and encouraged me in her own resolute way.

Everyone has a Dave in their life, and mine is my brother. He and his family are shining stars in my life.

My mum, wonderful in every way. Sorry about the swearing.

Prologue

Strongroom with a view

The night in the city of Triana was a dark and silent thing. Lights were not allowed after curfew, and any noise would bring the merciless guards running to your doorstep. No-one was allowed to disturb the queen's sleep.

Mitsey Boo sat on the narrow ledge and looked down upon the sprawling rooftops of the fairy queen's palace. Her perch was four-hundred feet above the palace walls. Above her, and within her reach, were the pink tiles that covered the tallest of the palace's five spires. The tower's white-stone walls were almost flawless, but Mitsey was an accomplished climber. She had climbed slowly and carefully, taking most of the night to accomplish the mammoth task. Now that she had finally reached the ledge, she took a moment to catch her breath. Mitsey had perfect night-sight, and so from her viewpoint, she could see the whole royal complex and the small circular city that surrounded it.

The pink tower upon which she was sitting sprouted from the centre of the gaudy palace; the other four spires were on each corner of the walls surrounding it. Each had a different pastel shade – blue and yellow looked north out onto the city's trade district, and green and terracotta coloured the south wall.

Many terrible things happened in the terracotta tower. Horrific things, only spoken of in hushed tones behind closed doors. No prisoner ever came out of it in one piece, let alone alive. Mitsey knew full well that she would spend the few remaining days of her life inside that terrible place if they caught her today. She was anxious to avoid that fate, but the abject fear of it fuelled her. It made her feel alive.

Anyone looking up at the ledge would never have spotted her. She had taken every precaution possible to avoid detection by the palace's numerous security patrols. She'd covered her light green skin in night-time camouflage, and her bright eyes hid behind tinted goggles. Goblins were known for their abilities to evade detection. Among her kind, Mitsey was the best and had no trouble avoiding even the exceptional hearing and sight of the fairies. For this mission, Mitsey was employing her talents as a thief. If she succeeded, her place in faie history would be assured.

Tonight, Mitsey was on vital Defiance business, a nickname given to their resistance movement hundreds of years ago. The name had stuck despite their leader, Sintra's, preference. She felt it much harder to find something that wasn't officially there.

Mitsey sat there, chewing on some moistened fruit, a rare treat these days. The energy she had used getting to this point had been considerable, so she needed to take a little time to replenish some of it, despite there being a lot left for her to accomplish before the sun came up.

Mitsey broke her reverie and got back to business. She carefully removed four of the large, oval tiles from the edge of the spire's roof and slipped silently through the hole she'd created. She fished around in her pack, and once she'd found the special hooks she'd prepared, she quietly restored the roof to its previous state. Before she hung the last tile, she took a long look at the surrounding city. She sighed and made a wish that she would see it again tonight.

The sun hadn't broken the horizon yet, so she still had time. The climb had gone well.

Using all her skills, she stealthily made her way out of the tower loft. Mitsey crept down the spiral of the white-marble staircase until she reached the door to the fairy queen's trophy room. It was a heavy, thick metal door with a spoked wheel in the centre, guarded by two heavily armoured palace guards. These creatures were orcish elite, a large, particularly vicious breed of regular orcs raised as killers from birth. They were fierce, vindictive fighters that Mitsey had no hope of defeating alone. Over four-hundred of them were in the employ of the queen, along with another one-hundred ogres. They guarded Triana, a city with a population of only three-thousand, and most of those were slaves.

Sintra had warned her these monsters would be here. Such an important room would never be left unguarded. The problem was, no-one Mitsey had spoken to could be confident that her solution would be effective against such creatures. They were a tough breed.

The goblin donned her custom-made breathing apparatus and withdrew a heavy demijohn of green liquid from her pack. She carefully removed the bottle's cork, making sure it didn't make a noise and betray her presence. She laid it down horizontally on the inside edge of the stair's spiral. Olive coloured goop started to glug out from the jar's wide neck and flow slowly down the steps. As the liquid touched the stairs' pure marble, it reacted, and dense smoke erupted from the stone. The corrosive goop oozed down further until it reached the landing upon which the guards slouched.

Satisfied that she had released enough of her concoction, Mitsey carefully lifted the bottle upright and recorked it. There was about a quarter of its original contents remaining. She allowed herself a small smile as the smoke spread, engulfing the stairway. After a short while, Mitsey heard coughing as the miasma began to overcome the guards. Then she heard two loud thuds as her victims succumbed to the fumes. The guards hadn't managed to utter so much as a squeak in alarm. The goblin knew that the smoke would reach the tower's base in about ten minutes, and its appearance would raise the alarm. The clock had started; she needed to get this next part done with all haste.

Using her natural mana-sight on the door, she saw what she had expected, the delicate webbing of a powerful protection spell. The lock was magical, built to defy everyone who did not have access to its power. This place was inside the queen's mana-restriction dome, a shield constructed to keep magical energy in and restrict what got through to the outside world. The magic here would be active.

That is how the fairy queen had enslaved all the faie. Mitsey could feel her anger rising at the thought. Her people had fled to this world when the humans threatened to eradicate them from their original homes on Earth. The queen had offered them safety in her realm, and the faie had readily accepted her offer. However, almost as soon as the waygate they'd fled through had crumbled away, the evil creature created a magical regulation dome that encapsulated the realm's one source of power and only allowed enough energy to escape to permit the faie to stay alive. The rest, the winter fairies hoarded – evil, greedy bastards, every one of them. The queen then decreed that unless the faie submitted to servitude, she would cut off the energy flow altogether and destroy every creature beyond the dome.

Mitsey admonished herself severely. She had stupidly let her mind wander. After a deep breath to steady herself, she began to concentrate hard. Using a technique that had taken her many months to perfect, she syphoned off the mana used to create the door's protection spell. She shivered as she absorbed the casting's raw power. The luxury of having spare magic inside her felt decadent. It was for this feeling that the resistance was fighting. It was a shame the mana was useless to her.

She heard the lock mechanism clunk as the spell finally died, and the locking wheel released. Mitsey then wound the door bolts open and pulled the door, which swung outwards smoothly on well-constructed hinges. Mitsey slipped inside. She knew that she had taken two-hundred and thirty-three seconds to open the door because her internal clock kept track. It irked her that she'd spent at least sixty of those seconds lost in her thoughts.

Staying pressed against the circular wall, she eased herself a third of the way around, clockwise. Mitsey inhaled sharply when she spotted her objective. There it lay in all its glory, underneath a delicate glass hood. Even in its dormant state, it was beautiful. The intricately cut keystone-crystal glowed with a deep blue light. A finely crafted golden frame encased the magical gemstone, and a delicate chain attached to the encapsulation turned the crystal into a pendant. It was amazing to think that a priestess had found someone capable of holding this artefact. At least, so she claimed. If true, though, there may yet be hope for all of them.

She took a few deep breaths to slow her quickening heartbeat and stuck her jaw out in determination. Mitsey steeled her nerves. She reached into her pocket and fished out the enchanted velvet pouch that the elders had prepared for the task. Any mortal that touched the crystal would instantly crumble to dust, a victim of a dire curse that the fairy queen had placed upon it. The queen was a master of curse magic, and Mitsey did not doubt the dire consequences that could befall her. The small pouch was the only thing that would save her from becoming a desiccated pile of powder.

Mitsey took another deep breath. In a heartbeat, she'd flipped the dome up and away, not caring that it shattered noisily on the floor. With a swift movement, she pulled the pouch over the glowing pendant and pulled the drawstring tight.

A high-pitched wail sounded throughout the palace, its tone rising and falling. That was her signal to flee. On her way out, she grabbed the remaining goop in the bottle and threw it down the stairs as hard as she could manage. She didn't wait to hear it shatter. Instead, she fled like a breeze, back up the twisting staircase.

Mitsey had prepared for this mission over the last few months, and her focus had been mainly on her escape. She was an accomplished engineer and had worked hard on something new that would enable it. At least, that was the plan. When she made it back to the tower's attic, she removed the tiles again and took off her jacket.

She climbed back out onto the ledge and pulled a cord hanging down from the harness she wore. Wings mounted on her back, unfurled, and extended outward. Mitsey took a deep breath, crossed her fingers, and leapt outward into the air. She sighed deeply with relief as her invention took her weight, and the wings bore her quickly away from the palace.

Now all she had to do was land safely.

****_****

The room smelled dank and abandoned. Many years ago, its original occupants had been dragged off to the terracotta tower by the royal guards. The floorboards were just as warped and twisted as the rough plank door that hung loosely in the corner. The wattle of the walls had long since dropped most of their daub onto the floorboards.

Sintra hefted the velvet pouch in her hand. The small drawstring bag was covered in sigils and wards, protecting everyone from the object inside. While her acute elven eyes could easily see the tiny, intricate runes, she had no idea what they meant. She looked at it thoughtfully as she considered what Mitsey had gone through to retrieve it.

The queen's screams of rage had been heard throughout the city when she learnt of the pendant's theft. Entwaine, the queen's sadistic advisor and second in command, was already out on the streets with hundreds of elite orcs, fairies, and ogres. They'd flooded the city, searching door to door for the item and the culprits that stole it. Corpses of many servants and slaves already littered the streets as rough justice was applied without hesitation.

"All of that suffering for this thing," Sintra said as she held the pouch up for the other elf in the room to see. "They will be searching for this for weeks. Hundreds are likely to suffer as a result."

The elf standing in front of Sintra was standing rigidly to attention. She had long raven hair, softly curved features, and radiant eyes that were a vivid shade of azure blue. Her expression was severe, though. She was currently looking over Sintra's shoulder at something.

"Isabelle? Dammit! Are you even listening to me?" Sintra asked, the frustration evident in her voice.

"Yes, of course, Sintra. Blah, blah, people are dying, blah. People are dying every day. One day those winged psychopaths will run out of people to murder. That is what we are fighting to stop. Is it not?" Isabelle replied, her gaze flickering briefly to look at Sintra. Her voice was snarky, her natural cynicism radiating through her words.

Sintra looked at Isabelle sternly. She shook her head and clasped her hands tightly in front of her. Then she thought about what her friend and co-conspirator had endured throughout her life, and her look softened. She had every right to be angry at the life into which she had been born. All she had ever known was the resistance. Sintra had rescued her when Isabelle was just a young elfling. Her parents had once lived here in this house until they had been dragged off to the terracotta tower, never to return. She'd been forced into a life she had grown to hate, but it was that hatred that made her one of their best operatives. She was not only a fierce, relentless fighter, but an academic and dedicated priestess of the Wayfarer too. It was Isabelle that had spent many years tracking their old god down and creating a desperate plan to retrieve him.

"Isabelle of Triana. I have answered your summons. Your plan is rash, but it has my blessing. I have seen the possible outcomes, and most end badly for you," a mature, stern voice said from behind Sintra.

Sintra jumped and spun around to face the unexpected voice in shock. Stood there was a lady of slightly advancing years, clad in flowing silver robes that sparkled when she moved. The woman had radiant golden eyes and seemed to be only partially there. No wonder Isabelle had been distracted.

"Uhm! Uhm! My sincerest apologies, Lady Fate. I did not realise you had already joined us." The elf's mind wanted to crawl away and hide under a rock as the goddess' golden eyes seemed to pierce her entire existence. Fate scowled at her and then turned her stare on Isabelle.

Sintra knew that this was an auspicious occurrence for the elves. Gods and goddesses could not usually leave their Pantheon, but Isabelle was a priestess and had issued a powerful divine summons in the temple earlier. Isabelle needed divine assistance for the next stage of her plan, and so she went out and got it. Her friend was single-minded in the extreme.

"Are you certain this is something you are ready to do, child?" Fate asked Isabelle.

"Lady Fate, I wish to strike a bargain. I offer you my soul when I die, in exchange for taking me to him," Isabelle said, without bothering to answer the goddess' question.

The goddess snorted in disgust at the elf's words. Her eyes flared a brighter gold, and she looked annoyed. "I do not want your soul, foolish elf," she said. She shook her head as she said the words. "You have no value to me. I want our Reaper back. You already have my goodwill for finding him. Now fetch him for me. Fail, and I might yet take your life, simply out of spite."

"Isabelle, if this goes wrong, you will surely die," Sintra said. Her face was full of concern for her friend, knowing that she would never back down from this. She also knew that Fate's ultimatum would only drive Isabelle harder. She was stubborn that way.

Fate closed her eyes, and her image faded slightly. "You have two minutes to say your goodbyes. It is nearly time."

Sintra dashed through a nearby door and quickly returned with a battered-looking satchel. She opened the flap on top and dropped the magical pouch containing the crystal inside. "This contains everything we can offer him. Be lucky, my friend. We will pray for you."

"To the street," Fate said urgently.

The two elves dashed down the grimy stairs of Defiance's headquarters, and the door-guard opened the outside door to let them pass. The guard never saw the goddess pass her by, but she yelped as she felt it happen. Fate grinned mischievously; spooking mortals was one of the only pleasures she had left.

The elves stood beside the road and waited. Sintra's heart fell when she heard the marching of heavy feet approaching their position. A squad of elite orcs by the sound and stench of it. The street corner obscured their approach, but her acute elven senses could easily pick them out from the city's daytime hubbub.

She hastily handed the satchel to Isabelle. "Good luck," she said. "We are all depending on you." Then she sprinted off down the road, away from the approaching troops. There was nothing more she could do for Isabelle. Now, self-preservation was all that mattered.

"Your friend is wise to flee. Take a half-step to your right and a full step forward," Fate instructed Isabelle.

She did as Fate had told her to and nervously listened to the approaching troops. They would be rounding the corner in seconds. Then she heard it. The sound of a heavy horse's hooves moving quickly across cobblestones. The sound came from the opposite direction of the troops' approach, but there was nothing there when Isabelle looked.

"Pay attention and get ready to jump upwards. I can only guide you, not lift you," Fate said.

The source of the pounding hooves should have been in sight by now. Then Isabelle saw a mist in the middle of the street that swirled and quickly darkened. A vertical, swirling disk of darkness engulfed an area twenty feet in diameter and out of that hurtled a huge, black horse. The horse's eyes were wild, and foam flecked its mouth and flanks. It was evident that it had been running hard for a while.

The troops rounded the corner at that moment, and a cry went up. Heavy, orcish boots pounded towards them, seemingly unafraid of the wall of equine muscle that was thundering their way.

"We are leaving," Fate said. Her voice was bright with amusement. "Three, two, one, jump."

Isabelle felt firm hands grip her under her armpits, and she leapt as hard as she could. The world had gone mad, and she was just going along with it. She shot upward and saw a robe-clad arm shoot forward from behind her and grab the pommel of the horse's saddle just as it arrived within the goddess' reach. The forward momentum of the animal and the upward inertia from her jump created a beautiful arc that landed her firmly in the horse's saddle –perfectly timed poetry in motion.

As soon as she had touched the saddle, everything started to fade from view. They passed right through the rampaging soldiers, and some of them toppled over in fright and confusion. Then the world around the elf went black. She could sense the motion and hear the creak of the saddle as the horse pounded through the void around her, but she could see nothing. There was just emptiness.

Isabelle began to feel the arcane vacuum pulling at her form. Faie creatures could not maintain their shape outside of a magical field, and in the void, there was nothing. She hastily stuffed the bag into the horse's saddlebag, hoping that it was a safe place. She would not be capable of holding it soon, which was a severe oversight. She prayed to the god she was searching for that this would not turn out to be a serious flaw in her plan.

There was a loud roaring of something approaching fast and then a thump. The void winked out of existence, and Isabelle found herself floating above the horse in her manifest form. Whatever world she was now in, it had no magical energy. If mistaken about her objective, death would claim her within a week. She didn't have enough spare power to keep her cohesion for longer, even as a pinprick of light.

Isabelle glanced behind her and saw that Fate had disappeared. *If I die, at least I died trying*, she thought bitterly.

Chapter 1

Casting the first stone

The driver of the slave wagon swore loudly. He had just hit someone. He knew it because he got a brief glimpse of the startled man in the van's dim headlights just before he heard the loud thump. The vehicle slowly came to a halt as poorly maintained components squealed and protested. He looked across at his companion, who shrugged.

They sat there for a minute, getting over the shock, contemplating their next move. Eventually, they both reached the same decision. The driver drew his knife while his companion began inexpertly loading the crossbow he'd only recently acquired. If the man they'd hit lived, then they'd take him as a slave. If he died, then no one would lose any sleep over the incident.

Nearby, Isabelle's manifestation, which was a tiny, glowing orb of light, pulsed green with relief as the battered body landed close to where she hovered. She watched as the last remnants of life left the man's body. At the exact moment of death, a mighty curse shattered within him, sending out a turbulent shockwave of decaying magic that rippled away from his torso. Isabelle felt sickened when it passed through her. Only then did she understand the obscene amount of mana that must have gone into casting such a wicked spell. She knew that his nemesis, the fairy queen, had put the curse on him, but the power of it still surprised her.

As the curse magic faded, a pinprick of utter darkness appeared and began to expand rapidly. Its edges swirled and protested as they were forced outward until they'd formed a rough circle, nearly ten feet in diameter. A human form made entirely of shadows stepped out, followed by a scintillating ball of energy that pulsed between blinding luminescence and sheer darkness. Isabelle watched in fear and fascination as the humanoid shadow turned to face the strange form. She also noticed how much magical energy was flowing through the portal and wasted no time in soaking as much of it up as she could.

<It appears one of your favourites has been waiting for you,> the ball of energy thought to the shadow man. There was humour in the words it spoke.

Isabelle was a gifted telepath, a rare thing among elves, so she could overhear the telepathic conversation between the strange beings. All faie creatures could communicate using thoughts, but only a telepath could read minds, allowing them to eavesdrop on mental communications and thoughts not intended for them.

<She seems to be able to hear us too,> it thought. <No matter. I have placed your beloved box on wheels in the primary nexus not far from here. She has been sitting in a void for millennia and needs to replenish some energy before she can be helpful to you. I believe the elf has brought your keystone crystal with her, so you should find your way there easily enough. You have much to do, son. It is time to get off your arse and get to work.>

There was a mental chuckle from the human shadow. <Father, there is such a thing as too much relaxation. Living with you has been so dull. While it was nice to spend so much time together, you really need to create better games. Nearly two-thousand years of chess is just too much.>

The entity snorted derisively. <I believe you were at least five-thousand games down at the last count. You go and play with the mortals. As you're a god, they might even let you win a few games.

I will let the Pantheon know you are back in business. Do not forget that you have less than ten days before your energy fails, so fix that nexus quickly.>

<I was not created yesterday, father; I will get it done, I promise,> the human shadow said. With that, it moved over to the corpse and lay down so that it engulfed the entire body with plenty of shadow to spare.

The ball of energy sank back through the portal, then both the progenitor and the gateway vanished with a loud pop.

Well, that answers that age-old question, Isabelle thought. Their god's origin was the single most argued point within the elven priesthood. Now she knew. He really was the son of the creator.

An intense, white light poured from the corpse, encasing the body, which began to writhe and convulse as its divinity was forcefully restored. After a few seconds, the light transformed. It became a softer, golden colour that lovingly caressed the prone figure. Bones began to knit, and lesions healed. All damage became undamaged as the divine magic worked its miracles. As the spectacle came to its conclusion, the glow changed to an energetic blue. The body began to grow, and musculature swelled to fit the shadow that engulfed it. By the time the magical light had faded, the body almost gleamed with vitality. The enforced humanity from the curse was utterly gone.

Isabelle's god had reawakened, and she examined him more closely. Her light inadvertently turned blue as she gawked at the magnificent body lying in front of her. Her vision wasn't up to the standards of her usual form, but she could easily recognise that he was an extremely handsome creature. His six-foot-three frame disguised the sheer broadness of his powerful-looking shoulders. His whole body was muscular, yet in an athletic way. His face was toned, with a rectangular shape, created by pronounced cheekbones and a strong jaw. His striking white hair matched his steely eyes that were so intense it was as if they could see straight into her soul even in his unconscious state. She would have to do some repentance chants to make up for the impure thoughts she was having.

****_****

Consciousness slowly bubbled up to the tranquil surface of his thoughts. Misty stars and shapes popped and swirled drunkenly around his brain.

What happened? His first conscious thought posed the obvious question. He waited for an answer to come to him; nothing arrived. Neither did his body offer him any clues. There was just; nothing. Was this even his brain?

Start with my name. My name is—is—. A word floated up to the surface. *Devon? Okay, at least that's something.* It was an excellent first step. He could remember his first name. Then he wondered if Devon was his first name at all. Maybe it was his surname? Again, his mind remained silent on the matter. Everything felt changed. Devon was sure that something terrible had just happened to him; he just had no idea what.

<Wake up!> A feminine voice screamed. The words didn't enter Devon's head in the usual way, though. Devon realised they had just appeared straight in the forefront of his mind.

<Wake! Up!>

Devon was fascinated by these words entering his brain. This time the words were louder. They appeared in flashing, neon-pink letters, along with a sense of extreme urgency. He perceived the speech without using his ears. The words even came with imagery and emotions too. Panic was the emotion he'd just received. *What fun!*

<Get up, you moron! They are coming towards us, and they do not look friendly,> the feminine voice shouted directly into his brain again.

She just called me a moron. She must know me then. Quite rude, though. Opening his eyes, he faced the world. Only the world he could see was dark, or was that the sky? Verticality was needed. After all, he wasn't getting any peace, lying on his back. He managed to rise to his knees and then clamber to his feet. He looked around. He located a ball of light flitting around and then focused on a massive, black horse. The horse gazed expectantly at him.

<Behind you! Idiot!> The urgent-sounding voice in his head sounded angry. She didn't seem impressed with him either.

Devon turned around and immediately saw two heavyset men eyeing him with wary hostility. *Ahh! So that's what that woman's shouting was about. She's right, though. They don't look friendly!* One of them was brandishing an old long-knife, while the other was aiming at him with a crossbow. There was a click and a metallic sound. The noise triggered some instinct within him, causing him to tilt his right shoulder sharply back. The crossbow bolt sped past him.

"Rude! You need to die first," Devon muttered angrily, designating the crossbowman as his primary target. The thug was now trying to reload. Devon reached down to the ground and scrabbled around until he found a suitably sized stone. He quickly hefted it to check its weight, then drew his hand back at waist height, and threw; hard. It left his fingers with a sound like an angry pigeon and almost instantaneously struck his target in the left eye. There was a wet, splintering sound, and then the man collapsed lifelessly.

"Well, that just happened!" Devon looked at his right hand in absolute shock. From where had all that strength and accuracy come?

Devon looked toward the other thug, who was staring down at his dead colleague with an expression of horror. He glanced back at Devon; his face wrought with fear. Not liking his new circumstances, the man turned and fled.

In a heartbeat, Devon was after him. A new strength launched him into the pursuit, pounding the ground as he ran. It took him seconds to reach his terrified target. Sensing that he was about to be caught, the man desperately spun, slashing his knife in an arc wildly. Devon caught the man's knife-arm with his left hand and twisted sharply. He struck the man hard in the face with the flat of his right palm. The thug's eyes crossed, then rolled as he collapsed. Devon grabbed the man's knife, and with one swift motion, slit his throat. No thought or emotion came to him as the man fell, bloody and lifeless. A strange feeling of familiarity washed over him. Every move he'd made felt well-practised and almost automatic.

Something spiritual sparked in his mind. Devon watched in fascination as his right arm involuntarily reached forward, fingers facing upward. The two corpses began to glow as shadows resembling the two dead men rose through the men's chests and began to drift lazily toward his outstretched hand. They sank into his palm as soon as they reached him. He felt a strange effervescence spread down his arm then onwards until it tingled throughout his body.

Everything just got a whole lot stranger, he thought.

<Wow! That was amazing,> Isabelle thought to him with added feelings of pride and relief. It was the most she could think to say. She was his priestess and had spent years trying to find him, but now that he was near her, her mind had frozen. In her opinion, he was a bit of an idiot. However, she ought to try and be a little nicer to him. Her naturally abusive nature needed suppressing, lest he turn hostile. Her snarkiness could alter the course of her people's history.

Devon sighed. Now he had removed the threats to his life, there was time to take in his surroundings. His attention fell upon the wisp, floating in circles nearby. It now glowed a bright, shocking-pink colour. He chose to leave that inquiry for later.

Instead, he walked the short distance across to the enormous, midnight-black horse. He stood and gazed at it in wonder. It was huge. It turned its head to stare steadily at him. Without a second thought, Devon bowed. The horse blinked at him, then dipped its head in response.

<What do I call you?> Devon asked the horse. He realised that he was trying to talk to a horse, but it just felt right. Things appeared to go a lot better when his consciousness didn't interfere; something else inside him took over, and knew what to do. He'd bide his time then go mad later when events had more time to catch up with him.

The horse tilted its head and narrowed its eyes at him as if to say, 'really?'

<Okay, you want me to choose your name?> Devon asked.

The horse nodded its enormous head.

He thought hard. Shadow was just too obvious a name for a black horse. <How about Jet then? That's a black stone and sounds good.> It was a name that just popped into his mind and seemed to suit the large animal. He wondered if that was already the horse's name, and he'd just remembered it. He certainly felt like this wasn't the first time the two of them had met.

The horse seemed to be happy with his suggestion and dipped its head briefly.

<Jet it is then. May I?> Devon asked Jet, pointing behind the horse. The horse didn't seem to object, so Devon slowly made his way around the beast. He wanted to avoid the embarrassment of getting the creature's gender wrong, so he planned to check subtly.

He paused to admire the horse's saddle. It was black and made of plush, well-worked leather. The saddle's seat looked comfortable, and behind the cantle, it dipped to form a second, smaller seat to accommodate a pillion. Saddlebags were slung behind the pillion and tailored to lie snuggly against Jet's sides. All the items were finished with subtle, decorative stitching and etched with delicate patterns.

He wondered at the sheer size of Jet. The horse's spine was over ten inches above his head. A thought suddenly struck Devon with a jolt. *Wait, what? Did I get taller?* How tall had he been? No idea, but he certainly felt taller now.

<Yes, genius, you are taller. You are also broader, stronger, faster, and, believe it or not, far more intelligent than you were,> the voice thought. <Which means you must have been even dumber before you woke back up.> Isabelle mentally kicked herself. She had only just promised to go easier on him, and here she was abusing him for being, understandably, disorientated and confused.

<Cute; which of you keeps thinking at me? The overgrown sparkle or the nag?> Devon asked. He needed to know who his tormentor was and, if possible, stomp on them.

The wisp sped around Jet and stopped abruptly to hover just in front of Devon's nose. Devon's eyes crossed as he tried to focus on the tiny thing.

<It is me, you ret… I mean, my lord,> Isabelle thought. Being tolerant was going to be a lot harder than she first thought. She would have to try harder. <I am talking to you mentally because I cannot communicate in the usual way.>

Devon made a swipe at the wisp, attempting to grab it, but it dodged his attempt with ease.

And now she had upset the one person that could help her. <I will save you the effort,> Isabelle thought, with a hint of amusement. <Jet is a mare – a girl horse. So, you don't need to keep walking around to her backside to check.>

<I wasn't–> Devon started to protest, but then he stopped. Suspicion rose in his thoughts. <Can you read my mind?> He had been wondering about Jet's gender, and he had been on his way to check subtly. Devon began to suspect that the wisp had some mental skills.

<Not much to read in your head now, I am afraid,> Isabelle said. Her thoughts tinged with regret. She could easily see the turmoil inside his head. <I am sorry, but I suspect all the memories of your human life have disappeared. That part of you is dead now. All that is left is instinct and whatever your soul brought with it. There are magical blocks on parts of your memory for some reason.>

Another glance inside his mind told him that she was right. He'd noticed it earlier. A more thorough search of his mind still revealed nothing but his name. Although, if Devon looked carefully, there were shadowy clumps in there, upon which he couldn't focus.

<And Devon is not your real name, either.>

<Oh? That's a shame. It's the only thing that came to me, and I quite liked it. What is my name then?>

<I do not know what your human name was,> the wisp replied. <Devon is where you are, not who you are. It must have been the last thing on your mind before you got hit by the van.>

Devon looked around and saw the van to which the wisp had referred. It must have belonged to the two men he'd killed. <So why aren't I in a lot of pain? I've heard that getting run over really hurts.>

<That is a long story. You have returned to your original divine state now that the cursed human part of you is dead,> the wisp replied.

<Okay, that doesn't explain anything; thanks for that. Does it matter what I call myself?>

<It is your life and your choice,> the wisp replied. While that statement was true, she needed to make sure his choices suited her.

<It's not a conversation for right now, but I expect you to tell me all about what happened here,> he said.

<Go f– Yes, of course, my lord.> She was trying to consider her responses before sharing them. Her aggressive personality was proving hard to bury. <I will explain to you as much as I can. I risked everything to find you and to help you through this.> She turned purple and settled on his left shoulder. Isabelle knew that her mission was to assist him and coax him safely back to her people. She had to try to be tolerant and patient with him.

Devon felt a light tingle where the wisp landed. He considered what could have caused the wisp to go from antagonistic to subservient. She said she was here to help him. Hopefully, that meant there might be some answers for him.

Chapter 2

Trouble is free

He turned back to face the vehicle, which had ended his life once already, then strained his neck to look at the wisp. <By the way, Jet has a name, now what about you?>

<Isabelle,> the wisp replied.

Devon nodded. <That's a beautiful name. I love it. A bit long though.> After a moment's consideration, he added, <how about Izzy?>

<I hate it,> she replied. <I would prefer Belle, but I suppose you intend to call me Izzy from now on then?>

<Yep!> Devon grinned.

<Well sh– it will do, I suppose.> Isabelle had grown up amongst freedom fighters and slaves. She had been called much worse.

Jet let out a loud whinny which sounded a lot like laughter.

<Wait!> A thought slammed into Devon's battered brain. <Jet can hear you talking to me mentally?>

<Of course. You share a bond with her. She knows what you know.>

<You mean she can read my mind as you can?> Devon responded.

Izzy sighed. Be nice to him. <Listen re– no, my lord, she can hear your mental speech. There is a big difference. Think of it as overhearing a conversation between two people.> Her voice perked up as she added, <well done, by the way. You have grasped mind communication. I did not think you would be able to manage it so soon.>

<Sorry, I did what now?>

<Yes, st– silly. Do you realise you have not said anything verbally since you killed those men? No?> Isabelle sighed inwardly. He might be easy on the eye, but he seemed a bit thick. She hoped that it was just the confusion of reawakening that was addling his brain.

Stunned, Devon thought on that for a moment. Like everything else so far, he'd just done it without thinking. This will all make sense someday, he surmised, so ride with it for now.

<Well done,> Izzy laughed, trying not to sound patronising. <A positive mental attitude. Very healthy. Onwards and upwards. You have a lot of catching up to do. I can help you with that.>

Devon ventured towards the abandoned van. He noticed he was walking on the verge of a broad, concrete road, clearly in a state of disrepair as cracks and blemishes riddled the surface. The larger cracks had grass growing up through them, and the edges of the concrete were crumbling badly.

<How do I know about concrete and yet not have any idea about what I did yesterday?> Devon pondered.

<Your mind will settle soon enough. Try not to worry. Your brain is getting used to your original form once again,> Izzy said. <It will take a little time.>

Isabelle was a feminine name. Devon wondered how she could designate herself female when she was a blob of luminescent attitude. She just doesn't have the necessary equipment for the gender.

<Guess again,> the wisp snapped. <My necessaries are just fine, thank you. Not that it's any of your business.>

Devon shook his head. He didn't like somebody being able to read his every thought. It was invasive. <If you don't like my thoughts, stay out of my head,> he snapped back, annoyed.

<Yes, my lord. I apologise,> Izzy replied meekly. She had to accept his point, knowing she'd overstepped the mark.

He reached the van and investigated the cab but saw nothing of interest amongst the rubbish and grime. The vehicle had once been white, but it was so old and rusty that the original colour was hard to find. Its better days had seen better days.

He carried on toward the back and was shocked to see a sizeable metal cage roped down on the van's flatbed. In contrast to the dirt and grime that clung to the van's exterior, it shone with a clean, steely gleam.

Devon realised that, even though it was night-time, he could see perfectly well. Colours were a little harder to distinguish, but apart from that, it was just as clear as day. He looked up and saw that the moon was almost full. Its radiance reflected off the metal bars of the cage. The smell of blood from the two dead men still filled his nostrils, but he could also smell something living nearby. He didn't even understand how he knew that.

He leaned over the side of the van's cargo area and peered into the cage. He wasn't too surprised when he saw a female dressed in jeans and a leather top curled up on the cage floor.

"Hey! You in the cage!" Devon shouted. He appeared to have no issues switching between mental and physical speech now, which was a bonus. "Are you okay?"

He smacked his forehead with the palm of his hand – what a supremely dumb thing to say. Too late, Devon wondered what the best way to address someone locked in a cage was. 'Are you okay?' probably wasn't it.

The lady in the cage lifted her head and swept her long, matted hair away from her face. She peered down at him. Her eyes were tear-streaked and her face puffy. She'd obviously been crying for a while. She was quiet, though, her eyes blinking in confusion.

"Hang on a second. I'll be right up," he said, trying to make the smile he gave her as reassuring as possible. It dawned on him that he didn't have anything he could use to open the cage. He thought for a second, then remembered the two corpses lying on the floor nearby. He bent down and started searching them. The prospect of harvesting the possessions of the dead didn't bother him in the slightest. That surprised him. After a lot of rummaging, he'd managed to loot a poorly maintained long-knife, some small amounts of cash, a black, plastic card with some sort of logo printed in the centre of it, and a hip flask containing some potent, evil-smelling liquid.

The man who'd had the crossbow also had a quiver containing more quarrels, strapped to his right thigh. Usefully, it also had a thin sheath stitched to its outer face that held a long survival knife. Its blade was robust, sharp, and curved on one side, serrated on the other. Devon liberated that too.

Finally, he found what he'd been searching for; a key. He grabbed it in triumph. He left the other items in a pile next to the bodies, but he took the survival-knife with him, just in case. Devon carefully tucked the blade into his belt, diligently trying not to slice through it as he did so. He'd grab the other things on his way back to Jet.

<Are you going to rescue yonder fair maiden then?> Izzy thought happily. She was now floating above his left shoulder. Maybe, if she encouraged him to do something like this, he would start settling back into his original divine form. Helping people was what her god was famous for.

<You think I shouldn't, perhaps?>

<Not at all. I believe you should,> Izzy replied. <Rescued maidens often turn into rampant love interests further down the road.> While

she had no personal experience in the subject, she had read romance novels. That was how these things worked.

Devon spluttered at Izzy's comment. He walked over to the side of the van and hopped up easily into the back. He marvelled at how his jump had effortlessly cleared the side of the vehicle. From a standing start too. He wondered what he could be capable of; perhaps Izzy would be kind enough to explain how he'd acquired such physical prowess.

The woman in the cage watched him intently, like a mouse eyeing a cat about to pounce.

"Don't worry," Devon tried to assure her. "I'm not going to harm you. I promise." The lady was unlikely to trust him, which was understandable given her current predicament. His words hadn't assuaged her fears.

<After all, the last person she met threw her into this cage,> Izzy thought.

Devon nodded sadly. The cage's door was facing the rear of the vehicle, so he stepped around to examine it. The cage was secured by a sturdy mechanism built into the door. He fished out the newly liberated key and inserted it into the lock. The key turned smoothly, and the door swung open.

"Yes!"

If it hadn't worked, it probably would have been the end of his rescue attempt. He simply didn't have anything sturdy enough to break through the cage's thick bars.

<Be gentle,> Izzy thought. She turned a purple colour.

Devon had no idea how he should take the wisp's words. He had started to feel as if she might be entertaining to have around, though.

<Oh, you should believe it,> she thought. She used the most seductive voice Devon had ever heard. Her wisp turned blue, and she started to orbit his head.

Ye gods! Izzy was terrible for his concentration

Izzy considered her actions. Was he changing her already? She had never been like this with anyone before. There had never been anyone to be like this with. It just was not her way. Being around him was starting to become enjoyable, though. That, too, felt strange. Men were an alien species for her, and Devon was no mere man. All gods and goddesses had a natural allure to mortals. They drew mortal devotion to them like moths to a flame. It was in their nature, but was that all this was?

Devon stepped into the cage and held his hand out toward the woman. Now that he was closer, he could see past the grime and tear streaks. She looked to be in her early twenties. Her prominent cheekbones and narrow chin gave her face a gently curved diamond shape, enhanced by the long fringe of her ginger, shoulder-length hair. She had wide, hazel-coloured eyes and a small, rounded nose that turned up slightly at the tip. Her lips were full but not pronounced. The lady sat up and stared at Devon's hand, then up at him with a slightly hopeful look, liberally laced with mistrust.

"Don't worry. I'm not going to hurt you," Devon said in as soothing a voice as he could manage.

"What happened to the slavers?" she asked him. Her voice had a gentle, west country accent.

"Uhm, I happened to them. They're dead," Devon answered. Her question had caught him a little off-guard. "Let's get you out of this cage and away from here before more of those people arrive." Devon waggled the fingers a bit on his outstretched hand to emphasise that it was still there, waiting to be accepted.

The lady eyed the waggling fingers with distaste and then sighed. She took Devon's hand and hauled herself up. She gave him a curious look when, despite leveraging her full weight against him, he hadn't moved at all.

"Nice outfit. Is that some sort of fashion statement?" she asked, her voice full of sarcasm.

Devon blushed. "Uh! I'm in a bit of a transitional period." Her comment struck him as an odd thing to say. He'd expected at least a thank you. Now that she was standing, he guessed that she was about five and a half feet in height. Although maybe his assessment of her size was a little skewed. His height felt wrong, so it was challenging to judge hers fairly.

"Would you like me to carry you out?" he offered.

<Very smooth,> Izzy laughed.

"No, I definitely wouldn't," she snapped at him. "I'm neither injured nor crippled. Keep your hands to yourself." The woman dropped his hand as if it had scalded her, then with a few easy steps and a light jump, she was over the edge of the van and standing on the ground.

Hell! That didn't go as I'd planned. I guess rescuing somebody doesn't guarantee they'll be polite. Devon chided himself. *Stupid!*

<Ha! Lancelot strikes out,> Izzy teased him. <Looks like chivalry caught the pox and died.>

Devon stood in the cage, looking down at her, feeling awkward and a little silly, while fighting the urge to snicker from Izzy's words. The woman reached out to him and waggled her fingers.

"Would you like me to jump back up there and carry you down?" she said. Then her face lit up with a radiant grin. She stuck her thumb on her nose and wriggled her fingers.

You try and be nice, and this is what you get. Now I've got two females pulling my chains, Devon thought to himself.

<Oh, yes!> Izzy cooed. <I like her, can we keep her?>

<You can bloody have her,> he replied. <Be my guest. I hope the two of you will be very happy together.> He joined the woman down by the bodies. She was examining the loot pile that he'd made earlier. "That's my loot, by the way. Although you're welcome to take what you need."

"You can keep their stuff, but I'm taking my gear back," she retorted.

Devon shook his head. *Why is this woman so hostile? What did I do wrong?* More confusion was the last thing he needed in his life. He had no issue with her taking whatever she needed from the rubbish pile, and he'd done his good deed. It was time to get out of here. This woman could go her own way, and may she have all the luck in the world.

<Who are you kidding?> Izzy said. Her voice amused. <You are just sulking because she did not throw herself at you.>

Devon ignored the wisp. She was probably right, but he was damned if he was going to admit it.

<Hah! I can read your thoughts, remember?> Izzy reminded him.

"The least you can do is tell me your name," he said to the woman.

She stood up and turned on him. She held her hand out. "Knife?"

"Knife's a strange name," Devon said. He thought he was being funny, but the woman just glared at him. He sighed and gave up. "You know what? It has been a real displeasure to meet you. I should have left you in the bloody cage."

He could see that she already had the crossbow and its quiver, so he knew which knife she meant. It was a shame, though; he'd wanted to keep it. He carefully withdrew the blade, flipped it around, and handed it to her, handle first.

The woman snatched the knife and quickly tucked it back into the quiver. She then started strapping the quiver to her thigh. "I have to travel on, to their camp, and rescue my friends," she said, indicating the dead slavers. Her voice sounded tired. "Come the morning, they'll be taken away to one of the prison compounds. Once that happens, I might never find them."

"Not sure why you're bothering to tell me but good luck with that." Devon wasn't having a good day and was tired of her aggressive attitude. He turned his back on her and made to walk back to Jet.

The woman scowled. "If you wanted to be gallant, you could help me retrieve them."

Devon spun back around to face her with a look of incredulity on his face. "What? Seriously?" He was confused. She obviously disliked him, yet she was still asking for his help. "Maybe you think your radiant personality has won me over?"

<You have been given a quest. Help Elizabeth rescue her friends. The reward is an increased reputation with this human female,> Izzy said to him before laughing uproariously. <Bonus reward: make your gorgeous wisp companion happy,> she added with a laugh.

Devon was trying to be angry, and so he suppressed the smile that threatened his face. Izzy could read minds, and she'd evidently been rooting around in this woman's head. <So that's her name. Cheers, Izzy. Why do you care about this woman anyway? Are you two linked in some way? I still don't even know why you're here.>

<You need to settle back into your god form. Helping her will be good practice,> Izzy replied. <And no, I have no affiliation with her.>

"I suppose I could help you, Elizabeth, but could you try and be a little less hostile perhaps?"

She looked at him with shock and suspicion. "I don't know how the hell you know my name, but if you must use it, please just call me Beth," she said, "and thank you." Her face softened. "Thank you for getting me out of that cage. Also, thank you for being willing to help my friends even though I was horrible to you." She gave Devon her best attempt at a smile, despite her anxiousness for her friends.

Devon's attitude toward her thawed a little when she smiled at him. *What the hell's wrong with me? I'm not a smitten teenager. It was a gorgeous smile, though.*

<Not a teenager,> Izzy thought to him softly. <Not so sure about the smitten bit.>

"What should I call you?" Beth asked him.

"You can call me Devon." He felt himself blush a little and gave himself a mental slap.

She arched her eyebrow at him. "That's a coincidence. Real name?"

That caught him by surprise. "I've no idea," he replied. "It'll do for now."

Beth tilted her head at him. "You can explain that another time perhaps. For now, Devon it is."

"How far away are your friends?"

"Their holding camp is about a mile further down the road," she replied, pointing down the road in the direction that the thugs' van was facing. "These bastards were taking me there." At that point, she gave the corpse nearest to her a hard kick.

"How do you know that your friends are already there?" Thus far, Devon didn't have any cause to believe what Beth had told him, but he felt it wise to learn as much as he could about her situation. As far as he knew, these men had just been thugs who'd tried to kill him. *Slavers? Did those even exist? What sort of world had he woken up in?*

<She is not lying. You will soon find out that slavers are very real. In this world and mine,> Izzy said.

"I was on my way back from scouting the holding camp when they caught me." She gave the nearest corpse another kick. "I killed one of them but got jumped by this one. The other one is just the driver." Another kick landed on the body. "You can guess the rest." Beth gestured to the cage. She walked around the van to the passenger door and reached in through the open window. After some rummaging, she pulled out a small rucksack. "By the way, you need to work on your looting skills, Devon. All the best stuff is in here." She raised the rucksack she was holding and smirked.

<Izzy?> Devon thought to the wisp.

<Yes, dear?> the wisp responded.

Devon wondered about the term of endearment. Was she being sarcastic or genuinely friendly? Considering everything he'd heard from her so far, it was most likely sarcasm.

<I can read your mind, remember, dumbass?> the wisp said. <I am trying to be nice, should I stop? You and I need to work together; so we ought to be friends. You need my help, and I certainly need yours.>

After all the insults the wisp had thrown at him, he still doubted Izzy's true intentions, but he'd take friendship if it were offered.

<Have I got any equipment?> he asked Izzy. Devon didn't know much about his current circumstances. Indeed, he hadn't woken up with much to his name. Or even a name for that matter.

<Before we arrived, I had to stuff all the items I brought for you in Jet's saddlebag. I cannot carry anything in this form. Check in there,> Izzy thought. <Your horse can cross realms without magic; I cannot. I just hitched a ride. You have probably got your original equipment in there too.>

Well, well! That's the most helpful Izzy has been so far, Devon thought.

<I can still hear you, numb-nuts.>

<Ah! There's the wisp I know,> he thought with a smile.

"What are you so happy about?" Beth asked.

Oh crap! Devon hadn't considered the issues he'd have to face, trying to maintain an internal and external dialogue at the same time. "Just thoughts. Nothing special," he replied, still trying to stay distant from this woman. Something was telling him that she was trouble.

Beth eyed him suspiciously. After a moment, she just shrugged. "Whatever."

"Do you want to drive the van while I follow with Jet?" he asked. Devon wasn't sure whether he even knew how to ride. Furthermore, would he be able to get up on the horse's back? She was an enormous creature.

"Jet being your horse over there?" She indicated the place where his horse waited patiently.

<Is she my horse, Izzy?> Devon thought.

<She is, and you are hers. You are bonded. She was created to be your companion and is a lot more than just a horse,> Izzy thought. <However, can you really own a living creature? I guess not, so take that as a partial yes.>

Devon didn't have time to consider the moral implications of what the wisp had just told him. "Yes. That's her," he responded to Beth.

"Not a bad plan. However, I'll stop the truck about half a mile up the road; then we can ride nearer to the camp together." Beth paused thoughtfully and then nodded to herself. "It'll be a lot quieter if we approach on horseback."

"Okay. Give me a few minutes and then lead on," Devon said. He turned quickly and strode back to Jet.

Chapter 3
Trappings

Thinking about Beth's comments on his outfit, Devon looked down at his torn and filthy clothes, something he hadn't bothered to do until now. He was wearing black, cloth trousers at least six inches too short for him and a tight, black T-shirt with a picture of a wizard on it. Like the trousers, the shirt was far too short, leaving his midriff exposed. The upside was that it showed off his muscular abdomen. Devon stared at his chest in wonder. *Was I ever this fit? I've got the physique of a god, yet my whole body is a stranger to me.* His shoes were a canvas-like material with rubber soles. They were travel-worn, dirt-covered, and extremely tight. He checked his pockets and found a large, multi-bladed knife, some matches, and a grimy handkerchief. Judging by his clothes, he hadn't been a wealthy man. Devon froze when he noticed the 'Hello Kitty' watch on his left wrist. *What the hell? Hello Kitty? What am I, six?*

<It suits you,> Izzy thought. She was currently orbiting his head and had gone back to her shocking pink colour.

Devon glared up at the wisp then shook his head. Acquiring better clothes had just been added to his to-do list. *Wait! How can I know what 'Hello Kitty' is if I have no memories?* he pondered. *My mind might contain some things deeply buried somewhere. Maybe there's a hope they'll come back eventually?*

It seemed his best hope of acquiring a better outfit was raiding the horse's saddlebags. He looked up at Jet. She was a beautiful creature with a coat of the darkest black that shone with vitality. Her mane was long and lush, as was the shaggy hair on her head and fetlocks. Now and then, he caught sight of her ample tail as it swished. She'd been watching him contently since he'd woken up. Jet's big dark eyes seemed amused with what occurred around her, and she appeared to have all the patience in the world. Devon felt an unexplainable closeness to this creature that went way beyond mere friendship.

"Is it okay for me to clamber on board after a rummage through your bags?" he asked Jet.

She nodded her horsey head and seemed to smile at him. He felt a feeling of affection radiate into his mind from her. <Trust us. We be good.>

Devon stood and stared at the horse. Just as when Izzy communicated with him, the words had simply appeared in his mind. These words were slightly different. They felt bestial. There were more images and emotions associated with the thoughts and less grammatical form. His mind seemed perfectly capable of translating all the parts into one exact meaning, though.

<Jet talks too?> he thought to Izzy.

<I have no idea.> She changed red and started to orbit Devon's head. <I only met her today. Her origin species are said to be able to, though,> Izzy replied.

This night just keeps getting weirder. I hope I remember this dream when I wake up.

<You are wide awake,> Izzy thought. <Get Beth to pinch you if you want proof.>

<No thanks,> Devon thought. He could imagine the response he'd get from Beth. <But I'm telling you this now. I'm only accepting any of this because I have no memories to compare it to.>

Izzy mentally giggled at him. She turned a dark shade of green and perched on his shoulder. <Relax, you are doing fine. Just think, you died less than an hour ago. It can only be up from there.>

Devon didn't know how to take that idea. So, like a lot of things recently, he ignored it. He walked around Jet and reached into one of the saddlebags on her back.

Feeling around in the bag, he didn't manage to find anything. It was empty. *Typical! I had a fifty-fifty chance to discover the full one.* Frustrated, he walked around Jet to the bag on her other side. He still couldn't believe just how big she was. What did she eat? He reached inside and, once again, rummaged around for any contents. As Jet was so tall, the bag's top was above his eyeline, meaning he could only search using touch. The second saddlebag seemed to be just as empty as the first.

<Izzy?> he thought loudly.

<What?> she responded. <Having trouble, oh moon of my life?>

Devon refused to be put off by her odd terms of endearment. <My bags are empty. I thought you said there'd be some gear in them?>

<These are magical bags,> Izzy said. <They are called void bags, and they can hold a great many things, much more than their physical size would suggest.>

<Magical? What? You mean magic exists?>

<Oh yes! Of course it exists. You are a god with exceptional talents and many times more magical ability than most. At least, you will be when we get to the nexus.>

Devon considered everything that had happened since he had woken up. He wondered about the telepathy and the changes to his body. Could 'magic' be a real thing? He certainly hoped it was. <Fair enough, but my bags are still empty.>

<You won't be able to interact with anything magical just yet,> Izzy said. <We will need to get the magic flowing in this world first. That is priority one; as we will both perish without it. For now, you will just have to trust me.

If you want magic, then we need to fix a few things. One thing at a time, though. Put your hand in the bag and think the words 'equip armour',> the wisp explained. <Think hard and clearly. Hopefully, that should be enough.>

Hopefully? That didn't fill him with confidence. He was contemplating stripping the two nearby corpses and taking their clothes, but he decided to give this a try first. The worst that could happen was that he ended up feeling a little foolish.

He tentatively reached into the saddlebag again. As he did so, he visualised the words 'equip armour'. At first, nothing happened, but as he closed his eyes and began to concentrate harder, he felt his existing rags disappear. He felt a cold breeze against his naked body. Then thick, well-fitting garments embraced him snugly. It felt as if he had grown a second skin. One much warmer and tougher than the original. The garments fitted perfectly. He opened his eyes wide and gasped. He was now dressed in tight, black leather armour and the most comfortable pair of tall boots he could imagine. Bracers and fingerless gloves finished off the ensemble; all black, all beautifully made.

Devon shifted his weight around and tried a few stretches. The clothes moved and stretched with him. They didn't constrict him in any way; they just continued to fit perfectly, no matter what pose he struck. Devon was thrilled.

<Now, put your hand back in the bag and think 'equip weapons,'> Izzy prompted him.

Devon jumped. He'd been so busy admiring his new armour that he'd forgotten about the world around him.

He reached back up into Jet's saddlebag and thought 'equip weapons' as instructed. This time it happened instantaneously. He felt a slight weight materialise on his back, under his arms, and on either side of his waist. He cautiously lifted his right arm and looked at his armour. There was a scabbard, aligned almost vertically under his arm that he hadn't noticed before. A textured handle protruded out of the bottom of the sheath, defying gravity somehow. He carefully pulled the handle, and a vicious-looking straight blade slid cleanly down and out. Devon didn't need to look to know that he had an identical dagger underneath his other arm too. He felt it nestled there.

The blade was made from a sinister, dark metal that gleamed ominously when it moved. It had tiny symbols etched along the ten inches of its narrow length, and its double edges looked wickedly sharp. Its handle was jet black and made of a slightly pliant material that produced an excellent grip. With respect, he slid the dagger back into its sheath.

He examined two pockets near his waistline that he'd felt fill with something. Sure enough, now each one had a handle sticking out of it. The handles were within easy reach of each hand.

He pulled on the two handles and examined the knives they belonged to. They each had five-inch diamond-shaped blades that looked wickedly sharp. Like his other blade, they were black. The edges tapered sharply to a slim handle that ended in a hollow circle and was nicely weighted for throwing. He went to replace one of the blades in its sheath, but he saw that there was already another handle protruding from it.

<Good, isn't it?> Izzy said. <Every time you draw one, another takes its place, magically. At least that is how the books tell it. My people have always been fascinated by you and we have some really detailed histories.>

<Histories? How old am I?> Devon asked, in shock.

<That was a much-debated subject, but recent events have proved to me that you are older than time itself. The scholars who got it right believe that your father formed the multiverse in which we live and then created you. There is speculation that you also have three brothers, but nothing is known about them. We are reasonably sure that you are older and more powerful than the gods and goddesses of the Pantheon,> Izzy replied.

Devon shook his head. That was way too much to dwell on now. More for another time. A glance behind him revealed the handle of a sword that protruded above his shoulder at an angle. He reached back and grabbed it, then felt it snap free. It wasn't in a sheath. A look over his other shoulder told him that, like the daggers, he had one on either side.

The sword was lethal looking, which was a good start. It had a double-edged blade, slightly over two feet in length from tip to shoulder. The inside edge curved gracefully back to the hilt, while the outside edge was straight. The width stayed narrow for nine inches, then the outer edge stepped outward a little and continued back to the shoulder. It was forged from the same sinister, dark metal as the daggers, which seemed to absorb any light that dared to venture close. The blade was covered with inscriptions arranged in tight patterns. Its hilt was also jet black and sculpted to fit a single hand, then expanded to become a streamlined handguard before it met the blade. It was a work of deathly art.

He gave the sword a swing then instinctively accomplished a stylish riposte and a swift lunge. He replaced it with reverence taking care not to cut his head off.

<Do I know how to use these things then?> Devon asked Izzy.

<You should do. That is your equipment, not anything my people gifted you. Thanks to the wonders of your soul's memory, you have instantly become very skilled with all types of blade combat. You were famous for it,> she replied.

<More explanations for later, I assume?> he asked.

<Afraid so. You have work to do right now.>

As if prompted, Beth shouted over at him from beside the van. "Are you going to stand there all night, or shall we get going?"

"On my way," he replied to Beth. *Now for the moment I've been dreading.* He took a deep breath then turned to eye the stirrup that hung at Jet's side.

<Just relax,> Izzy coached him. <Everything you need to know is already there, inside you. It'll come to you naturally if you try not to overthink the how of it.>

Devon took another deep breath. With a swift action, he leapt up and landed cleanly astride the saddle. Happily, he even managed to end up facing in the right direction. *Bonus!* Still working hard not to interfere with his instincts, he grabbed the reins, struck a pose, then gave Jet's sides a gentle tap with his feet. A glance down revealed that he already had his feet in the stirrups and at the right height too. He experienced a deep sense of happiness, sitting in Jet's saddle. He felt as if he had spent many happy years sitting right here. *A memory, perhaps?*

He looked back at the saddlebags to make sure they were now closed securely. He knew he'd forgotten to do it, but the bags were sealed and tightly fastened as he'd hoped. It might be weird having mysterious stuff in his possession, but he could get used to it.

Mercifully, Jet seemed to sense where Devon wanted to go and at what speed. <I think you and I are going to get along splendidly,> he said to his horse.

The horse looked back at him without slowing and whinnied happily.

Beth still stood by the van, and now she was watching him and Jet with great interest. "That's a beautiful horse you have there."

"She's gorgeous, isn't she?" Devon replied proudly. "Her name's Jet."

Jet lowered her head and nuzzled Beth's shoulder gently.

Beth giggled, then blushed.

"I think she likes you," Devon said, trying to be friendly. He felt self-conscious and automatically ran his hand back through his floppy hair.

<Jet shares your thoughts, and she will respond to your emotions too,> Izzy thought to Devon. <She has sensed that you are attracted to Beth,> she added, with amusement. <She's showing off for you.>

<Thanks, Jet. I owe you for that,> Devon thought to his new winglady. *Winghorse?* Just as he'd finished his thought to Jet, he received his first sense of a faint but growing bond between himself and the horse. It was tangible, like a spiritual rope – another oddity.

In all honesty, he was starting to enjoy himself. His human sense of self, now deceased, was fading, along with his confusion.

"You've dressed for the occasion, I see," Beth said, eyeing his equipment warily. "You look like a one-man army."

"You said you needed help. I'm the help," Devon replied. "Now, are you going to stand there all night, or shall we get going?"

She looked up at him and grinned. "Touché."

<You look good,> Izzy said. <If I could sustain a body in this realm, I'd jump you.> *What? I just said that to my god. Where did these urges come from?* Izzy wondered incredulously. *Is it even allowed between a priestess and her god? This is all happening far too fast.* She was extremely grateful that Devon couldn't read her thoughts as she could read his. Mental communication was not telepathy. It was just an alternative way to chat. Devon was no telepath, and so at least she got to keep her secrets from him. Right now, that was a mercy.

Devon went crimson. Luckily, Beth missed his embarrassment as she turned toward the wagon at that moment.

Beth forced the creaking door of the van open, then clambered into the driver's seat. Seconds later, the engine reluctantly spluttered to life while belching a large cloud of black smoke from its rear. There was a loud crunching of poorly synchronised gears, and the vehicle lurched forward onto the road. She was on the move.

Devon guided Jet to trek after the vehicle with a gentle squeeze of his legs. The van wasn't going anywhere quickly in its current state, and Jet easily kept pace with it. It didn't seem like Devon's input was required at all. The horse knew what he wanted and just got on with it. The exhaust fumes overwhelmed his sense of smell, and he got Jet to speed up a little so he wouldn't have to inhale them.

Ten minutes later, Beth pulled a fair way off the road and then turned the van around to face back up the road. She cut the engine and leaned out of the window. "It's getting lighter," she said, scanning the horizon. "I suppose dawn is coming. We'd best hurry if we want some shadows to lurk in when we get there." She scrambled out of the van and stood there, waiting.

Devon guided Jet over to her and grinned down while reaching out his hand. Beth looked up and frowned at Jet's sheer size. He knew she was debating whether she could manage the jump without his assistance. She sighed and reached up; Devon closed his fingers around her wrist and pulled. Beth shot upward and landed neatly astride the pillion seat.

She laughed in a way that revealed her inner little girl. "I could probably see my house from up here," she giggled. "Shall we go?"

"Same direction as before?" Devon asked Beth whilst looking over his shoulder.

"Yes. I'll tap your shoulder when we need to leave the road."

A naughty thought occurred to Devon. "Hold on tight," he warned her. Two taps on Jet's side sent her off at a swift trot, and he felt a pair of arms wrap around his chest.

<Are you going to help me out here, girl?> he thought to Jet while grinning to himself. Jet shot forward as if she'd been stung and began to gallop hard, gaining speed with ease. Sure enough, Beth squeezed him more tightly, and Devon revelled in her closeness. If this were his new life, then he'd take it.

****_****

Beth tapped Devon on the shoulder a few minutes later as they raced along the side of the dilapidated road. Her hand reached in front of his face and pointed left toward a well-used dirt track. Devon nodded and pushed his heels in and back against Jet's side. Immediately, she started to slow down to a brisk trot as they followed the track.

After a short while, the track wove into a wooded area that had been skirting the concrete road. Soon, trees walled the rough road, hemming them in on either side. The weak dawn light disappeared into shadow, and they were back in partial darkness once more.

Not far into the woods, Beth tapped his shoulder again, and Devon brought Jet to a stop. She leaned forward and whispered into his right ear. "The slaver encampment is just a few hundred feet up ahead. The track bends left then heads deeper into these trees. It ends where the trees open out into a clearing."

"What's the plan?" Devon asked. As far as he was concerned, he was here as 'the help'.

"Oh!" Beth sounded like she'd been caught with her hand in the biscuit barrel. "I planned to go in and get my friends." She paused, then confessed, "I hadn't gone as far as the details."

"We could leave Jet just at the point where the track bends left. I suppose we could sneak to the edge of the clearing and have a look, then make a plan?" he offered. Devon didn't know what skills he had to call upon. Apart from being able to kill a man with a pebble at thirty paces, that is.

"That'll work for starters," Beth replied.

Does she even want me here? Devon contemplated.

<You are so caught on her,> Izzy said. <Such a big softy.>

<I wondered if you were around somewhere,> Devon said. He wasn't sure if the wisp had to follow him around or whether she just chose to. <I'm really fighting it, Izzy. I don't want that complication. She feels like trouble. We do this and get gone.>

<I'm here to help. I want to be near you,> Izzy replied, turning a redder shade of pink. She hadn't meant her words to sound quite so sentimental.

<Any chance you can have a look at the clearing?> he asked. <Maybe let me know what we're facing?> He felt like he needed to add something because he was asking a lot of her, and she had helped him a lot already. <Pretty please?>

<You are lucky that you are handsome,> Izzy hmphed at him. <That will be a favour you owe me.>

<Yes, indeed. Thank you, gorgeous,> Devon grovelled.

<Ooh! He flirts too. Nice.>

Devon turned his attention to Beth. "Up for an adventure then?"

"Uh-huh," Beth replied. She was trying to hide her fear but failing.

Chapter 4

No good deed goes unpunished

Without him asking, Jet walked quietly along to where the track sharply curved to the left, then stopped. Devon took a breath, then swung his left leg over the horse's back and jumped down. When he landed, he turned and reached up to help Beth down, only to hear her land just behind him a moment later.

"Looking for me?" Beth whispered to him.

"Not really," Devon answered, then wearily turned to face her.

Beth put a finger to her lips and pointed into the trees.

With a sigh, Devon followed her into cover. <Can you stay out of sight, please, Jet?> he thought to her.

<No worries. We be safe. We be fine,> Jet replied.

Devon was able to put concerns about her safety to one side. The way she communicated with him always came with a sense of friendship and warmth. He still marvelled at how his brain could assemble the stream of images and concepts Jet sent him and translate them into her words.

It took a few minutes to skulk up to the edge of the slavers' camp. At one point, Beth turned and stared at him. "How can you move so quietly?" she demanded in a whisper. "You're a large man, and yet you move without any noise at all."

Devon just shrugged. "You probably can't hear me over the noise you make." He motioned for her to move on. Fortunately, Beth didn't press the question, and so he was saved having to invent a response.

The trees ended abruptly. They found some large bushes to use for cover. With a bit of manoeuvring, they managed to wriggle under one and obtained a fair view of the small camp without being too visible.

Fortunately, they still had the cover of partial darkness because their position wasn't brilliant. In front of them was a large floodlight illuminating the grass-carpeted clearing and the camp itself. A generator squatted beside the light. It rumbled happily to itself, generously providing some noise cover too. There were several roughly constructed wooden huts clustered around a large, central campfire. One had its door facing them, another off to the left, and the last just to the right. Stones encircled the campfire to stop it from spreading out, although the fire smoked listlessly rather than burnt at this time of the morning. The musty smell of smoke, damp clothes, and sweat reached Devon's nose. Just off to the right, past the hut, was the beginning of the rough dirt road that led back to the road. Beside the track sat three empty cages identical to the one Devon had found Beth locked in. Near them, another flatbed van was parked. He saw wheel marks in the grass beside the truck, so he guessed that the vehicle Beth had taken was usually parked in that position. The place looked deserted apart from two men who sat on a long log to the left of the fire.

<Oh! You are hiding in there.> Izzy laughed inside Devon's head.

Devon scrambled out from under the bush and grinned at the wisp. She was spinning excitedly and had turned a shade of vivid pink. <What have you found for me?> Devon asked her.

<Straight to business? You're no fun,> Izzy replied, turning grey. She managed to convey a pout through her thoughts, and her wisp puckered.

<Sorry. I want to get this over with and move on. I thought we needed to be somewhere urgently?> Devon's muscles had started to feel listless, and he could feel his mood darkening. He was beginning to tire. It felt that he didn't have much to spare before his body called time. <I think the adrenaline from earlier is wearing off.>

<You'll get plenty more adrenaline soon enough,> Izzy replied. <Apart from the two men on the log, you have another four sleeping in that shack on your left. There's one more in the hut in front of you.>

<Wow! Good job on the intel.> Devon was impressed that she'd managed to find out so much in the short time she'd been gone. He swept his hand through his long fringe while thinking about what Izzy had told him. There were a lot of targets to deal with. Especially when his abilities were utterly untested unless he planned to throw rocks at them.

<It is easy when you're invisible to anyone without magic,> Izzy replied nonchalantly. <It was a cakewalk.>

<Any sign of Beth's friends?> More than anything else, he hoped she'd found them.

<If her friends are two women and a man who look scared out of their minds, then yes. They're in the building on the right. Those men are sitting on that log so they can watch the door.>

<What can I say? You're an absolute star, Izzy. Thank you.> He blew the wisp a kiss in an exaggerated gesture.

Izzy's wisp turned a deep red colour. <Stop! You've made me blush,> she thought back to him. She was still amazed that she had started reacting that way to him. If this continued, things would get complicated.

He shook his head in wonder at Izzy. *The changing colour thing is cool,* he thought. *My life may have become weirder than I dare to contemplate, but it has some perks.*

Then he realised the situation he was now in. He had all the information about the camp but no right way to explain to Beth how he'd got it.

He reached back into the bush and tapped Beth's ankle. She twitched then scrambled backwards out of the bush.

"What?" she snapped, glaring at him angrily. She was annoyed that he had dared to touch her.

"Woah! Calm down, you crazy female," Devon responded. He wondered why Beth was so quick to turn hostile toward him. "I just wanted to talk to you. I couldn't call out to you."

Beth sighed and mussed her hair. "I'm sorry. I overreacted. I'm not handling any of this very well. What did you want?"

"I don't suppose you know which hut your friends are in, do you?" he whispered to Beth.

"I think they're in that one." Beth pointed to the one on the right.

Right answer! "Okay. Assuming that's where they are, we ought to also assume that the other two buildings have hostile occupants," Devon said.

"That would be fair." She nodded.

"Here's the stinging question, Beth. How many hostiles do you think you could fight at one time?"

She looked at him worriedly. "Uhm! None, maybe one at a push – possibly. Sorry, Devon. I'm a scout, not a fighter. I've got my crossbow, but I only carry it for defence. Once I fire it, it takes me forever to reload."

<Little help, Izzy?>

<What do you need?> Izzy asked.

<Can I throw these throwing knives well enough to kill someone?>

<Yes, you can,> Izzy chirpily replied. <Have some faith in yourself.>

"Beth, have you got a plan yet, or would you be open to a suggestion?" Devon thought it prudent to let Beth lead. This was her party, after all.

Beth looked a little crestfallen and shrugged. "I'll take suggestions."

"Do you think you could sneak into the room where your friends are?" Devon swallowed hard before committing to the next part. "If I could drop those two on the log without raising the alarm?"

Beth blinked at him in shock. "You could do that?"

"Well, you've just told me you couldn't. I won't know if I can until I try, but I have a feeling that I could," Devon hazarded. He wasn't confident in himself at all.

Looking at Beth, he gave a little shrug and sighed. "Are we going to try this?"

"I don't have a choice," Beth said. "I can't leave them in there. I'd never see them again. If I must risk my life to get them out, then I have to try."

"Your life won't be in any danger if I can help it. You've got this, Beth," Devon said, trying to reassure her. He could sense the pressure that Beth was putting on herself to rescue her friends, understanding why she had to do this even though she didn't feel up to it. Helping her was just the right thing to do.

"Wait here and watch the two on the log. If they topple and stay down, and if no-one starts reacting, sprint across to the hut where your friends are and try and get them out," Devon said.

Beth nodded gravely.

"If you free them, lead them back here. If I'm not here waiting for you, just keep going and get back to the van as quickly as you can. Then head for wherever it is you call home. Don't stop to wait for me."

Beth looked as if she was about to say something but instead reached over and touched his arm. She nodded and moved back into the bush to watch the two sentries.

Devon crept a short way around the edge of the clearing, trying to be as quiet as possible, until he had a clear view of the backs of the two men. He drew a throwing knife into each hand and readied them. He carefully assessed the range, and his instinct took over. Understanding of how the blades would rotate at that range and how to adjust his hold to compensate for the spin was all there in his head. He revelled in the knowledge of such things.

He drew his arms back with a quiet exhalation and threw both knives at the man on the left. The daggers spun away, and in just a fraction of a heartbeat, both embedded themselves deeply, just below the man's skull. The target fell forward, his life extinguished.

A heartbeat later, Devon had more knives in his hands and had thrown them too. Realising his partner had fallen, the target just had time to move slightly, and the left blade missed him; luckily, the other hit and sank deeply into his neck. The man managed to cry out in surprise before he fell off the log and lay still.

A few tension-laced seconds passed. Devon waited for the pandemonium to erupt. Instead, he heard footsteps inside the building to the left, where Izzy had said the four other slavers were.

Shit! Here we go.

He looked right and saw Beth darting across the clearing to the hut where her friends were. She, evidently, hadn't heard the footsteps. Devon needed to act before someone emerged and saw her. He quickly ran out into the clearing, feet moving swiftly, then bolted for the side of the building.

His destination reached without trouble; he tucked himself flat against the wall, perpendicular to the door. He carefully withdrew the swords from his back. His muscles sang, and his heart pumped rapidly. The feeling of the blood racing through his arteries elated him. Devon felt built for this type of action. He breathed deeply, then focused. The door opened, and Devon waited another second before jumping out and spinning to face the door, side-on. The tension that had built in preparation for a fight died a little. No-one was there. Whoever had opened the door must be standing just inside.

"What? I'm just going to see what that bloody noise was," a male voice grumbled from inside the doorway.

Devon couldn't see anything from his position as he was looking at the door from the side. Instead, he took a chance. Devon reached around at stomach height and stabbed his sword hard into the doorway, withdrawing his blade upon hearing a pained grunt. Something heavy and well-padded collapsed onto the floor. Devon's nose twitched as he scented the man's blood. Looking at his sword, he saw six inches of gore coating it. Strike one.

"Ben! What's wrong? Fuck, he's bleeding," another voice shouted from inside the hut.

Aaaannnd action! Devon raced through the door and only just managed to jump over the prone man who lay there in his vest and underpants. Quickly taking in the scene, he saw two other men in their underpants running toward the door, each clutching a knife. The fourth was just scrabbling out of his bed at the far end.

Devon leapt forward to close the distance to his charging assailants. He lunged at the one on the left, who was slightly ahead of the other. The man swung at him with his dagger hand outstretched, and Devon swung the blade in his left hand without a thought. His sword swung up and across in a diagonal motion knocking the incoming blade aside and severing the man's hand. Thrusting forward with his right blade, he impaled the now screaming man through the chest.

By this point, the other man had got within attacking range and aimed a low blow intended to impale Devon in his right kidney.

Devon stepped back with his right leg, thus angling his body toward his latest attacker. The man's wild lunge glanced harmlessly across Devon's armour. Using his assailant's forward motion, he brought both blades up and crossed them in front of the man's neck. He then uncrossed the swords forcibly while pushing them forward. The man froze. His head tilted and toppled sideways while his body collapsed. Blood flowing freely from both.

"You bastard! I'll fucking kill you," the last man screamed at Devon. He charged madly at him with a short sword outstretched. Just as the man reached him, Devon stepped to the right and stuck his left foot out. The man tripped over it and fell flat on his face. Devon was on him in an instant, two blades piercing the man's back.

Again, Devon felt the urge to reach out with his arm. He replaced his blades and allowed his right arm to reach forward, palm cupped and facing upwards. The bodies began to mist and sparkle, then four shadows sped to him, disappearing into his waiting hand. A second later, two more rushed in through the door and joined the others.

<And Death walks among us.> Izzy's thought to him was sombre, her wisp now black. <All mortals should fear the Reaper.>

Devon sank to his knees, his body shaking as shock and understanding washed through him. Tears flowed unbidden from his eyes, down his blood-spattered face. Ignoring the gore that coated the floor, he bowed his head in shame and wept. <Six lives extinguished all too easily, Izzy. Is that who I am now?> Recent events and emotions caught up with him all at once. He didn't know how he knew, but he was sure that the Reaper Izzy had referred to was him. The human he had been cursed to be was gone. His mind felt no confusion or doubt now. Death was who he had always been, and Jet was his horse.

<Welcome back, my lord. It has been too long. You must carry on, though. Pick yourself up from the floor.> Izzy's thoughts were both regretful and apologetic. <You are not finished yet. There will soon be time for answers, I promise.>

Sniffing, he sighed hard and got back to his feet. The hut reeked of blood and effluent from the bodies. The floor was sticky and gruesome, and he was done in here.

He retrieved another two throwing-knives and crept back out of the door. Once outside, he saw Beth emerging from the building accompanied by a woman and a man.

<I thought there were three friends, Izzy?>

<There were,> she replied, her thoughts were grim, and her wisp turned black.

He saw Beth glance across to him, and her face froze in horror. It wasn't a surprise. He was coated from head to feet in blood and gore from his last encounter. His swords were still dripping blood down his back, and he was in a defensive crouch with knives in his hands. He must be a scary thing to behold. Her friends saw where she was staring and followed her gaze. Their faces took on the same terrified visage.

At that moment, the door to the last occupied building was flung open. Devon saw a tall, heavyset man emerge. Like his colleagues, he was trouser-less, but unlike the others, he had a pistol. *Double shit! Not good.* He didn't have a good answer for guns. He needed to close the gap.

There was a moment's pause, and then there was a gunshot.

In the same instance, Devon launched both of his knives at the man and jumped hard to the left. He rolled when he landed and then emerged from the roll on his feet, going straight into a weaving sprint toward the gunman. Devon drew another knife and threw it as a second gunshot rang out. He felt an intense pain pierce his left shoulder and another erupt from his back.

Devon was knocked off-balance slightly, but he gritted his teeth and pushed hard against the agony that was trying to claim him. It yielded somewhat, allowing him to run on. *Owwww, that smarts!*

A loud exclamation of pain came from his target just before Devon managed to reach him. His third throwing-knife had found the man's chest. The man winced but managed to aim his gun again. In an instant, Devon unsheathed both daggers and dived into another roll, attempting to avoid the next shot. He was so nearly there.

Sure enough, another gunshot echoed around the clearing, but no more pain found him. Instead, he emerged from his roll on one knee, both daggers piercing steeply upwards into the man's groin. His momentum pushed the blades deeper, forcing them up to the hilt. He pulled the knives back quickly with a spiteful twist, and a fountain of gore followed them out. Rolling to the side, he got to his feet again.

"Eeeeeeeeeeeeeeeyeowwww!" the man screamed while sinking to his knees. He gave Devon a hate-filled look and then fell backwards.

<Take that for the team, baby!> Izzy squealed. <That has got to hurt.>

Devon stepped inside the last hut and was grateful for the lack of any other hostiles. He did notice a girl, prone, on the bed, sobbing; her clothes were mostly intact, so he hoped he'd got there in time. The thought occurred to him to help the stricken woman, but maybe the last thing she wanted to see was another man. Especially one coated in blood. He turned and stepped back out.

Looking back over to where he'd last seen Beth, he noticed that she was still standing there, staring at him with the same horror. "Beth, I think your other friend is in there," he said, pointing back into the building.

Devon cleaned his daggers on the man's clothes, then re-sheathed them. He bent over the corpse and pulled out his throwing-knife while, at the same time, surreptitiously harvesting the man's shadowy spirit. Devon was reasonably sure that Beth hadn't seen his actions. No need to reveal more than necessary.

<Those are souls I'm harvesting, aren't they, Izzy?>

<Yes. It is what you do. You use them as a currency.>

He was happy that he would be parting ways with Beth and her friends. He would be glad to have a little time to gather his thoughts and work out who he was now. Blood dripped from his shoulder. The bullet had passed through, but he'd need to patch himself up somehow.

Devon considered looting the bodies but decided he had no interest in anything they had, including that man's pistol. Guns had no fascination for him, and he certainly had no ambition ever to use one. Instead, Devon went over to retrieve his other blades from the bodies by the log. After wiping them and stowing them away, he slumped down and let exhaustion take him.

<Enough with the good deeds. I'm done, Izzy.>

<Quest complete! Reputation increased. Your gorgeous wisp companion now reveres you,> Izzy thought to him. She'd turned a soothing beige colour, while her thoughts brought sympathy and care with them, and Devon felt grateful.

Then something hard hit him across the back of his head, and the lights winked out.

Chapter 5

While you were sleeping

The small room smelled of dampness and neglect; nobody had lived here in decades. Paint flaked off the walls where ancient wallpaper wasn't peeling from them instead. Bare, ill-fitting floorboards covered the floor while plaster sagged listlessly from the ceiling. Beth stood beside an old, iron-framed bed; its slightly mouldy mattress creating a stark contrast to the tanned Adonis that lay atop it. The cords binding him looked weak, insufficient to secure the strapping man's ankles and wrists. The bed wasn't quite long enough to fit his frame, and it only just contained the breadth of his shoulders. His striking white hair was trimmed halfway down his neck, and he sported a floppy fringe that would meet his eyebrows if allowed to fall straight. His silver eyes were currently closed and peaceful. When they were open, they were intense and hypnotic. There lay a man that she could so easily fall for – was, so easily falling for.

Beth had no intention of permitting such a thing to happen. She didn't want any sort of relationship. She could never trust anyone enough to commit to them, least of all Devon. Here was someone shrouded in mystery. He couldn't be with the Hextaine corporation. All consortium employees had implants and numerous biotech nodes inside them; Devon had none – she'd checked, thoroughly. Beth had also searched through the corporation's database for his face, but that had revealed nothing. Yet he fought like a super-soldier. Even a gunshot wound hadn't slowed him. After all that, he still looked so adorable while he slept. So peaceful and – gorgeous.

Stop it! Beth thought to herself angrily while taking a deep breath and ploughing her feelings below the surface. *I can resist this. I'm strong.*

Unfortunately, the village had no concern for her feelings; they needed him. They were a group of misfits and refugees who had discovered this abandoned village and stayed. Their hatred of the system and fear of the establishment were the only things that held them together. Their biggest problem was their desperate lack of individuals who could defend them. They weren't fighters; the village was full of ex-academics, runaways, and displaced families. They only had one capable fighter amongst their entire population, and that was Gwen. Probably the oddest female she'd ever met. Her friend, Beks, had been a sapper in the army, but her ordeals had made her commit to pacifism for life.

Gwen was currently leaning against the far wall. She was guarding Devon while he slept off the drugs they'd injected into him. Her pixie-cut, black hair appeared tousled through lack of sleep and her habit of running her hands through it when boredom struck. She was currently using her spear as a prop.

"If you're tired, then go and get Steph; she can cover for you while you get a few hours rest," Beth said to Gwen.

Gwen glared sulkily at her. "You just want to be alone with him. I want him. I'd be good to him, not knock him out and drag him back to this dump," she said, then slouched off sulkily to find Steph.

Beth knew that Gwen wasn't happy with village life, so she ignored her outburst. This place bored her, and the people here bored her even more. Before she ended up at the village, she'd been in one of Hextaine's many armies but deserted when her regiment received orders to attack a civilian encampment. While the dull existence had helped her readjust to the world's new order, it was too quiet for a live wire such as Gwen. The world didn't have a place for a woman who mostly lived in the fantasy books she read and had ambitions of becoming a witch, not these days. After the army, Gwen had become fascinated with the occult. She claimed that she was now a follower of Wicca. Whatever Wicca was, it wasn't a science, and so Beth wasn't interested. Gwen and Devon would probably get along splendidly, though. Gwen was not afraid of violence and inflicting suffering on those she disliked.

Beth grimaced to herself. Devon's victims didn't suffer much. They tended to get eviscerated and spray gore everywhere. That thought brought recent memories back to mind, and she shuddered. Regardless of how strange Gwen was, if she left, they'd have no-one to protect them. Beth knew that Devon would be the perfect person to assure the safety of the entire village. They wouldn't need anyone else. That man could single-handedly keep every resident from harm.

Beth felt that she'd already burnt that bridge, though. While Beth did like him, she couldn't see past what he'd done in that slaver camp. He was a killer with outdated ideas. Both were a turn-off for her, yet she couldn't look at him without wanting him.

****_****

Consciousness floated back to Devon once again. *What happened?* He rifled through his memories and found the one he wanted. That gave him a slight sense of achievement; his memories hadn't been reliable lately. He remembered a sharp pain after being struck from behind. He'd fought hard and killed all the slavers, and then someone had hit him. *Who the hell could have hit me?* Images of the fights, getting shot, and Beth's horrified face flooded back to him but still no obvious culprit for the blow that knocked him out. *Did I miss one of the slavers? Am I a prisoner now?*

He was about to open his eyes to look around when he had a better idea. <Izzy? Are you there?>

<Right here,> Izzy replied.

Devon searched for his recently discovered bond to Jet; mercifully, it was still there. He tugged at the link.

<We be near, waiting. Ready and waiting,> Jet responded, along with a sense of well-being and contentment.

<What happened back in that camp? Who hit me?> he asked Izzy.

Izzy's thoughts revealed a copious amount of anger and a hint of sadness. <I hate to be the bearer of bad news, but that fickle bitch, Beth, hit you with a piece of pipe. She had it stowed in her pack.>

Annoyance turned to anger which flared to rage as emotions flooded through him in a torrent. <I'm, so, bloody, stupid!> A hundred sentences queued up to be voiced, and he knew that each one would include the word 'bitch' and probably some choice profanities. *Not. Bloody. Cool!*

<Just so that you know, she is standing in the room. You are tied to a bed, and she is out of reach.> Izzy's anger was getting more intense. <The ropes binding you are old and not tied very well.>

"Got anything to say for yourself, Elizabeth?" he said aloud without bothering to open his eyes.

"What the…?" Beth said, her voice incredulous. Her relaxed demeanour snapped to attention.

Devon opened his eyes. After taking a moment to blink, he found her leaning against a wall in the far corner. A closed door was just to her right, and, on the left, there was a woman dressed all in black. She wore tight hot pants, a t-shirt, and a black leather jacket, finished off with thigh-high, hold-up stockings, and heavy leather boots. Devon admired her fashion choices. The woman's hair was jet-black and just short of shoulder-length. Her eyes were an intense, dark green which bored into him as she stared right back. He tried not to let himself become distracted by the other woman. Instead, he focused a hateful glare on Beth.

"Thanks for the assistance back there. Very sweet of you. Devious bitch!" Devon said. He tried to convey all the dark thoughts that he was experiencing in the latter two words.

Devon checked his arms and legs and found that he was, indeed, tied to the bed. He trusted Izzy's estimate of the ropes' effectiveness, though. They felt neither tight nor robust. The metal bedframe he was secured to was rickety and old. Escape wouldn't be tricky; it would just need a little effort.

He noticed a bandage on his left shoulder and remembered the shot that had wounded him. He also recalled the pain it had caused. Devon winced as he rotated the joint a little to see if it still hurt. The bandage was clean, and didn't show any blood traces, so somebody must have recently tended the wounds. He was divine and would heal rapidly, but not even gods were immune to damage. It just meant that life would return to their dead body as they repaired themselves. Assuming their soul remained in place.

Devon turned his attention to the room in which he was being held captive. It was dilapidated, damp, and mould pocked the decaying walls. His eyes landed on Beth once again; he glared at her and growled. He hadn't meant to make the noise, but it had just escaped from his lips unbidden. It was a low, feral sound, loud and full of threat.

The black-haired women smiled broadly. "Cool! Awesome growl."

Beth stood up straight and looked at him in shock. "What the hell are you, Devon?"

"What am I?" he choked. "I'm not even important enough to be a who?"

"You remember what you did back at the slaver camp, right? All those men? I've never seen so much blood. You killed seven of them in less than half as many minutes. Not to mention the other two you wiped out before that."

"And?" Devon couldn't understand what Beth's problem was. "You'd rather I let them kill you and rape your friends? Those men deserved to perish for what they've done to people like you and the others. You asked for my help, remember? What did you expect me to do; swear at them?"

"You cut someone's fucking head off, Devon!" Beth's voice showed hints of hysteria and fear. "How do you even do something like that?" Her voice was rising in pitch now. She paused, took a deep breath, and tried to calm herself.

He glowered at Beth in a fit of fury. "By my reckoning, I saved your worthless arse many times over. A thoroughly pointless task, as I found out. Do you think you have a right to hit me and tie me up? You're worse than the fucking slavers. Your friend was about to be raped. Should I have just let that happen? You think they'd have let you just walk in there, say 'oh, excuse me, please,' and just take their prisoners away?" His anger had reached its zenith, and he knew that he ought to try and regain some sense of calm, but he just couldn't.

<No good deed goes unpunished,> Izzy interjected.

Beth sighed and hung her head. "No. I couldn't have got them out had you not done what you did. For that, I thank you."

"You damn well got that right. And save your thanks. You worthless, untrustworthy bitch." He was shouting now. "You showed your gratitude with some forcibly applied plumbing to the back of my head. I could do without your form of appreciation."

Beth's jaw dropped. "How the hell do you know all this stuff? How could you know I was in the room without even opening your eyes? How the hell could you know what I used to strike you? I mean, how could you possibly even have known that it was me that hit you?"

<Tell her nothing,> Izzy said. Her thoughts conveyed hatred for the woman she'd earlier been promoting as a love interest.

"How I know is none of your business. I am none of your business. Why would I tell you anyway? As of now, you are the enemy." Devon managed to force himself to take a deep breath and calm down a little.

"I'm not your enemy, Devon. Not now, not ever," Beth said. Her voice was soft and sad. "Were you a soldier before? An assassin, maybe?"

"I'll be the judge of who my enemies are. You certainly don't get a say in the matter," he said. He tried to keep the petulance out of his voice. "I told you the truth when I let you out of the cage. I have no memory of anything from before I woke up by the road. I couldn't even remember my name. All you have done so far is make my life worse."

<How long have I been unconscious, Izzy?>

<About twelve hours, since she knocked you out,> Izzy replied. <Beth and her buddies loaded a cage onto the other van and between them managed to bundle you in. They tried to find Jet but couldn't. When they had moved on, your wonderful horse followed them back to this village."

"I swear you're talking to someone else when you tune out like that," Beth stated. "I've scanned you for trackers, tracers, implants, nodes, genetic mods, even nano-meds. Nothing."

Devon gave her another hateful glare which made her wince. "You must think you're a real genius. I bet you're so proud of yourself," Devon taunted her, doing his best to convey the maximum malice he could muster. "I wish I'd left you in that damn cage."

"No, you don't, Devon. I knew you were a good person when you held your hand out to me." Beth kept her voice gentle. She just ignored his spite and ploughed on. "Then you wiped out an entire slaver camp by yourself and painted the walls with their blood and guts." She closed her eyes and breathed deeply. "What you did scared me, and I panicked."

"Poor baby. How you've suffered," he muttered, lacing every word with as much sarcasm as he could. Devon could tell that just the memory of his work sickened her. He looked at his clothes and noticed that someone had dressed him in a T-shirt and loose, cotton trousers with an elasticated waist. Almost the exact outfit he'd been wearing before he got his armour.

<Izzy, where did my weapons and armour go?>

<Your equipment is enchanted,> Izzy replied. <If anyone tries to steal it, then it goes back into storage.>

<Wow! That's useful.> The clothes he'd been dressed in fitted him a little better than the stuff he'd woken up in. They were a generic blue, though. "Was it you that changed my clothes?"

"No." She blushed.

<What the hell?> Izzy screamed in his mind. <Red has feelings for you. Cheeky ginger cow! When I get my body back, I will scratch her fucking eyes out.>

It amused Devon that Izzy had named Beth 'Red'. It might have been a good nickname for her, but he didn't plan on hanging around for long enough to worry about that.

"Madison changed your clothes when she treated your injuries," Beth continued. "She's our camp physician and leader. She stitched and tended your wound, then gave you antibiotics. Without you, she'd be a slave by now." She shook her head and sighed. "So would I, if I'm honest." Her eyes flicked to his left shoulder. "Does your shoulder hurt?"

Devon felt his anger evaporate but tried to hold on to it. He still wanted to hate her but try as he might; he couldn't. "Why do you care?" He saw a flash of annoyance cross Beth's features which she quickly quashed.

"I care. Believe it or not. I truly care. Not just that, we're all grateful for what you did for us." She collected her thoughts, then pressed on. "Fighters like you only exist in elite, corporate death-squads. Soldiers capable of doing what you did are genetically modified brutes. Hextaine corporation fills them with implants and stimulates them intravenously, often well beyond safe limits."

Beth knew she was fighting a losing battle trying to win Devon around, but they badly needed him. She also knew that she deserved every harsh word and thought he had for her. Right now, she hated herself for what she had done to the only man in the world willing to help her. "You have to understand, Devon. We're just a small group of refugees. We don't have anyone that could stand up to a destructive force like you. I weighed the options and did the safest thing for us. I added the facts up and felt that you had to be working for the enemy. Nothing else made any sense. I got it wrong. I'm sorry."

"You could have just left me alone." He shook his head and sighed hard. "I just wanted to help you, but you made sure I learnt not to do that again," Devon said.

Devon noticed that the black-haired lady had been grinning during the entire exchange with Beth. "What's so funny?" he asked angrily, focusing on the woman.

"Devon, this is Gwen," Beth said. "She's supposed to be guarding you, but instead, she's decided you're some sort of superhero."

"Damn, Beth! If he'd saved my life multiple times, I'd be more grateful than you're being. Much more grateful," Gwen said, giving Devon a smouldering look.

<Uhm! Devon, that woman is part faie. There is something magical, sleeping inside her; I can feel it. It is powerful but dormant.>

<Is that good or bad?> Devon asked.

<That depends. I would say good, probably.>

"You can't keep me here, Beth. I've got places to be," Devon said. He strained against the cords that bound him, and they all gave way. He undid the poorly tied knots and flung the rope to the floor in distaste.

"Can I go with you?" Gwen asked. Her face became animated; emerald eyes sparkling as she locked them upon Devon.

Devon looked closely at her for the first time. He admired her heart-shaped face, with its slightly pronounced cheekbones. He felt like her attractive, green eyes looked straight into his heart as they gazed questioningly at him. Her right eyebrow raised slightly as she waited for his reply.

"'How grateful are we talking, Gwen?" He raised his eyebrow in response.

"I'm open to negotiate all aspects of the deal. For the right offer, I'm up for anything," Gwen said. She gave him a predatory smile. "You seem like my type. Will your wisp be jealous?"

Izzy squeaked, and Devon's jaw dropped. He put his finger to his lips, hoping that Gwen would get the message and keep the existence of Izzy a secret.

Beth shook her head. "You two seem made for each other. The world better watch out," she said, with a deep note of sadness in her tone. Her brown eyes softened and became damp. She took a deep breath and made her best attempt at a smile. "I'll go and pack you both some food. I'd hate for you to go hungry, Devon. You've not eaten since I met you." She turned and left the room, leaving the door open as she went.

Devon was confused. His emotions were in turmoil. He may be mistaken, but Beth had just been nice to him. It appeared there were now three females in his life, and the one that he understood best was his horse. He refused to count Beth, and nothing his libido said would count as evidence.

"Well, you're an enigma, Gwen," Devon said with a warm smile.

"Thus speaks a fellow enigma," Gwen replied happily. "I can join you both then?"

"We're three in total. You've not met my horse," Devon didn't feel like keeping anything from this woman. She was such a contrast to Beth.

"Give me twenty minutes. I've got to grab my stuff. I have some books I just can't leave behind, and I'll need my blades and some food. Oo! I'll need clothes and –"

"Go and get your stuff, Gwen. We'll wait right here," Devon chuckled. "And don't worry about bringing too much. I've got space in my bags."

Gwen made him go gooey with the smile she gave him. Then she bolted out of the room.

<She saw me,> Izzy said; her thoughts were part worried, part impressed.

<I sense we've just gained a valuable member of our team,> Devon said.

Chapter 6
Under attack

Devon breathed in deeply as he emerged from his makeshift prison. He looked around and found that he was standing on a crumbling pavement that ran alongside a broken road. When Beth had mentioned her village, he had imagined a cosy little group of houses nestled in the countryside somewhere. In reality, the settlement consisted of tightly packed concrete boxes in an advanced state of decay. It depressed him to think that people could be so desperate for shelter that they should choose to live here. The whole place smelled of mould and... *blood? Why blood? How could that be?* Then he heard a gunshot and a female voice scream his name loudly. He knew instantly that it was his red-haired bane.

<Jet,> he thought to her through their bond. <Come quickly. We've got trouble.> A moment later, he received a positive response from her. A shadow bloomed against the house across the street, and Jet materialised out of it. *Wow! That horse has skills.* Seconds later, she was next to him, and he was reaching into her saddlebags and thinking about equipping himself. Once he was back in his armour with his full complement of weapons, he reached up to the pommel and propelled himself upwards and into the saddle.

Jet knew precisely what he wanted, and as soon as he mounted, she whirled around and galloped further into the village. Devon wondered if she'd already spent time familiarising herself with the area. She was far more intelligent than he'd imagined possible.

<Izzy, can you check around, please?> Devon thought to her.

<Already on it,> she replied.

Even though the road was uneven, Jet thundered forward. It took her less than a minute to erupt into a clear area that looked as if it had once been the village's centre. The crumbling road orbited an overgrown, central circle that was about one-hundred yards in diameter. There was a hulking, lichen-covered obelisk of some sort in the centre, with a low surrounding wall that was in the process of crumbling away. Rough grass sprouted in clumps where it had managed to break through the stone.

<Four slavers are loading the villagers into two covered lorries. There is also a driver in each cab. Three of the guards have handguns. I will check for others nearby,> Izzy reported. <They are parked on the other

side of the monument. No-one has seen you yet. Red took a gunshot, but not fatally.>

<I badly need a bow. Closing the distance to a shooter is painful,> Devon moaned. He received a warning from Jet and shifted his balance forward as she stopped suddenly. The momentum and his jump took him over her head. After a neat somersault, he landed cleanly beside the monument. He still couldn't see the slavers yet, but his gaze found the canvassed rooves of the two lorries. It didn't even occur to him that the dismount he'd just executed was majorly impressive. It had just happened.

Devon was happy to see the dilapidated wall nearby had shed numerous lumps of stone. After choosing a few that were just small enough for him to throw effectively, he ducked down and inched around the stone obelisk. He could see the back of the closest lorry and a man holding a pistol standing by the tailgate. There were no other slavers in view.

Izzy's wisp fleeted across the village's central area and came to rest above Devon's head. <You have four more who are searching the houses. Two groups of two,> she reported.

<Impressive intelligence work. Thanks,> Devon replied.

Without pausing, he adjusted his aim a little then threw his first rock as hard as he could. The rock slightly veered as it flew, yet still hit the man exactly where he'd aimed, between the eyes. Devon wondered if his brain had somehow expected the difference of trajectory and allowed for it. He felt a grim pleasure when the man's head slammed back into the lorry's tailgate and his body collapsed.

The next moment, he heard rapid footsteps as another man emerged from the side of the vehicle. Devon's missile was already airborne. The man looked at his fallen comrade and joined him when a sizeable stone, moving at speed, struck him, collapsing the right-hand side of his skull.

<I will keep an eye on the men searching the village,> Izzy said.

The wisp sped off as Devon sprinted toward the back of the rearmost lorry. Inside, he could see frightened faces peering out at him. Before he reached the vehicle, someone stood up and pointed a gun at him. *Shit!* He leapt sideways and grabbed a throwing-knife in each hand. A shot rang out, and something pinged loudly off the monument's stone. *Hah! Missed!* He launched his two blades at the gunman and heard the soft squelch as they found their target. Before he had time to dodge, his victim was pushed forcibly out of the back of the lorry. The corpse hit Devon and knocked him to the ground.

"Rats! Sorry about that," a man's voice said, apologetically, from inside the lorry.

Devon ignored him and clambered back to his feet. If the man was apologising, it was unlikely that he was hostile. The situation would probably seem funny to him later, but right now, he was just annoyed. These villagers were nothing but trouble for him thus far. He took off at a sprint down the side of the lorry to the cab. Izzy had said that each vehicle had a driver. Sure enough, the off-side door was just swinging open, propelled by a khaki-clad arm. Devon grabbed the arm and pulled hard, then quickly unsheathed his daggers. The driver yelped and tumbled out of the vehicle, landing heavily on the floor. A blade pierced his throat, and Devon was off, running again.

He got to the front lorry's cab door and saw that the window was open, but there was no-one inside. He heard a movement close behind him, and he reflexively jumped straight upward. His feet found the sill of the driver's window, and he launched himself backwards. As he performed a graceful backward somersault, he saw a chunky man pointing a gun at the point where he'd just been. "Too slow, asshole!" he growled as he slashed both daggers downward. The man screamed in pain as one dagger bit deeply into his shoulder and the other cut into his face. The slaver collapsed to his knees, blood pouring from his upper body. Devon deftly landed behind him and ended the man's life.

His hand shot forward and collected four souls. According to Izzy's intelligence, he was missing two more. They'd be here somewhere. Devon dropped down to lie flat on the ground and then peered under the lorry. Sure enough, he saw two pairs of boots stalking around the front. The vehicle had ample ground clearance, and Devon noticed an opportunity. He rolled underneath and waited. The slavers took their time, pausing to inspect the dead guard, then carefully looked around for whoever had done this to their colleague.

Devon thrust both daggers through one of the men's knees when the two finally came close enough; then struck again, slashing the other slaver's thighs deeply. They both yelled in agony and tried to stumble backwards. The first man's damaged leg joints gave way, and he collapsed sideways. His life was cut short by a knife piercing his heart. The other rapidly met his demise as he fell and instantly had his throat cut. Devon added two more souls to his collection and then rolled back out from under the lorry.

<Nicely done, hero,> Izzy said. <You will be pleased to hear that Gwen has speared two of the remaining four. The other two are

sprinting toward your position. Twenty seconds and they will reach the centre.>

<We need Gwen on our team. If those idiots weren't so spread out, it would have been more brutal.>

<They are probably unaccustomed to people fighting back,> Izzy said.

Devon ran to the back of the lorry. "Stay in the vehicle for now," he said urgently to the villagers. Then he repeated his instructions when he got to the other one. A muscular man walked around the back corner of the vehicle. He had a badly bruised eye, but Devon didn't have time to notice more. His daggers were up and ready.

The man raised his hands. "Woah! I'm on your side, I swear."

"Then get out of sight now; we're about to have company," Devon snapped. He may have sounded a little forceful, but he didn't need this idiot's death on his conscience. Thankfully the man nodded and ducked back out of view.

Glancing around, Devon found and grabbed the blood-covered rock he had used to kill the first slaver. He turned in time to see two heavyset thugs lumbering into the centre from the road he'd ridden in on. Devon wondered how they'd missed each other. He loped across the street and concealed himself behind the monument again. Tiredness was seeping into him, probably due to lack of sustenance. Beth had been right about one thing; he hadn't eaten since he'd awoken. As if he'd reminded his stomach of its plight, it grumbled noisily.

Peering around the obelisk, he saw that one of the remaining men had a handgun and the other a long dagger. The rock he'd been holding whizzed away from Devon's hand and struck the man with the gun, toppling him instantly. The last slaver looked shocked at the death of his colleague, then shouted when he spotted Devon. He started to charge at him, dagger outstretched. His momentum was interrupted when a spear travelling at speed hit him in the back. The man hit the ground face first and lay still.

<I agree. We want her on our team,> Izzy said as Gwen jogged over to the corpse to retrieve her weapon.

"Nice shot. I think I'll stay on your good side," Devon said to Gwen.

She gave him a broad smile and flexed her bicep at him.

After collecting the last of the souls, Devon walked back to the lorries. The man he'd met earlier was standing there waiting for him.

"What the hell did you just do?" Gwen shouted after him in amazement. "Did you just… No way, that's unbelievable. Did you just take their souls or something?"

<Busted, hero,> Izzy thought with added smugness.

"Yes, but keep it to yourself," Devon hissed back at her. "I'm still not clear on the details. My memories are all screwed up right now."

"Mmkay," she replied. "Wow! Shit just got interesting!"

"That was incredible. Thank you, thank you, thank you," the annoying man said to Devon as he ran up to him. His face looked tired and beaten, yet pleased too. The bruising around his eye was darkening rapidly, but Devon noticed that he had handsome features and a smile that made him want to smile back. "How rude of me – my name is Finn. I am Madison's husband. You've saved our lives twice now. How can we ever repay you for what you've done?" He stuck his hand out.

Devon reached out to him, took his hand, and shook it, paying him some attention for the first time. Finn was about six feet tall, with a muscular, square build. It was clear he'd led a physical, outdoor life because he had a deep tan that he'd accumulated over the years. He had short cut, salt-and-pepper hair and some facial hair growing in. Devon suspected that it would be gone in the morning, though. His powerful jawline put him on the handsome side of rugged, and his piercing, grey eyes made him striking to look at. In all, he was a good-looking man. Finn spoke with a well-educated, upper-class accent, which sounded out of place around these parts.

"Nice to meet you," Devon said with a smile. "It's a shame the circumstances weren't better. As for repayment, I haven't eaten in over twenty-four hours, and I've been a prisoner here for nearly that entire time. You could start by fixing that oversight."

"Oh my days! You must think of us as such terrible hosts. Leave that with me. By the way, could you teach me how to throw as well as you do? I have never seen anything quite like it."

A lady poked her head out of the back of the lorry. "Is it over?" she asked.

"Yes indeed, dear," Finn responded.

"Where's Red? Sorry, I mean Beth," Devon asked. He hadn't forgotten Izzy's new nickname for her or that she'd reported her shot earlier.

"In here. She's in pain but not in any danger of passing away. Although you would think she was if you heard the fuss she's been making," the woman replied, motioning to the dark interior of the slavers' vehicle. "The bullet clipped her neck. She is fortunate the slavers cannot shoot straight."

The villagers started emerging from the lorries as they realised their ordeal was over and they were safe. They blinked and looked at the corpses with fascination rather than horror. A few even kicked them.

"Do not wander off, everyone. I'm calling a village meeting right now," the lady shouted.

"Not interested, lady. I just want some food; then I'm leaving," Devon grumped. He noticed that most of the villagers were giving him grateful looks, and a few even looked him up and down approvingly. Their ordeal must have been traumatic and, from the appearance of the bruises that a few sported, rough too.

Devon felt a nuzzling at his neck and realised that Jet had walked around the circle and moved right up next to him without making the slightest sound. He heard a few appreciative noises when the others noticed her. He sent a feeling of pride to her and scratched her head affectionately.

He looked around him at the gathering crowd. These were just ordinary civilians, not a fighter among them. There were a few younger candidates who could learn, given the inclination and a chance. Finn seemed willing, at least. Thinking back, he remembered that Beth wasn't a fighter either; he'd just assumed she was from her aggressive demeanour. Gwen was the only one that appeared willing to fight back. Maybe stealing her away was unfair to the village, but that guilt would not stop him. An arm encircled his waist, and he found Gwen now standing next to him. Izzy sent him a smug thought, and, surprisingly, he also received a similar sentiment from Jet. He had to assume that Gwen now had their full support.

"Nicely done back there," he said to Gwen.

"I just got three," she replied with a grin. "It looks like you got the other seven. Impressive."

"It wasn't too bad once I'd recovered from Finn throwing a corpse at me," Devon chuckled.

Finn looked mortified when he heard Devon's words. "I am so sorry. Please forgive me. I meant to push your attacker out of the lorry. I didn't realise you had already killed him."

Devon grinned wolfishly at him. "A good plan. Apology accepted."

"Quiet down, please," the woman shouted above the villagers' rising hubbub – everyone seemed intent on comparing notes about their ordeals. Silence slowly descended on the gathering. The woman walked over to Devon. "First of all, I would like us all to thank our saviour for his timely efforts despite our treatment of him." The woman shot a displeased look at Beth, who was standing nearby having her neck bandaged. "Can someone please fetch him some food? He has not eaten since we took him prisoner, and we owe him our lives."

A smattering of applause started, interspersed with a few cheers and whistles. Devon was a little underwhelmed, but he hadn't expected any thanks at all; saving these people had happened without thought. It had just felt right to him.

<Devon, this is neither the time nor the place for long explanations, but believe me, saving people is one of the things you are famous for,> Izzy interjected. <It is what you do. You will remember that part of you in time. Being the Reaper is your job; you are not a killer for killing's sake; you are a bringer of justice. Do not let that bring you down. You are a merciful god and the one hope for anyone with nowhere else to turn.>

"All of us are in your debt, Devon. I am Madison, but please call me Madi," the woman, who was clearly in charge, said to Devon, offering him her hand. Numerous hand gestures accompanied her words, and the tone of her voice rose and fell exaggeratedly.

Devon gently shook the offered hand, surprised when she held on to him. He remembered that Finn had mentioned that this woman was his wife, and Beth had told him she was the village leader. Madison was almost the opposite of her husband. She was petite and good looking in a classically feminine way. Her face suggested she smiled a lot but had seen a good few years of worry too. It was a kind face with soft cheekbones and a nicely rounded outline. She had shoulder-length, hazel coloured hair and dark brown eyes that drew you in. "I suppose I have you to thank for patching me up?"

Madison dropped her gaze and looked guilty. "It was the very least we could do. Maybe one day you might tell me how your armour just disappeared when we tried to take it off, yet here you are, wearing it again."

"Don't hold your breath. I'm still not thrilled about the way certain members of your village have treated me. I was about to leave when I heard Beth scream out."

Madison looked distressed at his words but continued to hold his hand in her grasp. "I beg you not to judge us too harshly. You have witnessed the dangers we face. Paranoia is second nature to us."

Devon looked pointedly at Madison's hand to hint that it was past time to release him. Instead, Madison covered his hand with her other and held on to him more tightly. He wondered what her intentions were.

"Please stay for a short while longer. Our provisioner has gone to fetch you some food, she is a fabulous cook, and I hope you'll forgive us for not feeding you sooner. However, I am afraid we must ask you for a little more."

<You would be wise to familiarise yourself with her techniques of persuasion,> Izzy said. <She is well-practised at getting what she wants, and your good nature precludes you from refusing her requests.>

<Damn it!> How could he ever leave these people now?

<Devon, we have urgent business not far from here. If you must, bring these people with you. Do not offer to stay here with them, I beg you. Both of our lives depend on us getting to where we need to be.>

<I know. Well, I feel like I know. Things are still fuzzy. Details are proving tricky to focus on.>

Chapter 7

Yay! Presents

Devon pulled the pack from Jet's saddlebag as Izzy had instructed. When he had woken initially, she had told him that she'd brought gifts from her people, but he'd forgotten about it in the chaos that followed.

<I had been searching for you for many years,> Izzy explained to Devon. <Most of our people despaired and believed you had been destroyed, but not the priesthood. We always felt that you were banished somewhere, and we sought to find out where the queen had abandoned you. The book in the satchel is full of the notes I made of every tiny piece of information I could find about you during my years of searching. It might help with your memories.>

Devon thought about Izzy's words while he wandered over to the monument's crumbling wall and sat down. His promised food hadn't arrived yet, and so he was trying to catch up with the things that most urgently needed his attention. He was perturbed when Madison walked over to where he was seated and sat down beside him. She smiled warmly at him.

"Don't mind me. We normally have our village meetings here," Madison said. "By the way, everyone was very impressed with your use of stones as weapons. My husband is very taken with you; I sense some early signs of hero worship in him."

"I just did what had to be done. Look, Madison, while I am still annoyed at being held captive, I am willing to let that slide. I am grateful for the offer of food and will be more so if I eventually get some." Devon knew that the last comment was a bit of a low blow, but he hadn't been able to prevent the words from slipping out. He shouldn't judge the rest of the villagers by his experiences with one red-haired lunatic.

Madison's smile didn't falter at Devon's slight jibe. She knew how to get what she needed, and a little justified petulance from this man was understandable. Beth had been foolish in her actions, but she had brought him here. His unexpected presence had saved all of them. She was one of the people he had rescued from the slavers' camp and she knew what he was capable of. With this man in her clutches, they could start to feel safe and make a real go of creating a new life. Now all she had to do was keep him interested.

Gwen walked over to them with Jet following her. She sat down on the other side of Devon and sidled in so that she was touching him. "Alright, boss?"

Devon's stomach growled, and he winced. "At ease, soldier," he said with mock formality. "Although we're off to do some hunting soon if this promised food fails to materialise."

To distract him from his hunger, he opened the pack up and started to rummage. He drew out a few coils of the lightest, silkiest rope he could imagine. The fibres in it glistened with a silvery sheen, and it was soft to the touch.

<That is a gift from Mitsey, the best thief throughout the realms,> Izzy explained. <She is a member of our resistance in the fairy queen's realm. It is enchanted goblin rope. The more mana you feed into it, the longer it will become. It is one of the few remaining goblin artefacts.>

Devon didn't know how to respond. <Why? You said she is a thief, right? Why gift to me something of such value to her?>

<The rope is a token of her race's faith in you. The goblins, gnomes, and elves are the most downtrodden of all the species in that realm. Although everybody suffers, even all the fairies that aren't born in the winter. There is a pendant in the bag that is of vital importance to us. Mitsey risked her life stealing that from a high-security vault in the middle of the queen's most secure tower. She did it so that you would help us to be free of the queen's tyranny.>

<I wish I had that much faith in me.> Devon put the rope down and reached into the sack again. He pulled out a miniature model of a campfire. He admired the craftsmanship. It was intricately detailed and accurately painted so that the flames almost looked real. He could even see the woodgrain on the unburnt logs. <Wow! That's pretty. Is it an ornament of some kind?>

Izzy laughed. <Not as such. However, wealthy wizards were said to collect such things thousands of years ago. It is a magical, elven charm. It is a gift from my race to you. A token of faith. With it, you can make a comfortable camp anywhere you go.>

"That's pretty," Madison said. She had been observing Devon. He seemed to be full of surprises.

<How many people can the charm accommodate, Izzy?>

<Up to fifty, but there is only enough magical energy stored inside it for one application of that size.>

"It might come in handy," he replied to Madison.

"Are you happy for us to have a brief meeting while you eat and recover?" Madison asked him.

"It's your village. I have no problem with that," Devon answered with a smile. His food had just arrived, and he was thrilled to see that it was a sizeable tray, stacked high with cooked chicken dripping with sauce, accompanied by a substantial stack of fresh bread. "Thank you so much," he said to the smiling lady who had proudly laid the tray on his lap. She blushed and hurried off. If all the other villagers were this friendly, then he might enjoy keeping their company. Gwen reached in and grabbed a hunk of bread and dipped it in the pool of gravy around the meat platter. Devon gave her one of his feral growls, which made Madison jump and stare at him in shock. Gwen just grinned and bit into her gravy-soaked bread.

Madison stood up and began to discuss the villagers' situation as Devon demolished his long-awaited food with fervour. Gwen helped a little, but Devon knew she was only doing it to keep his attention. His stomach sent happy messages to his brain as it swelled satisfyingly. He noticed Madison constantly watching him out of the corner of her eye and realised that she had been waiting for him to finish because as soon as he set his tray on the ground, she dropped her bombshell.

"We have to leave this place and find somewhere else where we can be safer," Madison said. "It is a hard decision to make, but the slavers know where we are now. The next time they come, there will be more of them."

Devon had another issue that he thought they should be discussing. "Do you know how they found you in the first place? Beth told me that she knows I don't have any trackers on me, so have you discovered who has? Were you followed on your way back from the slavers' camp, perhaps? Did you check?" He fired one question after another at them, knowing they didn't have the answers. "If you move and they are tracking you, then they will just follow you again."

Madison looked at Devon with respect, surprised that this man was more than a mindless fighter. He had raised some good points. "Beth, can you tell if anyone here is being tracked?"

Beth nodded and hurried away.

"Tonight," she continued, "we will check to make sure that none of us is being tracked and then get some rest. I would beg Devon to stay here tonight."

"Is he coming with us?" the lady who had delivered his food asked. "I know I won't feel safe for little Lorna or me unless he is nearby."

There was a loud murmuring of agreement from the others. They all knew what he had done and the skills required to do it.

Devon looked at 'little Lorna.' She looked to be nearly twenty, and athletic enough to handle herself if given a bit of guidance.

<Would it hurt our mission if they came with us?> he asked Izzy.

<If we are confident that they aren't being tracked, then all they will do is slow us down a little,> Izzy replied. <We have a little leeway, and there are some energy crystals in the pack that would keep us alive for another few days if we had to resort to that.>

<Realistically, how much leeway are we talking about?>

<We have both been in this realm for about twenty-eight hours. I cannot be exact as I cannot track the passing time. If you take out the pendant, we might be able to judge how far away the nexus is from here. When you came back into this world with your father, he mentioned that it was nearby. My estimate is we have six days to get to the nexus and get down into the cavern. There is energy down there that would keep us both alive indefinitely, but it is deep underground. Once inside, you can restore your magic and then fix the nexus. That will restore magical energy to this realm's surface. There are a lot of variables that could affect the time any of those parts might take.>

Devon thought about the implications of what Izzy had just told him. He felt they had enough time to comfortably find this nexus thing and escort the villagers if they were all going in the same direction. Returning to what he'd been doing, he reached into the pack and fished around. <There's a book in the bag, Izzy. Is that the one you mentioned with all your research in it?>

<Yes. It's for your eyes alone. A lot of my private musings are shut away between those pages. With Madison watching your every move, it would be best to leave that in the pack.>

He fished out the next thing from the bag. It was a pointed stick – just that. A ten-inch piece of wood sharpened at one end. <Eh?>

Izzy laughed at his confusion. <That is a gift from the dryads who are some of your most fervent followers. In the past, you have championed them on many occasions. You are known for being very sweet on their species and their goddess, too, as they are all voluptuous and female.>

That last remark interested Devon. <Oh? Have I got a reputation?>

<You are a gorgeously put-together, male god, Devon. It comes with the job. Women want you, and men want to be you. Call it a perk. There

is no harm if it is not abused. All gods and goddesses have an aura that attracts mortal creatures, and all mortals have a built-in attraction to the divine,> Izzy replied.

Devon was blushing as Izzy laid it all out so bluntly.

Izzy chuckled when she saw his response. <The dryads' gift is a lot more special than it looks. If you stick it in the ground, it will produce a protective wall of thorns around you, one-hundred yards in diameter. Or so they tell me, I've never seen it in action.>

A hand curled around his inner thigh, and a voice whispered in his ear, "come back to us. You tuned out for a while there. They've just asked you a question," Gwen said.

"I'm sorry, what?" Devon blurted out, emerging from his reverie. "I was miles away."

"No matter," Madison replied. "I asked if you would be willing to escort us on our journey."

"I have to be somewhere urgently. If you are going in the same direction, then you are welcome to join me. Do you know where you are going?" With that, he reached back into the pack and found two pouches. He gripped them both and drew them out.

<The blue one has magical energy crystals in it; they can go back in the pack. Let us hope we do not need them. The red velvet pouch is a lot more critical. Be warned; no mortal can ever touch the pendant inside the bag. Your nemesis, the fairy queen, cursed it.>

<Why would I trust something she has cursed?> Devon asked.

<Because it belonged to you until the queen stole it. She cursed it to stop mortals from stealing it and possibly using it. She thought that she had dealt with you permanently. That arrogance will be her downfall. You have a debt to settle with her.>

Madison put her hand on his shoulder then leant down to whisper in his ear. "All we know is that we have to go; we don't know where. Please, Devon, lead us somewhere that isn't here. They want to follow you; I want to follow you."

Devon looked up at her in surprise. He hadn't expected her to be so candid about their predicament. "What time is dawn?"

"It starts getting light enough to see at about six," Madison replied. "Do you want us ready to leave by then?"

"Yes. Can anyone other than Beth drive a lorry?"

"I can," Gwen and Finn said in unison.

"We'll drive a good distance from here, then abandon the lorries and head off in a different direction. Probably safest if Beth checks the lorries for trackers too." Devon looked over to where Beth was using a box-shaped device with a circular antenna attached to it to scan each villager. As each villager produced a negative result, they shuffled off to grab as much sleep as possible before the morning.

"When I take this thing out of the pouch, nobody can touch it. Understood?"

Gwen and Madison looked confused but nodded. They looked at the red pouch with a mix of fear and curiosity.

Devon loosened the tightly pulled drawstring and tipped the contents of the pouch onto his outstretched palm. It sizzled against his skin for a second, then settled harmlessly. He breathed a sigh of relief and heard Izzy do the same through his thoughts.

<So many of us relied on you being able to hold that pendant safely. It is the keystone pendant, the only one in existence as far as we know. It opens a seal called the keystone, which reveals the entrance to the nexus. Nothing else can open the keystone. Do not lose it.>

Devon looked at the trinket closely. It glowed a deep blue in his palm, but a white dot shone brighter than the blue. He moved the crystal around to see if it was some sort of reflection, but surprisingly the light stayed fixed to a direction. When he rotated it by one-hundred and eighty degrees, the spot went red. <Is this some sort of compass, Izzy?>

<That is interesting. Yes, it appears to be. All I knew about the crystal was that it could show us the way to the nexus. I suspect that, by the dot's brightness, the nexus isn't too far from here.>

<That seems far too convenient.>

<The goddess of fate did me a favour and helped me find you. If she is involved, I doubt whether convenience has anything to do with it. I think the gods and goddesses have been at work to put us here and now. We should be grateful the Pantheon is so keen to get their Reaper back.>

He considered that. He had begun to remember a few things about who he had been. It was far too early to say he had clear memories, but he understood that he was older than the realms themselves. Then something floated to the surface. A word, *'Wayfarer.' I'm the Wayfarer. What is a Wayfarer? I am. What does a Wayfarer do? I wander. I am master of the waygates,* he thought. *What's a waygate? Damn!*

<Izzy! I know who I am. I remembered something.>

Izzy sent him a feeling of relief and happiness. <My lord Wayfarer. Welcome back. I bring greetings and a desperate plea for help from my people.>

<Woah! Hang on there, wisp. I just remembered my name. I'm still just me.>

<You have many names, but I still like Devon,> Izzy replied. <As your priestess, I am supposed to call you 'my lord', but I have become attached to your new name.>

<Sorry, what? Priestess? You haven't mentioned that part before, have you?>

Izzy laughed.

A circular aerial poked toward him aggressively. "You're talking to someone. I know it. It must be you that led them here," Beth said, accusation dripping from her tone.

"Oh, goody! You're back to ruin my day again. Find anything, detective?" Devon retorted while glaring at her.

"Elizabeth!" Madison snapped. "I told you to leave him alone. I agree it looks like he is talking to someone, but you said he was clean of devices. Has that changed?"

"No," Beth said, her head downcast. She'd been so sure. She yelped as she felt her scanner pulled sharply from her grasp.

"I am talking to someone. It isn't my problem that you cannot see her. Anyway, what happens when this thing finds a device?" Devon said, inspecting the lights mounted to the top of the box. "Let me guess, green for clear, amber for maybe, red for yes?"

"Smartass," Beth grumbled. "Yes," she grudgingly confirmed.

Devon ran the scanner up and down Beth as he'd seen her do to the villagers. The light stayed green until he reached her belt, then it flicked to amber and then red. "Hah! You were the only person remaining not scanned. It had to be you. They had you in a cage and probably put a tracker on you in case you escaped or got rescued. You owe me yet another apology, it seems."

Beth unbuckled her belt and looked carefully at the inside of it. Her face dropped, and she reached into her pocket and pulled out a pair of tiny slim-nosed pliers, then carefully applied the pliers to the belt and pulled something off the inner lining. Beth held the pliers close to her face and inspected a minute object the shape of a flattened egg. She sighed deeply. "I'm sorry, Devon. Yet again, I have been rotten to you. It's no wonder you despise me." She glared hatefully at the tiny device that she held with her pliers, then squeezed the tool hard until the tracker shattered. A whiff of smoke emerged from it as something died inside.

Devon noticed the tears start and acted quickly. He stuffed everything else back in his pack and hung the pendant around his neck, tucking it safely under his clothing, then stood. He wrapped Beth up in a hug which she returned. Her tears changed to full-on weeping as she reached around him and returned his embrace. He wondered why he'd felt the need to comfort her at all, but it had just seemed like the right thing to do.

"I don't hate you, Beth, and I'm not your enemy. I'm sorry I said that before. It was in the heat of the moment. My only issue with you is that you're a royal pain in my arse," he finished wickedly, and felt her shudder with a laugh before beating his back half-heartedly.

"I'm genuinely sorry about everything. From the beginning, you were just too good to be true. Can we start over again?"

"You do realise that I'm still going to tease you? I can go with starting over, though," he replied.

Chapter 8

That's how they roll

"We're not leaving our homes, and you can't make us," one of the sixteen angry villagers said. "We didn't agree to this."

"If you stay here, the slavers will most likely come back and finish the job their colleagues failed to do. Are you willing to take that risk?" Madi asked. She was trying to keep her cool but was losing the battle.

"Make him stay; then the slavers won't stand a chance," an older, severe-looking woman said, arms tightly folded in front of her in aggressive refusal.

"Can you hear yourself? May I ask how you propose to make Devon stay when he has already told us that he must leave?" Madi said.

They didn't realise it, but Devon's heightening senses could hear every word of the heated argument from where he was standing. It was good entertainment.

"Can't we offer him a small harem if he stays?" one of the other women suggested. "I'm sure some of the looser women here would be willing to lay with him. He's a man; they're all simple and easy to keep happy. Give him sex, compliments, and food, and he'll willingly do whatever we ask of him."

Madison choked then started to shake her head emphatically. "This conversation ends now. I pray he didn't hear you. If you want to stay, then do so. Get a radio from Beth so that you can call for help if you need it. We're leaving, with or without you." She turned, and her heart sank when she saw Devon doubled over with hysterical laughter.

"You'll have to introduce me to these looser women," he chuckled.

Madison walked up to Devon, put her arm through his, then steered him over to the loaded and waiting lorries. "I must apologise for her; she doesn't have any social filters."

"No need. I'm sure there are lots of men that would accept such a tempting offer," Devon laughed, "just not me."

Thirty minutes later, the lorries rumbled out of the village. This time, the villagers crammed inside were neither restrained nor frightened. Instead, there was a quiet expectation among them and even a little hope for a better future. The few horses that the settlement possessed trooped out after the lorries. Beth had been unable to find any form of transmitter or tracker on the trucks, so they took a chance and used them, at least for some of the way. Of course, Jet was at the front, proudly leading the procession.

In the end, forty-seven villagers had chosen to join their exodus, while the sixteen older members of the community decided to stay behind. He hoped they'd be okay, but his hopes weren't high.

Devon was amazed that the villagers had managed to get the lorries loaded and then clamber on-board within an hour of dawn. It saddened him to think about it, but these people were evidently accomplished refugees, ready to flee at a moment's notice. He hoped that he might be able to improve things for them but wasn't going to make any promises yet. He still needed to understand what his capabilities were.

His memories were slowly gaining focus, and he was starting to recover his original sense of self, which was a relief. He knew that he had a tyrannical fairy queen to remove before relaxing back into his role of Wayfarer. Before that, he had to get his magic back, get the nexus repaired, and reopen the Earth realm waygate. He was looking forward to the former most of all.

Izzy had said that he would probably never be able to remember his previous life in Earth realm; yet he had a history here that nagged at him. The 'Hello Kitty' watch suggested some unknown ties to someone, but he couldn't linger on such speculation. There was no way for him to find out anything about that. What gave him hope was that he knew what 'Hello Kitty' was. If he had no memory of his past in this realm, how did he know that?

It was early, and everyone was still bleary-eyed. Jet ambled happily along, seeming to know exactly where she was heading, which left Devon with plenty of time to bury himself in his thoughts. He admired the lush and verdant countryside that sprawled around him. Hills rolled away as far as the eye could see, and it was abundantly clear that nature owned this land and had set her mark everywhere. Where there weren't trees or bushes, there were swathes of grass liberally sprinkled with sizeable black granite boulders.

As the altitude increased, so did the size and frequency of the rocks. Now and then, they would pass ruins of houses or some business long since forgotten. Nature had reclaimed them too and was trying her very best to remove the taint of civilisation from her land. Trees thickly covered the area to which they were heading and spread as far away as he could see. Fluffy white clouds wandered across the azure sky as the day gradually took over from dawn. The air was invigorating, and today the sun had decided to make an appearance. It felt like a good day to be alive.

The first six hours passed peacefully while the lorries and horses followed Jet at a reasonable pace, steadily climbing up into the tall hills. Every mile or so, Devon checked the pendant. Each time he pointed it at the towering rock that formed the peak of the nearby hills, the white dot would change to bright green.

He didn't plan on stopping for a break until they had made the cover of the thicker forest. Trees loomed on either side of them now, and the left-side had begun to drop steeply away. He had taken a chance and chosen to travel along the road until they reached its highest point. The aim was to veer sharply off to the right, into the trees, climbing higher toward the tallest peak, which would be quicker than finding a route across open country and up into the rocky hills. While there were two lorries in working order, they would use them.

They had made significant progress and had reached the point where they would have to leave the road and head into the hills. Another forty-five minutes or so would see them safely out of sight.

Finn had introduced Devon to their grown-up daughter, Beks, this morning. She was an ex-army engineer and sapper, and he noted her credentials down in his head for future reference. He'd now sent Finn and Beks off to scout for a possible path into the hills that would be suitable for the lorries. If they abandoned them here, a passing patrol would see them and grow suspicious. The last thing they needed was search parties nosing around.

Gwen tapped on the back of his head. "Knock knock, you awake in there?" she teased him.

"Deep in thought, sorry. What's up?" Gwen had chosen to ride pillion with Devon, and Jet had thoroughly approved. Jet and Gwen seemed to get along well.

"Where are we heading?"

Devon pointed off to the right at about seventy-five degrees. It was the tallest point of the local hills, where a granite peak jutted high above the trees. He was considering travelling along a more accessible slope to find a better way to reach it.

"Up there," he said to Gwen, "where the trees start to bunch up more tightly. If we can find a suitable place up there on the high ground by that rock, we will be able to see people approaching for over a mile in every direction."

<I wonder if Gwen could talk to us using mental communication? Should I try?> Izzy asked Devon.

<It's worth a go. Do you have any idea what type of faie she is?>

<She has no magic, so I cannot read her faie core. I can just see she has one.>

<Gwen?> Izzy thought to Gwen and Devon.

"What? Who said that?"

Devon could feel Gwen wriggling around behind him as she looked around to see who was talking to her. <Calm down, Gwen. That was Izzy. The wisp you spotted yesterday. Welcome to mental communication,> he thought to her.

<Glad to meet you, Gwen. I apologise for not being myself at the moment,> Izzy sent to Gwen.

<Uh! Can you hear me?> Gwen thought.

<Now you know who I'm talking to when I stare off into space. Beth thinks I'm talking to my spy headquarters,> Devon thought with a laugh.

<Wow! I knew sticking around you would get interesting. Yesterday you were harvesting souls; now, only half a day into the journey, I become a sodding telepath. That's awesome.>

Then he heard it. His senses had been improving since he'd awoken, and he now picked up the faint sound of a heavy vehicle. <We've got incoming. Izzy, head further along the road quickly. Let me know as soon as you can see something. I can hear an engine coming at us,> he thought, trying to convey a sense of urgency with his words.

<Gwen, head back down the convoy and get everyone to head up into the trees quickly. Fast as they can.> He gestured further up the hill in the direction he'd sent Finn and Beks.

Devon looked around for a suitable place to watch the road while staying out of sight. Just up ahead, he noticed a crumbling inn that had a forecourt outside surrounded by a wall of about five feet in height. It had collapsed in places, and ivy was slowly pulling the rest of it apart, but it would offer good cover and some good ammunition – hopefully. Gwen had already slid down to go and get the others moving, so he urged Jet into action, and she galloped the two-hundred yards to the ruins.

Jet jumped the wall with ease and then stopped. Devon patted her neck and sent proud thoughts to her, and she responded with happy anticipation. She also chose this moment to send him memories of the two of them frequently doing this sort of thing a very long time ago. They'd both had magic back then, and because of that, Jet was able to change her form to suit the situation. He saw images of them fighting side by side and felt her pride in doing so. Sadly, this time, she couldn't, and she was away as soon as he dismounted. The Earth realm had no magical energy for her to use, so her form must remain as it was. She needed to find somewhere much more suitable to use for concealment.

The two lorries containing the villagers protested their way across the soft, grassy terrain, doing their best to avoid any boulder that would ground them. Devon hoped the poor villagers inside were holding on tight as the ride had become extreme for them. The horses had already made it safely into the trees and must have been tied up out of sight because their riders now came back to guide the lorries safely undercover. The smell of diesel smoke hung heavy in the air as both drivers struggled to keep the engines from stalling.

Satisfied that they would be out of sight in time, Devon concentrated on building his ammunition pile. Throwing rocks would be far more effective at this range. He could use his knives, but the stones had a much more devastating effect when he was close enough to hit something at full force.

A heavily breathing Finn vaulted the wall and landed next to him on his left. "What do you need?" he asked while coaxing a handgun out of the satchel he was carrying. He laid the bag down on the floor and placed two spare ammunition magazines on top of it carefully. He then ejected the clip that was currently in the gun and checked it had ammunition in it too. He almost looked like he knew what he was doing. He spoilt that illusion when he failed to push the clip back correctly and it jammed. Blushing, Finn had to repeat the action to properly load the gun.

"Can you safely use that thing?" Devon asked. "Could you kill someone with it?"

"I have never killed anyone before, but today I plan on changing that. Thanks to your inspiration, I'm ready to do what I have to, to protect the people I love," Finn replied. He stuck his chin out and made a determined face.

"Good answer," Devon said with a grin.

Gwen jumped the wall and landed on his right, clutching several spears. She nodded at Devon as she lay her spare weapons next to her and flattened the angle of the one she held so it wouldn't stick out above the wall.

Devon listened. The vehicle was getting close now, and he wondered why Izzy hadn't reported back. "Scooch to the right a bit, Gwen; I need space to throw." He chose his first rock carefully, testing its weight in his grip.

"Why don't you use a gun, Devon?" Finn asked.

"I don't know how," Devon answered simply.

Gwen and Finn looked at him in shock.

"Well, that explains the rock-throwing thing," Finn said. "I'd prefer to do it your way. I bloody hate these things," he nodded towards the gun.

<Five men in a sizeable, open-topped vehicle,> Izzy reported. <One man is standing in the back, holding on to a strange-looking weapon on a stand. I advise you to make sure he dies quickly as that thing looks very modern and dangerous. I will follow them in.>

"There are five men in an open-topped vehicle," Devon repeated to his companions. "Take the one at the back out first, both of you. Once he is down, you can work forward. Stay down until they're almost beside us."

The roar of the engine was very close now, and Devon readied himself. It was approaching fast, so he couldn't wait long. "NOW!"

The three of them sprang to their feet and took an instant to spot their targets. Just as Izzy had said, the vehicle had two rows of seats, five passengers, and cargo space at the back. Devon didn't know what the weapon mounted in the truck was, but it was grey, the shape of a squared-off tube, and about four feet in length. He saw the man in the back begin to aim the weapon their way. Devon launched his stone directly at the driver, who was now looking his way in shock. The rock hissed angrily through the air and struck the man on the jawbone, forcing it violently back into his skull.

The man in the back of the vehicle pulled the trigger. A searing bolt of superheated plasma shot out of the barrel and screamed off toward the wall, buzzing angrily and igniting the air as it went.

Finn wasn't having quite so much luck. He had aimed and been brave enough to squeeze the trigger just like Beks had taught him, but the trigger seemed stuck. It wouldn't move. He was in a panic, trying to remember what could be wrong. Then he remembered the safety catch. He found it after a second and clicked it off. Unfortunately, his trigger finger was still trying to squeeze the trigger, and the gun went off twice, recoiling hard both times before he had a chance to release the mechanism. He heard Devon grunt as Finn realised where his gun was pointing. Then he realised where his other bullet had gone as Gwen yelped in pain. He gulped and prayed for the ground to open beneath him and swallow him whole.

Gwen picked out the man at the back, but just as she was about to launch her spear as hard as she could, she felt a searing agony in her left shoulder as a bullet passed cleanly through it. She cried out loudly in pain.

The plasma blast hit just to the group's right, nearest Gwen. There was a loud explosion as the nearby wall erupted in a shower of stone shrapnel and molten debris. The force of the blast flung them all to the ground, peppering them with minor wounds in the process.

Devon swiftly picked himself up and winced as his latest gunshot wound made its presence felt. Looking across to where the vehicle had been, he saw it just finishing its last barrel roll, ending up back on its wheels, devoid of occupants. Devon was over the wall with a leap and running toward the nearest man who had just landed.

Gwen saw Devon ignore the wound inflicted by Finn's dumb actions and leap the wall. She realised he was going after potential survivors, and so she too was over the wall quickly and on her way to the stricken jeep, determined to ignore the pain of her wounds just as effectively as he evidently could. "Stay here and put the safety catch back on," she barked at Finn. The last thing anyone needed was him waving that gun around anymore.

Devon decided to throw caution to the wind and reached out and summoned as many souls to him as would come. He eventually got four which left one survivor. "There's one left alive, Gwen. Be careful."

Finn had stayed behind the wall, and Devon was grateful for that. While he didn't want to make Finn feel worse, he could do without his type of assistance. He sprinted after Gwen, knowing that this first corpse wasn't going anywhere.

Eventually, they tracked down all five of the vehicle's original occupants. Gwen finished the last one, who wasn't in any fit state to retaliate. Devon was impressed by how coldly she ended the man's life. There wasn't a moment's hesitation.

<Where you at, Izzy?> he asked.

<Right above your head. Tsk! Wounded again, this is becoming a habit,> Izzy thought with annoyance. <Friendly fire this time as well. These villagers will be the death of you.>

<The man was trying to protect his people. I can't blame him for that. He just needs practice. He's a good man, I can tell; I like him.>

<You liked Beth too. You should choose your friends more carefully. The only competent one is Gwen, and she vowed she'd have you before you even woke up.> Izzy laughed at him.

Devon had to smile at that. She made a good point. <Let's hope that when you get your body back, you don't decide to wound me somehow.>

<Like Gwen, I chose you. You are safe with me – at least, safe from any damage,> the wisp replied.

After a few minutes, Devon heard a horse approaching fast and spun to see Madison riding toward him. While waiting for her to arrive, he inspected her husband's damage to his shoulder. What annoyed him most was the graze his armour had suffered. The wound was barely a wound at all, just a scratch that bled quite freely. He staunched it with his right hand as Madison dismounted and grabbed a tubular green bag out of her saddlebag.

She rushed over to him, an apology already on her lips. "He's so sorry, Devon. It was an accident."

Devon held up his hand to stop her. "Relax, it's just a scratch, and I know it was an accident. He wants to protect you and the others so much, but he just doesn't have the skills yet. We can work on that."

Madison looked at him as if he was mad, then reminded herself why she was there and got to work on his wound. She marvelled at Devon's fortitude when he didn't even blink as she stitched his skin back together. She stared at him and gently shook her head. "You are a wonder. People like us cannot comprehend just how special you are. Whatever fate brought you to us is generous and kind."

Devon shook his head, uncomfortable with such a compliment. "What brought me to you was a red-headed attitude on legs, but you're closer than you think. I have it on good authority that Fate had a hand in our meeting. Now, perhaps you would be kind enough to administer your skills to poor Gwen? She got shot too."

"He's a god, Madi," Gwen said from behind him. She had a bloody hand clutched tightly over her wounded shoulder. "He is too modest to tell anyone, but he has an assistant that most of you can't see. She explained it all to me."

<Assistant? Pah!> Izzy snorted indignantly.

Madison looked at Devon closely. "You know what, Gwen. I could almost believe that."

Chapter 9

It's tough at the top

Fate stood on the golden sand; the warm waves gently lapped against her bare feet, and salty air filled her lungs. She looked down at her hand and noticed a tall glass of blue liquid containing ice, pineapple, and a cocktail umbrella that skewered two fat maraschino cherries. Considering that a moment ago, she had been relaxing quietly in her realm, this was a change of scenery. In front of her sat thirty-one gods and goddesses, each one unique in form and size, meaning that her fellow Pantheon members had summoned her. Fate knew precisely what this was about.

An officious little man walked toward them along the sand and came to a halt at a right angle between Fate and the row of her fellow Pantheon members. The man wore a formal, dark grey suit. His tie was done up in a fussy little knot and was a slightly lighter shade of grey than his outfit. His shoes were charcoal grey, his skin was light grey, and the air around him had become a greyscale shade of the colour it had been moments before.

"Lady Fate, you are hereby charged with the contravention of Agreement 12.b of the Non-intervention Pact," the grey man said in an officious, condescending tone. "Your actions caused the failure of my client's curse, and predictions indicate that you have now endangered her life. By divine right, my client demands you undo your actions and make reparations immediately."

"I am Fate, you pompous little peasant. That is what I do. Who gave you the authority to even be here?" Fate was livid. The Pantheon had been choking with laws and red tape for over a thousand years. The more they tried to rid themselves of it, the more tangled in tape they became. None of the gods or goddesses could put their finger on when it started or how the lawyers got their teeth into their dominion. It had just happened.

"Tsk, tsk, madam. There is no need to take that tone with me. I am merely a conduit of the law."

There was a thunderclap, and the scene abruptly changed. All the Pantheon members found themselves in a luxuriously appointed boardroom with old-school décor, including plush wood-panelled walls and a thick, deep blue carpet. The gods and goddesses were seated in comfortable upright chairs around an oval meeting table made from beautifully polished walnut. At the head of the sizeable table was a giant, glowing orb that scintillated with energy and every conceivable colour.

There were even colours in there that no living creature could ever imagine. Power oozed from its being, bathing the room.

Fate winced. Things must be bad if the progenitor had summoned them.

"What the hells have you moronic dumbasses been doing?" the ball of energy shouted. It expanded and turned a threatening red colour. Its voice sounded extremely angry and desperate to thump something, if it had had appendages with which to do so. "I leave you alone for a few millennia, and you make a bollocks of everything." The Pantheon didn't know, but Devon's father enjoyed swearing. It was something he didn't get the opportunity to do often. He'd been practising by swearing at Devon until he'd finally dumped his son back in Earth realm.

Fate had been around for long enough to fear a visit from the boss. This summons was only the third that had ever occurred, but the first two had gone badly enough that they were memorable.

"Which one of you halfwits let the lawyers in?" the orb demanded.

Everyone stayed silent – each one glancing around at the others who all slowly shook whatever passed for their heads.

"Hmm, that's what I thought. Little grey bastards just turned up, and not one of you was bright enough to question them."

"Uhm, sir, some of us questioned their authority frequently, but they just kept coming, and we couldn't stop them," Missy said timidly.

Fate didn't blame her timidity. She felt the same when facing their progenitor.

The ball of energy turned blue, and a circular shockwave of reality-altering magical energy rippled out and away from him. A line of twenty-five grey humanoids forming five neat lines appeared at the back of the office. They all looked shocked and confused, although it didn't take them long to start 'really must protest'-ing and begin quoting various regulations and sub-clauses. They all looked indignant and well within their rights.

"Silence, worms," the orb boomed. His words shook the room and caused the lawyers' images to shimmer and glitch a little. Instantly, silence filled the area.

"My lord, according to regulation 447.d: sub-clause 12, you are acting against protective orders securing the sanctity of the law. The fairy queen has set out the divine statute which we are within our rights to enforce," one of the more expensively dressed lawyers stated. His voice was adamant and sure of his authority.

"Oh! So it was that fat butterfly that created this fuck-up for my people. That's a primary misdemeanour point for her then." The progenitor's displeasure radiated outward then settled on the lawyer who'd spoken. The man began to glow a fiery red, eventually growing so hot that he felt obliged to loosen his tie. He didn't utter a noise as he met his demise. His body erupted in a cloud of red sparks, and the lawyer instantly ceased to exist. There was a rustling of ties loosening as the other lawyers began to glow as well. Within seconds they had all met their leader's fate.

"I want that bovinesque fairy bint dealt with. I want agonising torment followed by extinction. She's light-years past the naughty step, that one. It was her that caused my son to end up loitering around me for centuries. I congratulate Fate for doing something about that, and I am putting her in charge of a taskforce to mentor my son and personally make sure he doesn't end up in my domain ever again. We are paying top price for that fairy's soul. Do I make myself crystal?"

"Yes, sir. Thank you, sir. I will not let you down," Fate grovelled. She felt pleased with herself for a change. That, and she had just watched her boss atomise those accursed lawyers.

"Save it. Your taskforce is authorised to intervene within reason. If you must bind my son to a collective to protect him, then do so. I do not want him back. Oh, and give him his bloody realm back. He has done nothing but whine about losing that since he turned up on my doorstep."

"Yes, sir." Fate bowed.

"The rest of you had better get busy. I want all the realms cleaned up. They're a mess. It's as if you've all been sat on your metaphysical arses since I was last here. You've got your Reaper back; use him. Keep the little bugger busy. Pay him well and use his talents. Don't play chess with him either; he's a sodding embarrassment to the family."

The ball of energy started to fade, and the thirty-two gods and goddesses began to breathe again, happy that they remained intact this time.

The globe solidified again, and everyone breathed in nervously. "That reminds me. I was in Earth realm a short while ago. The bloody place is lousy with demons." He focused on an older man trying to sink under the table, out of sight. The orb pulsed red, and the elderly-looking god vanished in an explosion of photons. "I already told that idiot what would happen if he kept that pacifistic nonsense up. Fate, use your taskforce to sort that shambles out once that fairy bovine is out of the picture. Nature, help her out. My idiot son's soft on your lot. Anyone else want to get on my good side?"

Two hands went up: one was a humanoid creature made entirely of shadows, and the other, a lithe, humanoid goddess with pure white hair and a costume to match.

"Shalim and Theia; yes, you'll do. I will authorise expenses within reason. Bribe him, cheat; I don't care. Just keep the little sod out of my way."

The orb winked out of existence. The thirty-one gods and goddesses breathed a collective sigh of relief. They had all avoided the latest round of redundancies, and the boss's son was back. They all liked him. He was entertaining and easy to manipulate, unlike his despot father.

****_****

Devon used some leaves to wipe the worst of the blood from his armour.

Their group had been wearily making their way through the upper reaches of the forest when a herd of wild boars had run them down. The animals had come hurtling through the bushes straight toward them before anyone could raise the alarm. Some of the villagers had suffered injuries from the stampeding creatures but nothing life-threatening. Devon and Gwen had despatched five of the animals swiftly, once they'd got over the surprise of the pigs being bold enough to attack nearly fifty people. The other animals had fled once they realised that their prey was fighting back.

To the amazement of the villagers, Devon had stashed the corpses away in Jet's saddlebags. Izzy had talked him through the process and explained that items were stored in a void, and so decomposition of any sort was impossible. Devon was impressed that the storage could double as an eternal meat fridge.

They'd abandoned the lorries about a mile ago. They had all worked hard to conceal the vehicles as best they could. They'd parked them well into the forest and entirely out of sight of the road.

It was evident to him that the villagers wouldn't be able to walk much further. They were all tired from a long, eventful day and laden down with their worldly belongings. Izzy had reported back a few minutes ago, saying that she had found a nice place where they could stop. She also said she was sure that the nexus entrance was only a short distance away from it. The pendant was glowing enthusiastically, which Devon took as a good sign.

The clearing they found was perfect. Numerous springs fed a deep, fast-flowing stream nearby. The surrounding beech trees offered comprehensive cover from above, and on the forest's floor, rhododendrons and holly bushes hid them from casual view in every direction. Nearby, a vast rock formed the local hills' tallest peak; its proud, granite angles stood out prominently among the trees. The cliff face it created rose over one-hundred feet at its highest point, then sloped away steeply down to the other side of the hill. The group had hauled themselves up and down some strange artificial striations probably created many hundreds of years ago. This whole area appeared to have once been some sort of primitive fortification. It was unsurprising, though, as the location was a defender's dream.

"Welcome to your new home," Devon said. He was spinning around with his arms outstretched. "It needs a little work but think big. Finn, I'm told you were a civil engineer. Why don't you and I work on some ideas for a new settlement?" Devon had come up with the idea as they were trekking through the forest. For everyone's safety, Madi's husband needed a project that wasn't learning to fight. Madi had been clear that she wouldn't allow her husband anywhere near combat.

The shadows were lengthening, and they needed to make camp and get some rest. Everyone looked dead on their feet.

"Please stand out of the clearing. I need to make camp," Devon said to everyone with a raised voice.

<Okay, assistant. How do I work this camping charm thing?> he thought to Izzy.

<Naff off! You can cut that assistant nonsense out. I may be your priestess, but I am not obliged to tolerate any nonsense from you, mister,> Izzy barked and then giggled. <Just kidding. Concentrate on the charm, then think 'position camp', move it to where you want, then think 'set camp',> Izzy replied.

Devon shook his head. The wisp had some loose screws, but that was a big part of her charm. Following Izzy's instructions, Devon thought, 'position camp'. Immediately a wireframe made of light appeared all around them, highlighting where the camp would be. He found that he was able to move the wireframe around to choose the perfect location. He needed to ask Gwen to move as the overlay highlighted her in red. Once she'd left the circular grid, the overlay went green, allowing him to set the camp.

Devon revelled in the many 'oos' and 'ahs' he overheard as a large, circular campsite appeared. It was resplendent, with a large campfire in its centre and fifty identical camp beds and camp chairs neatly positioned around it. Each bed had a sleeping bag, pillow, and blanket. "Make yourselves at home," he said with a grin.

'Light fire,' he thought while concentrating on the charm, and sure enough, the campfire burst into warm, welcoming flames. Devon noticed that the fire even had a spit assembly above it. That brought the boars to mind.

<Izzy, is there rope in the saddlebags?>

<Probably. Try thinking of it while reaching into the bag then specifying the length you require. I expect you will get it,> Izzy explained. <It is the same for a few things like leather strapping, cleaning equipment, cooking utensils, and all sorts. You are the Wayfarer, a traveller at heart who needs equipment designed to help you along the way. You have another powerful item that our lore frequently mentions. From what I heard your father say, it awaits you in the nexus below us.>

Thinking about what Izzy had said, Devon retrieved the rope he felt he'd need and set about hanging and preparing the boars' corpses. His daggers made handy tools for the job, but it took him a while to do it well. Gwen helped him, but they had chosen not to ask the villagers for assistance because he knew they were all tired. The pair of them were like an old couple, wincing and complaining about their various wounds as they got on with the task at hand. One piece of good news was that his constitution was improving because it was getting easier to carry on for longer before needing rest. When finished, they trudged down to the nearby stream and washed up. The work had taken them a little over two hours.

When they got back to where Jet stood, Devon started to wonder about what he'd just done. <Izzy, how do I know how to do all these things? I just prepared five animals as if I'd been doing it all my life.>

<I only know what I have read in books about your history. Before your curse, you led a mostly solitary existence, travelling from place to place, dispensing justice where necessary and harvesting souls at the behest of the Pantheon. Eventually, you chose to remain alone because you had outlived every companion that ever pair-bonded with you.> Izzy's thoughts seemed to convey a little sadness. <Knowing that everyone you ever chose to love would eventually fade and pass on must have been awful for you. You decided to stay lonely to avoid the grief – you poor thing. Our books never managed to convey that emotion, but I can feel it inside you.>

<You are the 'Reaper,'> Izzy continued. <No laws of any realm could touch you while going about your business; the gods and goddesses demanded it. I would say that you are the only genuinely free spirit. The Pantheon trusted you to deliver their justice. Your love of spit-roasted boar is probably thousands of years old,> she giggled.

Devon walked back to where the five boar carcasses were hanging. Jet was standing beside the corpses, looking hungry. <Do you eat meat, gorgeous?>

Jet gave him a full smile for the first time. It was not the smile of a horse but a hybrid of a shark and a leopard. She certainly had a lot of teeth. Thick triangular teeth at the back, then thinner, razor-sharp teeth towards the front. Surely not the smile of a herbivore. It was a smile that you would dread to meet in a dark alley.

<You want a whole carcass, or shall I cut you some chunks off, girl?>

Jet moved toward a boar, bit cleanly through the rope that suspended it from the tree, then dragged it off toward the campfire.

<I guess you'll be joining us for dinner then.> Devon laughed.

He pulled a dagger out from its sheath and cut several large chunks of meat. He decided to let the villagers cook their food as he considered that he'd done enough for them today. He walked back to the fire and threaded the meat onto the spit bar. Once he'd placed the spit back on its rack, it began to turn itself slowly. Devon grinned a happy grin. Magic was just the best.

<Hey, Gwen,> he thought to his dark-haired shadow. She'd barely left his side since they had evacuated the village. <Can you sort us out a couple of chairs and beds a short way from the others?>

Gwen grinned back at him enthusiastically. <Sure, do these single beds convert to a double?>

Devon had to laugh out loud, startling a few villagers around him. <Not with an audience, no.>

Gwen shrugged, went over to a quieter corner, and began sorting out their sleeping arrangements.

He walked over to where Madison and Finn were sitting in camp chairs, whispering. They both looked around and smiled as he approached.

"Can you organise the cooking of enough meat for everyone for tonight and tomorrow morning?" he asked. "Gwen and I have some serious work to do in the morning. Then I might have something important to show you all. I suggest we plan to make a settlement here, but that choice must be yours. My journey ends here for now. The meat is hanging nearby. Don't panic when you see Jet eating one of the boars. She's not an average horse."

The looks on the couple's faces were a picture of confusion, wonder, appreciation, and thoughtfulness. All emotions passed across their visages, some more than once. In the end, they both managed a dumbfounded nod.

Madi stood and addressed the hubbub of the excited yet still slightly fearful villagers. All had marked their territory amongst the camp beds and chairs – refugees to a one. By now, the smell of cooking boar meat was making them very hungry. "Devon has prepared the boars he killed earlier and requests that we take as much as we need for two meals. Finn, would you be a love and do the carving?"

Madi raised her hand for continued silence as the chattering rose again. "I ask every one of you to consider our future; tomorrow we will take a vote. Devon will be staying here but welcomes us to stay, and with his help and protection, we can build our new homes here. Or we can continue on and see if we can find somewhere else. The vote will be: stay or travel on without Devon. I urge you to think about it carefully. Finn and I think this spot is a beautiful, perfectly located area where we could make a lovely home. It will need a lot of work, but we believe it will be worth it."

One of the village women, with two children clinging to her trouser legs, stood. "What does Devon want to do? I vote we stay with him. When he is with us, I feel safe and secure. We're not scared of hard work. What we fear is being taken for slaves or body parts."

There was a loud mumbling of agreement, and another lady, younger than the first, stood up. She was blushing and looked at Devon, moon-eyed from under her fringe. "What would you have us do, Devon?"

Devon was surprised to be dragged into the proceedings so quickly. "Your lives are your own. I will say that I am staying here, and I would welcome you all to stay as well. If you remain here, I promise that you'll see things you never thought possible. The decision needs to be unanimous as I would hate to see your community split further, based on my words. If you all have open minds, then I suggest you stay. Finn and I will work out some ideas for housing over the next few days. With your efforts, we could forge a small paradise among the trees. Maybe even in the trees. I have some exciting ideas about that. Have you ever fancied living in a treehouse?"

There was another round of murmuring and some laughter. Devon spotted a lot of nodding and positive gestures and began to suspect they'd stay.

Chapter 10
Going down

Devon inhaled deeply, revelling in the freshness and bite of the morning air in his lungs. Mist gripped the hills below them, leaving the campsite floating in a wispy nest of white and the forest smelling damp. The atmosphere muffled the sounds of waking villagers and birdsong that reached his sensitive ears. The leaves of the beech trees were starting to turn a radiant copper colour while their mast littered the floor and crunched underfoot. He could feel that autumn was beginning to take hold. That got him thinking about the time it would take to build insulated shelters for all the villagers – assuming they decided to stay with him, of course.

Today was a big day for him and Izzy. He was already up and busy, as was Gwen, who always made sure to keep Devon in view. Izzy was a rich shade of purple and whirled around his head excitedly. There was a heavy sense of anticipation in the air.

The three of them left the camp as quietly as possible, but several villagers watched them with interest. He saw several of the teenagers urging their guardians to wake up and get dressed. Others were only just starting to stir.

He walked the fifty yards to the enormous rock that was the peak of the hills. Gwen was next to him, and Izzy floated on the other side. Vegetation had left the sheer granite cliff face alone, and it stood out among the trees and bushes in its rugged glory. They stood right against the base of the black rock and looked up at the towering monolith. Devon knew this had to be the right place; it felt magical and somehow familiar.

He reached into his shirt and pulled out the pendant. It shone with a brilliant, deep-blue light that illuminated everything around, including the cliff face. Across the rock, hundreds of intricate symbols lit up and glimmered in the gem's glow. The symbols rotated and writhed as the light hit them. In the middle of the sigils was a five-pointed star, and an exact representation of the pendant's crystal occupied the centre of that star.

"Wwwoooowwwww," Gwen whispered breathily, drawing the word out in wonder. "It really is magic. Proper, magic." She could hardly contain her glee at discovering that all her dreams had just come true. All her life, she'd buried her head in every fantasy book she could get access to. She had always adored comics and books on the occult. Genuine magic was her dream, and here it was, happening right in front of her. "Life next to you just keeps getting better."

Devon smiled to himself, sharing Gwen's awe of the moment. He reached out and placed the crystal in the indentation, aligning it carefully with the glowing sigil. There was a deafening crack, then the thundering sound of rock scraping against rock as a vertical gap, more than thirty feet high, appeared in the cliff face and started to widen. He hastily retrieved the crystal from its seat and tucked it inside his shirt with reverence. The rumbling continued for over a minute until colossal doors finally pulled back into the surrounding rock. Ancient air rushed past them, and he could smell ozone.

In front of them was a large entrance over thirty feet square. Inside was a spherical cavern about seventy feet in diameter that stretched back into the granite. The base of the cave was flat and covered in moss of a greenish silver. There was an impressive doorframe over thirty feet square, built from finely carved, gold-flecked obsidian blocks in the centre of the cavern. Gold inlaid, arcane symbols covered every surface of the stones.

Behind the doorframe on the far wall was another glowing rectangle that was a mere twenty feet squared. It glowed with the same deep blue as the crystal did.

<I believe this is the primary waygate,> Izzy thought. <Like all the others, it's dead. My people suspect that this one is the power source for all the others; so when the fairy queen destroyed the nexus below this one, every gate died. Only you truly understand how they work, though. They are your creations. On the wall behind it is the keystone that leads down into the nexus.>

<He built this?> Gwen asked in shock.

<Yes, the elves certainly believe he did. You need to realise that Devon is the son of the progenitor. Creator of all things. These sacred waygates were part of the universal machinery he and his father formed at the beginning,> Izzy replied. <He is the Wayfarer, keeper of these ways. These gates span all the realms allowing travel between them. If you truly want adventure, stay close to him.>

<I intend to do precisely that,> Gwen said with determination fortifying her thoughts.

Devon had nothing to add to Izzy's words. He had no memory of building this place, but that came as no surprise to him.

He walked through the empty, black-stone frame and over to the keystone. Again, he fitted his crystal into its designated lock-space, and another sharp crack echoed around the cavern. He was tucking the pendant back under his shirt when the rumble of stone on stone ceased. The opened door revealed a road winding steeply down and away to the right. As he looked, hundreds of golden domes, fixed in various places on the cavernous ceiling, began to glow with a warm light. The light reflected off walls that were made from some sort of crystalline material, making them glisten.

Looking behind him, he noticed every single villager looking at the newly revealed cave and him with equal parts awe and unease. Mouths gaped in wonder.

Madi walked up next to him and smiled. "You are something more than we can comprehend, but being around you is the most eye-opening experience we could ever imagine. I feel like Alice looking down the rabbit hole. Please, Devon, may we come with you to wherever that goes? Maybe share your adventure?" she asked, gesturing to the road that spiralled down into the depths of the hill. There was pleading in her voice that she was not ashamed to reveal. "We have all decided that staying with you will be far more interesting than anything else we could ever do in a hundred lifetimes. We have a new leader, Devon. Please guide us well."

"Madi, I can't," Devon started to say, but Madi placed her hand on his arm and shook her head.

"Just keep doing what you do. Finn and I will handle the rest. I promise."

Devon's brow furrowed as he thought about what Madi had asked of him. "Fine," he huffed. "But please let us work all this out before everyone starts asking questions," he said. Devon trembled with excitement for the coming events. He grinned at Madi. "I hope you all believe in magic."

For nearly an hour, they wound their way down the road and into the depths of the granite hills. There had been a few moans from some of the children about the walking, which was fair enough. They'd spent the previous day travelling too. Devon had ended up giving piggybacks to at least five. The problem was, when he offered to do it for one of them, they all wanted a turn. It soon turned into a game, and Devon caught himself gambolling around while the children laughed uproariously. Seeing the person they were so in awe of behaving like a giant child put everyone at their ease. Even Izzy laughed along.

Some forty-seven villagers had joined him; nine of them were children. Another seven were young ladies who were just waving their teen years goodbye. Also strange was that there were only a few males among them. He had been distressed to learn that slavers always snatched the men first because they fetched a better bounty on the market. Whoever else they could grab was a bonus. The more he heard about the life they endured, the angrier it made him. There was no doubt he would do everything he could for these people, but he had a fairy queen to destroy as well. Izzy's people were in just as much need as these villagers after all. Maybe he could combine the two? This place would make a perfect sanctuary for a lot of refugees. Not just humans, either.

He was also concerned when he learnt that none of the children had received an education other than that which their guardians could offer them. Izzy, Gwen, and Devon had talked about that last night, and Izzy had promised to speak to some friends she had after the fairy queen's demise. She was sure that setting up a good school would be easy. Many elf children were in the same situation. It would also aid the integration of multiple species and cultures to the settlement. He was getting ahead of himself, though. There was a lot to do before schools became an issue.

The road continued to circle downward in a broad curve until he finally spotted where it straightened and the walls angled away. As they rounded the last bend, his mind nearly broke with what he saw before them. They found themselves standing in a cavern bigger than he had ever imagined possible.

"Bloody hell! Would you look at that," Gwen said in wonder. Other villagers shared her sentiment in hushed tones of awe.

Multifaceted, crystalline shards entirely coated the walls, bouncing and refracting the light from the golden domes. Rainbows shimmered within the walls to form a mind-numbingly wondrous effect. Devon felt as if he'd just entered a cathedral dedicated to the beauty of light itself. "Now this is where I would worship."

"Wow! This place is just – wow!" Gwen said, awe saturating her words.

<My god! I never imagined it would be this beautiful,> Izzy thought.

<You've never seen one of these places either, Izzy?> Devon replied.

<No, never! Only in history books. Woodcut prints could never do this justice. The nexus is a thing of faie legends,> Izzy replied. <Aeons ago, you and your father built this, and all the other such structures in Earth realm. This world is blessed by more raw magical power than any other, and it flows deep beneath the surface in rivers known as the Ley

channels. These structures pooled the energy and channelled it up to the surface, thus helping the magical creatures known as the faie thrive all across the world's surface. That was back when the faie ruled Earth realm; before the humans forced us out.>

He went back to gazing at the magnificent view. Memories stirred in his mind, but nothing he could properly focus on. A lake of shimmering water stretched from wall to wall on the far side of the cavern, and five waterfalls cascaded into it after descending down the lake's surrounding walls. The water made a strange hissing noise as it tumbled down; it didn't sound like water at all. Like a veil lifting, a memory suddenly came into focus. *Ley channels! That's right! That isn't water. It's dust formed from concentrated magical energy. I remember this place.*

In the centre of the lake, there was a stubby column made of crystal mixed with obsidian. On the ceiling, directly above the pillar, was a stalactite of the same material. Devon knew that they were all that remained of the conduit that carried magical energy from this cavern to Earth realm's surface. He also could now remember just how to fix it.

A low wall bordered the lake, preventing the dust from spilling out into the cavern. Devon strained to look more closely at the lake. He could see wispy creatures swirling around in the water's depths — the mana-wyrms, he remembered. Earth realm was the only world blessed with enough raw magical energy to sustain such ethereal creatures.

The cavern floor was solid granite, but here and there, it had crystals embedded within it. The crystals contributed to the chaotic light patterns. They were absorbing the light in some places and reflecting it in others.

He walked down the last of the sloped road onto the smooth granite floor. He heard a noise behind him and looked back. He saw Jet, now a fraction of her former size, coming down the steps backwards, pulling the remains of her meal from last night. The villagers parted the way to let her through. A wise choice when confronted with a creature with that many teeth.

Izzy intercepted his pending question. <She can get to magical energy now. The second the keystone opened, the power could get back up to the surface. You, me, and Jet are pure faie; we need it to survive. She's an uble, a creature that can be any size or shape she chooses. The Pantheon created her to be your companion.>

Jet craned her head around to face him and gave him a wide, bloody smile, then went back to dragging her snack over to a gipsy caravan parked beside the wall on the far right.

As soon as Devon saw the caravan, more memories slammed into focus in his brain. "HAVEN! My gorgeous, gorgeous girl, you're alive!"

Everyone jumped as they looked across to what had excited Devon. All they saw was a twee little caravan, done out in gaudy yellow panelling with red trim. Sure, it was a relic of a bygone world, but nothing to get excited about. They'd think very differently soon enough.

Devon made himself relax and forced his excitement away from his beautiful home. Haven had been his refuge and friend for thousands of years, but right now, he had bigger things to keep him busy.

<Can you feel it, Izzy? This place is full of energy,> he thought to her.

There was a loud, communal gasp just as Devon felt an arm slip around his waist. "My lord," an extremely feminine voice purred below his ear.

Devon looked down toward the origin of the arm. What he saw was the most beautiful elf he had ever laid eyes upon. She was petite with raven-black hair that reached down toward her waist. Her features were softly curved and gentle, with narrow, full lips that underlined a small, strong-looking nose. Her pointed ears were prominent, but her most striking features were her softly glowing eyes that shone a deep shade of azurite blue.

"My gods and their tiny angels... Izzy?" he uttered. After that, he was silent because his words had simply fled.

"You're Izzy?" Gwen asked excitedly.

"I am." She beamed a happy smile at Gwen, who couldn't help but return it. "I needed magical energy to take my natural form. Up until now, I have had to resort to a tiny manifestation which Devon calls a wisp."

"Are you the one he has been talking to when he goes all distant?" Beth asked from the front row of the villagers.

"Yes, indeed. Gwen, Devon, and I can communicate using our thoughts," Izzy said. "He is no spy."

"I know that now. It's all so hard to comprehend. None of this should be real, and yet here we are."

"Okay, Izzy," Devon said. "We made it here. Shall we get our magic first?"

"I have never experienced or dared to imagine what it would be like to have more magical energy than I needed to stay alive. I am so nervous," Izzy said. She sounded scared, too.

"So how does he get magic?" Beth asked.

Devon marvelled at the fact it had been Beth who had asked the question first. He had imagined that she would be the most sceptical of all the villagers.

"I think the best thing to do first is to explain what magic is," Izzy said. "Magical energy is what anything magical, such as Devon, me, or any faie creature, needs to survive. We need it to live just as you need oxygen."

"Is that the same power you use to cast spells?" Gwen asked, her voice bursting with enthusiasm.

"No, casting requires a much stronger magical power called mana. It is a power that must be created by concentrating the raw magical energy in the air around you, then refining and purifying it. Only then is it strong enough to change the world around it. Its purity and concentration define its power."

"How does it change the world?" Beth asked. "There is no room for magic in physics. It's all actions and their reactions." Her astute scientific mind was focusing on the one thing that bothered her most.

"Magic does not change your physics. Your sciences have no concept of magic, and so they ignore it. I am afraid I am not an expert, Beth, but I can tell you how I understand it," Izzy said.

Devon marvelled at how she already had everyone here focusing on her every word. The elf was a natural at teaching.

"All things are made from tiny particles that like to cling together," Izzy explained. "Your sciences struggle to break matter apart or form new substances using various particles. Sometimes it requires vast amounts of energy or lengthy, complicated procedures. Magic is a power that can easily break apart and reform matter in any way just by structuring its power in prescribed ways. That's how I understand it anyway. Let me ask you a question, Beth. I believe water is made from two different substances. Hydrogen and oxygen, correct?"

"Yes, we call them molecules," Beth answered.

"Semantics. What would you have to do to persuade water to change back into hydrogen and oxygen?"

"Normally, we'd apply electricity to the water and use special metals to catalyse the breakup. It's called electrolysis. It's not a very efficient process, though."

"Raw magical energy is not strong enough to change matter, but apply the right structure of mana to water, and it will instantly split into its component pieces. No mess, no fuss. That is what mana-powered magic can do."

Beth mulled Izzy's words over and seemed slightly mollified by what she had heard. If this power could affect things in any way at a molecular level, the possibilities were limitless.

Izzy hadn't finished, though. "Most creatures cannot process raw magical energy into usable mana. Not even gods or goddesses can do that. Mana is the power that you will need to utilise your spells and magical abilities," Izzy explained. "Because you need mana but cannot make it, you need to team up with something that can. You need an assistant, something that will take the magical energy in the world around you and compress and purify it into mana. That something is called a symbiot, and that lake is swarming with them," Izzy finished, indicating the vast pool in front of them.

Izzy's last words must have triggered alarm bells for some people.

"Something?" a young lady asked. Her face was red, but she looked giddy with excitement.

"Yes, something," Izzy replied. "If you could all line up along that low wall by the lake, I will continue."

Chapter 11

Pain is the price

Devon stood between Gwen and Izzy, in the centre of the long line of villagers, assembled along the low wall. Memories of this place were coming slowly back to him, prompted by seeing it all again.

"Ahem!" Izzy rounded up everyone's attention. "Note that the substance in this pool is magical dust, not water. You will not get wet in there. Now, there is no easy way to break this to you all, so just take a deep breath and listen," Izzy said. She stepped up onto the wall and turned to face her pupils. "A symbiot is a creature that lives with another creature; the two of them live a mutually beneficial existence. Each creature provides something that the other needs. You need mana, so you need to find a creature willing to provide it in exchange for something you have to offer. If you look down into the magical dust, you will see just such a creature. Look closely, observe what these creatures are doing."

"Miss, they are just swimming around in circles. Do they do that all day?" a girl of about sixteen said.

Devon kept his laughter in his head. The girl had even put her hand up. Izzy already owned the crowd. Even Beth hung on her every word; he noticed that she had even started fidgeting. *Was she excited?*

"Exactly. The wyrms don't just swim in circles during the day; they do it constantly. In here, there is no day or night. These creatures never sleep. They are intelligent, and some are thousands of years old. Just close your eyes and imagine swimming in circles for hundreds of years. Just that, swimming and swimming and swimming. How would you feel after a week of doing that?"

"Very bored, miss," Finn said without even an iota of sarcasm in his voice.

Some of the children giggled, but Finn looked sincere. Izzy had him in her grasp too.

"Exactly. So, what could you offer these poor, bored creatures in exchange for large amounts of mana?"

"Entertainment, miss?" a young male villager asked.

"Entertainment; precisely. Your body also provides a few mineral salts that they crave, but your system has an excess of those and won't miss the tiny amount your symbiot might take."

"Must I walk around with one of these creatures holding my hand the whole time?" Finn asked.

"No, it lives inside you. Those creatures in the mana-pool are called mana-wyrms. Without a host, they can only survive in these mana-pools, which only exist in this world. The faie refer to this world as Earth realm, and it is just one of many worlds that exist in parallel. The taking of a symbiot used to be a big event in a person's life. Creatures would travel great distances, through the waygates, to places such as this to receive their symbiot and gain the ability to wield magic. It was the first step of their journey into the mystical world. Large ceremonies took place to celebrate the 'taking of the wyrm.' When you and the wyrm become bonded, it provides you with mana converted from the magical energy that will soon fill this world again. You will give it nutrients and a more interesting life than just swimming in circles for eternity."

"That doesn't sound too bad. Will I see it swimming around under my skin?" Finn asked.

Izzy laughed. "No! Mana-wyrms are ethereal creatures. They don't have a physical presence, only a magical one. You are corporeal, the exact opposite," she said, "I can't emphasise enough how bored these poor creatures get. Serving you will be like experiencing the best theatre compared to their lives in the mana-pool. Your symbiot will want to please you. The wyrm that chooses you will know that its talents are best suited to the type of person you are. A pacifist will never attract a wyrm that likes combat. The wyrms will do their utmost to give you the magic and abilities that best suit you. It will never turn you into something you are not."

"This is all so amazing. There must be thousands of those things swimming around in there," Gwen said, staring at the long, ghostly, eel-shaped creatures circling deep below the surface of the mana-pool.

"Miss? Are we allowed to have magic too?" a young lady asked hopefully.

<I could melt,> Izzy said mentally to Devon and Gwen. <I would love to teach children.>

<Then you're hired. I was already planning to ask you if you would.>

"If you are under sixteen, then your parent or guardian needs to agree, but yes, of course. In our new world, everyone gets an equal chance," Izzy said with a warm smile. "The dust clings to clothes, so if you want to do this, then strip down to your underwear and stand on the wall. Everyone must have a partner. One goes in while the other oversees them in case they faint. Then swap if your partner is taking magic too."

Finn put his hand up. "Why would we faint? Does it hurt?"

"A good question. Yes, it does hurt. A lot, but only for a short time and only once. Having mana within you will change your life forever; it will empower you, make you healthier, and prolong your life. Unfortunately, something that good comes with a price. Step forward, all those who want to take magic now. Do not feel forced. We will be doing other sessions should you wish to wait."

In the end, twenty-seven people stepped onto the wall in their underwear. Finn and Madi were having a quiet argument which consisted of Madi telling Finn that he couldn't and Finn ignoring her and stripping to his underpants.

"I want this; this is my chance to protect you and the others. Don't take that from me," Finn said.

"Fine, then I'm taking it too. Maybe I'll be able to heal you when you get hurt," Madi said petulantly as she started to strip too.

And those two make twenty-nine, odd number, not good, Devon thought. He was amazed to see Beth standing on the wall, practically hopping up and down.

He carefully removed his weapons and then stripped everything off except his tight undershorts. He even took off his 'Hello Kitty' watch, the last reminder of his past. He looked at the watch. The tiny thing made him feel melancholy. Then he noticed something written on the inside of the watch's strap. He looked closely; it said, '2 daddy with luv'; and the bottom instantly dropped out of his world. *DADDY? Did that refer to him? Was the watch a gift? If so, who from? Had he stolen it? Was there a little girl out there that missed him, or just her watch? Why was he assuming it was a girl? Was there a memory buried in his head somewhere?*

<Devon, what is the matter?> Izzy asked; her thoughts were worried about him. She had sensed his mood drop suddenly. She used mental communication to keep the conversation private.

He held out the watch for Izzy and Gwen to see.

<Oh! Wow! That certainly creates a mystery. Does the message mean anything to you?> Gwen asked.

<No. I can't even remember how I got the watch. For all I know, I stole it or bought it in a junk shop. The trouble is…> Devon paused and looked sadly at the tiny pink and white thing in his hand, <now I have a head full of unanswered questions.>

<Put the watch away in your pouch and forget about it for now. We will come back to it when we have means to investigate it,> Izzy said. Her thoughts were calming yet firm.

He knew Izzy was right, and Devon did as she had suggested. He couldn't find out anything now; wondering about it would just eat away at him. He took some deep breaths and tried to clear it all from his mind.

"Do you all have a partner? Line up in your pairs," Izzy called out.

Devon's acute hearing picked up someone weeping, and he quickly looked down the line for someone in distress. As the Wayfarer, that sound always started alarm bells ringing in his head, sending him straight into action. The girl that had spoken up earlier was trying to hold back her tears. Devon strode down to where she was standing with a lady that looked about thirty years her senior. Just before he arrived, the younger lady turned away and began wiping her eyes with her sleeves.

"Is she okay?" he asked the older woman. He realised that the woman was the same lady who had brought him all that lovely food the other day. She had rich brown hair that hung down to her shoulders and a rounded, friendly face. She was of a slightly heavier-than-average build and curvaceous. Her eyes were large and a soft hazel colour; they looked kind. Devon thought she must be in her early fifties. He knew she was a great cook, which made her a wonderful person, in his opinion.

"I know you. That food was delicious, by the way. I meant to thank you personally." He gave her his most winning smile. It seemed to have the effect he wanted.

"Oh, heh! Well, I mean, wow! I'd gladly be cooking for you whenever you wanted me to. You are something proper special," the lady said. She cleared her throat and tried to regain her composure. "This young madam doesn't have a partner, and I'm not sure I want her to take part. She's my niece, and I promised her mother I'd keep her safe. Lorn's mum was killed last year."

Devon took her hand and softly said, "I'm desperately sorry to hear about your sister. What about if I promised to mentor your niece through this? She could be my partner if you'd permit it. You could join us just to make sure everything is okay."

"Uhm. Well, I suppose that would be fine, but you have that beautiful foreign lady to care for and young Gwen, who seems to have become your shadow."

Devon snorted. "I suppose she is foreign. I never thought about it that way. She is an elf from a different world," he explained. "And now I have two more beautiful ladies to care for. It would be my pleasure. By the way, what should I call you both?"

"Ahem! Yes, names; my name is Juniper, no, no, it's June, not nobody that calls me Juniper these days. It's a silly name. This young lady here is Lorna, but she insists we call her Lorn. She's a headstrong young miss but has a heart of gold. Far too reckless for my liking but can run like the wind itself." She went red as she realised she was rambling.

"I'm honoured to meet you both. Just so that you know, I think Juniper is a lovely name."

"Ohhh, now stop it!" she said, blushing even more deeply. "I'm old enough to be your mother. If you were older, though."

Devon snorted with laughter. "Oh! I'm older. I promise you that I am older than everyone here combined," he whispered in her ear conspiratorially, all the time grinning broadly.

June looked at him in shock but kept silent.

Devon glanced at Lorn to find her staring at him in the same adulating way that Finn sometimes did. She looked to be nineteen or thereabouts and quite tall for her age, partly thanks to her long legs. She had a diamond-shaped face with pronounced cheekbones, intense blue eyes and a button nose. Her pale skin had freckles which Devon thought made her look younger. She had long, honey-blonde hair down to her waist that was intricately braided around her head then in patterns down her spine. It must have taken a lot of work. Her figure looked athletic.

"Are you coming, Lorn?" he said to the girl. "Let's get you sparkling." Devon practically dragged a shocked June back to where Izzy and Gwen were standing, watching him with amusement.

<You are so good with them all, my lord,> Izzy thought to him.

<They already love you and are desperate to follow you. There's just something about you that pulls us in,> Gwen added.

It was Devon's turn to blush. <I think both of you are biased in my favour. Can you two pair up while I pair with young Lorn here?>

<Yes, boss,> Gwen said.

"Right, everyone listen carefully; this is not a game," Izzy said with a raised voice. "You are about to join forces with a living, intelligent creature. In your pairs, choose which one of you will go in first. The first person in the pair should sit on the wall and slide into the powder, do not jump in. You will float, so do not thrash about. Stay near the wall and concentrate on the wyrms. Eventually, you will catch one of the creatures' attention, and they will come to you. Relax, do not panic, no screaming, and get out of the pool when you have finished," Izzy instructed.

Devon leant down and whispered in Lorn's ear, "you had better strip, young lady; everyone else is waiting."

Lorn smirked at him then stripped down to her underwear without breaking his gaze. "Shall I go first?"

"Fine by me, hop in and do it just like the elf instructed."

Lorn sat on the wall and spun around, then slipped straight into the fine silvery powder that flowed just like water.

Devon stepped up to take her place on the wall and saw fifteen nervous people floating in the pool staring down into the dust, their eyes wide with apprehension and varying degrees of fear. He was surprised to see one of the mothers floating in the dust. Her daughters were standing on the wall, watching her nervously. Devon wondered if the woman felt as Finn did and wanted magical power to protect the people in her care.

One by one, mana-wyrms detached themselves from their fellows and made their way towards the people awaiting them. Izzy stood beside him, watching Gwen closely. The wyrm that was headed toward her appeared to be quite a bit larger than its fellows.

Devon realised that only fourteen wyrms were on their way toward the surface. That meant someone was going to be upset very soon. He had a feeling he knew who. There was now a pronounced gap between Gwen's wyrm and the one heading for Finn. That gap was where Lorn waited nervously.

He decided to intervene. Like all faie creatures that couldn't speak conventionally, the wyrms used mental communication. <Oi! Wyrms, remember me? I am looking for a new symbiot, but before I get in and choose a candidate, I want my friend here to join with one of you. Whichever of you she chooses will have my blessing. This girl is officially in my care,> Devon mentally shouted to the wyrms. Vague memories had surfaced of his father originally populating this pool and of the queen's curse that had killed his previous symbiot. One lucky wyrm was going to get a very prestigious posting today. He smirked when he saw six wyrms detach themselves from the circling throng and immediately begin fighting with each other on the way up to the girl.

Grunts and cries rang out as the first fourteen people began to assimilate their symbiot. It was obviously excruciating, and people were only suppressing their exclamations because Izzy had told them that there was to be no screaming.

"Devon! Devon, what's happening?" Lorn cried out while worriedly watching the six bickering mana-wyrms swimming towards her as fast as they could manage.

"You seem to be extremely popular, Lorn. They must see great potential in you. Don't worry. If they all present themselves to you, then you will need to choose one. It is a great honour to be chosen by more than one symbiot."

Izzy looked at him and grinned. <Gwen and I heard what you said just now. That was a lovely thing you did for Lorn.>

<Shh! Don't tell anyone. I don't want her to know I intervened.>

<Oww! It hurts so much,> Gwen moaned to them. Her thoughts conveyed not just pain but suffering too.

They both looked to Gwen, who had started to look very ill. She appeared to be near to passing out.

<Devon, get her out, I will watch Lorn,> Izzy said. She added a sense of urgency to her thought.

He reached out and grabbed Gwen's outstretched arm, and with some effort, he managed to pull her body out of the dust. Once she was clear of the wall, he laid her gently down on the floor nearby. She was still breathing, but her skin was ashen.

<I think the human part of you is dying, Gwen,> Izzy thought. <The faie part of your soul has woken and is fighting for dominance. I think we might lose you for a day or so, and then you'll come back to us much stronger.>

Devon looked at Izzy in horror, but Gwen smiled happily. <Good riddance. Nothing good about being human. See you soon, guys.> With that, she closed her eyes, and her breathing slowed right down.

He remembered Lorn, and rather than dwell on Gwen's predicament, he refocused on her. She seemed to be having a silent conversation with the remaining four wyrms that had reached her. Eventually, she nodded and pointed at the largest one on the left. It seemed different from the other wyrms, as if its mother had been part dragon. He was impressed by how decisive she was. He instinctively reached out to June because the poor lady looked terrified as she watched Lorn's ordeal. She came to him and happily wrapped herself into his friendly embrace.

"She will be alright, won't she?" June said, looking up at Devon with wide, frightened eyes.

"Yes. She will be fine. Nothing will harm her. You have my word," Devon replied.

They both stood there watching Lorn, enjoying the intimacy of the moment.

Lorn squeaked loudly as the wyrm wrapped itself around her and started to sink through her skin. He could see that this part caused the most pain. The girl began to emit a strange, strangled groan as whatever ailed her became more intense.

Devon glanced down the line and saw that all the other people who had gone first had extracted themselves from the pool. The following candidates were already easing themselves in. Finn was looking straight at him with a look of happy triumph on his face. Devon winked at him and gave him two thumbs up.

<Devon, can you watch me, please?> Izzy asked.

<Yes, of course. In you go, gorgeous.> Devon hadn't meant to add that last bit, but it had slipped out. Besides, the elf was beauty personified.

<I can read your thoughts, idiot, but thank you for the compliment.> Izzy mentally smirked back at him. Then she slipped into the mana-pool with a nervous smile back at him.

"You can talk to them using your thoughts, can't you, Devon? We can all tell when you are talking to them even though none of you speaks. Can anyone do it?" June asked.

<Hang on, I just need to fetch Lorn,> Devon thought to June.

June looked at him in wonder. "I heard you, but I can't answer in the same way."

Devon pointed to the mana-pool. "Get magic, then it'll work for you. You'll be healthier, stronger, and live longer too."

"I'm seriously considering it," she replied. Her voice sounded wistful.

Devon leaned forward and whispered in June's ear. "Don't let fear rule your life. Seize the moment."

He turned, reached into the pool, then fished out the unconscious Lorn. She had chosen the biggest, most powerful wyrm which had probably offered her great things to become her choice. However, the price of great power seemed to be an overwhelming pain that was too much for her. He checked on Izzy and noticed that she was already in silent discussion with two candidates. When Lorn was safely lying beside Gwen, he returned to watching the elf.

"She'll be fine, June. Watch over her until she comes around," he assured her. He ran his hands back through his hair and tried to hide the look of concern on his face.

June nodded to him and bustled over to begin her vigil.

Ten minutes later, Madi was lying next to Lorn, entirely out of it but certainly not in any danger. All the other villagers were anxiously waiting for their teacher to finish her turn. Izzy had an audience. She assimilated her symbiot without much fuss, swam back to the side, and clambered out of the pool by herself. She flashed a victorious grin at him.

"Your turn, my lord."

Chapter 12

Sometimes life gives you diamonds

It was Devon's turn to suck up the pain and be brave. Everyone still conscious was standing on the wall, watching him expectantly. He was as ready as he was ever going to be, so he sat on the wall and slipped into the powder. The first thing he noticed was the dry tingle of the powder against his skin.

"Now, observe the mana-wyrms. You've certainly got their attention," Izzy instructed.

Devon stared down into the silvery dust and saw what Izzy meant. Rather than swimming around in a circle, all the creatures had stopped. They were all facing him now. Then the chaos started as the wyrms began squabbling amongst themselves. His attention fell on something far below the arguing wyrms that was rapidly increasing in size. Devon realised it was a head that was rising straight toward him. The squabbling mana-wyrms scattered like skittles when the rising beast swam directly through them, heading upwards at speed.

Gasps and exclamations came from the villagers as they began to realise the sheer size of the creature hurtling up towards Devon.

"Oh my! You attracted a mana-dragon. Oh, Devon!" Izzy said, her words filled with awe.

"Is that bad?" June asked.

"No! My goodness, no, not bad. Far from it. If Devon can bond with a mana-dragon, then this moment will become a thing of legend. These dragons were thought extinct, just like he was."

Devon was apprehensive before he heard Izzy's words. That had now turned to fear. He watched as the mana-dragon continued to swim upwards. By the time it reached him, it was evident that the dragon was more than ten times his size. "Uh! Izz? That will never fit inside me."

"Shh! This is a big moment. Don't scare it away," Izzy said. There wasn't any sympathy in her tone, just unadulterated awe.

"Me scare that! Are you kidding me?"

<YES?>

Devon felt the question ram itself straight into his brain. It wasn't in a language, just a concept. He knew the thought came from the monster in front of him.

<Yes,> Devon thought back, trying his best to imitate the same concept the mana-dragon had used while adding welcoming thoughts to it. He took a moment to admire the beast. Izzy wasn't joking when she called it a mana-dragon. It looked like the dragons from western myths but elongated and ghostly. The dragon grinned at him. It was a smile very much like Jet's; there were lots of ethereal teeth. *Oh crap!*

The mana-dragon licked its ethereal lips and gave Devon a hungry look.

"I'm gonna die. I'm gonna die!"

"Shh! Stop being such a big wussy baby. It is just being friendly," Izzy said, still without sympathy.

The dragon started to move. Its tail came around him and continued to circle until Devon was wrapped from toe to chin by seven loops of the monster. The dragon's head rose until it was looking straight down onto his head. Devon looked up, straight into its maw. The dragon winked at him before dashing its head downward.

"Eeeeeeeee!" Devon squealed uncharacteristically.

"Shh!" Izzy hissed.

"Crikey!" Finn said, his face full of shock. "I've never seen him look scared before."

Devon watched in horror as the dragon's mouth enveloped him. The mouth disappeared inside him, and the rest of the body began to follow it. The sensation of the monster merging with him was almost beyond description.

Then it started to hurt as well. Devon fought back the urge to scream as pain, more intense than anything he could ever remember, engulfed every nerve in his body. It felt as if every cell of his being was rudely violated and then roughly repaired an instant later. Despite his resolve, Devon shook violently from head to toe. Every muscle spasmed then contracted fiercely as the sensations ripped through him. He gave in and screamed. His neck tightened, and his voice cut off as the feeling swept upwards and started to wreck his brain.

His mind warped and twisted and then, like the other pain, was repaired and passed over. Devon was sure that every molecule had been examined and affected by the faie dragon's melding with him. He could feel that there was now something very different about every tiny part of him, including his consciousness. The only way he could describe it was miraculous.

Devon could feel aspects of his being coming alive, radiating power and response. His forehead ached, and he felt a sharp pain emerge from it. He reached up to touch the spot that hurt and felt something hard and shaped like a diamond. As he touched it, he felt a shock engulf him, and for the second time in as many minutes, his nerves tingled angrily and shouted at him.

"Devon, you must listen to me," Izzy shouted. "Climb out of the pool. Now! You're about to pass out. You can't stay in there."

A moment later, he felt arms wrap around him, and someone dragged him from the pool. It was at that point that Devon's thoughts went dark.

He opened his eyes moments later and found himself lying beside the unconscious form of Gwen. Devon felt worn out but at the same time bursting with power. He reached into himself, looking for a bond like the one he had with Jet. What he found was the dragon sitting in his consciousness, grinning happily at him.

<'Ow do, yung un!> the dragon thought in a mischievous but amiable way.

A Somerset accent? Seriously? I have a mana-dragon from the West Country. Devon laughed hard. <'Ow do yourself, dragon. So how do you and I work then?>

<Tis proper simple. You tell I what ee needs an I fetch it up to you.>

"You okay in there, Devon?" Izzy asked.

Devon grinned. He also smiled internally at his dragon. <You and I are going to have some proper fun, dragon. You give me the mana, and I'll provide lots of entertainment.>

<Proper job. 'Ang about. Gotta do this first. This might 'urt a bit.>

Devon screamed again as the agony coursed through him. He felt four burning paths sear their way from the dragon to his forehead. <Ow! Steaming crap, that smarts! What did you do to me?> he asked the dragon.

<Your mana be flowin' now, yung un. Now we can 'av some proper fun.> The dragon's words came with a great sense of amusement.

<Uh, Devon! Are you okay in there?> Izzy asked with concern. <Your thoughts are coming through scrambled. I can't read you right now.>

Devon opened his eyes and blinked a few times. "I'm fine. Just chatting to my mana-dragon, who happens to be a proper wurzel." He laughed.

<Proper wurzel, an' proud.> The dragon laughed.

<What's a 'wurzel'?> Izzy asked, confusion filling her thoughts.

<A nickname given to country folk from this area. At least, that's what he tells me,> Devon replied. <I now have a mana-dragon with a thick West Country accent, who seems like he might be good fun.>

"Ooh! I love your diamond. Very mystique. I wonder if that is a god thing or a 'look at me, I've got a mana dragon' thing." Izzy laughed. "Probably both, as I have never seen anyone else with a crystal that protrudes through the skin. Most creatures with magic have a crystal embedded in the skull that is just under the skin. The only way to tell is to press the skin above it. Trust you to be different."

"Is having my dragon a good thing?"

"The stuff of legends, Devon. The power he can create for you is beyond amazing. If you can handle him, then we're in for some exciting times."

Devon thought about what Izzy had told him. Then he thought about what must happen next. It might be better for everyone to stay down here for now. "Izzy, can you please fetch the camp charm from the surface and bring it down here. It's warm and dry down here, and Haven will have plenty of food and water, I expect."

Izzy seemed like she was about to scowl and swear at him but thought better of it. She bounded off up the road instead. She'd realised that, apart from Devon, she was the only one that knew how to strike the camp and transport it down into the nexus.

Devon clambered to his feet and accepted the many offers to shake his hand and hugs he got in congratulations for surviving the mana-dragon's assimilation. Those that had taken magic looked euphoric, and those that hadn't were firing eager questions at them. The villagers all looked excited and hopeful. The tired, hopeless look that had dogged so many of them before had disappeared. He wondered if they realised how much more their lives were about to change.

His gaze fell on the ruins of the magical energy conduit. His brain informed him that he knew how to fix it. He wondered if his dragon could provide enough power to do it.

<Ee be 'avin plenty. Let's be givin' it a try,> the mana-dragon enthused

<Do you have a name, dragon? We've got a long time together, and it would be easier if you did.>

<I fought ee'd never ask,> the mana dragon thought happily. <I be Brack and me sisters are Draska an' Preeta.> The dragon knew his remark would confuse Devon and seemed to enjoy the prospect.

<Go on then, I'll bite. What sisters?>

<Da yung un 'oo said yu'd be sponsorin' 'er or sumut. My sister told 'er that I was getting yoo, so she said yes. Clever girl that un,> Brack said. <Preeta chose the little un with the blonde 'air. Yu'd best be watchin' that un; she's proper powerful.>

That explained why Lorna was still out for the count. She hadn't assimilated a mere mana-wyrm. She'd got his mana-dragon's smaller sibling. He was pleased to see that Finn was attending to an awakening Madi. That meant one less casualty to be concerned about.

He looked around. Trying to spot the other girl to whom Brack had referred. If there was a promising mage around, Devon wanted to know about her. He saw the girl lying on the floor next to Lorna, unconscious. He'd keep his eye on them both.

Devon walked over and stood back up on the low wall by the mana-pool. Beth came and stood next to him but indicated that he should ignore her. He smiled when she spoke anyway.

"I'll tell you a secret," Beth said. "Magic was my dream when I was a little girl. Thank you for sticking with me and allowing me to fulfil this fantasy."

Devon gave her a warm smile. "You and Gwen had something in common after all. You're welcome."

He reached out his left hand and asked his dragon for a thirty-percent flow through half of his channels. If he started this repair any faster, he would damage the foundations. He reached under his shirt and pulled out the pendant. It was still glowing the intense blue that it had been on the surface. Devon felt two of his channels swell and deliver mana to the mana-crystal embedded in his forehead. He forced his will against the mana stream and directed it through the pendant and out towards the lower portion of the broken conduit.

As it left the pendant, the mana stream's soft blue light expanded away to form a holographic overlay of the column's original appearance. The image swelled until it engulfed the ruins from the base to the top, then when it had reached full size, the hologram began to solidify slowly. The construct creaked and popped as matter was pulled in from other planes and forced to form the desired structure.

Devon asked for all channels to open and increased the flow to sixty percent. He had to fight hard with the vast amounts of energy that flowed through the pendant. Trying to keep the mana in an orderly stream was like wrangling cats. By sheer strength of will and bloody-mindedness, he managed to keep the flow tidy and concentrated on the solidifying structure in front of him.

The conduit started to look corporeal and began to take on the details of its final form. Patterns of runes became visible, etched into the obsidian and crystal of the reforming column. Hundreds of fine channels took shape, flowing vertically up the shaft. These would contain the power as it flowed upwards through the stone. He knew that hundreds of other structures just like this were taking shape simultaneously, all around the world. This was the key-nexus. What happened here was reflected throughout the Earth realm. Progenitor magic possessed world-altering creationist powers beyond comprehension.

Finally, the forming process was complete. Devon stopped his mana-flow and waited with bated breath. For him, this moment was huge. He had never had to fix a nexus before. They were supposed to be infinity engines that would pump for as long as magical dust was there to shift. He used to repair waygates all the time. Every tinpot dictator or power-hungry king would try and damage them just to stop reinforcements from getting through. Nobody could get near a nexus, though. Not until that pox-ridden fairy queen had stolen his pendant and cursed him, that is. He intended to make her pay for that, though, and soon.

Devon jumped as a rumbling started. The vibration spread outward until the whole world was shaking. Every occupant of the Earth realm felt the ground jump; closely followed by the loud, prolonged thunder of five-hundred infinity engines powering up and beginning to pump magical energy back up to Earth's surface. Of course, no-one could see the results, but everyone experienced the seismic event. In the nexus, everyone squeaked as the whole cavern shook, and an ear-splitting thump rang out. The intricately detailed column began to glow with a warm, golden light. Enchantments and runes began to perform their tasks in harmony, and energy started to flow cleanly through them. Everyone jumped at the 'whoomph' sound as the pillar began functioning fully and radiating with a light too bright to look at directly.

<Bloody' ell!> the dragon said, then sent Devon a mental double thumbs-up. <Flash bugger, int ya? I'm bloomin' luvin' yu.>

Everyone in the cavern was further startled when Devon leapt high into the air and cheered loudly. "Oh, yes! I've still got it." When he landed, he started to do a little jig that looked more like a dad-dance. "Yes, oh yes, oh yes, ohhhhhh yes!" When his euphoria had calmed a little, he looked around and saw nearly fifty shocked, confused faces and one filled with awe. Izzy was back.

"I cannot even begin to understand what just happened," Beth said.

"Earth realm just got its magic back. Now things will get interesting," Devon replied.

Izzy stepped forward to stand in front of Devon, then sank to her knees with bowed head and clasped hands. "My lord Wayfarer, I am your humble priestess in name alone, not by bond. I beg you, take my soul in binding as your disciple. Grant me your power that I might show the worlds your might and grant me your wisdom that I might guide your followers. I swear my lifelong fealty and devotion to you, in front of witnesses."

Devon felt a tight tug at his soul as if something was trying to get his attention. His response came to him without a thought. "My bond is yours, priestess. My values are now your values." When his words had finished, a bright golden light enveloped them. He felt a tight bond form between them and saw Izzy's beautiful blue eyes turn golden momentarily.

"Wow! What the hell was that?" Beth asked in amazement. She looked deeply into his eyes as if she'd find answers in there. "You're not seriously a god, are you? You can't be; gods are just mythical beings. They have no basis in science or reality. You're just a… just a… Fuck! You really are."

"I'm just me, Beth." Devon blushed. "The god thing is no big deal. Feel free to grovel, though." He snorted.

Beth caught him with a hard punch to the arm and grinned at him.

Devon and Izzy had set the camp up in the nexus for that evening. He'd asked Jet nicely, and she had agreed that they could undertake the task of pulling Haven out of the nexus tomorrow so that he could safely seal the lower cavern once again. More villagers had asked if they could take a symbiot too, and Izzy had supervised another session of pairing people up with willing mana-wyrms. In the end, only three of the older villagers refused magic.

****_****

They had finally found a quiet moment and slipped away to Haven. Izzy put her hand on his back as he stood at the back of the gipsy caravan and looked up at the door. He'd been nervous about entering his old home again. His memories of time spent inside it were still sketchy, but he knew how much he loved the place. Devon ascended the three steps and respectfully turned the golden doorknob. The door opened outwards, and behind it hung a black beaded curtain that wholly obscured the view inside.

Devon hesitantly pushed his way through the beads and found himself standing in the familiar living area. It was just as he remembered. The colours offered a warm and cosy feeling, with a plush, dark, wine-coloured carpet setting the scene. Darkly-stained, wooden panelling rolled outward from the floor and then back in as it rose to meet the wood-vaulted ceiling. When the two of them entered the room, its dimensions changed. Once in the room, it was bigger than it had been when he'd been looking inside from the steps.

There was an entrance in a dividing wall at the far end of the room, concealed by a thick burgundy curtain. Devon knew that behind that curtain was a very nicely appointed kitchen, dining area, and a door that led you into the bedrooms and bathing area. Each bedroom had very generous facilities, but this caravan also had a communal bath and a spa. To the right of the entrance hung a large, golden-framed, full-length mirror. On the curtain's left sat a luxuriantly upholstered armchair. That was his chair. Now that Izzy was in the room, there was a companion armchair next to it. The caravan was clever like that, adjusting its size and furnishings to suit the guests present. Devon wondered if it could stretch to fifty.

To the left of the armchair was a wooden bookcase, about five feet wide and spanning from floor to ceiling. Its deep shelves supported books of all sizes. The books were all leather-bound, not damaged or dusty, but they did look old. The bookcase was mostly for show because it concealed the entrance to a well-stocked library, that got bigger as more books were stuffed inside it, and there was a magical study area at its centre.

On the opposite wall from the bookcase was another curtained entrance that offered access to all Haven's other rooms. Next to that were four capacious, double-doored cupboards. The cupboards lined the entire length of the wall not taken up by the entrance. Beneath them were four equally deeply shelved cabinets. All the furnishings were made from the same dark wood that seemed to be a recurring theme throughout. An intricately carved, wooden coffee table sat in front of his armchair.

The last thing of note was Jet's favourite spot. It was a large fireplace with an ornately decorated surround and mantle. It protruded slightly into the room from the middle of the left wall. At the fire's base was a deep, spacious hearth and atop that sat a sturdy firebox, iron trellis, and spit assembly. Jet was there now. She'd changed into her petite form and was currently fast asleep. This place was just as much her home as his.

The gods had provided for him generously. They wanted him to reap souls for them, and they'd enticed him to agree by offering him Jet and Haven.

"Devon, it's beautiful. A bit small, but lovely," Izzy said. She didn't sound convinced.

"Oh, Izzy, how can my priestess have such little faith?"

Chapter 13

Come over to my place

"You there, Abi?" he called.

"Master!" a happy sounding female voice answered.

Her voice brought more memories into focus. "It's been far too long," Devon replied. Abi was the housekeeper for Haven. She represented the caravan's sentience and managed everything concerning his home for him.

"Yes, indeed, master. Your father made sure that I am back to full functionality with some significant upgrades, too. While I have been awaiting your return, I have been researching current technologies, materials, and fashions."

Devon walked over to the mirror and tapped the surface. The reflections vanished, and the glass seemed to gain depth as swirling mist filled the view. The mist coalesced into a group of gently rotating cubes and a cog that span at the bottom. Each cube was labelled. They said: 'Hub', 'Hospital', 'Training area', 'Workshop', 'Games/VR room', 'War room', and 'Prison'. The cog had the word 'Other Stuff' floating beside it. The 'Games/VR room' cube was greyed out presently, but he'd soon sort that out.

He reached into the mirror and touched the 'Hub' cube, which turned red, and a sliding noise came from behind the curtain. There was a clunk as something heavy settled into place. The 'Hub' cube turned green.

"Be my guest," he said to Izzy, motioning to the curtain he was holding to one side. Izzy stepped through into an enormous, circular room. It was at least one-hundred yards in diameter and twenty yards high. Everything in this room was alien to her, and she felt as if she had stepped into a different world. She gazed around in amazement. A perfectly smooth, white compound covered the walls, floor, and ceiling. The material radiated a glow, making other light sources completely unnecessary. Fine channels made from a transparent material crisscrossed the ceiling. Now and then, different coloured globules of light would travel slowly through them and disappear somewhere else. The whole place smelled clean.

Haven's cylindrical core rose from floor to ceiling in the hub's centre. It was formed from a strange, semi-translucent black crystal and was nearly fifteen feet thick. Deep inside the column, Izzy saw thousands of bright little lights of every colour. Sometimes they flashed; other times, they stayed lit or just disappeared completely. The whole column emitted a thin, shadowy mist that dissipated mere inches from its source; it hummed faintly.

On the left side of the circular wall were two doorframes. The far doorframe had been constructed from dark steel with a pillar nearby, supporting another full-length mirror. A dark gold formed the other frame. Both were empty, and Devon gazed forlornly at them.

"The gold portal is for my realm," Devon said, indicating the gold frame.

"All gods and goddesses have a personal realm. I read about it," Izzy replied. "The Pantheon closed your realm's access when they lost you. Is that right?"

"Sadly, yes; although once I kill the fairy queen, I'll take hers too. I was preparing to liberate the fairy queen's realm just before I was cursed and had built a huge city in my realm. If I could get my realm back, everyone's housing problems would be over. The other portal I can use to select a waygate and use it from here. I can also set portals wherever I need to if I get Abi to make me a portal charm."

"You should set one in this nexus, master. If the portal stays open, I can now pull magical energy through it and use that to maintain myself."

"Is that one of your upgrades, Abi?"

"Indeed, master. It will allow me to continue functioning should we run out of points. I think your father wanted to avoid fixing me again."

"Right you are, Abi."

Izzy continued to gaze around at the wonders contained in this strange room. Her eyes fell upon a silvery square on the floor, near the far wall. It was about thirty feet across but was only about ten inches thick. Izzy noticed a narrow line travelling horizontally, all the way around the square, suggesting that the platform was two platforms, one on top of the other. Izzy walked over to it in curiosity. The construction consisted of thirty-six smaller squares, all tightly slotted together. "What does this platform do?" she asked.

"Abi? Is this a new design for my mana-forge? Why is it so much bigger and segmented?"

"Yes, master. It can create far bigger designs now. The old cylinder design was limiting the size of your creations. It is segmented to enable transportation to a larger area. You may now purchase more segments for it, thus allowing you to expand it further. It is as big as it can be in this room."

"I have not heard of a mana-forge. What is it?" Izzy was surprised that there were things about the Wayfarer's life that she did not know. She had tried to learn everything she could in readiness for meeting the god to which she had devoted her life.

"Ah! My pride and joy and utterly unique. It utilises ancient creationist magic to pull matter from other dimensions and uses large amounts of mana to form that matter into designed objects. It can create anything if you have a design for it. Because it is a fundamental truth that you cannot make something from nothing, Haven acts like a giant recycling system. All waste is fed back into the forge to create new matter, and any shortfall is pulled in from elsewhere.

The construction is the easy bit, though. The hard work is all in here," Devon said, tapping his head. "Designing requires a high amount of mental strength and good mana control. You create things in your mind and must mentally hold on to your creation throughout the design process. If you lose concentration, you lose all of your hard work."

"Abi, where has my scanner gone?" Devon asked while looking around. "With all these new people and new technologies around, I'm going to need that soon." He paused, and then a concerned look crossed his face. Another memory had popped into focus. "This isn't about that last incident, is it?"

"No, master." Abi tried to conceal the amusement in her voice. "The Pantheon chose to let that pass if you recall. The scanner is built into the mana-forge so you can scan much larger items."

Izzy noticed that Devon looked relieved, but he didn't elaborate, so she decided not to pry. Instead, she continued to gaze around the room. She spotted ten recliner benches arranged in an outwardly facing circle around the core. Izzy hadn't noticed them earlier. Each seat had a white leather covering over plush upholstery. They looked exceptionally comfortable, and Izzy wondered why anyone might choose to relax in such a place. Ten someones relaxing was an even bigger mystery.

Devon saw her looking at the benches and smiled. He knew from experience that they were very comfortable and easy to fall asleep on. He'd done so many times. "They are the design benches, Izzy. You lie back and create things in your mind, using the designer and your imagination. Whatever your design, it can be constructed using the forge. They are right next to the core because Abi needs to interact with the creation in your mind. You need to be coated in a fine mist of mana for that to happen. Haven is one big magical energy conversion engine."

Izzy nodded and stared again at the benches with a fresh look of awe.

Devon remembered why he had come in here. He held out his hand and reversed the soul summoning process. Shadowy souls billowed from his palm and formed into the shapes of their originators. Twenty-four humans and five boars. The shadows were drawn away toward the room's core, where they were absorbed.

"Thank you, master. All souls accepted. No additional bounties from those. Would you like a points report?" Abi asked.

"I'll look at that in the front room. Thanks, Abi. We'll also need a room list." He gestured to Izzy, and she led the way back into the front room. They both settled into their cosy chairs.

Just then, a familiar face poked its way through the bead curtains of the entrance.

"Hi, Finn, what's up?"

"Uhm, well, we were wondering what is happening," he replied.

"Oh yes, hah! Sorry, Finn, I was just settling back into my old life. I completely forgot that I have you all to think about now."

"We imposed ourselves on you, Devon. Never feel guilty about being who you are."

"Actually, can you organise some help and bring Gwen in with Madi and Beth? I have a hospital in here, and she can rest in there. We can discuss what happens next, too. Are Lorn and Grace awake yet?"

<Lorn and Grace are now playing host to my mana-dragon's sisters, by the way,> he thought to Izzy.

<Oh, wow! There were three of them? I was amazed you found one,> Izzy replied.

"Yes, they woke up a few minutes ago," Finn said.

"Master, I would like to scan your new companions. They may have skills we can utilise, and I will need their sizes to make clothing. Also, I have added a farm upgrade to the room list so that I can supply fifty people with produce."

Finn looked startled and glanced around.

"Don't worry, Finn, that's Abi. She oversees my home. Now, about Gwen?"

"Oh, yes, right. On my way." His head disappeared back through the beads.

“Displaying your earnings report now, master.” Light swirled in front of them. Gradually the particles of light assembled into a floating list above the coffee table.

Haven Points Earned: Devon-001

Deed	Qty	Score	Total
Soul of Enemy: Level 1	10	250	2500
Soul of Enemy: Level 2	9	300	2700
Soul of Enemy: Level 1: Elite	1	300	300
Soul of Enemy: Level 2: Elite	4	350	1400
Soul of animal; Boar	5	150	750
Nexus matrix repair (500x50)	500	50	25000
Assimilate mana-dragon	1	2500	2500
Residual points from previous occupancy	1	27550	27550
			62700

“Woah! That’s a lot of points. It should be enough to get you fully updated, Abi, and have enough left to start building items for the new settlement,” Devon said, thrilled that Abi had managed to retain his previous points. That would help to achieve his plans that he had been working on. Abi would need to run through some significant technological upgrades too.

“Would you like the ‘Rooms and Upgrades’ list now, master?”

“I certainly would. Let’s get spending.”

Izzy looked at him in fascination. “You lead such a wonder-filled life. I cannot comprehend how much you could do with the resources you can control. I would dearly love it if you taught me to craft. Would you?”

“Yes, of course! It would be my pleasure. Crafting was always a passion of mine, and I think you would make an excellent crafter. The designer allows people to work together on creations as well, which might be fun. I need to make you some priestess’ garments and a suitable weapon. Maybe a magical staff?”

“You would do that for me?” Izzy said.

“Izzy, you act as if you are not part of my life now. Are you planning on leaving me?”

“No, my lord. I am bound to you as your priestess,” Izzy said.

“If you don’t want to stick around, then go, my priestess or not,” he said with a hint of testiness in his voice. “I don’t expect you to stay if you don’t want to be here.”

Izzy was shocked at how generous Devon could be and how coldly he could dismiss her if she did not want to stay. For her, that was strange, but she understood that his past was to blame. He had been hurt too many times and was cautious with those he was attracted to. Did that mean he wanted her in that way? Izzy usually acted out of obligation, rarely by choice. She had to admit that her feelings toward him had become intense, both physically and emotionally. He was her life now. Staying with him was all she wanted. However, her obligations to the resistance and her people were also essential commitments.

"Devon? Where shall we carry Gwen?" Finn shouted through the bead curtain.

"Bring her in here, Finn," Devon replied. He jumped up and hurried over to the mirror. When it lit up, he selected the 'Hospital' option and waited until the cube went green. Finn and Beth struggled in through the entrance holding an inert Gwen between them. Devon pushed the curtain aside and guided everyone into Haven's hospital. "Just rest her on one of the beds."

Madi looked around in wonder. Sterile, white material that she didn't recognise lined the floor, walls, and ceiling. It was a purified marble paste in resin that Devon had invented millennia ago, but Madi wasn't to know that. Deep cupboards lined the walls and supported extensive work surfaces; glass-fronted cabinets were located higher up. They contained various bottles, assorted bandages, and other medical paraphernalia. Devon was no expert, but Abi knew what she was doing.

<Master, I have quietly scanned these individuals. They all have valuable skills.>

Devon had forgotten that Abi could communicate mentally too. With so many people around, that would come in handy. He had to smile at Abi's resourcefulness. She worked for his benefit beyond anything else.

Madi started opening cupboards and rifling through the contents. Beth joined her moments later.

"Devon, this place is great. You badly need some robotic units in here, though," Beth enthused.

"Master, I have added an item to the room list that includes such upgrades. I have included an upgrade in the hospital's size too."

Beth and Madi looked around in shock. "Who said that?"

"Devon has a housekeeper," Finn said, proud that he knew something the women didn't.

"I'll have a cook too if I can persuade June to move in," Devon smirked.

"You've already got her wrapped around your finger." Beth laughed. "All we've heard is Devon this and Devon that. I don't know what you said to Lorn, but she is suddenly your biggest advocate. She's only nineteen, so watch her. I had some serious ambitions when I was her age."

Devon felt pleased to hear that. He was contemplating taking Lorn and Grace under his wing, since they were also living with powerful mana-dragons and needed to learn how to harness that power. "Is Gwen comfortable? Can we leave her to sleep?"

"She's dying, Devon," Madi said sadly.

"The human part of her is dying," Izzy said. "She is part faie, which are magical creatures and cannot live without magical energy. While there was no magic on Earth's surface, the faie part of her was dormant. Devon has returned magic to Earth realm, and that part of her has woken up. In a day or so, the faie side will win the battle, and she will reawaken and be a stronger, healthier version of herself."

Madi gawked at Izzy. "Devon, is there a way we can learn about all this? June said you mentioned building a school."

"Yes, let's retire to the front room. We have lots to discuss."

****_****

Abi had set out another three armchairs, arranged in a semicircle around the roaring fire. A list of upgrades for Haven hovered above the coffee table in front of them.

Haven: Rooms and Upgrades: Devon-001	Cost
Hub upgrade 1: Capacity upgrades: Higher Capabilities	410
Hub upgrade 2: Modern Processing, Interfacing, surveillance	435
Hub upgrade 3: Digital infiltration, Information acquisition and compilation	550
Hospital upgrade: Robotics and tech enhancements plus extended capabilities	370
Hospital upgrade: Size upgrade. Treatment facilities for up to 20 people	550
Portal - Fixed gate - 20' Diameter	200
Portal - Fixed gate - 40' Diameter	450
Waygate Installation Kit	750
Mana-forge upgrade - Segment. Can expand or create new mana-forge	250
Design area: Mana-forge Upgrade - Laboratory + raw-mana sculpting	250
Design area: Mana-forge Upgrade - Masterwork Alchemical Laboratory	300
Design area: Mana-forge Upgrade - Artisan weapons factory	500
Design area: Mana-forge Upgrade - Artisan vehicle factory	500
Design area: Mana-forge Upgrade - Artisan munitions factory	500
Mana-forge Update - Modern Earth realm materials, compounds & templates	1250
War-room upgrade: Scanners (Long range)	120
War-room upgrade: Aerial downfacing scanner relay, transponder	279
Haven upgrade: External communications 2-way	200
Games room / VR Units for up to 25 persons	400
Games Room: Size upgrade. Capabilities for additional 25 people	450
Additional 30 permanent bedrooms: Includes luxury bed, facilities & storage	1150
Dormitory / Barracks - Sleeps 50: Includes luxury bunks, facilities & storage	3150
Self Sufficiency Farm Upgrade +50 persons	750
Medical Pod - Automated Emergency care for up to 50 people	1950
Training Room / Gymnasium Pod - 100 people	1875
Library and study rooms pod - 50 people	3750
Mana-forge output pod - 25 segments	4500
Farm Pod - Quality produce for 1000 people	7450
Expanded Catering Pod - Communal cooking facilities for up to 1000 people	3950
School Pod. Educational & VR facilities for 100 students.	4750

Finn and the three ladies stared at the list with rapt attention.

"That's incredible. Can this little caravan do all that?" Beth asked. Her eyes were wide, and her face radiated fascination. "Do you want me to run your war-room? I could do that if you think it would be useful."

"Yes, please, Beth. I don't know what's coming, but that would be very helpful. I'll have to get you into the library and put you through a course on how to use the room."

<Master, I have taken the liberty of creating some new items called pods. They are self-contained, pocket dimensions that can have various Haven-styled rooms constructed within them. I thought the technology might prove helpful. Large constructions will fit into a small outer form. Following your thoughts on education, I took the liberty of including a school pod as well.>

<Abi, you are an absolute star. You've solved my settlement problems before I could even ask you for your help. How many points would the upgrades and the pods cost me?>

<That will cost forty-one-thousand, two-hundred and eighty-nine points, master.>

<Please start work on all of that. Build the pods after everything else. These villagers will need to eat, so Haven's farm upgrade comes first.>

<Of course, master. I will have a few more mana-forge patterns ready soon. Some of the villagers have a wealth of new information in their heads.>

<Go right ahead. The villagers don't even realise you're doing it.>

<Commencing now. Master, Haven has been producing food for a long time in your absence. There are enough reserves to feed everyone for at least ten days, all stored in the kitchen's food storage facilities.>

Beth started looking around the room. "He's talking to someone again. Izzy is here, and Gwen is out of it. Who can he be talking to?"

"Abi, the housekeeper," Devon said. "I've asked her to build everything on that list. She tells me that there is enough fresh food to feed us all for ten days. By then, I will have the larger food production facility working, as well as some other interesting projects Abi has just started work on."

"Can you afford to build everything?" Madi asked in concern.

"It's costly, but I think you might be worth the expense," Devon said. He swept his fringe back with his hand and gave Madi a small smile. Now that he had achieved his first objectives, the next step was to get back at the fairy queen and her entourage. There would be many deaths along the way. Points for the settlement were the least of his worries.

"Devon, you're doing so much for us. How can we ever repay you for this?" Finn asked.

"There's still plenty of work for you all to do, Finn," Devon responded. "I will not be running this settlement. I want that absolutely clear. That is for you all to sort out between you. I'm just helping in the ways that I can. My role means I must travel often. However, I would like to share this place with you and make it my home, too."

"Of course. We promised that we would take care of all that," Madi said. She stuck her jaw out in the same way that Finn did when he was determined about something.

"It won't just be for the forty-seven of you, Madi. There will likely be thousands of other refugees from at least two different worlds. I haven't worked everything out just yet," Devon said.

Everyone but Izzy looked at him in shock. This was the first they knew of his ambitions for the settlement.

"Relax, these are just my thoughts, and they still need work. Besides, I happen to have grown quite fond of you all, so I'm simply helping my new friends, even that ginger one there," he laughed, pointing at Beth. "Now, I've got plenty of food stashed away, and we all need to eat tonight. Does June do all the cooking?"

"June is our main cook, and Dawn helps out. She's the lady with the two daughters," Beth answered. "I think I can speak for everyone when I say we've grown to find you quite tolerable too. Most of the time. Although you can be an insufferable show-off sometimes." She gave him a wicked grin.

Devon chuckled and shook his head. "Can we get the cooks in here and get them busy with the meal then?"

"On that?" Madi asked, her voice incredulous. She pointed to the small spit assembly above the fire.

"He's probably got a massive kitchen stashed in here somewhere," Beth said.

Chapter 14
Ye gods!

Devon awoke somewhere unfamiliar. Clouds billowed around a well-worn rectangular stone plinth, upon which he stood; on every side of the platform, steps led infinitely downwards. Ornately sculpted marble pillars surrounded the platform, and a flat stone roof sat on top of the structure. Carvings and runes covered every surface. The décor left him feeling chilly, although he felt no sensation of temperature.

In the middle of the rectangle stood four identical stone thrones that faced him in a semicircle. The seats looked poorly made and uncomfortable, but the occupants were far from ordinary. Sitting on the mid-left throne was a mature-looking lady surrounded by a silver shimmer that seemed to flow away from her edges like mist. She wore silver robes that sparkled whenever she made the tiniest movement. Her face was that of a goddess with severe lines that made her seem strict yet just. It was her long, gently curled, silver hair and glowing golden eyes that were the shock.

The lady sitting on the mid-right was smiling seductively at him. She was one of the most alluring women he had ever seen. She was tall, voluptuous to the point of obscenity, and had a perfect heart-shaped face. The most striking part was that she was green all over. She wore leaves that kept her modesty but only just. She had lustrous, dark-green hair that flowed in ringlets down to her curved rear. On her head, she wore a crown of flowers.

The details of the man on the far-right throne weren't apparent because he was made entirely out of shadows. He was on the large side of a humanoid form, and the only parts of him that weren't shadow were his eyes. They shone with the piercing orange glow of the setting sun. Devon looked more closely and noticed that the form was smiling.

On the far-left throne was a young goddess who was overdoing the virginal look somewhat. Her eyes shone with pure white light. Her dress was pure white and diaphanous. Her hair was pure white and reached down like a plush curtain to the backs of her knees. She was barefoot and wore a pearl tiara. She looked as if her adolescence was a recent memory.

"Ah, finally! Our Reaper returns," the silver lady said.

"I'm sorry I don't have all my memories back yet. Do you know me?" It was so frustrating when he could see some of his memories, yet others remained stubbornly out of focus. It was as if something was preventing him from seeing them.

"We do indeed know you," the lady said. "The whole Pantheon knows who you are. You caused quite a stir when you disappeared and again now that you have reappeared. Your father has broken all precedent and authorised us to form this consortium to mentor you. Now that you have told me that you lost your memories, I understand why he was concerned. A divine entity with your power and without the memories you require is a dangerous thing indeed."

"I don't mean to be rude, but I still don't know your name, miss."

"Miss! You are utterly adorable. I always did like you. Forgive my rudeness; I am Fate, the goddess of destiny. To my right is Missy, the goddess of nature, and far-right is Shalim, the god of twilight and shadow. The young lady on my left is Theia, the goddess of light."

"Uh, Missy? An interesting name for a goddess, may I say," Devon said. His brow furrowed, and he gave Missy a sideways glance. He felt a faint feeling of familiarity when he looked at her.

Fate grinned. "Missy is not your average goddess. She has always been a fan of yours, though; and you have always been fond of her dryads."

Missy smirked and gave him a knowing nod.

"Our colleague of the shadows is keen to champion your cause and is an old friend of yours," Fate continued. "He is the ultimate authority when it comes to shadow powers. The same powers your Reaper skills utilise. Mistress Theia was very keen to meet you as she joined us after you disappeared. She is interested in a power bonding with your Wayfarer talents as she is of the light."

"I sincerely apologise," Devon said with a bow. "I had no idea I was in such esteemed company." Devon imagined four silver cushions and a pair of white slippers as an experiment. Sure enough, they appeared in his hands. It pleased him that he still possessed his divine skills. He stepped forward and handed them a pillow each, then gave the slippers to Theia. "Those seats look very hard. As you are here for my benefit, I would hate for you to be uncomfortable. Mistress Theia, I would feel personally responsible if your feet became cold on this stone."

Theia beamed and clapped her hands excitedly. "You said he was adorable, Missy, but this is just too much. I love him already," she said in quite a childish voice.

"Oh, he's just too cute. Just like he always was. Not many gods have such lovely manners. We have missed you, Wayfarer," Missy enthused.

"We, being the Pantheon?"

"Yes, dear," Fate replied. "I'm afraid we've become a bunch of old fuddy-duddies during your absence. The fun disappeared when you did. People don't believe in us anymore, and so our might fades with each passing millennium. We are hoping you will liven things up again. Just as you used to."

"I have a few plans that are certain to do just that. Earth realm has its magic back, and the resurgence of the faie is next on my list," Devon responded.

"Perfect! The fun begins. To business then," Fate said, her face a picture of anticipation. "We have promised your father to mentor you from now on. He has an extensive list of jobs he wishes us to pay you to do. To assist you, we are authorised to reopen your realm and use some of our resources where required. If you agree to resume your duties as our Reaper, then Shalim here will help you with that faulty memory of yours. Would that offer be acceptable?"

"Yes, of course. I would like to know how that arrangement would work, though. The knowledge of my roles is blurred in my mind."

"Yes," Fate sighed and shook her head. "At this point, I could be naughty and lie about that, but you'd know, wouldn't you, Wayfarer?"

"I would." Devon couldn't be sure of his words, but if Fate said he would know, he wouldn't argue with her.

"It's all straightforward. In the Pantheon, material wealth has no value to us. Instead, we trade using favours. Your little box on wheels uses points for currency, so we can offer you favours or the points equivalent, whichever works for you. In return, you bring us back the souls of those who have committed crimes against the Pantheon. Your housekeeper has been upgraded and can now administer the whole thing," Missy explained.

"We have dull lives, and you will be a tonic for all of us, I'm sure. We are your mentors now. Our relationship will be slightly more, shall we say, mutually beneficial," Fate added.

Devon grinned. "That does sound fun. The fairy queen is already on my list. How much for her, and how do I deliver your prize?"

"We will pay extremely well for the queen's soul. Shall we say a favour each or twelve-thousand points for your little box? As for delivery, you're the Wayfarer; use a portal."

Devon blushed. "Of course. I wish I could remember these things."

Shalim stood up and walked over to Devon. While his form was an ordinary shape for a humanoid, Devon could see right through him. He was twilight, anthropomorphised. When he reached him, Shalim placed a shadowy hand on Devon's forehead. <Relax, Reaper. I intend to remove the blocks the fairy queen left in your mind. She did this to you because we sent you to claim her soul for us. She challenged you to a duel and cheated. She hoped you'd forget all about her. Take a deep breath; this will be painful.>

Devon took a deep breath just before his mind seemed to explode. He scrabbled at the air, baffled by his very existence, as large chunks of magic shattered from his mind, followed by more agony as his brain pieced itself back together. Mangled memories floated through his consciousness. As they warped and reformed, his thoughts solidified, and so did his identity. And then there were his memories, in perfect order. He grinned at the feeling of completeness that settled into him.

<Shalom, old friend,> Devon thought to Shalim with a slight bow. <Thank you. You have done me a great service.>

Shalim gave him a wide, shadowy smile and returned Devon's bow. <Shalom, Reaper. It's so good to have you back. People have stopped fearing the shadows. Let us re-educate them with prejudice. You should show yourself to others in your were-cat form. Put the fear of a real god into them.> He turned and returned to his throne.

Devon could now remember that, before the curse, his usual form had always been a shadow-pumine – a manifestation of pure shadow energy with magically enhanced teeth and claws. The pumine were were-cats, which was a proud humanoid race that had originated from pumas. No mortal would ever have realised that though; they always saw him as they imagined he should be, unless he chose otherwise. It was the same for all deities and a closely guarded secret among the Pantheon. People imagined what a god should look like and would always see gods or goddesses in that form unless the deity chose otherwise.

"We have passed the Pantheon's list of soul bounties to your housekeeper," Fate continued. "She can pay bounties in points, or you can accumulate favours. She can keep the book on our behalf."

He looked at Fate and nodded.

Then the introspection started. All Devon's old memories were there now. There was still nothing from his centuries on Earth realm, his wilderness years as Izzy now called them, but he now knew who he had been. Reaper, Wayfarer, Traveller, Death, Lord of Souls, so many different names, used by every species imaginable, yet in his heart, he was now Devon, and that was who he wanted to remain.

<Well, yu got my respeckt yung un. I iz proud to be yur dragon. Right proud,> Brack thought with a sniff. He sounded emotional, caught up in the moment.

Devon sent Brack warm thoughts of gratitude. Apart from Jet, Brack was the only creature that would still be there with him when the realms ended. Even the deities would fade away in the end. Already, Devon realised that his ability to remember his past meant that the heartaches came back to him along with everything else. With them came an understanding of why he'd travelled all the time and shunned attachments, both physical and emotional. Yet now, history was repeating itself. Now he was wrapping himself up in emotional attachments that could only ever end with loss and yet more heartache. Should he close himself away and reject everyone again, or should he enjoy it while it lasted and try to steel himself against the inevitable? Neither choice sat well with him.

His thoughts veered away to somewhere less uncomfortable and landed on the Pantheon. Before everything had gone wrong, most of them had been his friends. They'd always engaged in bartering, information trading, some harmless banter, and maybe a little quaffing and divine karaoke now and then. The gods and goddesses could only manifest in their ethereal form outside of their domain. Although, he remembered that Fate could become slightly more corporeal for a short time if she expended a lot of energy. He still wasn't sure how she managed that.

As the Wayfarer, Devon was the only one capable of travelling throughout the realms. He was the progenitor's son, older and more powerful than the lesser deities of the Pantheon. That was why the gods and goddesses had often asked him to collect soul debts on their behalf. After centuries they ended up creating his Reaper role, thus making it official. Mortals who had wronged a god or goddess would forfeit their lives, and Devon would get paid to collect their soul. It was a mutually beneficial arrangement that suited him because, being an eternal entity, he needed the distractions. Besides, it paid well. He searched his mind for the mental tab he kept for each deity. When he found it, he couldn't stifle his grin.

He went back to what Fate had said. "Please call her Abi. 'Housekeeper' is so derogatory, don't you think? You'll give her a complex. Although now I have my memory back, I recall that all of you are in debt to me for my previous services, except for mistress Theia," Devon replied, leaving his smile in place. "I think it would be best to discuss what you can do for me in exchange for all this work you have for me. Very soon, I will have thousands of refugees who will need our support. I trust you will do your best to help me help them?"

Fate laughed loudly. "Ah hah! He is back. You always were canny, young Reaper."

Devon ignored the remark. He had never understood why she insisted on calling him young when he was older than all of them. Devon continued to press his point. "All the liberated creatures would be potential followers. All grateful to you for your beneficent support. All in exchange for a little effort from you at the beginning. You are authorised to use your resources, so I have an excellent use for them. If you want your Reaper back, you have me, but this time there is other work to do, lives to be saved, and you will help me do it. Agreed?"

The god and three goddesses looked shocked, not used to this approach from him. Once they started to consider his words and what they stood to gain, they all agreed eagerly. For a deity, followers meant power and the influence it brings. Theirs had dwindled over the centuries, and they had suffered in its absence. It appeared that an enforced sabbatical had done their Reaper good.

"Considering your words, I have an offer for you, Wayfarer," Missy said. "If you take my whining daughter off my hands, I will be extremely grateful. Combine that gratitude with my assistance for your new colony and the debts I already owe you and let this be my contribution. I will offer five-thousand moon-willow seeds and as many species of flora and fauna as you would need to get your delightful, little forest on Earth realm up to the standards of the one we created in your realm. In exchange, my slate is clean, and you pair-bond Aria – anything to stop her moaning at me about how lonely she is. Since you disappeared, that blasted girl has done nothing but mope around with her sisters, fantasising about your return. She adores you, and you can bet your tasty behind that she will be waiting with anticipation by the waygate as soon as you reopen it. Consider this an arranged marriage. I'll even throw in a troop of her sister dryads to tend the forest and grow your settlement. They wanted to go to you anyway as you've championed them for centuries, but this way, I get shot of Aria. Please, Wayfarer, she drives me crazy, and I want my solitude back."

Devon smiled. He remembered Aria only too well now. She was a pacifist, yet the best shot with a bow he had ever known. It was Aria who had taught him how to shoot with such esteem. "While that sounds fair, I think the scales tip toward you, Missy. You are the goddess of nature, and increasing your presence on Earth realm benefits you, too. If you add the best bow enchantment you can create for my new weapon, once I get around to making it, then we can wipe the slate clean. Agreed?"

Missy huffed but nodded anyway. "Fine! My daughters will meet you on the Triana side of the gate three days from now with the seeds and as many animals as they can lure. I'll send the rest through the gate as soon as I can after that."

Devon nodded and turned his gaze on Shalim. <I need to see my enemies coming. The dark sight you gave me long ago has gone. A victim of the curse, I suspect, but I need it back. I believe you owe me three favours. Would you trade those for my dark sight and an upgrade to my shadow magic? You must have some improved spells by now. I remember how studious you always were.>

<I do have some very 'interesting' spells that you won't have ever seen before, and the dark sight reaches further now. It took a lot of effort and study to modify it to work so efficiently. So much work, in fact, that I feel it to be worth at least five favours alone, with another three for the new magical patterns.> He was smiling as he said it.

Devon spluttered, fighting to keep his face impassive. <Hmm! I believe my father mentioned demons that needed culling and the necessity for you to assist me? You still collecting demon souls, Shalim?>

<I am,> the god of twilight replied. <I do not see ho—>

<—The price of eight favours is ridiculous, and from a friend too; I should feel insulted that you asked so much. Zeus is a fellow collector of demon souls, and he always paid more generously than you. Should I offer future trophies to him?>

<No! No, Reaper.> Shalim knew he had been outsmarted. <I knew it was a mistake to give your memories back.> He laughed. <You always were far too shrewd. Perhaps we could meet halfway. I give you the shadow powers and sight you requested in exchange for a clean slate and a reduced price on my choice of demon souls.>

Devon grinned. He liked this part of any deal. His position as their senior gave him a slightly unfair advantage. <Souls? Come now, Shalim, that's very vague. I offer you the deal as you stated but suggest you revise the last part to one demon's soul at half price.>

It was Shalim's turn to huff, but he yielded the battle and accepted the price. He swiftly crossed the floor and placed his shadowy hand on Devon's forehead. Devon felt the changes rush into his mind and the painful spikes that attacked his brain and eyes for a few moments. When he could see again, Shalim had retaken his seat.

He grinned at Fate.

"I know what you want and how much I owe," Fate said, her voice sounded friendly but a little weary. The glow of her golden eyes flared briefly. "You look at me hungrily, like a wolf, and yet, to me, you will always be my little lamb. As I promised your father that I would assist you, I will agree, partially, and grant you a limited version of my power of anticipation, but my debt of seven favours is my price and don't try and reduce it. I know the outcome already."

Devon always thought it unfair that Fate could pre-empt any negotiation by knowing how it ends in advance, or maybe that was a bluff? She never lost, either way.

"Agreed. You drive a hard bargain," Devon conceded.

Before he had finished speaking, Fate was in front of him with her hands covering his eyes. He remained motionless as warmth and golden light flowed into his mind through his retinas. The sensation of his mind being warped as his perception skills were remoulded and enhanced was beyond strange. Understanding twisted and writhed until finally, it ended.

"Wow! That was intense. Thank you, Fate," he said. His thoughts were a little dazed and confused, but everything was rapidly returning to a new normal.

Fate nodded and retook her seat, which left Theia.

"I wish us to merge our powers, Wayfarer. Your justice magic combined with the light of mine would make a formidable power. However, I will discuss that with your high priestess when the time is more appropriate. For now, I shall observe."

Devon gave Theia a slight bow. "As you wish. I agree with the merging but feel that your observation is just delaying your assistance. It would be a shame to remove you from this new group when we could become such good friends and both benefit from your support. I will discuss it with my priestess. Don't delay for too long, though."

Theia looked surprised by his poorly veiled threat but stayed silent.

"There; deals made; prices agreed," Fate said. "Goodbye, Reaper. Thank you for coming back to us. It's been too long," she added with new happiness in her tone.

"Yes, it certainly has," Devon replied.

The dragon gave him the magical pattern for the portal spell, which he loaded into the spell crystal embedded in his forehead. He sent mana through the crystal and directed it to a point just in front of him. When the swirling black disc appeared, he stepped through, straight back into the Hub on Haven.

Chapter 15

Knowledge and fealty

Devon yawned as he wandered from the Hub to the front room.

"Good morning. Are you off to the kitchen?" Finn asked from one of the armchairs.

Devon grinned warmly at Finn. "Good morning to you, too. Yep, breakfast is calling me."

"Would you mind if I tag along?"

"I'd be delighted. Let's eat." He continued through the other entrance and turned left to get to the kitchen. The smells of cooking massaged his nostrils enticingly, and his stomach instantly paid attention.

In the kitchen, June was bustling around as if she had worked there her entire life. The room was a spacious, open-plan arrangement with the dining area in one half, a breakfast bar dividing the centre, then the kitchen and food storage was on the other side. A long pan-rack hung from the ceiling above the breakfast bar, and copious drawers and cupboards kept all the equipment and utensils tidy. June was currently frying thinly sliced and cured boar meat in a skillet with a horde of eggs cooking on the hotplate. The smell of freshly baked bread wafted across the room from a large batch of fine-looking wholemeal loaves that were sitting on a wide, cooling-trellis.

"Oh, June! I adore a lady who can bake. Where have you been all my life?" Devon cooed.

Finn guffawed when he heard Devon's patter.

June beamed across at Devon. "Good morning, you gorgeous creature. Sit at the bar. I'll get you two fine fellows fed."

Finn mouthed 'gorgeous creature' at him and grinned. "She will be eating you for breakfast before you know it." His comment was met with a rap across the knuckles with a wooden spoon brandished by the chef. Unfortunately for Finn, June had excellent hearing.

Lorn stumbled into the room, looking tired, followed by Dawn and her daughters. Devon had given bedrooms to all the guardians with children, plus Madi and Finn, Izzy, and Beth, while Gwen was still in Haven's hospital. Devon had his master bedroom. Abi was currently adding more bedrooms along with a dormitory.

"This place is beyond belief, Devon. You have a beautiful home. Thank you for letting us stay," Dawn said.

"You are very welcome. Until we can get your new residences ready, I would like you to treat Haven as your home. You'll find this place is full of surprises."

Lorn grabbed a stool and dragged it over until it was right next to Devon, then leapfrogged over it, landing squarely in the seat on her bottom. She smiled slavishly at him.

"Morning," she said.

"Hello, sunshine. Very impressive entrance. Hopefully, you ladies should start seeing aspects of your new magic soon. Maybe even today."

"Awesome! Will you be teaching me today? My dragon said that you are my master now, and you will mentor me."

"Did she now? Firstly, I'm not your master, but I would consider taking you and a few others as apprentices for a while. Secondly, I should explain that your mana-dragon is one of my dragon's little sisters. Grace got the other."

"I did," Grace said happily.

"All the dragons chat together. Their accents are funny," Lorn said.

"Well, now that's interesting. You can hear all of the dragons?" Devon asked.

"Uh-huh! Yours tells rude jokes."

Devon snorted. "He does. My dragon has a very rustic sense of humour," Devon replied with a smile. Lorn's abilities seemed to be emerging much quicker than expected. He wanted to take all these young ladies and create magical, frontline soldiers. He would need them for the trials to come. What stopped him was the ethical implications.

<I can see your thoughts,> Lorn thought to him. <I want to become that person you have in your mind and to fight by your side. I'm old enough to choose my path, Devon. Life as your apprentice would be a million times better than my life now.>

Devon gasped. <Lorn, have you got your magic already?>

<Yes, but I don't want aunty to be angry.>

<What have you become?>

<I am a fast-strike shadow warrior and a neuromancer. A shadow warrior must follow a dark god. My dragon says that you are the Reaper, and that part of you is dark. I want to choose you as my god.>

"Bloody hell!" Devon said, unintentionally out loud. Her mana-dragon was intent on pushing this intense young lady straight into his path. <I will speak to your aunt after breakfast. If your friends feel the

same, bring them and their guardians. If I do this, it will need to be quick as I have lots to do. I will talk to you and anyone else directly after that. Think very, very carefully, young lady. If you make this promise to me, it is with your soul. When you make promises to gods, they are unbreakable, and you'd better keep them. Do you understand?>

<I understand. I am not scared and want this more than anything. I just need your help to learn.>

The one mention of mentoring Lorn yesterday had started a chain of events in motion. Devon decided to go with it this time. He'd shied away from company for too long. Now felt like the right moment to cast aside the enforced solitude of his past.

****_****

Devon was so happy to have his memories back. It made him feel whole again. Knowing his past unlocked all the secrets of Haven, including his beloved library and his passion for literature. Over the millennia, he had read most of the books in here. With Abi's new connections to the outside world, she might be able to start obtaining more. He had decided to ask for a comprehensive library restock as a favour from the gods. Abi had promised to convey his wishes to his mentors.

He walked to the bookcase and reached for the blue book on the second shelf up, fifth from the right. He tilted it back, and the bookcase slid into the wall and then sideways to the left. Behind the door was a long corridor with a towering bookcase on either side, which opened out into the study area. Devon revelled in the enormity of his library, and he knew that it would just keep getting larger every time he managed to obtain more books.

Bookcases radiated out in every direction. Each double-sided bookcase rose over thirty-five feet from the floor. On both sides of every bookcase, there was a metal sliding ladder. The ladder wasn't what guests expected a library ladder to look like, though. Yes, it was designed to slide along the bookcase's length, but each ladder had intricate mechanisms mounted to its frame.

The décor of the library was straight out of the history books. It had dark parquet flooring that currently stretched for at least seventy yards in each direction, with the wooden panelled walls matching the floor in colour. The domed ceiling was fifty feet high and painted with a detailed depiction of the night sky. A warm glow from concealed lighting around the walls lit the area, and a plush, thickly piled rug of the deepest blue covered the floor in the centre of the room. The whole effect was one of subdued opulence.

The central reading area contained a wide circle of twenty armchairs, each facing the middle. Each chair had a low-slung side table made of mahogany and a tall, heavily shaded floor-lamp on the other side. In the centre of the circle was a matching table that was about six feet in diameter.

Devon sat and waited for the others. He had put June off for ten minutes to allow time to set his first students on their path; but the first person to arrive was Gwen, and she did so at speed. Luckily, Devon had stood to greet her before she reached him because as soon as she was near enough, she flung herself and landed in his arms in a princess hold.

"God, it seems like a lifetime since I passed out. Did you miss me?" She leant back so she could look at him, then she leant in and kissed him tenderly. "We've got some catching up to do, but first, put me to work. I am now a dark-witch and a master alchemist. I need to learn how to craft and so many other things too. Like you, for instance. I want to know everything about you. Oh, and my faie race is pumine. I'm a bloody cat-girl, Devon, and a bad-ass one at that. I've been reading comics about them since I was small."

"Wow! Aren't you talkative! And yes, I was worried, and I'm relieved you are okay. Are you officially joining my ranks then?"

"A witch is a dark-priestess, so yes. I'll be swearing a vow to the Reaper once I know what the words are. Anyway, don't be daft. I was yours from the start. You knew that. Absolutely, completely, yours. You're a god. Why the hell would I settle for anyone else? You make life fun. You're not hard on the eye either."

Devon coughed at her last remark. He blushed and couldn't help but grin shyly. Gwen wasn't the least bit shy, though. "You'd best take a seat then. You'll be here all day, probably through the night too. Abi will put you to sleep while you assimilate the knowledge.

Abi, can you fetch Gwen books on the Wayfarer, Reaper, the Pantheon, Haven's crafting system, materials, realms, all the faie creatures, lore, magic, witches, and everything you have about chemistry, alchemy, and potion making?"

"I don't have anything specific on realms, master. When your consignment of new material arrives, that will be rectified. I can help with all the other choices, though. I will have the books brought to you."

They watched as the library sprang to life. The library ladders got to work, sliding left and right rapidly along the shelves. A flotilla of library trolleys had appeared from somewhere. They dashed here and there between the bookshelves, while ladders used mechanical arms to pass books down to them. He watched with familiar fascination as magic and mechanisms worked together in harmony. It was a ballet of motion, and he loved it.

"This whole place goes way beyond cool, Devon. Can I live here?"

"Of course, you can. I've already organised a room for you. Welcome to your new home, cat-witch."

"Mmm! I like the sound of that name."

Soon a trolley, heavily laden with thick, leather-bound tomes, sidled up to Gwen's table and used a mechanical arm to place the books carefully onto it. When the trolley had finished, Gwen had five neat piles of books arranged next to her.

"Mistress, your reading list will take twenty-six hours and eleven minutes to assimilate. Do you wish to sleep for the duration?" Abi asked.

Gwen looked at Devon, and he nodded. "Yes, please."

"Certainly. Starting now," Abi replied.

Devon watched as the floor lamp behind her dimmed, and Gwen's eyes flickered closed. When he turned, he saw a crowd waiting for him.

The group that had assembled were all keen to try and learn the art of crafting. Izzy was there, with Beth, Beks, Madi, and Finn too. Beks was standing next to Beth, chatting happily with her. She was a little shorter than Beth and had short brown hair and big, dark eyes. Her face was slim, and her prominent cheekbones added an elegant touch to her features. She looked a lot like her mother, Madi.

Dawn was also there. She was the village seamstress and a good one, not only with cloth but with leather too. Lorn had, of course, insisted on being there, so had her best friend, Pip, and her sister, Grace. Dawn's two daughters both wanted to learn how to make clothes and other things they refused to disclose. A young lady named Ffion was also there. He'd cheated with her name as he'd asked Abi to mentally prompt him with information on people he didn't yet know. All the villagers had been scanned, and so Abi recognised everyone now. Even though Ffion was a little older than the other three, she seemed to be part of Lorn's crowd. The trouble was he knew nothing more about her other than she was orphaned at the age of three. That made him wonder what had happened to her parents, and it also made him a little sad.

"Everyone who isn't waiting to see me, please take a seat in the other room. The rest can join in a little later," Devon said. Grace, Pip, and

Ffion all had a whispered conversation with Lorn and Dawn. Lorn nodded quickly, then shushed them.

Devon waited until they were all seated and looking at him expectantly while glancing at Gwen. "Abi, please can you give everyone except Izzy the same reading list that Gwen has. Izzy just needs all of Haven's manuals along with the crafting and materials reading lists."

"Of course, master. Does everyone wish to have a sleep-induced study session?"

Devon looked around the circle. Everyone nodded except Izzy. "All but Izzy, Abi."

"Sweet dreams, everyone," he said as each floor-light dimmed, and they dropped to sleep. He looked at Izzy. "I'll see you later, priestess. When you have finished in here, would you care to join me in the design centre?" He kept his voice neutral. Until Izzy made her mind up where her loyalties lay, he would not allow himself to need her more.

"I would be delighted, my lord," Izzy replied with a warm smile.

"Commencing now," Abi said.

Devon wondered if his comments about Izzy leaving had startled her. She certainly had been acting more warmly toward him since then. He wanted her to stay but would never stop her from going. Putting those thoughts aside, he motioned to Lorn and the others, then walked back into the front room.

June was sitting there waiting for them.

As soon as Devon had sunk into his chair, Jet looked up, grinned, then launched herself into his lap. He automatically started scratching her head and making a fuss of her. The purr that Jet let out was noisy and blissful. Her swishing tail bashed against Devon's leg and told him that she was in her happy place. Jet was currently in her most diminutive form, which meant she looked just the same as she did in her massive horse form but on a much smaller scale. Now, she was just over two feet long and very fluffy.

"She's adorable," June said. "Does she live here all the time?"

Devon laughed. "I'm sure you've noticed that black horse I ride; well, this is her. Her name is Jet. She is a magical creature and can change her size; her shape too if she chooses. She seems to prefer her horse or cat forms, though."

Everyone's mouths went into an 'O' shape, and they looked at Jet with fresh wonder.

"June, even though Lorn is nineteen, I still want to ask you to allow her to become my apprentice. She would become my ward, and I will train her to become a soldier and fight for our cause. In the meantime, you would be welcome to take up permanent residence in Haven. If you'd consent to continue cooking full-time, then I would be an even happier man."

Lorn was watching him with intensity, and he turned his attention to her. "Has Lorn told you what her magical class is yet?"

"No, she just said that you would tell me and that I wasn't allowed to be mad," June replied.

"Did she now? Coward," he said, grinning at Lorn.

"For goodness' sake, just tell me, Devon. If this is what she wants, then she has my blessing. Nothing she does with you will put her in more peril than she has already known throughout her life. In fact, with you, she will have the protection of a real god. She is desperate to take this opportunity, and I'm not going to be the one to stand in her way."

"I appreciate your faith in me. Magic has chosen to make her into something called a 'fast-strike shadow warrior'. She also received a second class of neuromancer, a mind-mage. Lorn has already demonstrated that she is an accomplished telepath, and I expect telekinesis and empathy will be hers to utilise as well. She may even be able to do far more complicated things that I do not know of."

"And what does the shadow-warrior bit mean for her?" June asked. It was evident that she was trying to be brave about all this.

"It means that her mana will make her very fast, agile, and deadly for targets with anything less than heavy armour. If she tries to attack anything stronger, she'll answer to me. She will kill swiftly using whatever type of blade she chooses. Most likely, she will have concealment magic, shadow magic, and some minor location jump skills. She will probably also get one or two different forms to utilise. Sworn to me, she might be able to take on the same shadow-cat form that I do. A deadly predator that's very fast with large claws and teeth."

"Oh, okay. No man will ever hurt her again then?"

"Not if she's smart and doesn't stay still long enough to be grabbed. She'll have many ways to deal with that situation, though. Her neuromancy will be a blessing as a backup defence."

"Fair enough. Give me one of those fancy bedrooms near you, and keep Lorn as safe as you can. Deal?" June agreed.

"Deal." He grinned, leaning toward her with his hand outstretched.

June bit her bottom lip and shook his hand.

Lorn knelt in front of Devon, took his hand, and bowed her head to it. "Lord Reaper, I choose you as my deity. I beg you, grant me the powers to fight in your name and the strength to thwart any that oppose us. I offer you my vow of fealty in return."

"Oh Lorn, my little girl, I hope you know what you are doing," June whispered, her voice choked.

"I accept your vow, Lorn."

There was a flash of shadows that engulfed both Devon and Lorn. Lorn's eyes flashed black, and the bond formed. Lorn's form became shadowy at the edges as dark energy infused her. Nodding at the positive outcome of the oath, he turned his attention to Dawn.

"Devon, I wanted to ask you if you would accept Grace and Pip as your apprentices, just as you did for Lorn," Dawn said. "They want to join you so badly that they've begged and pleaded with me to allow it and to ask you on their behalf."

"Would you teach me too, Devon? I'm a hard worker and just want to learn and to fight," Ffion said.

"Okay! One at a time. Dawn, are you happy to release your girls into my care? They will live separately from you and spend most of their time working with me or training hard. The same offer I gave to June goes to you, too."

"Yes, they want this so much, Devon," Dawn replied. She looked serious and a little emotional. "I want my girls to be capable of protecting themselves and others, just like you do. I will happily live here and do what I can for the new village."

"That sounds fair. Yes, of course I will take them. It will never be dull, I can promise them that." He turned his attention to Ffion. "Now, to you, young lady. Are you absolutely sure that this is something you want? I demand loyalty from my apprentices. You would be placing yourself in my care. You'll need to work hard and make an effort to get on with everyone that's not on our shit-list. Does that work for you?"

"I'll work my arse off and do whatever it takes. You have my word," Ffion replied with a grin.

"Abi, please recognise Lorn, June, Dawn, Grace, Pip, Ffion, and Gwen as residents of Haven. They may spend points with my authorisation."

"Noted. I have marked the rooms with the names of each resident. Do you wish your students to use the barracks, master?"

His plan had been for the barracks to be a dormitory, but times change quickly. "Yes please, Abi. That's the new plan," Devon confirmed.

Once he had sworn the other three young ladies in, he sent them back to the library with a much-expanded reading list.

Time was escaping him; he needed to move quickly to set up a new waygate in the queen's realm, and he now had less than three days to do it. It would need to be created where the old one crumbled, just west of the city walls.

Now that everyone was peacefully sleeping in the library, he and Jet could begin the task of hauling Haven out of the nexus so that he could seal it back up. Later, he had a mountain of crafting to do. With a sigh, he grabbed a portal charm from the mantle and left Haven to begin his day's work with Jet closely behind him.

Chapter 16
New world army

Devon had packed up the temporary camp, and then he, Jet, and the other villagers who weren't in the library had spent several long hours pulling Haven out of the nexus. Now she was nestled against the granite wall, beside the entrance to the waygate. Once he'd made sure that the villagers all had accommodation within Haven and knew where the games room and gym were, he left them to their own devices and made his way to the Hub.

His new weapons needed to be remarkable. Devon had a few ideas and many new materials to utilise, thanks to Abi's research on new world technologies. He lay back on the design chair and took a deep breath. He hadn't done this for centuries. "Abi, please start the designer."

"Yes, master, misting now."

Haven connected to a designer by surrounding them with a fine mist of mana particles that acted as an interface between the brain and the design system. All Devon felt was a slight tingle as it connected. It always reminded him how much he loved creating new things.

He closed his eyes and imagined the design grid that he would use to guide his structure. He adjusted the grid size to be more suitable and then investigated the new 'weapons factory' feature that Abi had suggested. He was impressed to find a new menu system that allowed him to choose from various weapon templates. During his search, an interesting telescopic staff and spear combination caught his attention. He selected it and then went back to 'manual creation' mode, where the weapon's empty wireframe awaited him. There were five sections to the staff. The central handle contained two telescopic sections on either side, and the outer segments looked more like barbed spears.

While Devon could fight with any blade, his preference was a polearm. He found it better to keep an enemy at arm's length, and a polearm could outreach most other bladed weapons.

He chose his favourite metal, chornium, which was magical by nature, exceptionally strong, and very black. It was also dense and thus heavy, which suited him. He filled the wireframes of the inner three segments with the metal, and for the outer parts, he used mithril, a magical metal of elven origin. While chornium was an excellent holder of magical power, mithril conducted it better. It was just a happy coincidence that chornium's light-absorbing black and mithril's brilliant silver looked fabulous together.

To create magical blades formed from mana, he would need to move large quantities throughout the staff. For that, he would use mithril. Devon crafted mithril rails internally to stabilise the sections as they slid in and out and allow him to extend and retract the weapon magically. These would also serve as the mana conduits that he needed. He could do the same with daggers, too, but he stored that idea away for later.

Once done with the crafting, he began carving tiny, tightly-packed mana conversion runes into the mithril so that he could create blades from magical power. He then added patterns of runes to the shaft that would use some mana flow to create dark flames, a trick he'd noticed someone had used on his swords. After adding the last of the runes, there was nothing left but to name the weapon. He gave it the name 'Wrath'. It just seemed fitting.

Once he'd stored the design, Devon relaxed and took several deep breaths. It was easy to forget to breathe when you needed to concentrate that much.

"Abi, how much?"

"That will be one-thousand, one-hundred and fifty-one points, master. Shall I create it?"

"Yes, please."

Devon then got to work crafting his new compound bow. He wanted it to be the best he could make. Missy was an expert in enchanting this type of weapon, and she'd done so for all her dryads. After experimenting with almost every material he could, he found the perfect combination that suited his strengths and preferences.

He spent another happy hour creating a vicious assortment of metal-shafted and tipped arrows and a quiver that would sit high on his back. It was linked to Haven's magical storage, so he'd grow tired before he ran out of arrows. It would also act as a holder for his staff.

Devon then went on to build daggers, armour, and weapons for everyone. His prodigies would be confronted by a baffling mountain of equipment when they awoke. Correctly putting it all on could be their first challenge.

Once he had completed a new staff for Izzy and something interesting for Gwen, Devon decided to get some sleep. The new morning was fast approaching, and even his heightened constitution couldn't drive him forever. Abi would organise the enchantments for his weapons from his mentors, so he could take a break for now.

Devon just loved crafting. Having so many people to do it for was bliss.

****_****

After a huge breakfast, Devon was sitting in the Hub on the edge of his favourite bench, letting his bloated stomach recover a little. June loved to mother him, not comprehending that he was tens of thousands of years her senior. Devon didn't mind, though. If it meant he got fed well, then he was all for it.

Missy had said that her dryads, including Aria, would meet them in three days. That meant he had to be in the fairy queen's realm in approximately forty-four hours. He planned to take Izzy there later today to contact the leader of her resistance in Triana. Jet had agreed to ferry them through the void between realms.

The city's name always made him wince as the vain bitch-queen had named it after herself. When he destroyed her and took her soul, her realm would become his. Once he'd relocated the people, he'd level the city and spit on its ruins. That was for the future, though. There was still a lot to do before then.

The frown that had crept onto his face vanished when his gorgeous witch walked into the Hub. She saw him sitting there and deliberately upgraded her walk into a sashay. When Gwen got to him, she dropped to her knees in front of him.

"Lord Reaper, I choose you as my god and sponsor. I beg you, allow me to be your high priestess of shadows and grant me the power to destroy any that oppose us. I offer my unconditional devotion to you and your cause. Will you take me as your life bonded?"

Devon had never seen her look and sound this serious before. It went against her nature. "I gladly take you as my life bonded and welcome you, my high priestess of shadows." As expected, darkness rose from the floor and encased them both as the bond between them became established. Devon was quite surprised at how powerful the new bond was. When it was over, he felt a blast of ecstasy as her first emotions flooded across the link. He grinned at her and guided her up from her knees and onto the bench behind her.

"Now that is done, I have some presents for you. First, as one of the Shadow Elite, you need a uniform." He reached into his void pouch and drew out a set of black armour. Straight away, Gwen was on her feet, and a minute later, she was standing before him in her underwear.

"You never told me we had an official name. That's awesome."

"It's the name of an army that I helped create, a very long time in the past," Devon said. "Izzy's history books might mention them."

"It's got lore; kudos," Gwen said, then enthusiastically grabbed the items and proceeded to wriggle into them. Soon, the witch stood there twisting and stretching, trying to get a look at herself. Devon pointed to the mirror over by the portals, and she sprinted over to it. As he did so, he noticed that the doorframe to his Wayfarer's realm had a swirling golden mist that filled it. It was open. He felt his heart skip with pleasure at the sight, but it would have to wait for an hour or so.

He knew that Gwen would not wear a complete armour set, so he had gone with her preferred clothing style and, of course, maintained her signature all black colour scheme. He'd made her a high collared shrug, accompanied by a bustier style top. There was also an ankle-length split skirt with light leggings underneath and then the calf-length army boots that she always wore. Virtually invisible runes of power and protection covered every item.

Gwen turned round to him and smiled her beautiful smile. Her dark green eyes sparkled. "The outfit is gorgeous. Thank you so much. I can feel the power coming from it too. How many enchantments did you put on these?" She walked back over to the bench and sat down opposite him. She buckled on the long bracers and looked at him expectantly.

"Most of the enchantments should strengthen your protection. However, not being where the blow lands works best, I find. The other runes will empower your shadow magic," Devon responded. "I made you something a little different. I hope you like it," he added. Reaching into his pouch again, he withdrew a black handle, bound with a rubbery material. It had a two-inch spike at the pommel end to inject potions and was mithril coated on the other. "This is called 'Malice.'"

He stood up, walked a few paces into an open space, and turned sideways. He fed some mana into Malice's handle and twisted black mana-strands shot from it. Dark flames engulfed the ten feet of the strand's length, and black mist oozed from the tip of the woven magic. Devon brandished the handle and the magical cord arced then cracked with a vicious sound. A small explosion of intense darkness erupted from the point where the whip had struck. He cut the mana and walked back to his bench. He handed Gwen the whip. It was a divine weapon, empowered by the god of darkness himself.

Gwen looked at the whip's handle in shock that turned to awe as she turned it over in her hands. "I don't know what to say. This goes well beyond my wildest dreams. It is the darkest weapon you could ever choose. I adore it. Eeeek!" she squeaked and looked at the weapon in amazement. "It just bonded with me. How can a weapon do that?"

"You're a proper witch now. You have powerful bonded magic. I forged it specifically for you, and so it recognises you as its true owner. No-one can use it but you, now.

Moving on, you are missing one vital aspect of witchcraft," Devon continued. "I had to ask for Shalim's council on this."

"I know what you're going to say. I plan on finding a familiar as soon as I work out what species I'd be happy with. I can't make my mind up, though," Gwen said sheepishly.

"I may have an idea about that," Devon said. He was thinking hard as he was talking.

<Jet, do you think you could take Gwen through the void with Izzy and me?>

Jet considered her master's request carefully. She had to be sure about this, as getting stuck in the void was certain doom. His power was not at its original level yet, but it was enough. He was strong, so she was too. <We have enough power and like your witch. We be ready,> Jet responded. <Need long, open space, outside forest. No trees.> She needed a reasonable distance to stop after the velocity she would need to punch through the reality walls between realms.

Devon sent her back his gratitude and a big mental hug. "Get your stuff together for this evening. We're going on a journey. You might find a familiar on the way."

Gwen flicked to her pumine form and grinned toothily back at him. "I bloody love life with you."

The moment ended when a small troop of young ladies scampered noisily into the Hub. They were chatting and laughing and genuinely enjoying each other's company. These women had been refugees, living under the threat of slavery or worse. Now they were acting in the way he thought women of their age ought to be able to. It made him happy.

Izzy walked into the Hub behind them and gave the ladies a stern look before making her way over to Gwen and Devon. Her face changed from strict to happy in an instant. Finn, Madi, Dawn, and June came in then, and they also made their way straight over to Devon and the others.

Gwen flicked back to her regular form because her pumine state made humans fearful.

"Before we start our conversation, I have gifts for you, Izzy," Devon said while extracting everything he had crafted for her and placing it on the bench beside him. "Try all that on," he added, handing her the armour.

Izzy looked surprised, but, like Gwen, within a few minutes, she had donned the outfit. The armour was similar to Gwen's, but instead of all black, Izzy's was white, and every edge had detailed golden trim. Woven into the inside of the fabric were over a thousand runes of empowerment and shielding. He'd also made her comfortable shoes instead of the heavy boots Gwen preferred. It even had a matching cape attached to the top, which added further protection for her back.

"Devon, this is beautiful. I love it. Thank you."

Devon grinned. "You look fabulous, Isabelle, but as a priestess of the Wayfarer, you are missing something." He reached into his void pouch and pulled out a delicately carved gold-alloy staff, covered from tip to base with the intricately carved script of the Wayfarer's ancient language. It had four spirals of mithril inlaid down its length, with delicate mithril vines sprouting from the inlay in places. At the tip was a golden crescent shape that had a three-dimensional star floating in its crook. The star rotated slowly, occasionally emitting golden sparks that arced down the shaft. The staff glowed with a golden mist.

"Izzy, I'd like you to meet 'Faith.'"

Izzy reached out with both hands and took the staff, then promptly dropped it. "Eeeek! Devon, it spoke to me. It said something in your old language. How?" Izzy bent down and tentatively picked the staff back up. By the look of concentration on her face, she was probably listening to the weapon.

"Theia blessed your clothes and the staff," Devon explained. "I used the soul of a powerful priestess of the light called Tanwin. Her spirit volunteered to help you with your magic and empower you with blessings of the light. It is a mighty thing."

Izzy looked at him with such a dumbfounded stare that he had to smile. "You are special to me, Isabelle. I want you to know that. Stay with us. You truly belong here."

"But… I want…. Oh, my lord. Thank you so much," Izzy said, her voice cracking with pent-up emotion. She cleared her throat and took a deep breath.

"For a start, I need the old Izzy back. Stop being so formal. I also want you to be ready to travel at sunset tonight. You, Gwen, and I are going on a journey to Triana," he said. "I want to open the waygate within a day and a half, and we have some travelling to do before then. You need to make contact with your resistance group. They need to start sending people through to us, and I really need my dryads. I've got some big plans for our new settlement, and only they can assist."

"This sounds serious," Madi said.

"It is another step in what I'm here to do, Madi," Devon explained. "I want this forest to combine with my realm to become a sanctuary for all of you, as well as other creatures that need somewhere safe to live. Izzy here is an elf. She comes from another world. Over there, people have a life much worse than yours. Would you tolerate other races living together with your people?"

Madi and Finn looked affronted.

"Yes, of course we would," Madi replied. "You only have to ask. This place could easily be a sanctuary for so many refugees. How can we help?"

"Make a list of everything a city of two-thousand people might need. Include everything, from stationery for the mayor's office to mattresses, please. We can make it all right here," he said, patting his design bench. "You won't need to include building materials, but you will need furnishings. We have another god and three goddesses funding this venture, but we need to move quickly. I am going away for two days, and I need you to handle this."

"Two-thousand? Seriously?" Finn looked shocked.

Devon smiled amiably. "For starters, yes. It's magic, Finn. You'll see soon enough."

Devon stood up and motioned to the group of young ladies hanging around nearby. The girls stopped chatting immediately and started to look serious. They trooped over and lined up. He noticed something that had been gently nagging at the back of his mind. Yesterday, Lorn, Grace, and Pip had beautifully plaited hair that reached down to their waists. Today, their hair was cropped like Ffion's, who stood beside them. When they saw him looking at their new hairstyles, they each reached up to it and fiddled self-consciously.

"Good morning, ladies. Welcome to your first day as a Shadow Elite soldier." Devon grinned at their worried faces. "At ease, everyone, you're not on trial. I see you've turned up with soldiers' haircuts."

They blushed and nodded.

Devon indicated four large piles of equipment next to the mana-forge.

Finn eyed the piles. "What's all that for?"

"Ladies, there is a pile for each of you. Your names are on the top," he said. "Tell you what, Finn, you join us, and I'll make you a pile of stuff too."

"He won't be fighting anyone," Madi said, her words brokering no dispute. "He's an engineer, and now he's a hunter, too. I can't risk losing him."

Finn looked annoyed for a second, then concealed it and nodded his agreement.

June and Dawn followed his new students over to the piles and looked at them with some confusion.

"Is this all for me, Devon?" Lorn asked.

"All for you. You'd best practice getting into it as you'll be spending most of your time wearing it. I'll make some spares too." Devon smiled encouragingly at her. Everyone started sorting through their respective heap of armour and weapons with a look of determination. They soon started trying to outdo each other and made the process into a competition.

His army now had five sworn-in members and Izzy. He noticed that Grace's sister, Pip, was a sharpshooter, some sort of mana-assisted sniper. She also had some electrical-based attacks, which would add some spice to her talents.

The two that intrigued him the most were Ffion and Grace. Ffion was a shape-changing infiltrator, which he'd never seen before and assumed would be an assassin type. His mind was already racing with possibilities for what she might be able to do.

Then there was young Grace, the baby of the bunch at sixteen and the receiver of Preeta, his mana-dragon's other sister. She was an arch elementalist. He'd heard of the elementalist class, which were rare and renowned for their power, so he had to suspect that an arch elementalist would be even more powerful. She further surprised him by petitioning for the role of an evangelist for the Wayfarer. Of course, he had agreed, but what made him wonder was where she had heard about a class that hadn't existed for centuries. He didn't ponder for long, though. Izzy confessed to giving her the idea after Grace asked about some way of acquiring healing magic. The diminutive elementalist was ambitious and already making an impression on him.

He heard June clear her throat behind him. He turned, and there stood the four ladies, resplendent in their new armour. Each of them looked triumphant and proud. The girls that had seemed so nervous ten minutes ago had become empowered warriors, ready to leap into combat at a moment's notice. Unintentionally, his voice expressed his thoughts.

"Wow!"

Chapter 17

The hard sell

June handed him an enormous pack stuffed full of food and drink. She saw it as her duty to overfeed Devon at every opportunity she found. He added it to Jet's saddlebag and gave her a kiss in thanks. As usual, she became hot and flustered, which he loved to see.

Earlier, he had created a sizeable gateway into his realm that now hummed happily to itself nearby. The translucent mist inside the portal swirled, allowing occasional glimpses of Devon's domain on the other side. The gate opened out onto the vast hexagonal centre of the city he had built a long time ago for the refugees from the fairy queen's world. Devon wished he had more time to revisit the beautiful place he had created.

He had opened up his realm so that Madi, Finn, and the other villagers could start work on the new homes for everyone. There had been no time for a tour, sadly, but they'd find everything soon enough. Before his curse, he'd worked with the dryads to create a forest city in his world. They had built the entire settlement inside and among the trees, in the old elven style. There were many thousands of home spaces inside the giant moon-willow trees, just waiting to be finished, furnished, and occupied.

After Devon had opened the portal, he'd recruited Beks to work with Pip to create a unique weapon for her sharpshooting abilities. Devon didn't want to get involved with making guns as he was positively clueless about their design, and Pip wouldn't be much use as a sharpshooter if she didn't have a quality sniper's rifle and customised ammunition to work with.

Once all that was done, Devon then spent an energetic afternoon training with Izzy, Gwen, and his students. He taught them tactics, the critical lesson of when to cut your losses and quit, and any other trick he could think of. They all practised with the new mana-blades he'd invented, and the overall results had been impressive. It was evident that everyone still needed more time to grow into their abilities and skills, though.

Lorn had begged him to take her on his journey, too, but that just wasn't possible. Jet was already overburdened. Instead, he instructed her to supervise the Shadow Elite's training tomorrow and ready them to move by midnight of the next day. Hopefully, they would have a chance to do some live training in the city. He was starting to think of Lorn as the leader of the other students. She fitted the role so comfortably.

Jet stood proudly in the centre of the settlement's clearing, her coat gleaming in the approaching twilight. Her plush tail swished, and the long black hair around her fetlocks swirled as she stomped impatiently. She had Devon in her saddle and Gwen positioned awkwardly in front of him. When Izzy jumped up behind him, Jet knew they were finally ready to depart. The light was fading, and the conditions were perfect. Devon, Gwen, and Jet were creatures of the shadows. Darkness empowered them.

Jet stomped around in a circle. Devon knew she was checking to see if she had a sufficient runway. It took energy and momentum to punch through the reality barriers that encased a realm. She made her way to the far edge of the clearing and turned on the spot again. Devon noticed that they had an audience, as usual. Watching his antics had become a new theatre for the villagers and kept them well entertained.

<We be ready. Prepare the others,> Jet thought to Devon with suggestions of warmth and reassurance.

"Brace yourselves. This is going to be fast," Devon said to Izzy and Gwen. He felt Izzy's arms fasten tightly around his waist, and he did the same with Gwen.

Jet reared up then launched herself forward with a leap. Her huge muscles began pushing hard against the soil as each powerful hoofbeat propelled her faster, kicking up earth and gaining momentum with every step. Halfway across the clearing and she was nearly at her full speed. The wind whipped around, trying to unseat them, and the trees on the far side of the clearing were approaching fast. Thinking they were going to crash, Izzy began to squeak loudly. Jet finally reached her target velocity, released a powerful magical pulse, and leapt hard into the air. There was a loud boom as the reality barrier had a Jet-sized hole punched clean through it, and then they were out into the void.

"Wow! What a rush. That was awesome," Gwen shouted over the noise.

The broken reality membrane struggled to heal itself behind them as the horse fled on through the emptiness. For the three riders, the sensation of movement had ceased altogether. There was no atmosphere to pass by and no gravity to pull at their bodies. In the void, there was nothing except a witch, a worried priestess, an uble, and a god. He was grateful for Jet's unerring sense of direction because, to him, it all looked the same.

After a few minutes, they heard the rush of something approaching fast. There was another thunderclap as they smashed through a different barrier and into another reality. Jet's hooves finally made a slight noise as she fought to slow her pace as quickly as she could while keeping her footing. Her eyes went wide, and Devon felt her body tense. After a few more steps, she locked her legs, pointing forward, and skidded for the last ten yards. He sensed panic from Jet and then noticed the reason for her desperate attempt to slow down. They were fast approaching the mouth of a vast cave.

When they came to a halt, they were a mere five yards from the gaping cavemouth. Jet turned and trotted quickly away from it. Devon could feel her need to create distance from the ominous entrance. Once they were fifty yards further away, she stopped and turned back. He marvelled at the two long gouges in the flat ground, where Jet had fought to eradicate their momentum.

Devon looked around and grinned at the familiar place in which they had landed. Rolling grass-covered planes stretched as far as the eye could see. They were standing in a shallow valley that contained nothing else remarkable other than the cavemouth that faced them. The warm zephyrs that ruffled Jet's mane smelled of hay and late summer. The sun was shining down from its zenith, meaning that it was a completely different time here than it had been on Earth realm.

<You wonderful, clever, magnificent girl,> Devon cooed to Jet, reaching down to pat her neck enthusiastically. <You found him. I'm going to spoil you rotten when we get home. Thank you.>

Jet looked back at him and sent weary thoughts of happiness. She gave him a toothy smile. <We be good to you,> she projected to him and gave him a mental wink.

There was a rumble, and a heart-trembling roar rent the air around them. Thunderous footsteps were approaching them rapidly, and each step shook the ground.

"Okay! Time to disembark," Devon said to his two petrified passengers. "Whatever you do, don't hurt him. That would end badly for us, I promise."

"Hurt who?" Gwen asked. Then she saw it. "HURT THAT? You've got to be kidding!"

"Oh shit!" Izzy managed to squeak before a golden dome enveloped them. She'd cast her first ever spell and was feeling quite pleased with herself. It had taken a little time for her powers to manifest. Then her mind registered what was thundering their way. "Eeee! DEVON! Why have you brought us here, you idiot?"

"Shhh! You'll spook him," Devon warned, grinning at the giant black dragon stomping toward them, looking not only angry but extremely hungry.

When the dragon got closer and started to look like it might inhale at any moment, Devon acted. He raised his left arm to the sky, loaded the pattern for his 'divine truth' spell into the spell-crystal in his forehead and then, with Brack's assistance, sent a blast of mana through it, directing the spell's trajectory by channelling the mana along his arm. Golden light erupted from his left hand and coated the world around with its glow. White sparkles floated everywhere and settled on every living thing. This spell was unique to the Wayfarer and revealed the purity of the target's soul. While Izzy and Gwen glowed with a golden aura, the dragon's aura went amber. Devon felt relieved. Aura colours started with golden for the purest souls and black for the most rotten. Red usually meant deceit. Sulkiss was still good at heart, although slightly tainted in places.

"Sulkiss! You old fool. Don't you recognise a friend when he visits?" Devon said, raising his voice as much as he could without resorting to a shout.

"Reaper? That cannot be you. You are supposed to be dead," the dragon boomed. His voice sounded old, but there was a good-natured tone to it.

Gwen looked up at the dragon in awe. He was the most fantastic creature she had ever seen. He was at least sixty feet long from maw to spiked tail-tip with sleek, jet-black scales covering every part of him. His long neck had sharp spines all the way down either side that grew significantly in size as they continued down his back, then ended partway down his tail. Devon had called him 'Sulkiss', which she liked the sound of, in an odd way. His regal head was characteristically equine but more pronounced and angular. It was long and elegant. Bony ridges ran down to his nostrils which were large and occupied the front of his upper jaw. Massive teeth lined the beast's mouth, which was currently smiling.

"I think this young lady fancies me," Sulkiss cackled at Devon. "And well she should, for I am gorgeous."

"The years have piled high on you, old friend. It was over two-thousand years ago that we last hunted together," Devon said, sadness tinging his words.

"Has it really been that long, Reaper? Is that insect queen still running this rat-infested realm?"

"Yes, Sulkiss, although her remaining days can be counted on one hand if I get my way."

Izzy was surprised to see how much hatred crossed Devon's features. Now she could see that he wanted the fairy queen's demise as much as she did. That meant the day of the queen's death was nigh; Izzy could almost feel it approaching. A shiver of anticipation rippled down her spine as she thought about the world without that monster. Then her focus snapped back to the massive monster that loomed here in front of her, grinning.

"Need a hand?" the dragon offered jovially. "I haven't done anything even remotely interesting for centuries. The excitement would get the old blood pumping again."

"About that; I have a proposal for you, actually," Devon said. "Might you be interested in a lifestyle change?"

"Oh? Do go on, dear boy. You'll have to speak up a bit, though; my hearing isn't all that good these days," Sulkiss replied.

Devon raised his voice a little, knowing that Sulkiss was playing to the crowd. His hearing had been good enough to hear Jet land from inside his cave.

"Your age is showing, old friend, and your life has been boring for the last two-thousand years, I'll wager. Am I right?"

"Indeed. No living creature passes this way these days. They all know where I live and stay away. I don't have the magical energy to fly far, and my symbiot died of starvation just after you disappeared. I miss the old days, the adventures, the gold, and the pillage. What's happened to this place, Reaper?"

"The fairy queen happened. She cursed me and destroyed the waygates. She banished me to the Earth realm without memories of who I had been. That was then; now I have better news. I am back, the nexuses are working again, and soon the waygate will be restored."

"Yes, yes! That's all well and good, but it doesn't change my circumstances. Not a jot. I didn't hear mention of a lifestyle change in all those pretty words," the dragon said testily.

"I have come to offer you a choice, sir dragon," Devon said. He kept his words carefully enticing but vague. "I could offer you renewed life, an abundance of magical energy, a wyrm to replace your sadly departed symbiot, and as much adventure as you can handle, but I need you to do something in return."

"I'm not going to like that something, am I? The first part sounds absolutely marvellous." Sulkiss studied Devon for tells. Then he happened to glance at Gwen, who gazed adoringly back at him. The signs were all there, and the penny dropped. "OH NO! No, no, no, no, no! You cannot be serious, Reaper."

"Please, old friend, this powerful young witch is as dark as you are. The two of you would see so much and have so many adventures together. She has me as her sponsor, and you could be part of that. She's a master alchemist too. You could both swap recipes." Devon was going for the hard sell now. The dragon had caught on before Devon had buttered him up sufficiently. Sulkiss was a shrewd character, as were all dragons who managed to live as long as he had.

"Wait! You are serious?" the dragon questioned incredulously.

"Yes. Please, old friend."

Gwen looked at Devon with abject shock and amazement. Familiars were supposed to be small creatures, easy to transport and interact with. This creature's litter tray would need to be the size of a small field. What would she feed it?

Izzy had been trying to follow Devon's plotting, but now she felt he'd wandered away from all sanity and reason. She struggled hard to keep her silence, hoping that things would start to make sense again soon.

"And if I agree? I suppose you want me to lumber across this wretched land then squeeze through one of your waygates?" Sulkiss already knew that he was going to accept the Reaper's offer. He was slowly rotting away in his damp, rodent-filled cave. Most of his joints ached, and he was sure he'd pulled a muscle while he was charging at his visitors. He didn't want to fade away. He was a dragon, king of all beasts. More than that, he was a black dragon, master of magic and cunning. At least he had been. Now even the rats poked fun at him. His thoughts made him feel wretched. The Reaper must have known he'd take whatever deal he offered.

Devon sensed the depression settling on the dragon. "Sulkiss, I am your oldest friend. I offer you this partnership because I know it will be good for both of you. I would never do you down, I swear. This young lady will be devoted to you, and together you will carve your way throughout the worlds. Enemies will perish where they cower, and you may pillage to your heart's content if it is from our enemies. I must insist on that last part. Please, bond with this dark-witch as her familiar and live again. She's part of our new army, so adventure is assured."

"Yes, yes, yes! I hear you. Offer too good to decline, blah, blah, blah. I accept, you win," Sulkiss grouched.

Devon produced a pale blue crystal from his pouch and waved it under the dragon's nostrils. He had to hold on to it tightly when Sulkiss inhaled deeply and sighed loudly.

Izzy gasped when she realised that the crystal was one of the precious few her people had scraped and saved to collect. It was a magical energy crystal. One of those Defiance had gifted to her and Devon. Her thoughts caught up with her. Once Devon opened the waygate, magical energy would flood through from Earth realm into this one. Izzy did not need those crystals now, and soon, neither would anyone here.

"You'll need this to change your size. Whatever is left over is yours to keep." Devon kept waving the crystal under the dragon's nose. A swift, forked tongue lanced from Sulkiss' maw and wrapped around the crystal, whipping it away before Devon could react. There was a crunch as the creature bit down on its prize and then swallowed.

"Ahhhh! That tastes so good. It's been too long since I felt that tingle. A little old for my tastes, though. You better have plenty of the fresh stuff in this realm of yours."

"More than enough," Devon replied. "Now make good on your side of the bargain."

Sulkiss shuffled himself around a bit until he was directly facing Gwen. "What is your name, young lady?"

"Uh!" It was all the stunned Gwen could manage in response.

"Come, come! Don't be shy. This is the beginning of a partnership that they'll sing about in all the best songs," the dragon said with a huge grin.

Devon couldn't suppress his snort of laughter. The songs he'd heard about his friend had been written by the dragon's pillaged victims and didn't portray Sulkiss very kindly.

"My name is Gwen, mighty dragon. I seek your consent to become my bonded familiar. Equal in every way, our powers combined. The Reaper is my bonded deity, and I offer you a joint share in that bond," Gwen said. Her voice sounded like she was reading her words from a text, but they were all present and in the correct order. If the dragon agreed, the bond would be made.

"I agree, Gwen. I will accept your bond and the terms on which it is offered. I shall be proud to become your familiar. Let us treat our enemies as our playthings and revel in their demise."

With that, a thick cloud of shadows engulfed both him and Gwen. Devon and Izzy could see shapes writhing inside the gloom, but nothing more. The dragon's shadow shrank rapidly, and its bulk flowed into Gwen. There was a loud pop, and then Gwen screamed and fell to the ground. Devon's arm shot out and held Izzy back from rushing into the murky depths of the shadows to help Gwen.

"She's okay, Izz. The bonding between a witch and her familiar is a much more intense experience than our bonding was. The familiar can exist inside their bond as well as out. This is an auspicious day. Not just for Gwen, either. Sulkiss is the last and mightiest of his kind."

Gradually the shadows dissipated, revealing Gwen's prone form spreadeagled on the ground. This time Devon didn't stop Izzy rushing forward. In fact, they both raced over and knelt beside her. Devon placed his finger on her neck, sighed with relief when he felt her pulse, and visibly relaxed when he noticed the slight rise and fall of her chest. Poor Gwen had suffered over the last few days. Hopefully, this was the final milestone on her road to powerful magic.

Devon scanned the area and found no trace of Sulkiss. He had seen his shadows flow into Gwen so he could make an educated guess about where his old friend was lurking – probably making himself comfortable in Gwen's psyche. If Devon knew that dragon, he would emerge knowing a lot more than Devon about Earth realm after memorising everything in Gwen's mind.

Leaving Izzy tending to Gwen, Devon walked into Sulkiss' cave and set about retrieving all the dragon's possessions. His friend would never forgive him if he left his library behind, not to mention the large heap of precious metals that he slept on. Devon also spent time collecting the dragon's alchemy equipment, enchanted weapon collection, war trophies, and stacks of metallic junk that he'd accumulated over the years. All disappeared into his pouch. Fortunately, Haven's void storage allowed him to hoover up practically anything, and Abi would sort it all out neatly for him. Anything that wasn't needed would get recycled by the mana-forge. With the sheer quantity of items that needed to be fabricated for the settlement, raw materials would be at a premium.

Sulkiss would need a much smaller bed now, but Devon would wager that he would still demand a nest of gold before he would sleep. He grinned to himself when he wondered how long the dragon would take to train Gwen to administer to his every whim. Then the reality struck him. This was Gwen. More likely, the dragon would soon be rolling over or fetching sticks to please her.

After Devon had collected all of Sulkiss' possessions, he and Izzy struggled to sling Gwen over Jet's saddle so that Devon could hold onto her and ride at the same time. Izzy jumped up behind him once more, and they set out towards Triana.

Chapter 18
Food for thought

They had entered this world outside the dragon's cave on the outskirts of the queen's realm. Now their direction was almost due east toward Triana, this world's one and only city. It was a day's ride to reach the forest that skirted the western side of the town. Then it would take another few hours to trek through the trees to get to the city walls. Triana was a demigoddess, and her realm was small, matching her divine status.

Jet was trotting across the flat wilderness. Parched grassland stretched away from them as far as Devon could see. Wispy clouds scurried overhead while the unhindered wind waltzed across the plain, whisking up Jet's mane and tail as it went.

With Devon's help, Izzy and the now awake Gwen had found their spell lexicons. A mental list of spell patterns, taught to them by their mana-wyrms. That was one of the main reasons that the wyrm would choose a host. The creature would gravitate towards a host with identical affinities to themselves.

This realm was the worst place to discover you have spells, though. The level of energy here was barely enough to keep the structure of a faie together. Where most creatures in the Earth realm were organic lifeforms, the faie were magical lifeforms. Without magical energy, a faie would eventually just dissipate and cease to be.

They rode on for several hours, happy when the barren grassland became more attractive. Small hills rose in front of them, and scrub replaced the grass. It was evident that plenty of rain fell here. The vegetation became verdant and grew in abundance as they left the tundra behind. Devon noticed that as they got closer to Triana, the temperature decreased, but it was no surprise. The fairy queen was a winter fairy, and around her, it would always be colder. She always had been a powerful creature. Devon had been arrogant when he attempted to go up against her alone; something he regretted more than anything now. When they next met, he would have friends around him, and together they wouldn't fail.

He gave Gwen a squeeze. She looked pale. "You alright?"

Gwen looked back at him and gave a slight smile. She was still recovering from her ordeal, so she stayed silent. While she was conscious, she felt utterly weary. The weak magical energy in this realm didn't suit her either. Her curiosity still worked well, though, and she watched the environment pass by with fascination. She noticed a squat, sturdy building surrounded by a wide, fortified bailey and pointed it out to Devon.

Devon looked to where Gwen was pointing and noticed a hill at least twice as high as anything around it. Atop it squatted a wide, circular keep made from grey stone and surrounded by a thick wall. Devon looked at it with interest. The hill featured in his memory, but not the building. It was only a short ride from the path they were travelling, and he debated spending a little time investigating who lived there. He had taken a chance asking Jet to take them far from their destination to where Sulkiss lived. It had cost them a full day's ride, but he hoped that it would be worth it in the longer term. Having a kindred spirit like the dragon as an ally meant a lot to him. Devon couldn't justify this latest detour so easily.

"Izzy, what are your thoughts about investigating that keep? If the occupants are loyal to the queen, they'll need eradicating. Otherwise, they might make a valuable ally. I think we should investigate, but you should decide."

Izzy was keen to get to the city as soon as she could. She had to discuss so much with Sintra and the Wayfarer's high priestess, Mersia. The quicker the waygate was reopened, the faster they could begin liberating everyone. She couldn't fight the curiosity she shared with Devon, though, and it was evident that Gwen wanted to investigate. The ride hadn't been enjoyable, and a break couldn't hurt, could it?

"I think a short break might do us good. I need to stretch my legs," Izzy answered.

Devon nodded knowingly. That was a great excuse. "Yes, a brief stop would be just the thing. Good idea, priestess," he said with mock solemnity. He sent warm thoughts to Jet, who was already heading directly towards the keep.

****_***

'Ring the bell for service' were the words scorched into the wooden plaque above the verdigris covered bell pull. Heavy bolts fastened the sign to the thick stone wall next to the rusty iron gates. Fat chains wrapped around the two gates, making it clear that this place was securely fastened shut.

Izzy tugged the bell pull, and everyone strained to hear the subsequent ring of a distant bell. Elves have supremely sensitive ears, and if any one of them heard something, it would be Izzy. She looked back at Devon and Gwen, who were still sitting on Jet, and shook her head.

Devon looked up at the top of the wall. Stood on Jet's back, he could easily vault up to the walkway that ran along the fortification. They hadn't even got to the keep yet; this was just the bailey.

<Stay where you are! I can hear footsteps approaching the gate. Whoever it is, does not sound big,> Izzy thought to them, urgently. She knew that her impetuous god would vault the wall in seconds if she didn't rein him in. She also knew that Gwen would be right behind him despite her weak condition.

Eventually, even Gwen could hear someone approaching, and finally, a wizened dwarf shuffled up to the ageing double gates. He was so short that he peered out at Izzy from under the padlock that secured the thick chains. He was dressed in a dark-tartan dressing gown, matching slippers, and a cute nightcap with a fussy little tassel at its tip. The dwarf was elderly and had an unkempt white beard that obscured the rest of his face that was not already covered by the hat.

Devon realised that it must be just before dawn. Except for Izzy, they were all creatures of the shadows. Given that elves had night vision, none of them often considered those that slept at night. They must have dragged this poor individual from his bed.

"What do you lot want?" the dwarf barked, his voice angry and heavy with sleep. He looked at the three travellers and made an assumption. "I barely have enough to feed myself. I can't spare any for vagrants that wake me from my slumber."

Devon knew that Izzy would be sifting through the man's mind. While she did that, he wondered what this creature was doing here in the middle of nowhere.

<He doesn't have magic,> Gwen thought to them. <He's just an ordinary dwarf.>

<Cheeky cow. I can hear you.> The dwarf's thoughts were gruff and clipped as if he was speaking a language he wasn't too familiar with. <I suspect your elf is wondering why she cannot read my mind.>

<Devon, he tried to block me and failed,> Izzy thought to Devon alone. <He does not realise that I can read him without issue. He is too busy reading Gwen and cannot hear this. He regards himself as a scholar

of magic and keeper of scrolls, but his actual trade is a blacksmith and founder. He is frightened and starving.>

Wow! This dwarf has mental skills. The plot thickens. <See if you can persuade him to admit us voluntarily. Otherwise, we're going in anyway. I want to see just what he has stashed in there. If he's hungry, we have plenty of food to spare. Offer him some,> Devon thought back.

"Please, we are not vagrants, I assure you. We have plenty of food that we'd be happy to share with you if you would allow us to be your guests," Izzy said, doing her best to keep her voice calm and soothing. "This is the Wayfarer, and we are his priestesses."

The dwarf guffawed. "Now I know you are vagrants. Everyone knows that loser got beaten by the winged vermin that calls herself our queen. Now, begone and fast! Otherwise, I'll set my dogs on you."

Devon doubted this man had dogs. He could barely feed himself, let alone guard dogs. The more this person tried to get rid of them, the more curious Devon became. He slid down from Jet; Gwen automatically followed him down and appeared beside him.

"Sir, I am the Wayfarer. As you can see, I am very much alive. We are on our way to Triana, and when there, I intend to reopen the waygate," Devon said politely. He cast a 'divine truth' spell again and watched as the golden cloud descended and the white sparks began to settle on everything around. The man's aura was mainly golden but slightly tinged with red. "Only the Wayfarer could ever cast that spell. I grow curious about what you are doing here and what you are hiding."

The old man looked at the sparkles that clung to him with wonder. "That was real magic. As I live and breathe, you cast an actual spell. How? I have spent a lifetime reading about it and never truly believed it possible. Oh! Yes! Sorry, please come in. I have so many questions." With that, he started fumbling through his pockets. Eventually, he fished out a set of keys and unlocked the padlock. Several minutes later, he had untangled the chains, unbolted the rusty bolts on the gate, and pulled one of the gates open a little. "Please, please, come in. I am afraid these are dark times, and I rarely get a visitor that doesn't mean me harm."

"Those times will change very soon, sir," Izzy said. "The queen's days are numbered."

The man chuckled at her words. "If he truly is the Wayfarer, then his average is pretty poor so far. He didn't do so well the first time, did he? Why should he do any better this time?"

"In less than a week, you will see the results for yourself," Devon replied tersely. He looked around him on their way to the front door, made of thick, rivetted oak. Devon suspected that there would be a heavy iron plate on the other side into which the rivets were set. This was a place built to withstand a minor invasion.

As they walked, Devon noticed a large building further around the keep that hugged the bailey. The wide chimney suggested to him that it was a forge or foundry. "Do you do much smithing these days?"

The man looked at him with curiosity. "Are you a fellow artisan?"

Devon grinned. "Oh, I dabble. I could show you a crafting tool that would amaze you."

The old man snorted into his beard. "Well, you certainly talk a good game. We'll see."

Once they got to the keep door, the man pushed it hard, and they were ushered into a vast room that occupied the entire lower interior of the keep. Stone steps wound upward around the wall, and heavy wooden bookcases lined the outside of the room. Books and scrolls crammed the shelves, here and there spilling out onto the floor to form piles. Long wooden dining tables stood in three lines across the entire length of the circular room. Two and a half of them were stacked with yet more books or strewn with scrolls. The only seats in the hall were a shabby armchair and two benches that lined the only table not covered with some sort of paper.

"I suppose the library is upstairs," Devon joked. He already loved this room, it was full of books, and the scrolls excited him even more. He guessed the dwarf lived on a higher floor.

"Yes, I'm afraid it has overflowed down here. It filled the top two floors first, and then my grandad just decided to build more shelves down here," the man confessed. "The queen ordered all faie texts to be destroyed. Being scholars, my ancestors did their best to collect as many manuscripts as they could before they were found and burnt. I'm the last of our line and always wanted to be an engineer, not a sodding book nanny. I ended up here on my own with just Patricia for company."

Devon's jaw dropped. *The whole place is full of manuscripts!* Just then, an idea occurred to him, and he grinned.

"Oh, you're married then?" Izzy asked, trying to remain calm. She had often wondered where so much of the faie's literature had gone. Now they had discovered what was most likely all that remained of it, stacked haphazardly in a remote building. She had a powerful longing for the chance to delve into all the lost knowledge that filled this dismal place.

"No. It's difficult to meet anyone when you're stuck here all the time," the dwarf sighed. "Patricia! Here girl!"

"Yip! Yip! Yip!"

A tiny brown dog scampered out from under a stack of books and ran excitedly over to the man. Her tail wagged hard, making her whole body ripple. He scooped her up and cradled the small creature under his left arm, leaving his right free to continue gesturing as he spoke. "This is Patricia. Now, did someone mention sharing food? Times have been rough lately. I used to trade metalwork for food with the Chaibok, a silthrine tribe that lived nearby, but orcs came and took most of them a few months ago. Now they're just living wild in the forest. Probably just as hungry as I am."

Devon was upset to hear about the plight of the local silthrine tribe. He held the species of lizard-people in high regard. Hopefully, they would all be free soon. He thought of the food, reached deep into his pouch, and pulled out the enormous pack that June had given him yesterday evening. As expected, she had crammed enough food to feed all three of them for at least a week. There was probably enough meat in there to keep Jet happy for a while too. "You haven't told us your name yet. What can we call you?"

"Jeffery. I suppose Jeff would be okay, as long as the food is good." He smiled. "Will your horse be alright outside? There are bandits everywhere these days."

"Good! We won't need to feed her later then. She'll be fine. I'd worry more for the bandits," Devon replied. "I'm afraid we can't stay for long." He started pulling various packages of food from the pack. There were numerous packs of sandwiches, vegetable pasties, cooked meats, cheeses, biscuits, and raw vegetables. Wine and water were the last to be dragged out and placed on the crowded table. "Don't stand on ceremony, tuck in. We can talk business while we eat."

Everyone began eating their fill, but Jeffery fell upon the food like a wolf on its prey.

"Ye gods! This food is delicious. I would gladly marry whoever cooked this," Jeffery lauded without pausing his consumption.

Devon laughed loudly. "Sorry, I saw her first, but I will certainly pass your praise on to her. Or, maybe you could tell her yourself?"

Jeffery looked up, still chewing a considerable chunk of the chicken leg he was holding. "Oh?"

"I could offer you a very cosy new home, unlimited food, unlimited magical energy, and a symbiot so that you could cast your own spells."

Devon was back on the hard sell. This man had skills and knowledge, and that had given him an idea. "We could relocate your library and combine it with mine, and you could learn to become an engineer or teach magical lore in our school. Maybe a combination of both?"

Jeffery looked at Devon, his jaw dropped open, and the chicken leg fell from his limp fingers. Patricia was delighted by this turn of events and grabbed the chicken and fled with her prize. "You mean that? Could I learn to be an engineer and teach? Would you give me all that? Unlimited food and the ability to have true magic? In exchange for all this junk?"

Izzy choked on the vegetable soup that she was spooning from a wide-necked flask. "Junk? These records must be the combined knowledge of hundreds of species over untold centuries." Jeffery's words caused Izzy to dislike him instantly. These books represented generations of precious histories. *Junk? How dare he!* she thought angrily.

"Most of it is, yes. There are some good things in there too," Jeffery replied, his voice bored. "When can I move in?" he asked Devon, more anxious to make the deal than discuss the library with the elf. He was sick of the hunger, the cold, and the loneliness. He wanted to build things that went bang and play with true magic, not just read about it in these accursed tomes. Over the years, the books and scrolls had become his gaoler. He would not even bother to wave them goodbye.

Devon gave the little man a broad smile. The dwarf was hooked. *Excellent!* "I will personally teach you to be a designer and build anything you can imagine. When we have dealt with the queen, I will send a squad over to secure your library and escort you back to the new settlement. We'll leave what's left of the food, which should tide you and Patricia over for the few days you'll have to wait."

He held out his hand to Jeffery, who grabbed it eagerly and shook it hard.

"Excellent. I've secured my second teacher," Devon enthused.

"Second?" Jeffery enquired.

"Yes, I offered Izzy here a job not long ago, and she graciously accepted. She is an expert in faie lore, some ancient languages, and a lot more." Devon was very pleased with himself. His idea of a school for absolutely everyone was taking shape nicely.

Izzy looked at Devon in surprise. She had forgotten the conversation they'd had in the nexus about becoming a teacher. Now she considered the idea, researching all these texts and becoming a teacher thrilled her.

Once the queen died, her life might finally become her own for the first time.

Devon smirked at Izzy when he saw her surprise. "Be careful what you promise a god, Izzy. My memory is working fine now." He grinned at her and was happy to get a smile back in return.

"You won't regret this, Jeffery," he said to the dwarf.

"You're damn right I won't. Best deal I ever made. Just hold up your side of the bargain, and I'll be a happy dwarf."

"Yes, well, you'd best keep this lot safe for the next few days then," Devon said. "We should be going now. If you would be so kind as to see us to the gate and lock it securely behind us."

Chapter 19

Natural environment

They rode on, reaching the outskirts of the forest around mid-afternoon. As they continued toward the city, the undergrowth thickened until they were riding toward a dense treeline. Mist hung in the air, and they could smell the dampness of the approaching forest before they reached it.

As the trees loomed over them, the path narrowed. Devon's vision took on a red tinge, and a red line loomed toward him. Fate's anticipation ability was sending him a warning. <Everybody down, we're under attack! Jet, I need your help.>

Within the blink of an eye, three shadow cats and a snow-leopard were heading into the trees. In her snow-leopard form, Izzy faded into the undergrowth. Shade was abundant in the forest, and the shadow-cats magically jumped between shadows without passing through the area in between. Further up the path, they located a silthrine and her companion. Each was armed with a self-made bow and dressed in little more than rags. Their lizard-like features looked scared as their targets had just disappeared in front of their eyes.

<Bring them down, no casualties. I want to speak to these two.> Devon cast his 'divine truth' spell yet again. He felt it was the only spell he knew that was economical in this environment and a distinctive trademark of the Wayfarer. He didn't have time for long debates and discussions.

The silthrine ladies looked around them in awe as golden mist covered the surrounding area and white sparkles clung to them. Their auras were golden, and Devon sighed with relief. He had no desire to kill these two waifs. The two lizard women fell to their knees, fear contorting their feminine features. "Lord Wayfarer, could that truly be you? Have you come for our souls?"

Devon broke cover and stepped out of the shadow right beside the kneeling ladies. He felt sad when he saw how terrified they looked. They truly believed they would lose their souls for a little petty banditry. These two were young and looked starved. Their eyes wide with fear as the enormous black cat stalked up to them. He changed into his shadow-pumine form – a large humanoid cat-man. Like Shalim, Devon consisted of pure shadow; unlike Shalim, he could talk while in this form.

The silthrine ladies instantly pushed their faces hard against the ground. "Please, Lord, forgive us. Don't take our souls."

Devon reached down and gently guided the two girls back to their feet. They looked apprehensive about standing in his presence, but they obeyed without question. "You must do something for me if you wish to keep your lives," he growled.

A human, an elf, and an enormous horse appeared behind him, causing the girls to look even more scared. "A-Anything, lord," the smaller silthrine said, the red combs on her head twitching nervously.

"Go into the forest and tell your people what you saw. Give them this message. The waygate will reopen at midnight tonight. They should make their way there, and I will take you all to new homes in a place where you can be well-fed, safely housed, and free. Everyone will be welcome. The Wayfarer has returned to fulfil the promise he made to your people nearly two-thousand years ago. I am also looking for soldiers to join me." He delivered the message slowly and clearly, hoping that the petrified ladies would spread it far and wide. He couldn't search for each refugee, but these two probably knew where a lot of them were.

"Yes, Lord. We will spread the word, and they will come. We promise."

"What are your names?" Izzy asked.

"I am Darcia, and this is my sister, Braken. Would you allow us to join your army?" said the shortest silthrine. She was no more than five feet tall, which was short even for the diminutive lizard-folk.

Devon laughed. "Yes, I would. Maybe we can teach you to shoot straight once you get your magic."

The girls looked amazed but realised they had been given work to do, so without another word, they fled away into the depths of the forest.

Izzy looked at him and smiled. "Nicely done."

****_****

"This is Triana's outer wall. We are outside the slum area on the western side of the city," Izzy explained. "The forest borders onto that part of town."

"The wall's not too high. We could probably climb over right here if we jump up from Jet's back."

"Easily," Gwen added, looking up at the wall.

"You are not coming with me, Devon. The guards will notice you instantly, and even you cannot fight an entire city full of those brutes with just us by your side. I have things to do, and Gwen is still recovering." She laughed. "Although, from the historical records I read, you tried to do it by yourself last time."

Devon snorted. "I made it into the throne room, but by then, I was exhausted, and my symbiot had given up. It's no wonder Entwaine managed to incapacitate me with a crappy freeze spell, allowing the bitch-queen to claim a victory even though she technically cheated."

"Entwaine is still her second, and he still spends half his life whispering in the queen's ear. That is what Astley tells us, anyway."

Devon froze at the sound of that name. "Izzy, promise me that you will not tell Astley anything. Bring her with you when you return if you can, but please, don't tell her anything."

Izzy gave him a worried look. "I promise, of course, not a word. I will go in alone and bring a delegation to you. Mersia will be desperate to meet you, as will everyone else. I have spent my life in there being invisible to the guards. Your only dalliance inside those walls has become a thing of legend. You really should read that book I gave you. It contains ancient texts and histories about you. It is my notebook."

"Fine, but you had better come back to me," he said, then twisted in the saddle and kissed her gently on the cheek. "You're far too important to me, and I need you in my life." Devon reached into a pocket and withdrew a small crystal sphere. "Take this. Keep it safe, and do not give it to anyone. When the waygate opens, it will start to glow with a golden colour and will guide you to it. Only with that token will your group be able to pass through."

Izzy delicately took the sphere and tucked it away. She felt her face turn scarlet. Her emotions had done a backflip as soon as he'd said that he needed her. She loved him, ached for him, but she had never dared to dream that he might ever want her in that way. Because of that, she had been struggling to bury her intense longing for him. It was a new emotion for her. It made her feel hollow inside, vulnerable, but what she felt was incontrovertible. Did he love her? She hadn't dared to go looking for the answer in his head. Then there was Gwen. Why was all this so complicated?

Fortunately, the one person in the world she could talk to was on the other side of this wall. In a desperate attempt to save face, she grabbed his shoulder and stood up on the saddle. With a leap, she pulled herself up and over the wall.

"One day, Wayfarer, then I will meet you back at the settlement." Then she was gone.

"You'd better love me as much as you do her, or you're in big trouble," Gwen said. She looked upset, and there was anger in her voice.

"I love you both just as much. I can't help the way I feel about the two of you," Devon said. He had dreaded this moment, but he wanted to face it head-on. "You are the opposites of each other, and yet I need you and Izzy more than I can tell either of you."

"Hmph! I should be mad at you. I really should, but my heart itches every time I look at you. You make me stupidly happy, and you're the only person I've ever met that is just as dark as I am. The elf better be ready to share because I'm not giving you up. No chance."

"We will sit down and work it out. Can it just wait until the queen is dead, please?"

Gwen nodded. She had expected this moment, but it had still hit her hard. She had no intention of waiting, though. The second Izzy got back to the settlement, Gwen would have it out with her. If the elf was reluctant to share, then she'd better be prepared for a world of pain. She forced herself to calm down. Devon deserved her understanding. He had given her everything and asked her for nothing in return. He had too much on his shoulders already.

After Gwen had re-seated herself behind him, he guided Jet back into the forest, and they began searching for the waygate's original location.

****_****

Using his pendant to guide the way, Devon found the spot where the old waygate must have been. The location was a few minutes from the city's edge. Even after centuries, the ground was still scorched in a circle the same size as the gate had been. Nature hadn't dared to try and reclaim it. He and Gwen sat atop Jet in the centre and listened. It was nearly midnight, and they expected to hear the muted sounds of night animals going about their business, but there was nothing. If they were being stalked or watched by anything, they were good at their job. His shadow sight suggested that he and Gwen were alone, though.

He slid down from Jet's back, walked to the centre of the clearing, withdrew the waygate charm from his pouch, then placed it on the ground. Gwen came up to stand beside him. Devon reached into his bag and removed the last four magical energy crystals. "Hold those and feed them to me if I need them. This will need a lot of mana, and Brack can't pull enough energy from this weak environment."

"Let the rebellion begin," Gwen said, taking the crystals. Her voice was still sulky, but she couldn't stop herself from getting swept up by the thrill of the moment.

Devon stepped back to the edge of the trees, fished out his pendant from under his shirt, and began channelling a generous stream of mana through the pendant into the charm. It felt strange for him to be doing something like this and not have a curious audience of villagers. It was good to be with Gwen, performing deeds that would change worlds. He didn't miss the loneliness. The people in his new life filled a gaping space inside him that he hadn't realised he had. Right now, he needed Gwen and Izzy more than anything. Also, he needed soldiers. He would not face the queen alone a second time. He'd bring an army of trustworthy people, and they would flatten their enemies as they marched to the palace.

Devon watched the flow of mana happily as it poured into the waygate. It was always a good feeling for him. A new waygate meant new adventures, and he was confident that this gate would not disappoint. Very soon, the faie could cross back into Earth realm and take residence in the world that was originally theirs. Once established, they would take the Earth realm back together.

<Brack, how are you doing in there?>

<I av some rezerves put by but I can't be givin ee much, yung un,> Brack replied, apologetically.

Devon gestured to Gwen, and she popped one of the magical energy crystals in his mouth. It fizzed and dissolved as it slipped down his throat. Brack hungrily pulled all the power from it before it reached his stomach, and he felt his mana surge as the dragon converted the energy. The ghostly image of the waygate slowly started to become solid as his mana flowed into it. He nudged his dragon and asked him for all his channels to step up to ninety percent. Devon knew that this gate would connect to the key-nexus that was already powered up and active in Earth realm.

Devon made another gesture to Gwen and received another crystal in his mouth. This time Brack had drained it before it slid past his tongue. He nodded to Gwen again and received the penultimate crystal, which was swiftly sucked dry by his hungry symbiot. The gate was now pulling its power from him rather than requiring him to channel it. He supposed that the magic's weakness in this realm meant he had to supply much more of his power. He needed to invent a better way to store magical energy. Maybe even bottle the dust from the mana-pool in the nexus. Devon wrenched his mind back to the task at hand.

Still, the gate dragged more from him. He consumed the last magical energy crystal and hoped desperately that it would be enough. Gwen placed her hand on his neck and channelled what little mana she had spare across to him.

<I ain't got much left, yung un,> Brack warned him.

Devon started to panic. This gate would start dragging at his lifeforce if there wasn't enough mana to feed it and that never ended well.

<Dat's it. I'm out, I be sorry.>

Devon's blood went cold as Brack's mana flow ceased, and the gate started pulling at his own energy. The pain began to scream from every part of him. His lifeforce and vitality were sucked from him by the hungry waygate. Devon sank to his knees, cradled by a distraught Gwen, who was screaming at him to stop the flow. Her voice became more distant, and his sight started to tunnel and fade. He wondered if his body had broken when he heard a loud crack. Gwen spun to look at the waygate.

The gate's form had become solid. Devon was just able to dampen the energy flow, stopping it entirely before it killed him. He quietly thanked the elves and Defiance for sending Izzy to him with the crystals. They had proved valuable twice and saved his life this time. He vowed to create and store more for times such as these.

There was a thunderous *thwump* sound as the waygate flashed into operation. A bright blue haze filled the frame, its light flowing outward before gradually dissipating a few feet away. The gate was twenty feet tall and fifteen wide, and it hummed quietly. Devon had always thought his creations sounded happy, as if the hum was a sign of contentment. He felt the rush of the magical energy as it began to cascade from Earth realm through the gate. He and Gwen just knelt there, bathing in it as it flowed around them like rocks in a river. It would flood this realm within a few days, thus removing the hold that the queen had over the faie. Then they would strike her down. The countdown to Triana's demise had now begun.

<That feels so gud. I can give e az much juice as ee be needin now,> Brack said, basking in the abundant magical energy that washed over them.

Devon watched a golden beam of shielding energy flow out from the top of the gate and begin to spread out around it. The shield was an orb that surrounded the structure, protecting it from harm. As long as the gate had magical power, it would be shielded and hard to damage. Without mana, the waygate would just crumble to dust. The energy flowing from Earth realm's nexus would keep the gate running indefinitely.

"Take Jet through and get the Shadows ready," he said to Gwen. "I'll follow you through in a minute." He wanted to make sure the shield formed correctly and that the gate was set to refuse entry to anyone without a token like the one he'd given to Izzy. Otherwise, anyone could wander through, and that would compromise the settlement.

Gwen nodded and led Jet through the gate.

Once he'd set the gate correctly, he stood back and basked in the feel of the magical energy that washed over him. He already felt stronger.

Devon was pulled from his musing by the loud sound of shouts and numerous feet thumping through the trees toward him. The voices were loud and harsh, and he could smell their stench. Orcs! Some local guards must have heard the gate activate. He wasn't concerned, however. The darkness was his church; it empowered him. He shifted into his shadow-cat form, a sizeable puma-like creature with razor-sharp claws and teeth even deadlier than Jet's. This form was invisible in shadows, had perfect night vision, and still allowed him to utilise his magic. In this form, he exuded power and became a deadly predator.

Devon ran through the darkness. He wanted to get behind the incoming orcs and see what he was up against – no sense in taking foolish risks. When the hulking, green creatures came into sight, he could see that there were twelve of them, and they were the elite variety of the species. Being elite hadn't made them smarter, though. Only two of the creatures had the sense to grab a torch, so their ability to see was limited. Unfortunately for them, orcs couldn't see in the dark. Their smaller cousins, the goblins, could, but faie magic hadn't blessed these creatures with the ability. Two of the twelve were hanging back; they were carrying heavy crossbows. *You two need to die first*, he thought.

At night the shadows ruled, so he could appear and disappear in any place that was visible to him. He appeared behind the first crossbowman and pounced. His teeth bit hard into the back of the orc's neck, and then he pulled his head back hard. Its spine snapped, and the stricken creature collapsed. Then the shadows silently swallowed the monster cat back up. The second crossbowman yelled in horror, and the group halted their charge abruptly. They all drew their weapons and began to turn on the spot, trying to locate their attacker.

Black flames erupted from the floor where the orcs were standing and began to sear up their legs. Screams rang out as chaos ensued. The second crossbowman collapsed to the floor. Mind-numbing terror racked his body as he wept bitter tears, Devon's 'terrorise' spell overwhelming every sense the poor guard had. The largest, most heavily armoured orc became wrapped in a thick black chain which oozed a dark mist from its links. The chain contracted and forced him down to the floor. This was one of his most potent Reaper spells. 'Soul chains' would keep the target wrapped up and drained of mana for as long as Devon had mana to spare.

A colossal cat materialised behind one of the torch-wielding orcs at the back of the group. Claws sank deeply into its flesh, either side of its torso, then raked back hard. The torch was extinguished as the eviscerated creature collapsed and rolled on top of it. Then the cat was gone again, disappearing into the shadows like a ghost.

The orcs closed into a tight circle, each facing outward, brandishing their weapon. Terror gripped every one of the remaining creatures. Their heads twitched left and right, their poor vision desperately trying to pick out any detail they could in the pathetic light of the one remaining torch. A black-feathered arrow blossomed from the last torch wielder's eye, and a moment later, his head erupted with a loud explosion. Seven terrified orcs became covered in gore. They screamed as darkness engulfed them. Each guard made the same decision and ran as fast as possible, trying to add distance between them and the horror tearing into their ranks. The direction didn't matter; it just needed to be away.

One orc knocked itself out as it blindly ran headlong into a tree. Another had its throat ripped out by something it never even saw. The others fell one after another as Devon systematically hunted them down. Not one of the creatures made it back to the wall they had been patrolling.

The squad of guards had been unlucky to encounter a Reaper in its natural environment.

Chapter 20

News from the slug

The enormous chandeliers in the throne room shone brightly in defiance of the night outside. They hung from the high, vaulted ceiling and dripped with intricately facetted diamonds of the highest calibre. Their light gleamed off the white marble floor and delicately carved pillars that stood around the outskirts of the room, tightly regimented like sentries. Enormous tapestries created from the finest threads and silks covered the walls, proudly portraying scenes of the fairy masters subjugating the lesser creatures. A plush, golden carpet ran the entire length of the throne room, from the colossal double doors to a tall, marble stage where the queen's ornate throne resided. Ten broad steps led up to the queen's seat. Huge curtains that matched the carpet flowed down from the ceiling and draped across the floor, concealing everything behind the throne.

Over two-hundred fairy nobles congregated in pools of fine costumery and pomp. They would remain there until the queen felt like retiring for the night. An even greater number of well-dressed royal slaves, their faces expressionless, milled about seeing to everyone's needs. It was a noisy, perfume laden environment full of slander and intrigue.

Triana sat upon her golden throne, bored. Her iridescent wings moved listlessly as she listened to the latest gossip from the city. She sighed when she noticed Entwaine, her advisor, making his wizened way toward her along the carpet. One of these days, that old bastard would do everyone a favour and die, preferably while in a world of pain. Even though he was good at his job, he was ugly and looked like a prune. Triana despised anything that was not beautiful to the eye and would have had him tortured and executed decades ago had he not been so useful. He had a bond with all the guards and knew everything that happened within the city walls. The revolting fairy was still a constant blemish to her perfect throne room, though.

She arranged her immaculately curled locks of multi-hued golden hair so that they draped alluringly across her ample cleavage. Not for Entwaine's sake, of course. He was a slug. She did it purely for herself. Triana was thrilled by her resplendent beauty, and she was delighted to be looking particularly radiant these days. She had ensnared an attractive young nobleman who had been 'entertaining' her for several months now. He would wither and die as she drained his vitality, but right now, he was still so full of life. Triana was thriving on it.

Triana was a demigoddess and would therefore never age. Still, she had discovered that she could improve on her already wondrous appearance by taking the life force from others and channelling it into her looks. The technique gained effectiveness if the victim already had beauty, which her latest had in abundance. She glanced, once again, in one of the ornate mirrors nearby. She admired her beautiful face that was a softly defined heart shape. Gentle cheekbones underlined perfectly proportioned almond-shaped eyes of dark sapphire-blue. Triana particularly liked her cute button-shaped nose that was just slightly upturned and highlighted her features perfectly. She pouted her small mouth, defined by succulent rose-red lips. With a thought, Triana reddened her lips a half-shade and nodded in satisfaction at the result. Her small chin and daintily carved neck finished off her flawless visage that she prized so highly.

"Your most beautiful highness," Entwaine creeped, as he reached her dais. "I am sorry to disturb your, ahem, you-time, but I bring grave news."

Triana sighed heavily and dragged her gaze away from the mirror. She refused to look at Entwaine, though, because his face disgusted her, so she gazed instead at her beau positioned nearby for that very purpose. "Continue, slug," the queen said, with a disinterested wave of her dainty hand. She was careful not to allow her face to wrinkle in disgust and blemish her perfect features.

"Uh yes, thank you, your highness," Entwaine said. He was all too familiar with the queen's insults and ignored them. "I am afraid to report that a dark entity in the forest has destroyed one of our western patrols. I was too late to view what happened through their eyes, but I heard their thoughts before each was killed. Something came from the darkness and eviscerated them before they could see what it was. The only clue I got was a black arrow shot with extreme precision. They were all dead in less than three minutes. Nothing we know of could kill with such speed and ferocity."

Her eyes narrowed, and her face took on a look of horror. There was only one dark entity she knew of that could do something like that, and he was supposed to be eternally doomed to aimlessly wander another world. The pendant's theft and destruction of her lawyers had raised her suspicions, and now this confirmed it. He was back, and the Pantheon must be working with him. She took a short time to contemplate her next move. A few ideas came to her, and her expression changed instantly to malicious delight.

The queen clapped her hands twice, loudly. "Leave us! Now!"

The nobles nodded and began to file slowly out of the room, including Fran, her beau.

"Not you," she snapped. "Guards, take Fran to my bed chamber and feed him well. I will have him when I am ready."

The burly orcs rushed forward and grabbed the beleaguered nobleman. The poor fairy whimpered as the hulking creatures dragged him through the golden curtains behind the throne.

When finally she was alone with Entwaine, she forced herself to look at him. "Fetch my daughter and that miserable servant of hers. They have only been in the tower for a few days so they should still be alive. Also, fetch my guard and a wheeled cage. He can't resist damsels in distress, regardless of how much we've messed them up first. He'll soon wish he'd stayed banished."

"Thy will shall be done, your highness," Entwaine said as he inched backwards down the steps of the dais; a trick he'd perfected over the years.

"Oh! And Entwaine?"

"Your highness?"

"Send for that filthy elf, Astley. I have an important job for her."

"Yes, my most wonderful, magnificent queen," her advisor grovelled in an oily voice.

"Ugh! You revolting maggot. Be quick about it, or I'll hang you from a lamp post by your viscera."

Entwaine turned and ran. His stupid hat and baggy brown robes flapped as he hastened out of the throne room.

****_****

There was a loud *whumff* sound as Devon stepped through the waygate. His body tingled and his vision blurred as the energy took him from the fairy queen's realm back to the settlement. When his eyes regained their focus, he saw his four new students and Gwen lined up and standing to attention. When they saw Devon, they executed a perfectly synchronised salute. Well, four of them did; Gwen did her best to match the others while grinning.

Four of them were clad in black armour. Then there was Grace. She had begged for pink armour, and so, as he couldn't think of a good reason why everyone had to wear black armour, he'd made her armour in a light, baby pink. He was going to get a reputation for spoiling his youngest student.

"Wow! When did you lot become soldiers?" he asked. "I was only away for a day."

"I asked Abi to make us a knowledge pack on military training, sir," Lorn said. Her face was devoid of emotion, and she stood rigidly.

Devon grinned and changed into his shadow cat. <Let's see your travel forms. You should all have them by now.>

In the blink of an eye, he was facing two shadow-cats, a centauress, a small arctic fox and–

<Ffion, what the hell is that?>

Ffion, his infiltrator, had the polymorph ability, allowing her to change shape. He hadn't realised her skill was quite that flexible, and clearly, she'd been practising. He looked closely at the black creature. It looked like a shaved fox, but twice the size and streamlined, with a long snout filled with evil-looking teeth that overlapped. It currently didn't have claws, but he was sure it could develop some good ones if it wanted to. The most disturbing part was a black, scaly, muscular tail with three sharp spikes mounted to the end.

<It doesn't have a name, boss. I just made it up. You like?> Ffion asked. She was obviously proud of her latest invention.

<If it's deadly, then I love it,> Devon said while watching Jet wander over to Ffion and sniff her. She clearly didn't know what type of creature Ffion was, but intended to find out. <Jet, you can't eat her.>

His horse gave Ffion a toothy grin and nuzzled her in a gesture of friendship. Then Jet changed into a shadow-cat and meandered over to stand beside Devon.

<I just encountered twelve elite orcs on the other side of the gates. They are larger than your regular orc and twice as nasty,> Devon thought, his tone turning serious. <They're all dead now, but that bit of excitement gave me an idea. I thought I might take you through and let you have a bit of live practice. I'm sure we can find some more of them. Your travel forms have acute senses. Use them.>

He received five thoughts of enthusiastic affirmation, so he turned and led his troops back through the gate. Most of them had never travelled far from their place of birth, and now he was leading them to another world. He had promised that their lives would get interesting. Now, it was time to deliver.

Once his students had got over the sensation of travelling through the waygate, he got down to business.

<Grace, can you cast in your fox form?> he asked, then jumped as a tick shape made from stone rose from the ground in front of him then crumbled to dust. <I'll take that as a yes then.> Happy they were ready, he led them off toward the wall.

Six hours later, he'd taught them how to use the shadows to launch attacks and to come at the enemy from different angles. A confused, frightened enemy became fodder. Training with real enemies as targets made his students learn at a staggering rate. They quickly learnt to adapt and improvise and began to lose their nerves. Grace had developed a good tactic of sinking hostiles into the road by softening the ground beneath them then hardening it again. Then the group would go at them all at once.

Word of their presence must have got back to the palace as they intercepted one patrol after another, all heading to where they had last been. The group moved around constantly, and were impossible to track in the darkness.

Pip despatched one enemy after another with her new rifle. As he had suggested, she'd gone to Beks and got it custom built. Pip's new weapon looked more like a plasma-gun. Devon could see the mana trail left by the gun's ammunition as it left the barrel. It was an impressive weapon, but it didn't change his mind about guns.

His squadron gradually abandoned all their fear and began to fight with absolute faith in their abilities. They'd made him proud. Ffion had particularly impressed him; what she lacked in spell quantity she made up for in a long list of mana-fortified abilities. She was lightning fast and utterly deadly, changing her shape as she fought to best suit the situation. With her quick imagination, she created creatures with features that were best suited for dismantling the opposition. Her spider form had proved highly effective. She had also demonstrated a very nasty talent called 'ear worm', which allowed her to infest and subsequently control a target just by touching it.

By the time dawn touched the streets of Triana, they had wiped out no less than twenty patrols. That meant over two-hundred orc guards had met an assortment of demises as well as fifteen huge ogres who were escorting a caged wagon with two female fairies inside. They were both severely injured and looked like they'd been tortured for days. No one in the group knew who they were. Devon's 'divine truth' spell showed one to be purer than most, while the other had an aura that was a russet colour which he didn't know how to interpret. Fairies or not, they couldn't just let them die in a cage, so they carried them back through the waygate with them.

Chapter 21

Dryads and mimseys

His troops had begun to look tired as they walked back to the new waygate, even though he knew none of them would admit to it if he asked. He was jolted from his inner musings by the sight that met them when they arrived at the gate. In addition to the creatures he'd killed, Devon counted twenty-two more orcs and four ogres, all dead, all looking like pincushions. Nearly a hundred dryads were busy removing arrows from the corpses. The orcs and ogres hadn't stood a chance. Never one to miss an opportunity, Devon reached out and harvested every soul. When the dryads saw the shadows emerge and fleet away, they looked up.

A voluptuous dryad detached herself from the others and charged in Devon's direction. A lot of her moved alluringly when she ran, and Devon found himself mesmerised by the sight.

Gwen smirked from behind him as she saw where his eyes were focused. <She's a big girl. I can see why you like her.> There was a touch of bitterness in her words.

Devon thought it best not to respond to that.

The dryad hit him with force and engulfed him in a tight embrace. "Mother divine, I have missed you so, so, so much, my lord. I have been desperate without you."

"Hello, Aria. I've missed you too," he said.

Gwen looked disapprovingly at the buxom dryad and sniffed disparagingly.

He disengaged himself from her, which proved tricky because she was reluctant to release him. "Aria, I would like you to meet Gwen, Lorn, Grace, Pip, and Ffion." The women all changed into their usual forms and bowed. "They are all very special to me, so play nice with them. Same for the rest of you," he said to the sea of happy dryads that stood in front of him.

Aria looked the soldiers up and down and wrinkled her nose. "They're nothing to us, my lord. We can easily ignore them if that is your wish."

"I said play nice, and I meant it. You and your sisters need to be friendly to everyone in the settlement, or I shall send you back to your mother." Devon needed to head off any internal conflict before it occurred.

The dryad pouted and looked away as if she was contemplating an argument. After a short while, she looked straight at Devon and batted her eyes. "Yes, my lord. It will be just as you wish." She looked over the Shadows and gave them a saccharine smile. "It is nice to meet you."

"Thank you," Devon said, grinning.

"Mother gave us all the seeds she promised you. We've also brought some friends that wanted to come and live in your forest." Aria said, quickly changing the subject. She gestured to a beautifully ordered horde of forest creatures, smallest at the front and most prominent at the rear. They were all waiting patiently for the dryad's permission to move.

"Cute. I hope they'll be happy in their new home."

Aria looked at the creatures and pointed to the gate. She barked a few commands in her language, and the animals all trooped off in an orderly fashion. "Is it true what mother told us? The enchanted forests are ours to care for?" Aria asked excitedly.

"My realm is open, but I haven't done anything with it yet. It's just as you left it. The one on Earth realm is desperate for your attention. I want you to expand it in every direction, as far as you can. The forest will be where the resurgence of the faie begins. First, though, I need you to use those seeds to grow me an elven-style settlement around the gate. Be creative. Use your imaginations. I'm sure you already have ideas. All of you are very welcome to take both forests into your care," Devon replied.

There was a lot of hopping and clapping.

Devon raised his hands. "I want the seeds planted and grown soonest, so you need to get busy. Many people will desperately need comfortable places in which to live. I am looking to all of you for your best help with that. I need as many houses, halls, walkways, business spaces, and platforms as you can manage. The whole area is flooded with magical energy now, just right to restore the forest to its former glory."

The dryads nodded excitedly and sprinted through the waygate, grabbing more arrows and their void bags as they did so.

"Well, they're something else," Gwen said, the contempt evident in her voice.

Devon chuckled at her comment. "Relax, nothing changes with us. They are a little over-enthusiastic, but they work hard and are good to the core. They will be a serious asset to the settlement and the entire forest. Have faith."

Devon and the others all jumped when thick roots sprang from the floor, wrapped around the corpses, then dragged them back into the ground. The dryads must have planted several corpse-vine seeds, germinating when the guards' blood seeped into the soil. Anyone with ill intent near the gate would find themselves feeding the plants before they could flee. "Clever girls."

Gwen's expression turned from annoyance to reluctant respect. "I see what you mean. Useful creatures to have around."

****_****

The next morning, for reasons he didn't want to consider, Beth had floated into Devon's thoughts. He hadn't seen her recently. Devon wondered what she was doing. Abi knew where everyone was, and she had told him that Beth was currently working in the war-room, which is why he was just stepping into it now.

Devon was shocked when he saw the room. It still looked like the hub in shape and décor, but the raised areas around the outside had disappeared, as had the large map table that used to reside in the centre. Now, there was nothing in the room apart from some comfortable-looking office chairs and tall, metal cabinets along the wall. The cabinets all had smoked glass fronts, and inside he could see hundreds of tiny lights flashing in random patterns in a variety of colours. He had spent many points upgrading this room when Beth had offered to take charge of it. A battle coordinator had seemed like a very appealing option, especially as Beth was hopeless in close combat. Yet his points seemed to have reduced the features of the room.

"Don't look so shocked," Beth said. Her voice muffled by having her head buried deep inside one of the cabinets. Eventually, she removed her head from the cabinet and stood up to face him with a broad grin.

"I'm a technomancer which is something Abi said was completely unheard of before I arrived," she announced proudly as she approached him.

"That's nice. What does a technomancer do besides try to force themselves into cabinets full of flashing lights?"

Beth laughed and thumped his arm. "I was already a technology nerd. My mum and dad were high up in the Hextaine Corporation. As a kid, I wanted to be a witch or a unicorn, but they lectured that out of me. Instead, I received the best education money could buy and became a robotics and bio-tech prodigy. I rebelled and got caught hacking Hextaine's core financial database. They threatened to put me in a juvenile labour centre, so I ran away. Nearly bloody starved and would have perished if Beks hadn't found me and brought me back to the village. That's the short version of my life story."

"I had no idea you were smart," he said with a devious grin. "So, what does technomancy give you that you didn't already have?"

"The power to be in the wires, to become part of the whole system. Devon, it's incredible. I can exist inside the machines and have thousands of tiny displays lining my vision. I can bring any of them into focus and see any camera view or data display. I understand so much now. I can be anywhere," Beth enthused.

Devon noticed that Beth's brown eyes were bright, almost as if they were backlit, and there was constantly shifting glitter amongst the colouring. Looking at her was almost hypnotic.

"I understand all of Abi's systems now. We have been working to link her up to the outside world and pull in information from everywhere."

"Is that safe?" Devon asked with concern. "Can't other people get to her from out there?"

"Absolutely not. I'm the only technomancer that exists, and I have put protections in place that are magical, not made from mere algorithms. No-one is getting in or out without our permission," Beth said with triumph radiating from her face.

"Nicely done."

"My skills also allow me to combine magic with technology. That meant I could create thousands of these," Beth said, holding out her open hand, palm up.

Devon looked then felt foolish. "There's nothing there."

Beth scowled at her hand. "Go on," she said as if coaxing a reluctant puppy, "show him."

Devon watched her palm. Either Beth had lost a few marbles during her voluntary isolation, or he was supposed to see something that he couldn't. Then a small black egg shape appeared. It had two pairs of insectile wings protruding from its sides but otherwise was completely black. Oh, and it had eyelashes. Wait – what?

"Don't be shy. He wants to meet you," Beth coaxed.

The little creature opened its one large eye, which was almost as big as its body, and looked up at Devon. It blinked at him.

"This is the first creature and technology hybrid. I call them mimseys."

"What does that stand for?" Devon asked.

"Nothing, I just thought it sounded cute," Beth replied with a giggle. "I used the mana-forge to create two-thousand of these little guys."

"Abi, I didn't authorise that spend," Devon said in confusion. All spending had to be cleared by him.

"Beth said you had authorised her to spend what she needed. I'm sorry, master. She was very persuasive."

"You used your technomancy on poor Abi. That's just wrong," Devon said, not quite knowing whether to laugh or be angry. He had begun to see just how powerful Beth's new talents could be in today's world.

"Devon, I'm so sorry. I didn't think it would work. I needed a target to practice on. I can't exactly go down to the training room and work this stuff out."

"Well, kindly refrain from doing it to Abi again. She is strictly off-limits. If you need targets, we'll find you some. By the way, how much did you spend?" he asked, trying his best to sound stern.

"In total, three-thousand, three-hundred and twenty, master," Abi stated. "Two-thousand for the mimsey creations and the rest for war-room interface upgrades, plus a magical link to the new external uplink."

"Don't be mad. I know that sounds like a lot, but it's worth it, I promise," Beth said.

"That's more than the cost of a pod to feed two-hundred people, Beth."

Beth paled and looked mortified. "Really? Oh, Devon, I'm so sorry. I didn't know. I'll pay you back somehow."

Devon had to smile. Her face had become so troubled now that she realised the value of points in Haven. "Show me what all these points bought me. It looks like we've been burgled. Where did my war-room equipment go? How did you even get the table out of here?"

"I didn't. It is sunk into the floor now. The rest all disappeared when I upgraded the room to a technomancy design. Everything in Haven is made of mana-forged matter, which Abi can control as she requires."

Devon laughed and shook his head. Beth knew more about Haven than he did, and she'd only been in here for a few days. "You never stop surprising me."

Beth smiled a worried smile. "I'm proud to be part of the team, Devon. I really am. What you are doing for people is incredible. I want to help."

And that was it. Beth had floored him with a few words, and suddenly all was forgiven.

"Let me show you what your hard-earned points paid for," Beth enthused, sensing her victory.

Beth walked over to the pillar mounted mirror that was customary in Haven and started tapping options. The room went dark, and then the whole place became his realm, just inside the gate he'd opened. The view looked down on the hexagon and the magnificent, moon-willow trees, latticed with walkways and vine bridges. He caught the occasional flash of green as a dryad flitted from tree to tree and villagers carrying various items from the mana-forge to the next home they were furnishing. It was all there.

"Transferring mental controls to you, Devon."

Various controls appeared superimposed in his vision. After playing with them a bit, he got the hang of what to do and zoomed in on a villager. The resolution was phenomenal, and he could even see the texture of their hair. He tried looking around and discovered that the image was three-dimensional. Above him were the tops of moon-willow trees and then the sky. The view stayed still; it was him that moved within it. His controls just changed the point in space from which he was viewing it all. It was incredible.

"Gods and goddesses, Beth, how have you done this?"

Beth beamed with pride. "I was hoping you would find this useful. My mimseys are smart and normally completely invisible. They can flood an area, and each one sends what they see back to the uplink, which relays it all back to Haven. The war-room sends them instructions about where to be and then stitches all their views together to form this display. When there is a dark space, the system instructs a mimsey to go and look at it, then adds it in."

"You are an extremely clever woman. In an eternity, I have never met your equal," Devon said, and he meant it too. One person had no right to be that smart.

Beth went scarlet and bit her lower lip. "Thank you, darling. That's a lovely thing to say."

He looked at her with curiosity, then walked over and gave her the hug he had wanted to give her since he'd met her. The minutes passed, and they just held on to each other. This moment had been a long time in the making.

"Is there any chance your mimseys can go through the waygate and scan the city just beyond it? That's where we're going to be operating over the next few days. Izzy's resistance members will want to see this miracle of yours in action tomorrow."

"Mana flows through that gate thing, right?" Beth asked, disengaging herself from their embrace.

"Yes, both ways," he replied.

"Then yes, that'll be easy. I'll send them through now."

"You're a star. Do you trust me enough to bond with me yet? If we bonded, we could all share a mental link and be able to talk to you wherever we are. No point in having a coordinator we can't coordinate with."

Beth nodded. "Good point. I think I'm ready to commit to that."

****_****

After his visit with Beth, Devon had ordered his tired students to the training room and worked them hard for several hours. They needed to learn that war didn't stop because they were exhausted. After this, they would realise that using just as much energy as was necessary was also a life skill. The training room was the same size and shape as the hub but with a smooth, slightly padded black covering on every surface, including the ceiling. Ambient light came from a glowing strip that circumnavigated the upper wall. When active, the whole area could magically represent almost any scenario imaginable, allowing combatants to train against seemingly real opponents without risking death or serious injury. The room would even simulate spells and magical attacks, which gave Devon and his students a mighty tool to hone their skills.

Devon had dragged Aria in to teach them all how to shoot a bow with competence. Even though Aria had readily agreed to help, she still complained, simply because the task he'd set the dryads was so daunting. Moon-willow trees would usually grow to at least six-hundred feet tall and be over eighty feet across at the trunk's base. With an unlimited supply of magical power at their disposal, a group of five dryads could raise one of the mighty trees in less than five hours. However, Devon had also asked for rooms inside the trees, interlocking branches, platforms, natural steps, and ladders. It all took time and vast attention to detail. Even the daughters of nature themselves felt the pressure. What was more, there were five-thousand of the monster willows to raise and thousands of other forest flora to establish before the enchanted forest would begin to soak up the magic like a sponge and gain proper sentience. Things were progressing rapidly, though. It was just that teaching younglings to hold a bow correctly wasn't on Aria's to-do list.

Chapter 22

Reaper's gonna getcha

Devon stood in the old beech clearing where he and the villagers had first spent the night. The beeches that surrounded the clearing were now a beautiful russet as autumn called the changes. This morning the forest smelled musky and damp from the dew. He happily watched the bustle of so many lives all around him.

The villagers had been ever-present throughout the beginnings of the new settlement on Earth realm. Finn and Madi coordinated all the efforts, and everyone worked hard to assist with the enormous task. Often, they took time away from their work and watched with amazement as the dryads cast their spells and made seeds grow from almost nothing into trees more immense than they could even comprehend. Since Devon had entered their lives, every day had been full of wonder and promise. Fate had undoubtedly smiled upon them.

The enormous moon-willow trees already towered over the beeches. The forest in Devon's realm was well established, and all Aria and her sisters had to do to it was bring it back under their control. It had been doing its own thing for nearly two millennia. It was the forest on the Earth realm side that needed their full attention. It had been an enchanted forest thousands of years ago, but when the magical energy had stopped flowing, it had slowly died back to the mundane.

Moon-willow trees were magical. They survived by bathing in magical energy and absorbing it into their long, dark-green leaves. They used some of that power for nourishment, and the rest went to reinforce their structure and protect their exteriors. They were famous for their lengthy, drooping branches which created a curtain of leaves that reached from the topmost part of the tree all the way to the ground. This species was so coveted because the leaves emitted a protective aura as an effective method of self-preservation, creating a magical barrier that engulfed the entire tree.

In Earth realm, the dryads had already done exemplary work at the centre of the settlement. Devon gazed up at the thick branches that formed aerial walkways between the trees. The thoroughfare was all you could see. Each emerged from one curtain of leaves through an archway woven from the tree itself, then crossed into another. Similar arches were present on the ground in three separate places. They created entrances to walkways that left the floor and spiralled around the tree, up into the heights.

Over one-hundred trees wove together around the central circle to form the settlement's heart. The central clearing was now a thick carpet of short, lush grass interspersed with tiny flowers of assorted colours. Devon listened to the river's merry tune nearby as it scampered its way down through the forest. Joining the melody was the chatter of the villagers above him in the trees, distant birdsong, and the distant tinkling sound of the melodic bells dryads liked to wear around their ankles. Every breath he took was invigorating and fresh. Overnight, the dryads had taken this mundane collection of beech trees and turned the whole area into something magical. *One day soon, this will be close to how it all used to be, and it will live again.*

Tomorrow, the dryads were planning to plant many more trees surrounding the core plantation. They moved swiftly through the forest, their senses and speed enhanced by the environment. They worked hard while laughing and smiling happily, chatting excitedly among themselves. They would toil tirelessly for decades until the forest of yesterday became the wondrous enchanted forest it had been centuries ago, sprawling across thousands of acres and providing sanctity for all creatures. If someone the dryads didn't like the look of wandered into an enchanted forest, that person would never emerge. The flora and fauna would see to it. While dryads were pacifists, they had a very pragmatic opinion on defence. The moon-willow trees and sentient forest would become the settlement's best protection.

Devon had commissioned Abi to build customised pods that had greatly expanded capabilities. They had cost him and his mentors dearly but would allow them to feed, cater far, school, and provide hospital facilities sufficient for a community of over two-thousand. He had also commissioned pods that would offer large utility spaces for the community like a town hall, a guildhall, theatres, and meeting places. He suspected that all of this would still not be enough, but it was a good start. Enough for the new occupants to gradually develop the skills they'd need to become self-sustaining. The refugees from the fairy queen's realm needed sanctuary, and they would look to him to offer it. He had also commissioned a secondary mana-forge so that designs could be manufactured within the village. He was tired of people traipsing through Haven all day. It was playing havoc with his carpet.

Pods would be dispersed throughout the settlements in both realms. His realm housed the bulk of the fledgeling city, for now at least. That would even out as the settlement in Earth realm grew in stature.

Almost everyone stood and watched with fascination as the dryads magically manipulated vines to haul the pods up into the trees' boughs. Devon watched in wonder at the seamless way the dryads worked together. They called intentions and actions in their language, and gradually the pods were pulled into the trees and positioned perfectly on their prefabricated platforms.

When the last pod was in place, everyone watching burst into applause, cheering and whistling their appreciation. The dryads looked delighted and lined up to take a bow. It was a long line. The forests were blessed to have so many of these demi-goddesses, and more would be arriving soon.

Devon noticed five of the villagers, including Finn, sidle up to a few of the dryads and strike up a conversation. He wondered what they were chatting about because more dryads gathered around, all clapping and nodding enthusiastically.

<Most of the villagers have become either druids, hunters, or rangers, my lord. They are asking the dryads to teach them what they should know,> Lorn thought to him.

<They have already dedicated themselves to the goddess of nature and have received additional powers,> Pip added.

He looked proudly at his Shadows, then heard the *thwum* of the waygate bursting into life which instantly pulled his focus toward the origin of the sound. The noise meant someone was passing through the gate. Izzy was the only one with a token on the other side, so his priestess must be returning finally. Devon and his Shadows lined up in front of the waygate. Aria sidled up next to him. Devon hadn't seen where she'd materialised from, but she'd kept close to him since she'd arrived. He flashed her a grin. He was very fond of Missy's oldest daughter. Technically, all dryads were her daughters, but Aria had been the first. A possessive, green-skinned arm wrapped around his waist and squeezed. He stroked her hand softly as they waited. Finn and Madi sauntered over, and the crowd of villagers who had been watching the spectacle of the pod raising now wandered over to watch the next event. Life for them wasn't dull anymore.

Six figures walked timidly through the large waygate, looking around them in wonder as they emerged from the cavern into the forest. When they realised the sheer potency of the magical energy on this side of the gate, they all stopped and took deep breaths. Izzy hurried to Devon's side and turned back to face the newcomers.

<Welcome home,> he thought to her.

She smiled warmly up at him. <Thank you, my lord; it's good to be home. I take it this is Aria and her sisters? They have been busy, I see.>

<They certainly have.>

<From what I hear, you've been busy in the city too.>

Devon sent her a mental laugh. <It was just a training exercise. My troops needed practice.>

<That practice wiped out half the city guard. The queen is blaming April, her daughter. Someone told the queen that her daughter sponsors the resistance, which is true, but no-one should know about it. You may have inadvertently instigated that poor girl's execution, Devon.>

<We rescued two fairies during our exercises. Could she be one of them? They're both strapped down and sedated in the hospital. They'd been tortured for a while and weren't far from death. We'll discuss this later. I'm sorry if I caused trouble for your people. This is a revolution, don't forget. I just started it early. Forgive me?>

<Of course, idiot. I'm your priestess and will always forgive you – eventually,> she laughed.

Izzy had enjoyed a long and heartfelt discussion with Sintra, her boss and friend. Izzy had explained about her love for Devon, and how torn she was between her loyalties to Defiance and her need to be by his side. After some thought, Sintra had dismissed Izzy from her obligations to the resistance. She was now officially Devon's priestess, who just happened to have close affiliations with Defiance. Her task now was to look after elven interests with the Wayfarer. Izzy knew that wouldn't be hard because her Wayfarer, and he was definitely hers, would always take special care of the elven people. Gwen was the last hurdle. She needed to make peace with her new friend.

She snapped out of her reverie. Izzy had introductions to make. "My lord Wayfarer, may I introduce you to Sintra, head of Triana's resistance forces. High priestess, Mersia, leader of your faith. One of Defiance's finest operatives, Mitsey Boo. The distinguished head of the gnomish Tinkers' guild, Glimmer; and finally, Astley, our best spy," Izzy said. She had done her best to make sure everyone got the introduction they needed.

Devon's smile froze. He did well to manage to keep it on his face at all. Astley was one of his Reaper targets set by the Pantheon. Their eyes met, and he instantly felt her malice.

Everyone jumped when Astley leapt forward and screamed something that sounded like a battle cry. A finely carved bone dagger appeared in her grip, drawn from the folds of her robes. Her face contorted with rage as she hurtled toward Devon. She had the look of a thing possessed.

Devon stood rooted to the spot in shock. He knew Astley was an enemy and had long since prepared his plan for her exposé, but this had taken him completely by surprise. She had deliberately shown herself as a traitor by attacking him in front of everyone. Then he focused on the dagger she brandished.

"DEVON! THE DAGGER'S CURSED. MOVE!" Gwen screamed at him.

Devon was violently thrown to one side as Aria used her tight grip around his waist to thrust him out of danger. Dryads were a force of nature, and she had the strength to move him easily.

As he regained his balance, he heard a pained cry. He spun around and saw Aria fall to the ground, dark smoke rising from her skin. Tears streamed down her face. "Oh no! Aria! NO!" The dryad must have taken a wound from the dagger meant for him. He looked up to see Astley staring at the dryad in horror.

"Devon! Help! It hurts." Aria mewled pitifully.

<Capture the elf! No mercy. Keep her alive. I want her. Lorn, keep her quiet,> he ordered his Shadows.

Black mana strands hissed past him and ripped the dagger out of Astley's limp hand with a loud crack. The elf yelped and held her hand in pain, then collapsed on the floor writhing in agony from sources unseen.

Devon rushed to Aria's side, fell to his knees, and cradled her where she lay. Her skin was flaking away as the black smoke rose. "Oh Aria! What has she done to you?"

Gwen, Sulkiss, and Izzy arrived at the same moment.

<Don't touch her skin!> Sulkiss said. <That's an accursed bone dagger that stabbed her. The dryad has been cursed with something ancient that even I have never witnessed. Her fate is already sealed.>

Izzy quickly pulled her hand back. She'd been about to begin pumping healing magic into the dryad, hoping it might help.

"That bitch Triana is behind this. I can smell her influence. This curse is her work," Devon hissed. Anger seethed through him. He pushed his hand back through his hair in frustration. He felt the dryad go light and watched as she crumbled into dust. He felt the tears start as his emotions welled up and overflowed. Two arms wrapped round him, one from either side. Bizarrely that small gesture from both of them instantly broke his ire. He would grieve when he conveyed the news to Missy later. Right now, he had a debt to settle.

When Devon got to his feet, surreptitiously wiping the tears away from his eyes, Gwen joined the other Shadows, and Izzy retook her place by his side.

<Thank you, gang!> he said over the team bond that his students shared with him. <Wait for the sign, then stab the bitch through the back of the knees, bring her down, and hold her. Make it hurt a lot.>

<Yes sir,> they replied in unison.

Devon turned to the other four individuals who had emerged from the waygate. "My apologies for the interruption. It seems that not all of you are trustworthy. I wonder if the queen has influenced anyone else?" He flicked his wrist and cast a 'divine truth' spell. This was the most effective way to unmask a traitor. He already had one example to make and would soon be leaving a lasting impression on everyone here.

A golden cloud of light descended on everyone within a fifty-yard radius. Sparks of white coalesced around each body present, bestowing all but one figure with a beautiful golden glow. Astley's aura was dark red. Two shimmering mana-blades sliced straight through her legs from behind, both twisted as they were withdrawn, causing the elf to cry out in agony.

Devon cast a Reaper spell next. The 'soul chains' instantly wrapped Astley up in thick black chains that exuded a dark, mana-draining mist.

"Your top spy is, in truth, employed by the queen and is responsible for more deaths among your kind than any other elf in history. Now the piece of filth has cost me someone very special to me. I am disappointed that none of you realised exactly where her allegiances lay."

Sintra looked at Astley in horror. "My lord Wayfarer, we are mortified by what has just happened. I swear we had no idea." Anger flooded across Sintra's face as the implications finally sank in. "You traitorous whore!"

"Oh, Devon! We brought her through the waygate. I am so sorry," Izzy said.

Devon ignored Izzy for now. He'd asked her to bring Astley. This situation was of his engineering. "Astley, the Pantheon has issued a bounty for your soul after convicting you of mass race betrayal and genocide by proxy. Oh, and the goddess Fate asked me to make sure this really hurts. I suspect Aria's mother will want the same now. Lorn, if you'd be so kind. Do your absolute worst."

Lorn looked at him and grinned. Her brow furrowed, and Astley's scream rang out through the forest. Her body shivered and twitched as pain tore through her. After a few seconds, she looked like she was suffering so much that she was about to pass out, but Lorn sent a shock through her brain, forcing her to stay awake. The elf shook and spasmed as agony induced by her own mind wrecked her body. The scream turned into a defeated sobbing as every evil she had ever done became ghosts that cursed and tormented her from within her brain. Lorn hadn't had a chance to lash out with her neuromancy before, and she was making it count.

Devon let it continue for over a minute until he felt Izzy squeeze his waist. He knew his priestess wanted the torture to end. He raised his hand slightly to Lorn in a 'stop' gesture, and the elf slumped. Gwen and Ffi had her arms and the chains held her in place so she couldn't fall to the floor. Lorn relaxed. He leant down and cupped the weeping elf's chin and raised her face toward his. "I regard your crimes toward my people as a personal slight. What you did to that beautiful dryad has motivated me to make sure your soul suffers an eternity of torment. I will send your mistress the bitch queen along to join you very soon."

"Wait! Please! I will tell you everything that I know about the queen. She made me attack you. I can be useful to you. Let me make amends for my crimes. I'll do anything. Please! Just spare me."

"What could you possibly tell these people that could persuade them to forgive you?" Devon asked in a voice dripping with contempt.

"Uh… the queen's daughter! Yes! The queen's daughter; she's on your side. The queen just found out she is a sympathiser to your plight. She believes April masterminded last night's rebellion and ordered her execution tomorrow morning. April and her lady in waiting have been taken to the arena to be torn apart by wild animals. You see! I know lots of things that could help you. Just let me live, I beg you."

Hmm! That sounds promising. The fairies that we rescued could have been on their way to the arena, Devon thought.

"Where are they being held?" Mitsey asked. "The terracotta tower?"

"No. They were there, then the queen's guard took them to the arena last night. They will both die when the sun rises. The queen wanted their deaths to be entertaining, and so it will take place in public."

"And who told the queen she sympathised with us?" Sintra asked, not bothering to hide her hatred for the traitor.

"Not me, I swear."

Devon watched her aura turn an even darker shade of red as his Wayfarer magic judged her for the lie she had just uttered. "You are even stupid enough to try and lie to us while you are in a truth aura. Thank you for the confession of yet another betrayal, though."

His anger at Aria's death resurfaced. "Now die the death you deserve, YOU PIECE OF SHIT!" He put out his hand and summoned the elf's soul. Astley's scream chilled the blood of everyone within earshot. It was a terrifying thing. Agony coursed through her. She shook and spasmed as the pain overloaded every cell in her body. Devon watched dispassionately as the elf's soul violently ripped free from her living essence, and Astley's life instantly ceased. Dark mist oozed from her body and formed a floating shadow that represented the person she'd been. A creature's soul reflected the life they'd led. Astley's was black, disfigured, and brutally twisted. The girls let her corpse go, and the chains faded away. Her soul came to him meekly; deformed head bowed in repentance. He took the soul into his care, sighed, and ran his hands through his hair. They only ever regretted their actions when he caught them. No torture could compare to that of having your soul removed while you still lived.

Devon decided to try a new skill that Shalim had donated to his weapon. He touched Astley's body with his staff and watched in fascination as it sucked all the energy from every molecule out of her and into him. The body became dust in seconds. *There! Now you know how poor Aria felt, bitch!* Just for good measure, he stomped on the elf's dust.

Every eye watched him in amazement and shock. Finally, they saw the true power of the god that he had always been.

"Again, my apologies," Devon said to the four remaining visitors, who looked terrified and were visibly shaking. "I am afraid that I must deal with all traitors this way now that I have returned. Justice is only effective when it is seen to be done. The queen and a fairy called Entwaine will soon share Astley's fate."

Sintra nodded grimly. "It is right, lord Wayfarer. You are justice and death; that is why we are devoted to you." Then she and her friends sank to their knees.

Devon looked around in frustration and embarrassment. Not only were the delegates on their knees, but Izzy, the dryads, his shadows, and quite a few of the villagers, including Madi and Finn. "Oh, stop! We're all friends here," he shouted. "Please, just don't." His face had gone scarlet. People bowing to him made him feel icky. He hated it.

Slowly people started getting back to their feet.

Devon was desperate to change the subject and move things along. "Where would you all like to start? You can get a symbiot, have a meal, or we can talk about plans," Devon said, trying to smile and look reassuring. It proved hard to fake.

Four heads snapped up and looked hungrily at Devon.

"We could have magic? You would give us that blessing?" the goblin girl asked in amazement.

"Of course, most of the good people of this settlement have received it already. These five ladies behind me are fine examples of the magical skills you could possess." Devon checked behind him to make sure his Shadows had resumed their places. He smiled when he saw they were all there in the same order as they always stood behind him. He'd have to ask about that.

"The villagers are preparing the new homes for your people as we speak, lady Sintra," Grace said.

Devon could have wept with pride at his youngest prodigy's words. She'd just nailed the issue of elf-human relations. She was going to get the best magical staff he could make.

Chapter 23

The little things in life

<Beth?>

<Uh-huh?>

<Can you please inform everyone that we have refugees incoming?> Devon said. <I want welcoming smiles and friendly gestures all around. Those poor people must be terrified.>

<Yep! On it.>

Sintra had asked to bring the assembled refugees through the gate, and things weren't quite ready for them.

<Shadows, go through the gate and neutralise anything that acts in an unfriendly manner. Call me if it gets ugly. You've worked hard, so when the refugees are through, make sure someone is looking after them, then take the night off.>

His troops filed off in perfect step.

"Devon, those women are terrifying. What have you done to them?" Izzy asked with a concerned look.

"I haven't done anything to them but empower them to be the individuals they choose to be. Relax, they're very nice, intelligent young ladies," Devon tried to assure Izzy. "You know all of them, especially Gwen. They've just had a tough life so far. I had hoped you might have some understanding for them because of that." Izzy's reaction had annoyed him a little. He admitted that his students were a bit controversial, especially now, but they were wonders in human form, in his opinion.

"Ahem!" Sintra tried to interrupt this tiff between god and priestess delicately. Her deity had proved he could be a lot more ruthless than their history books ever suggested. "We would be honoured if you would gift us with magic, lord Wayfarer," she said. Her voice was still very formal and a little scared.

"Please, Sintra, relax. I want us all to be friends. We will need to work closely together from now on. After all, there is so much to do," Devon almost pleaded. He hated diplomacy, and he didn't want Astley's demise to sour the situation.

Devon walked the guests into the cavern and past the waygate, which was now fully active and humming happily to itself. He walked over to the keystone and started opening it with the Wayfarer's crystal. Aria's death weighed heavily upon him, but their guests needed his attention. He would deal with her loss later in solitude. "I believe I have you to thank for fetching this for me, Mitsey?"

"Yes, lord. I would have done it a thousand times just to get to this moment. It would be an honour to serve you further if you have a space for me in your guard," Mitsey said. Just getting her hands on a set of that magnificent armour the Wayfarer's troops wore would be a dream come true, but to become as powerful as them would be awesome.

Devon looked questioningly at the goblin. "I do owe you a debt that I will struggle to repay. Perhaps you and I should have a chat," Devon said.

A wide smile spread across Mitsey's face. "Of course, lord."

They began the long trek down the winding road that led into the depths to the nexus. The walk gave them some time to talk.

Devon looked across at Mersia. Many years ago, the elven high priestess had sworn her life to the Wayfarer while he was still wandering uselessly around Earth realm, cursed to be eternally human. She had stuck to his faith, and he owed her a debt for her loyalty. Izzy was right. She was always right.

Mersia was older than Izzy but still, like all elves in Devon's opinion, very striking. She had blonde, almost white hair that reached past her shoulders. Her face was narrow but gently shaped, and she had the look of too many years of worry about her eyes, which were a silvery blue. Her figure was a little fuller than an average elf's, but not by too much. The overall impression he got was a genuine person that anyone would be lucky to call a friend.

"Mersia, I believe I owe you my thanks. Your constant loyalty throughout my darkest years humbles me. I wondered if you might do me the honour of becoming my arch priestess? Now that I am back, I will need someone to take charge of our faith and advise me."

<Oh, Devon! Thank you so much. Nobody deserves that more than Mersia,> Izzy said secretly to him.

"My lord, Wayfarer, I... I... Yes, of course. It would be the highest honour. I thank you with all my heart," Mersia said. Her face lit up with glee.

"Then, it is done." A radiant explosion of golden light engulfed them both, and Devon felt a link appear. He sent warm feelings of friendship and gratitude to Mersia across the freshly forged bond. "In my realm, there is a temple that I built many hundreds of years ago. It has sat empty for all this time. I would like it to become the centre of our faith.

I also included suitable accommodation for my arch priestess. Would you be willing to take it as yours and make it your new home?"

Mersia looked stunned and almost apoplectic with delight. "Yes, my lord." The elf paused and looked worried.

"Just talk to him, Mersia; he is quite friendly and approachable," Izzy said.

"Well, uhm, you see, lord Wayfarer, I'm just a priest. I don't know what an arch priestess is supposed to do," Mersia admitted.

"Well, talking to me is a good start. Having the courage to speak up and tell me when I'm an idiot would be helpful. Izzy is very good at that," Devon said. He heard Izzy snort and grinned to himself. "Think of our faith as a school with you as the headteacher. Whatever you need from me, just ask. I want us to be friends and move forward as a team. You, Izzy, and me."

Mersia beamed the happiest smile.

Izzy looked delighted. <You are laying it on a little thick, but I am very proud of you. You have made Mersia so happy.>

<I'm enjoying myself. Besides, she deserves it.>

<Indeed, she does, and you deserve my thanks, but you will have to wait for my complete gratitude,> she said, with a sly smile.

<Oh, wow! Are priestesses allowed to do such things?>

<I have a very generous god. I'm sure he won't mind,> she replied.

"Isabelle, I hereby promote you to the role of my high priestess," he said.

"Thy will be done, my lord," Izzy replied with a slight bow, and another golden flash enclosed them briefly. <You're still an idiot, though.> She beamed a bright, innocent smile at him.

Devon tried to conceal his amusement with a slight cough. "Ahem! The first item on our agenda is the goddess of light, Theia. She has requested a merging of faiths. As it happens, Light and Justice align very well. I would like you both to discuss the matter and let me know your thoughts. I consider anything that makes us stronger to be good."

"Yes, my lord," the two priestesses chorused.

After all the walking, they were still only halfway down the twisting road. Devon still had two more guests to address, though. He turned his attention to the lady gnome.

"Now, Glimmer, I must admit that I am confused about what I can do for you," Devon said, smiling down at her. She had all the features of a fully grown human but on the scale of an eight-year-old child. She was a little over four feet tall with long, richly coloured nutmeg hair organised in the most complex network of interwoven plaits that he had ever seen. Her head looked a little larger by proportion than an adult human's, and her eyes were enormous. They were a striking golden brown that was hypnotic and drew his gaze straight to them. Devon had always liked gnomes.

"My lord, the gnomes have always been dedicated followers of the Wayfarer," Glimmer said. She was not shy by gnomish standards, and her mission was to secure her people's place next to their deity. "Our race is often more persecuted than others because of our size. We are tired of the constant oppression and seek sanctuary in your domain." She took a deep breath. "In exchange, I bring a pledge from my people. By your leave, we, the gnomes, wish to dedicate our lives to an alliance with your cause. We beg you to take us into your employ and use our skills." She looked up at him and gave him a beseeching smile.

"Truly, this is a favourable day for me," Devon said in all honesty. "I gladly accept. When can you start, and how many of you are there?"

Glimmer's face fell. "I'm afraid that is the bad news. The Tinkers number just ninety-two artisans. Our Ranters' guild numbers a sad thirty-six fighters, and the Boffs' guild have a mere seventy academics. As for our race, we number just shy of six-hundred."

Devon was instantly sad that one of his favourite races had suffered such decimation. "I am deeply sorry to hear such tragic numbers, Glimmer. Thank you for informing me. Have you brought your people with you today?"

"Every last one, my lord. Long ago, our Boffs prophesied this day, and no one would dare miss it. Today is an auspicious day for our history books."

"You have my word that you will all have good homes to call your own, the best magical protection we can offer, and the rightful freedom to be the wonderful people I used to know. We'll work hard to restore your numbers to their former strengths."

"Then you will have our oaths. We can start now," Glimmer replied.

"I have some fascinating things to introduce you to, lady gnome. I think you will enjoy my design centre and I will introduce you to a unique lady called Beth. She is a technomancer – a new ability that combines this world's technology with magic. I think you'll both become good friends. I have already created a guildhall for you and the others, and I have a few projects I would like to discuss very soon."

"Wow! You work fast. Thank you, my lord," Glimmer replied, excitement oozing from her words. "We will strive to learn everything we can and build you the best artefacts ever created by my people."

Devon nodded his thanks to the gnome and turned his attention to Sintra. "And that just leaves you, lady elf. I hope to remove the need for Defiance very soon. I need to make reparations to you for not being around when you and your people needed me. Tell me what I can do for you, my friend."

"My lord, my wildest dream was that this day would come to us during my lifetime. Now you offer me magic and call me your friend. It is already enough."

Devon smiled. This elf had spent a lifetime being austere and often felt the weight of the realm on her shoulders. There must be something he could do. <Izzy, help, what does Sintra want? Would she be a teacher? Retire? What?>

Izzy's laugh tinkled into his mind. <Relax, stupid. You worry too much. Let her have today, then ask her again when all this is over. I suspect she would love to be a teacher, though. She taught me well.>

Finally, the road straightened out, and Devon gave the guests a minute to take in the beauty of the nexus. "Take your time. Come over when you are ready." He guided Izzy onward, and they sat together on the low wall by the mana-pool.

"Devon, you know we have to try and rescue princess April from the queen's clutches. We can't let her die because of Astley's treachery. Besides, there are some very credible rumours floating around that she just came of age. With magic, she could be a powerful ally for us and a huge thorn in the queen's side."

"I am fairly sure that we already have her and her lady in waiting, strapped down and sedated in the hospital. I need someone who can identify her by sight to confirm my suspicions," Devon said. "Our foray into the city was part of my plan for fast-tracking the Shadows' training. I hope that our army will grow soon, and I need them to train others. Lead them too, when the time comes. They're becoming extremely talented, Izzy. The guards never saw us coming."

"Devon, I want to fight the battle for Triana with you, but I have decided that I want to become a teacher when all this is over. My days as a resistance fighter end when the queen is finally dead."

Devon was pleased that Izzy had made her choice. She'd fought for the resistance throughout her life, and he understood her need for change. Now all he had to do was persuade her to talk openly with Gwen about their relationships.

"I can still read your thoughts, idiot," Izzy laughed. "I don't want to fight anymore. The liberation of Triana will be my last battle. As for Gwen; of course I will talk to her. I see how you feel about each other and how you feel about me. Just relax. Gwen will want to fight by your side, and I will be here supporting you both."

Devon laughed out of sheer relief. "Thank you. That means a lot to me." He hadn't realised just how much the issue had been weighing on his mind. "Back to the original subject, we destroyed over twenty patrols last night and a squad of the biggest ogres I've ever seen."

Izzy looked at him in amazement. <The queen lost over two-hundred guards. Not only them but her elite force of ogres perished. That was a lot of training you did!>

<I told you they were good. I want them to become the best.> Devon grinned at her.

Izzy pressed herself closer to him. "I'll wager you are right then. That was the princess and her lady you rescued. Astley said she was being taken to the arena by the queen's guard, which, according to our intelligence, consists of fifteen of her most fierce and loyal ogres. Sometimes, you make it easy to forget just how powerful you really are. The strength you lend to those of us you have bonded with is beyond comprehension to my people."

Mitsey walked up to him and jumped up to sit on his lap. "Am I interrupting something?" the goblin grinned.

Devon and Izzy looked at her in shock, but Mitsey continued to grin. "You said you wanted to talk, boss. I get a crick in my neck talking to you tall people. Glimmer would prefer talking to you from here too. She's a short arse like me." She looked down at his lap. "Yes, I'm sure she'd like it here cuz I'm bloomin luvin it right now."

Devon snorted. Goblins were always fun to know, and he already liked this one. Her skin was a lighter green than the dryads, a more delicate shade. Her wild hair contrasted her skin as it was a flame red and cut to a length just longer than a crop. Her face had more curves than human faces, making it look a little more pronounced in the cheekbone area. Mitsey's eyes were as large as Glimmer's but a beautiful dark green, and they glowed as Izzy's did. Her entire being radiated intelligence and cunning. She had a small mouth that contained very sharp teeth. Her petite body was athletic, but there was no polite way to describe her figure. Her curves were lewdly exaggerated and buxom.

"You mentioned that you would like to join our team, lady goblin. Are you any good?" Devon asked her. He already knew he wanted her in his force but had to lead into it somehow.

"Devon, Mitsey is the best you could find and then some. She is an accomplished assassin, a talented engineer, and the best thief in the business."

Mitsey pointed at Izzy. "What the lanky one said, plus I am fabulous in bed. Very fertile and would give you strong babies."

Izzy coughed hard, trying to disguise a loud swear word. She'd forgotten how forthright Mitsey could be.

Devon choked at her words. "Wow! Goblins aren't shy, are they?" he laughed. He couldn't believe she'd just said that. He decided to cut to the business part. "If you want to join us, then I want you on our team. Now, why don't you strip to your underwear and climb into the mana-pool."

Mitsey grinned back at him. "I've heard some lines in my time, lord Wayfarer. That one is new, though."

"Down, girl. Just get in the pool. Go and find your mana-wyrm," Izzy growled at the goblin.

Mitsey touched her forehead in a mock salute and jumped down. Instead of stripping to her underwear, she took the lot off and did a twirl. She laughed raucously and slipped into the mana-pool.

<You will need to watch out for her, Devon,> Izzy said seriously. <She seems to like you quite a lot, and goblins don't often take no for an answer.>

<Maybe, but I've got enough on my plate right now. The queen is still breathing, and there's a whole city to liberate. I want all the innocents out, and the whole place flattened. Do you think Mitsey can lead troops?>

<Yes. I can't sing her praises highly enough. Goblins are super smart, but she is even smarter. Whatever you need to do, you can trust her to make it happen.>

<I need to know for sure who those two fairies are. If I assume it's the daughter and her lady and I'm wrong, two innocent lives will be lost, which will go straight on my conscience.>

<I would like to hear what they have to tell us,> Izzy said

<Beth?>

<Hello, yes?> Beth replied after a brief pause.

<What are the chances of us talking to those fairies we captured yesterday?>

<They're both awake. The anaesthetic wore off from their last surgery over an hour ago. The one who claims to be a princess refuses to eat common food, but the other is currently forcing some soup and water down. Those bastards messed them up good and proper, Devon.>

<You're my shining, ginger star, Beth. Can we meet you in the hospital in an hour? I have someone anxious to meet you. Bring Beks if she's free.>

<Ginger and proud,> Beth laughed. <No worries. We'll see you then. Beth out.>

He chuckled at her sign-off. Finn had recently explained to him what a 'nerd' was. Beth was what he'd used as the definition.

"Looks like we accidentally rescued a princess, Izz."

****_****

Devon stood on the stone dais with Missy and Fate. He'd just broken the news of Aria's death to Missy, and he wasn't sure if she was stoic about her daughter's death or just cold. She certainly didn't seem upset by the news.

"Don't mistake my indifference, Wayfarer," Missy said. "I am sad Aria has passed, but I also know that she will be reborn eventually. Do you have her soul?"

Devon handed Missy Aria's soul sadly. Regardless of Missy's emotions, Devon was upset at the dryad's death. He had made Astley suffer as much as he could, but it had still not been nearly enough.

"I will double the price Fate offered you for Astley's soul and another two favours for the queen's painful demise," the goddess of nature said firmly. "It will entertain me to make Astley's soul suffer."

Fate nodded her head to Devon so that he knew she was happy to concede the deal to Missy.

Devon handed over Astley's soul to Missy, and she took it with a satisfied snarl.

"Thank you, Reaper. The deals are done. You may depart," Fate said, ending proceedings in her usual abrupt manner.

Devon shrugged sadly, opened a portal, and left quietly. There was nothing left to say.

Chapter 24

Ending the decline

Devon's determination to destroy Triana drove him forward. The need for vengeance had been growing inside him since Shalim had returned his memories. He barely slept, and June had to nag him to eat properly. There were so many other things to do, but nothing else seemed as important when his sight was so intently focused on the fairy queen. He wouldn't be alone when he arrived in her throne room, not this time. This time the victims of her oppression would be there by his side, empowered by magic and trained to fight back.

Mitsey had sworn herself to become his student that same day, while Glimmer had officially pledged her people's loyalty and commitment to his cause. He'd left Mitsey asleep in the library after prescribing her a three-hour crash course of literature. He couldn't plan much without Mitsey, so he decided to work it out later when she woke back up.

Beth and Beks had agreed to take Glimmer and her gang of Tinkers under their wings, and the group buried themselves in the wonders of magic, technology, munitions, artillery, and biosciences. Tonight, they were going to sleep in the library. The gnomes were anxious to please, and they seemed desperate to cram their heads with as much as they could.

Izzy had taken Mersia into her care, which just left Sintra. There was a little time now for Devon to take the elf on a tour of the settlement, and then he'd asked Beth to demonstrate the war-room, during which they could talk about tactics.

The dryads were still scooting around, seemingly unaffected by their sister's demise. They were raising moon-willow behemoths and planting other magical plants and flowers. More of them had arrived overnight, and they had brought more bags full of many natural wonders. Magical mosses, fruit bushes, fungi, and herbs were all rapidly taking root as the druidesses' natural magic, infused them.

"They certainly seem happy here, my lo… I mean, Devon," Sintra said, smiling sheepishly.

Devon intended to use this quiet time with Sintra to get to know her better. She was a talented leader, and he needed her services when Defiance was no longer necessary. First, there was something that he had been aching to say. "Sintra, I am sorry that you had to endure such hardship over there. It wounds me deeply to think of your suffering while I was unable to help you and your people."

Sintra looked shocked. Warmth flooded her features. "Sadly, it is we who must be sorry. You were cursed while fighting for our cause. Our race has felt the guilt of that ever since. You will soon realise that every last elf follows you with devotion. It was the most triumphant moment for us when Isabelle told us of your resurgence."

He didn't have an answer for that. It had all gone so badly wrong back then. All because he chose to do everything alone and had assumed that a fellow deity would fight by the rules. It was a lesson hard to learn, but he wouldn't make that mistake twice. They both chose to walk in silence up the winding staircase that led high into one of the central moon-willow trees.

When Devon and Sintra emerged onto one of the aerial walkways that crossed from tree to tree, they looked out at the new forest. It had been dark for a while, and they could see the tiny, coloured lights of the pixies as they flitted in and out of the trees, hunting insects and playing wild games. The whole area was gently lit by the faint blue glow of magical energy that the trees exuded to protect themselves. It gave the forest a haunting feel which Devon loved. An enchanted forest at night was one of the most beautiful things to experience.

The new homes they found in the boughs were much bigger than they'd expected but still managed to be warm and cosy. Sintra was amazed when she saw a sizeable washbasin and a toilet in a small room. There were numerous cupboards and wardrobes which were part of the living tree, and the dryads had even formed shelving and benches along the walls.

Further investigation revealed a lovely bedroom with a sturdy wooden bed frame and mattress. There were two windows in the living area that looked out onto the walkway, which had glass windowpanes and brightly coloured curtains. The apartment's door even had a latch and lock mechanism. The new homes had basic furnishings, but all were well-made and practical. The villagers and his mana-forges had evidently been hard at work. Fortunately, people from the village had crafting talents, and their contributions had already been invaluable. They were working tirelessly for the cause. It was inspiring to see the new look of purpose that all the refugees had.

He then showed Sintra the new pods. They had initially been a source of utter bewilderment to the elf. The pods were considerably bigger on the inside, and Sintra stepped in and out several times in amazement.

He could tell that the elf was about to launch into another speech about how grateful the elves were, so he quickly changed the subject. That sort of talk made him squirm with embarrassment. He helped people because it was the right thing to do and didn't seek praise. He felt responsible for their plight and was convinced they deserved his best attentions. "Are you a fighter, Sintra?"

"Not anymore, lord. There is no point in fighting the fairy queen's soldiers in close combat. They always win. There are so few of us left that we cannot trade lives."

Devon felt sad that the fight had gone from her. She was content to lead the resistance, not fight for it. She had a point, he supposed. If you cannot win, then walk away. That was one of the first lessons he'd taught his Shadow Elite.

"How many of you are there?"

"Defiance has less than two-hundred members now. Recently, Astley's treachery has cost us dearly. They remain in Triana for now, protecting the refugees as they head out of the city to the gate. Your incursion the other night has resulted in the remaining guards staying around the palace. Now, they don't venture past the inner circle just outside the palace walls.

As for the faie races, the situation is not good. All the different species have suffered steady declines in their population over the centuries. The lifestyle we must endure, and the lack of magical sustenance, have bitten into our numbers hard. Of the wood elves, I know we have about two-thousand, but less than two-hundred of the survivors are male, which does not bode well. The dark elves have half our number, perhaps. Dwarves are rarely seen above ground these days, so I couldn't guess how many of them remain. Not nearly as many as the elves, I would wager. Goblins are notoriously fecund, but their males quickly die once they are bound in the fairies' chains, so they have suffered badly. Maybe a thousand of them remain. I believe Glimmer already discussed the gnomes' troubles with you. The fairies prefer male slaves of every race and take them wherever they can."

Devon nodded along sadly. Though a terrible story to hear, it was not dissimilar to the Earth realm's. Populations were predominantly female these days because the males didn't get a chance to remain free for long. It meant that his new city would, undoubtedly, become a matriarchy. Devon would not tolerate inequality in anything within his sphere of influence, and he would stomp on any that appeared.

"We cannot travel without authorisation from the fairies. Gathering information is dangerous, and so everything I know of the other races is hearsay," Sintra continued.

Sintra became lost in thought for a few moments. "You are the lord of justice, and therefore I feel it is right to tell you that not all fairies are evil. The season in which they are born determines a fairy's disposition. Summer fairies are warm and kind, while those born in winter tend to be cold and loveless. As you well know, the queen is winter born. She kills fairies born during the transitive seasons because they will inevitably become mystical creatures, powerful in magic. Those born of the summer lead a thoroughly miserable life of servitude and persecution. The queen is a jealous creature who has been persecuting her kind ever since she had them in her clutches. The fairies are dying out, too, although the queen is too arrogant to see it.

I would suggest you talk to the queen's daughter, April. She was born in the spring, much to the queen's shame. The queen chose not to murder her daughter but instead sought to enslave her. April's persecution is known to have been much worse than ours. I believe what Astley said about her impending execution. I hate to think that she might perish this close to the end of the queen's rule. Fairies are highly susceptible to arcane influences, and their forms are not as stable as other faie. We should not let them die out because of a vendetta."

Devon was disgusted and angry. This wasn't just an issue of persecution. Every one of the core species of ancient Earth was rapidly approaching extinction. Sintra's last words offered some hope, though. "It does my heart good to hear you consider the plight of the fairies as well. Maybe there is still hope for the faie to live peacefully and for populations to build again."

"It seems that even a god has dreams." She smirked. "Do you have plans to rescue the princess?"

"You need not worry about princess April. She is alive after her ordeals in the terracotta tower. She and her lady in waiting are both recovering in our hospital as we speak."

Sintra looked at him in wonder. "How? You haven't left this place since Astley told you about the princess." Sintra sounded amazed but a little confused.

"You know about our little – ahem – training exercise." Devon had the decency to look embarrassed. Their rescue of the fairies had been by chance, and it was sheer luck that the fairies they'd happened across turned out to be so important. "During our time in the city, we encountered a group of ogres escorting a wheeled cage into the western quarter, towards the arena. We killed the ogres and found two fairies inside the wagon."

"I am starting to think that Fate is a close friend of yours, lord Wayfarer. Finding the princess and her lady was fortunate indeed," Sintra replied, shaking her head.

"The good lady Fate is my mentor and a close ally currently. She and three other deities are committed to our cause and want the fairy queen dead almost as much as I do," Devon said. He wondered if Fate was intervening on his behalf. Good fortune had indeed smiled on him several times recently.

"Do you know anything of the other races?" he asked. "We ran into some silthrine during our trek to the city. What of them?"

"Many other races are hiding away outside of the city; the silthrine included, they don't survive well in the urban environment of Triana, so they are sent into the wilds to mine gems and harvest rare herbs. There may be as many as a few thousand of them remaining if you could find them."

"What of the cat-people? Yet another species to which I owe a debt," Devon said.

"There are cat-people living far out in the forest, but they hide themselves away. The fairies hunt them for sport, and if they catch one, they put it in the arena to fight. The Lionine, I am sad to say, were hunted to extinction, but the Leopardine species still exist in small numbers. There are still a few Pumine, and maybe even some other subspecies, but they are rarely sighted these days. Once Isabelle had departed for Earth realm, I sent messengers into the wilds and toward the mines, warning them all of what was to come. We received a few delegates last week, and they have returned to their lands to bring as many of their species as they can to the gate. Some had already arrived and came through today. I hope more will follow soon once they have seen that it is not a trap. Will you be able to house so many?"

"In this realm, there will be five-thousand moon-willows planted within the week. There are many more already grown in my realm, plus a large underground domain I created before the curse. It was going to be your new home, all those years ago, Sintra. Instead, I have linked my realm to this location and combined both sites.'

Sintra nodded but stayed silent, preferring to listen.

"Each moon-willow tree can provide housing for at least five families. Space will not be a problem in the short term," he said, forcing his inner musings onto an elf with so much already on her mind. "I also need to feed, clothe, and provide for all the people, at least initially. Once things settle, there will be even more to do establishing trades, guilds, administration, and facilities. I am not the one to organise such things as I have other work to do. This realm is filthy with persecution, and the gods have tasked me to begin the clean-up. All nexus-points are working now, so magical energy now saturates this world. It is time for a resurgence of the faie in the realm that was once their home."

Sintra turned sharply and faced Devon. "My lord Wayfarer, can I be of service? I feel you have been leading me to the question." Sintra smiled then laughed for the first time since she had arrived.

"I was starting to think you weren't going to offer," Devon answered in relief.

"The resurgence of the faie in our original homeland is indeed an exciting thought and a worthy cause," Sintra said. She hesitated and appeared to consider her next words carefully. "I will swear my services when the queen breathes her final breath. Fair?"

"I accept, and I am grateful for your offer. Now, madam elf, I'm recruiting for my new taskforce. I would like volunteers from a wide variety of species to set a good example. I'd like you to find some suitable candidates. How many refugees came through today?"

"Just over seven-hundred. There are some very suitable specimens that I could ask. Shall we meet at your box on wheels in three hours? I want to find myself a home among these gorgeous trees. I always dreamt I would get to live in one, one day. Thank you, lord Wayfarer, you have made an old elf very happy."

"Send those potential recruits to me sooner. I'll be in my box on wheels," Devon laughed.

****_****

Gwen finally tracked the two priestesses down in Haven's Hub. This was the first opportunity she had to go looking for Izzy since they'd parted company at Triana's wall.

"Izzy, you and I need to talk," Gwen said. She took yet another deep breath to try and calm herself. This conversation had already played out a hundred times in her mind and not once had it gone well. Mostly it ended with her losing her temper. Gwen did her best to stifle the hostility that bubbled in her.

Izzy whispered something to Mersia, who nodded and made her way to the Hub's exit swiftly, leaving her and Gwen alone in the vast, circular room. "I assume that this is about Devon?"

Gwen moved over to a designer bench and sat down. She motioned for Izzy to join her on the opposite seat. She arranged her face to convey a slight smile that she hoped looked less forced than it felt.

Izzy took the seat she'd been offered and tried to keep her body language open rather than just curling up into a ball, which is what she wanted to do. Devon's soldiers scared her, but Gwen was the one who terrified her most. Izzy could see the inner darkness that, while not evil, was cold and remorseless. Sometimes she even caught suggestions of Sulkiss' thoughts, and they were even blacker. The witch was an enigma to her. They had been allies and friends since they'd united against Beth at the village but had never become close.

"I know that you're roaming around in my head as we sit here, and I sort of want you to see what's in there. It will save me so many poorly chosen words."

"You are hard to read, Gwen. There are areas in your mind that are tightly closed and barricaded. I would guess that you have suffered so much that you have locked the memories away. I want to be your friend, not your enemy. Talk to me. It might help."

Gwen's face lost all discipline and fell straight to looking wretched. She bowed her head and sighed. "This conversation stays here. Nothing I tell you can ever reach Devon's ears, is that crystal clear?"

Izzy's mood became solemn, and her face echoed that. "I swear to that. Your secrets are my secrets," Izzy replied.

"I don't have anyone else that I can talk to. I never have," Gwen explained. "I've always managed on my own, never needing anyone else. Hextaine Corporation sent an assassin squad to kill my parents when they tried to flee from their jobs." Darkness crossed her features as that particular mental wound opened back up. She clasped her hands together and squeezed hard. "I was taken and raised in a corporate nursery and taught to be a fighter from an early age. They used torture, pain endurance, and starvation as ways to motivate us, and then, when they deemed us ready, sent us out to capture or murder anyone who the corporation considered a target."

"That's appalling – you poor thing. I lost my parents when I was very young too. Luckily for me, Sintra rescued me and raised me to become–" Izzy's thoughts crashed. While she had never endured torture or any cruel treatment from Sintra, her situation was almost identical to Gwen's in every other way. She had been taken at an early age and raised as a killer. Izzy had found her salvation in the priesthood and academia. It seemed that Gwen had not been so lucky. She reached across the gap and took Gwen's hand in her own. "Our situations are very similar. I was lucky, Gwen. I found religion and became a priestess of Devon's. From there, I learnt many languages and lost myself in literature. I have always adored history."

Gwen tried to force a conciliatory smile for Izzy. The elf meant well, but what Gwen had revealed so far was a small fraction of what she had actually gone through. It was doubtful they had anything in common at all other than their worship of Devon. However, Gwen needed a friend. She had pushed everyone away, all through her miserable existence, and maybe it was time to let someone through her barriers. Izzy felt like a light that had stumbled into her dark world yet was unafraid to be there.

"For me, it was comic books and fantasy stories," Gwen explained. "Tales of magic and sword fights. Superpowers and strange mystical creatures. Now all the fantasy is happening around me, and I feel like it's me who isn't real anymore. Devon has made me into some sort of hero way beyond my imagination, and I am proud to be the person I have become. For the first time ever, I am proud to be me, something I never dreamed might happen. I always despised myself."

Izzy squeezed Gwen's hand sympathetically, her face radiating concern for the dark witch's insecurities. "We have all become mighty through our bonds with him. He is the son of the progenitor, and we share his power, Gwen. Think about it," Izzy enthused, doing her best to raise Gwen's mood.

Gwen looked up and focused intently on Izzy. Her eyes took on a manic gleam, and she grabbed Izzy by the shoulders, gripping her tightly. "He is the light that has entered my world, and I will do anything I can to keep him there. Anything! Even kill, Izzy."

"Woah! Hang on, Gwen. Relax. I am not trying to take him from you." Izzy gulped and took several deep breaths. Gwen's grip was starting to become painful.

"You love him. Every look you give him makes that clear enough. We can't both have him, so it boils down to you or me. Aria is dead now, so she isn't a contender anymore. Rumour has it she wanted to marry him."

Izzy squeaked. "Gwen, you're hurting me. This isn't an argument. Please, calm down and listen to a suggestion I have. You have my oath that you will not lose him because of me."

Gwen looked at her hands in shock as if realising she owned them for the first time. She relaxed her grip and clasped them in front of herself instead.

Izzy breathed a sigh of relief. She stretched her shoulder a little and rotated her arms to allow the blood to flow freely once again. She reached over and took both Gwen's hands and held them gently. Izzy did her best to mimic the technique Madi had used on Devon back in the village. She looked intently into her eyes while softening her expression.

"He is a god, Gwen. Thousands already love and worship him. We are not the first to love him or want to offer him our affections either. If we want to keep him close, we have to share. Will you share him with me, Gwen?"

Gwen pondered Izzy's words. She didn't want to share him, but there was sense to what Izzy said. If she tried to eliminate the elf because she was competition, all she would succeed in doing is incurring Devon's wrath. At least by sharing, they both strengthened their hold on him. "We can share, but I am staying right by his side for as long time as I am able."

"Then we have an agreement. I aim to become a teacher and historian and stay right here. I will not fight you for your place by his side. I only want him, just as much as you do. We can care for him better as a team and each gain a friend as a bonus."

Gwen smiled her first genuinely happy smile in days. Relief washed through her. "Thank you. I think we can both benefit from this, and I need a friend at the moment."

Izzy smiled at her ally and friend. "So do I, Gwen. I really do."

Chapter 25

The Shadows grow

Devon was sitting in Haven's front room and thinking about the madness occurring around him. His Shadows were sitting with him. Mitsey was busy regaling everyone with the tale of when she'd stolen the Wayfarer's pendant. The others listened in fascination to the goblin's (only slightly embellished) deeds. He was pleased with how quickly they had all become friends.

<Master?>

<Yes, Abi?>

<Your account has been credited with the latest soul payments, plus the bounty Missy promised you for Astley. I have started work on the additional pods.>

<That's great, Abi. Thank you. There is just so much to think about.>

<Master, I recommend learning the art of delegation.>

<You are correct as always, oh wisest of housekeepers,> he replied. Mitsey had finished her story, and so he decided to share his musings.

"Firstly, I want to say how pleased I am that you seem to have become friends so quickly," Devon said with a smile. His smile faded when he saw a few uncomfortable looks exchanged between them. He noticed that Lorn glared at each one and gave them an almost imperceptible shake of her head.

"They argue like cats and dogs, but they work at it and bury any differences quickly," Izzy said, slumping down in a chair that had appeared for her.

Devon looked at Lorn in shock. Since he'd agreed to take them as students, he had got the impression that they were all the best of friends. Had he been naïve?

"Lorn?" he said, focusing on her with his eyebrow raised.

"What Izzy says is true, Devon, but we all made a pact never to trouble you with any disagreements we might have. We swear that it will never affect our duties."

The others nodded along as Lorn laid out the reality of life in the barracks.

Devon didn't know how to react to that. He was a little upset that they weren't getting along as well as he had thought, but also annoyed with himself for thinking it would be permanent sunshine and rainbows in their lives. He settled for a nod. "Fair enough, but if anyone has an issue, I want them to speak up. I don't want anyone suffering in silence. We don't fight for the freedom of others to be miserable ourselves. Is that clear?"

"Yes, sir," they all replied.

Devon grinned at them. "Now, to business. I am thinking about our future and want to include you all in this discussion. Soon, there will be recruits waiting outside. Our numbers will increase. We will become a small army, and with that comes challenges. So, I ask you for ideas."

"We need a name," Mitsey said.

"We have a name. Devon calls us his Shadow Elite. It's a name from centuries ago. I love it," Lorn replied, her voice proud.

Izzy nodded her head emphatically. "I think it is a perfect name. I have read about the original Shadow Elite. If you can walk in their footsteps, they'll write songs about your exploits."

"We need an emblem," Grace said. "Something awesome we can have emblazoned on our armour."

Devon held up his hand. "That I leave for you to discuss and decide upon, although I maintain the right of veto if I hate it," he said with a chuckle.

"Master, you have guests waiting outside," Abi announced.

Devon sighed. He'd wanted the chance to chat to his new team, but yet again, time was insufficient. He took a deep breath. "We'll come back to that discussion another time. Think about it. I'm open to all ideas." He grinned at them. "We have some recruits waiting for us outside, and I need you to run them through their induction. Give them their symbiot, get them scanned, and then to the library. You all know how it goes. Try and learn as much about them as you can, and I want your thoughts on our group's potential roles. I am trusting you to guide them through their initial training fast. We need to move on Triana soon, and I want those that suffered at the queen's hand to take a key role in her downfall."

"Yes, sir," they all said in one voice.

Devon walked out of Haven to find over thirty creatures standing by the caravan, looking lost, confused, and a little scared. Devon gave them his friendliest, most reassuring smile, and that appeared to settle a few nerves.

"Good afternoon. I assume Sintra passed my request for willing volunteers to you?"

He received enthusiastic mumblings and nods of affirmation. Devon scanned the crowd using his Wayfarer's aura skill and was relieved to see that they were all good at heart and loyal. He had the 'divine truth', which did the same to a large group, but he mainly used that for show. He had a divine talent for seeing people's auras if he had the mana to spare. He was impressed to see the rich deep-golden auras of five ladies dressed all in white.

<Unicorns in their humanoid form, my lord,> Izzy said. <You are blessed, but they won't fight. They are a race dedicated to the empowerment and healing of others.>

He looked around and saw her coming down the steps with the others.

"Welcome, everyone. I asked for volunteers because this is the beginning of our war against the suffering of others. Soon the faie will be ascendant, and we will need champions. We need dedicated people who will swear their lives to our cause. If you doubt the cause or do not desire to commit to it, walk away right now."

There was silence. Not one of the refugees moved. They continued to stare at him, expectantly.

"My lord Wayfarer, is it true that we could become part of your guard?" a young male gnome asked.

"Not just my guard, but your guard, and everyone's guard. Your role will be to defend our sanctuary and to fight for our cause. It will be my honour to fight alongside you. Soon we march on Triana, and I would like you to be there with us. You will see a lot of action here and in many other different places. I can promise you that. If you are willing to make the bond, of course."

"It would be a great honour, lord," one of the unicorn ladies said, "but we cannot fight. We could care for everyone's wellbeing, though. We are anxious to work for your cause. Could we be considered?" The five white-clad ladies looked at him, hopefully.

Devon grinned. "Yes, of course; we will need every kind of support. We would be very fortunate to have you with us."

The ladies smiled happily and started to chat excitedly amongst themselves.

“Ahem! Please follow the rest of my team. They will be guiding you through the induction. Feel free to ask them anything you need to know, but obey their wishes.”

The crowd trooped away, following Lorn and the others toward the keystone which stood open in readiness.

****_****

Devon sat on the temple steps and looked out onto his realm. It resided inside the biggest of the moon-willow trees, which the dryads had explicitly raised for the task. Once grown, they had created a vast area inside the base and wide steps leading up to a beautiful archway carved with animals and creatures. Then Devon had formed the interior, which was an ornate crystalline pyramid that filled the space. The ceiling glowed with a golden light which shone down onto clear crystal mezzanines. Seating occupied the centre, which faced a dark translucent crystal platform at the far end. It had two curved staircases, one on either side leading up to it. Later, he’d added two channels that guided water from an enchanted spring, located on the far side of the pyramid’s interior, down past the stage, then flowed out either side of the entrance steps. He’d engineered the channels so that the healing water tinkled and sang as it flowed through the hall.

He had called his city Sanctuary because that was its purpose. It was built from a forest of moon-willows accompanied by trees, shrubs, and plants from almost every realm. The dryads had worked hard to integrate so many species, resulting in the most magical of herbs existing happily next to the most mundane flora. This was the forest that Missy had promised to replicate for him on the Earth realm. The sheer variety of plants here was an alchemist’s heaven.

The temple sat on one side of the city’s enormous central hexagon, with the main archway that led down into the extensive underground section taking up another. Next to that was the waygate that led between the centre of Sanctuary and the clearing of the settlement. The other four constructions were also inside magical moon-willow trees. The large, multileveled city and guild halls occupied the following two sides, and the last two were a crafters’ centre and theatre. A dark green, marble-like stone covered the hexagon with a broad, shallow fountain in the centre. Devon had intended this area to become a thriving market, but it currently just looked lonely. Still, it was early morning, so it wasn’t a huge surprise.

A quiet hour passed while Devon allowed his thoughts to drift. His focus returned when he noticed Mersia walking toward him across the hexagon, accompanied by Izzy and Gwen. His witch had Sulkiss, her dragon, perched on her shoulder, and she was feeding him fruit. Devon guessed that the dragon was hungry after his life in the cave. His old friend seemed to possess a good sense of balance, which was probably for the best because Gwen didn't seem to pay much attention to the smoothness of his ride.

Elsewhere, Devon's Shadows were busy training all the recruits that had joined them yesterday. He had spent some time last night crafting their equipment, and now the trainees just needed time in the library and the training room.

The unicorns had been excused from the training because they were tending to patients. Some of the refugees had come through the waygate in a deplorable state of health. Of course, April and her lady in waiting were still recovering in the hospital too. The princess had refused to talk to anyone but had at least confirmed her identity for them.

"Good morning, my lord," Mersia said.

"It is a good morning, Arch Priestess. I was hoping to see you today," Devon replied. "This is the temple I mentioned yesterday. The facilities are on the upper levels," he added, indicating the giant moon-willow behind him. "I was wondering if it might be suitable for your new home."

Mersia looked past him and gasped.

Izzy smiled to herself. She knew that her old friend would love it regardless of how it looked. Her beloved god had created it, and that was all that mattered in Mersia's eyes.

"May I see inside, my lord?" Mersia asked, her voice trembling with anticipation.

"Of course. If you like it, then it is yours," Devon said with a kind smile. "I was hoping you might take ownership and turn it into the hub of our faith."

If it was possible to run while maintaining a solemn posture, then Mersia managed it. She was also struggling to conceal her wide smile underneath an expressionless mask. That attempt wasn't going so well.

What made Devon smile was Izzy trying to keep up with her. Every few steps, she had to break into a run. His smile broadened when a black-clad arm encircled his waist, and a sexy witch pressed herself against him.

"Good morning, gorgeous," Devon said to Gwen.

"It is now," she replied, pulling him into her embrace more tightly. "You look like you haven't slept much. Busy night?"

"Yep! There's still so much to do, and I'm anxious to move on Triana as soon as the new troops are ready."

Gwen glanced around at the vast trees and structures. "So, this is your world?"

"It is. Every god or goddess gets one, and we can mould and shape them to our will while we are alone there. Once sentient creatures arrive, our powers to shape the environment cease," Devon explained.

"I knew that. Your library is full of interesting things to learn," Gwen replied. "While I was in there yesterday, the whole room expanded. Does it do that often? The place is even more stuffed with literature now."

"Splendid! That means that the Pantheon granted my request for a restock. Hopefully, there will be some modern titles in there finally. I mustn't forget to send a team across to Jeffery's keep to escort him here along with his library."

"Well, when I told Glimmer about your library, the gnomes practically moved in. They're extremely keen, you know."

Devon had to smile when he heard that. If you asked a gnome about something they didn't know, they got a little upset. They hadn't changed at all after so many years. "Do you want to see this temple then?" he asked.

"Nope! Architecture bores me."

Devon snorted. "Shall we look in on the princess and the other refugees then?"

Gwen smiled, then nodded. She held on tightly to him as they walked. If she had her way, she'd never let him leave her side, especially after the incident with Aria. Losing Devon was now her greatest fear. She and Izzy had agreed to share his affection. They didn't want to, but Izzy had been right. If they didn't share, one would become the loser, and neither wanted to contemplate that.

****_****

Devon selected the hospital cube on the mirror and waited for the entrance to go clunk. He was surprised when April's lady in waiting came out through the door in a hurry. She jumped when she saw Devon and Gwen directly in front of her, then fell to her knees.

"My lord, thank you so much. How can I ever thank you enough for saving us? We would certainly have died a horrible death if not for your intervention," the lady grovelled.

Devon leant down and gently cupped her chin, then guided her back to her feet. "I don't need any repayment, and please, don't kneel in front of me. It's not necessary."

"But I owe you my life, lord. Let me join you, please. I desperately want to fight. I've always wanted to fight."

Devon was a little overwhelmed. He quietly examined her aura. It never hurt to check. People this keen sometimes had a motive, but this woman's aura was as pure as any he'd seen.

"I don't even know your name," he said while marvelling at the way the fairy's wings shimmered as the ambient magical energy reacted with them. Fairies had two sets of translucent wings that allowed them to fly in energy-rich environments. As she breathed, they opened and closed gently. Her hair was several shades of golden and clung to her features as it flowed down to her neck. Deep blue eyes flecked with gold shone back at his stare. Her face looked finely carved, and there was a deep intelligence behind her eyes. He thought her pretty, but that was the same for every fairy. She had the typical, delicate features that every fairy possessed. They were magical creatures and often used their looks and magically enhanced allure to influence others. You had to keep your wits about you when negotiating with these tricky creatures; a lesson he'd learnt the hard way.

"I am called Fern, my lord," she said, executing a perfect curtsey. Her face then transformed from grateful to determined in the blink of an eye. "You have used your truth aura on me, I can feel it, so I must tell you this. I am autumn born, not of the summer as my mother firmly claimed. I am a transient fairy, just as princess April is. Throughout my miserable, hateful life, I have wanted revenge for those that made my life hell. There is nothing that I would not offer you for that chance. Will you give it to me?"

Devon and Gwen stared at the little fairy in shock. That diatribe had come straight from her heart. Her aura plainly showed him that there was not a trace of deceit amongst her words.

"Will you offer me your bond and become one of our soldiers?"

"In a heartbeat, yes."

"Then let's go and see how your ex-mistress is doing. Maybe then, both of you can take your symbiot, and we get you sworn in."

"I do not know what that foolish girl has told you, but she is not permitted to speak on my behalf," princess April said haughtily, emerging from the hospital's entrance.

"Good morning, April. I'm glad to see you've recovered from your ordeal," Devon said, trying to keep his face from scowling at the fairy's attitude.

"Save it, Wayfarer. I am not one of yours," April said, looking at him with contempt. "I will forgive the one transgression, but in future, you will address me as your highness."

Devon wasn't in the mood for her attitude. They hadn't needed to rescue this overprivileged wannabe, but they had done so because it was right. None of this added up. She spoke to him with more contempt than her mother used to, yet she was supposed to be a sympathiser to the resistance.

"So much like your mother," he chided. "Unlike her, though, you were born mortal, and you ought to realise that you are nothing special outside of her dome. Your mother is doomed, and you are a princess in name only as of now. You have no rights or entitlements unless you choose to earn them first. If you dare talk to anyone here in the way you have just spoken to me, I will send your pathetic carcass back to where we found it." It was a bluff, of course, but she didn't need to know that.

April glared at him angrily then sagged. "Fine! Yes, I owe you a life debt, and I thank you for rescuing me, but I will not join your faith or bow to you in any way."

Devon snorted. "I have never asked anyone here to do either." He turned his back on April and spoke to Fern. "Let's get you some magic."

"I will take a symbiot too, Wayfarer," April said, her voice back to its aloof tone.

"You will not," Devon retorted, "and unless you change that foul attitude, you never will."

"You owe him your life, your high – April. Why are you so mean to him?" Fern said. Her chin stuck out, and she looked determined to stand up to the woman she had spent almost her entire life serving.

The princess suddenly looked sad as Fern's words sank in. "I do not know how to be any different. Fern is correct, though. Please, may I take a symbiot, Wayfarer?" she said, trying to sound civil. "I apologise for my behaviour. I am my mother's daughter; I have never known how to be a normal person."

Devon finally smiled. "How about we both make an effort to be nicer to each other? Who knows? Maybe we may even become friends?"

Chapter 26
She's gonna blow

Devon watched as the two fairies floated in the magical dust and peered down into its depths. He knew full well that the princess had endured a difficult life of abuse combined with inherited privilege. Devon was willing to tolerate her attitude as long as she helped their cause and tried to play nice most of the time.

April's bonding with her mana-wyrm was going smoothly but what Devon now focused on was the monster that rose straight from the depths toward Fern.

<Oh, bugger me backwards! It's only the bloomin' missus. Heck! Hide me, yung un, that female be bonkers,> Brack said, his thoughts riddled with panic.

<Seriously, Brack? There's more of you?> Devon responded.

<Ya daft, sod! There be loads of us down there in the arse-end of da pool. Me problem iz dat wun be crazy.>

Devon had to laugh. If he had understood correctly, his poor mana-dragon seemed to be in a panic because Fern was about to assimilate his wife. Maybe the creature had been enjoying his newfound freedom a little too much. He'd have to ask Lorn to tell him what they were saying. She was a powerful telepath and could listen in on the mana-dragons' conversations.

Eventually, April clambered out by herself, looking triumphant. "Those vermin in the palace are going to get what is coming to them," she stated.

"That they are, princess. Are you joining my group of soldiers then?"

The fairy started to look confused. "Uhm, forgive me, Wayfarer, I suddenly do not feel very well. Something is changing inside me." April collapsed down to one knee and held her head in her hands.

A thought occurred to Devon, and he examined her with his aura-reading ability. Her aura went straight to deep scarlet. <Gwen, HELP! April has just popped a curse! Her mother must have turned her into a trap.>

<Hold her!>

Devon leapt at April and grabbed her slim arms. <Chains?>

<Yep, let's get her neutralised. I think she's got a 'destruction' hex on her, triggered by her new mana,> Gwen answered.

Black chains wrapped themselves around the fairy princess, and the mana-sapping mist got to work. Devon held her firmly as what little magic April had just accumulated seeped away.

Gwen finished her chant and touched April's forehead, wincing as their skin met. <Bloody hell! That cow has turned her daughter into a living bomb! With the amount of magical energy that's down here, she could have destroyed us all.>

Devon remembered that they had two fairies in their care currently and shot a look back at the mana-pool. Sure enough, Fern was lying unconscious on the surface of the magical dust. Mana-dragons seemed to be a guaranteed knock-out when they assimilated with you.

<Have you got this for a minute?>

<Go, get her. This one's out cold, and I'm not sure she'll live through this. She certainly wasn't supposed to.>

Devon sprinted away toward Fern. <Do what you can, my love. What happens, happens.>

Once he'd laid Fern safely on the marble floor, he returned to Gwen.

Sulkiss had emerged and had a talon buried in April's chest.

"Sulkiss syphoned off the hex, so she's not going to explode. I've neutralised the spell pattern, but there's something very weird – oh crap! That's not cool," Gwen said, jumping back and grabbing her familiar as she did so. The shock was evident in her voice. "I think she's transitioning!"

A glowing golden sphere about twelve inches across emerged from April's chest with a mana-wyrm wrapped tightly around it. The creature looked at him and smiled a smile full of ethereal teeth. The orb, with the wyrm still hanging from it, shot his way with a flash of light and hit him in the chest, disappearing from view. There was no sensation of an impact, but it knocked him onto his back anyway. Devon felt like he was assimilating his mana-dragon all over again. Agony gripped him, and he wondered if this was the moment of his demise, outsmarted by the queen once again. Neither he nor Gwen had thought to check the two fairies for traps, curses, or spells, something they both now regretted with fervour.

Gwen raced to Devon's side. "No, no, no! Don't you dare leave me." She placed her palm on his forehead, and above the pain that coursed through him, he could feel the tingle as she sent one anti-spell after another into him.

Another sharp pain hit him in the chest, and he saw that Sulkiss' talon was now embedded in his torso. His old friend was trying to find malicious magic and syphon it away before it could do him harm.

"Whatever the hell that was, it wasn't malicious," Sulkiss pronounced.

"It's behaving in the same way a mana-wyrm would," Gwen said, shaken by these latest events.

The pain faded, and he was able to think again. "Whatever it's doing, it needs mana to do it. Its wyrm went with it." Devon felt a second bond wind around the one he had with his mana-dragon. It was April, and her intentions were friendly but determined. She had bound herself to the Reaper part of him. "Oh! That's new."

"What?" Gwen asked in alarm.

"It appears that I've inherited a djinn, and it's taken up residence inside me. The princess just bonded with me, and she did so without needing to receive my permission. I didn't even know that was possible. I think I can break the bond, though; it's weak."

A form emerged from his torso and hovered beside him. It was the djinn. Its upper half was a very rough outline of a humanoid, only twice as large. It consisted entirely of shadows as Shalim did. Its lower half tapered away into mist, and it didn't stand but hovered. The single clear indication that it was more than an apparition was its burning, red eyes. They had no detail, just two bright red beads of intensity, lodged within slightly corporeal darkness.

<Wayfarer.> The low voice that appeared in Devon's head was crackly and contained static. It lacked both gender and emotion. Where April's identity was in that new magical creation was beyond his knowledge. He just assumed she must still be in there somewhere. This voice bore no resemblance to the princess, though.

<Uh! April? Is that you?> he thought, lost in a state of confusion.

<I am Djinn. April is nought but a memory. Use me; command me. I am vengeance incarnate. My price for my services to you is that you grant me the queen's death by my power alone. I have a debt to pay.>

Devon thought about that for a moment. He needed to take Triana's soul. Killing her himself wasn't mandatory. He needed vengeance; the need gnawed at him. Now here was an alternative way to get it. By allowing this creature to kill the queen, he gained both the queen's death and an ally. <I can gladly offer you that payment without negotiation. Triana's soul is mine. She dies by your hand, or claw, or whatever you intend to use.>

<Then the deal is done, master.> With those few words, Djinn disappeared back into his chest.

Devon felt the weak bond he had with the djinn dissolve, and a new one form and strengthen significantly, becoming as strong as the one he had with Brack. The creature certainly lacked imagination when it came to names, though.

Gwen shook her head. "Never a dull moment around you, lover. The boredom of the village seems like a lifetime ago." She laughed wryly at her own humour.

****_****

Devon stood in the war-room with Beth, Gwen, and Izzy. He studied the three-dimensional representation of Triana.

Mitsey stood beside him. He'd put her in charge of the new sapper squad, a group he'd formed and equipped in consultation with her and Glimmer, consisting of ten engineers, all gnomes or goblins, with munitions expertise trained to get in and out of just about anywhere without being seen. Their objective was usually to leave strategically positioned explosive charges, but sabotage and havoc were also among their skillset. Red dots flashed on the map showing where they were to target their munitions during the final raid. Each sapper had a specially adapted vision enhancement that Beth had created. The implant would guide them to targets and highlight structural weakness, allowing them to improvise if the opportunity permitted. They even had their own specialist magical class, gifting them some very specific, destructive magic, which was slow to evoke but powerful. As a bonus, they were also accomplished sharpshooters. Devon regarded them as an elite resource to be used strategically and protected at all costs, so he had assigned them a group of five protectors who had infiltration skills. Mitsey had volunteered to lead the squad and, with her skills, she was busy turning them into petty thieves too. Glimmer had nicknamed them the Chaos Squad.

Beth was now busy feeding the agreed locations into their targeting systems.

Devon planned to take Triana tomorrow night, and he was working his troops hard with training today. Tomorrow, they could rest up and equip before moving out just before dusk.

He wanted the attacks to emphasise to the queen that her time was over, and she was powerless to stop him. It gave him pleasure to imagine her trembling on her throne, barking impossible orders for troops that were already dead or had surrendered. He hoped he could take as many creatures as possible alive, but that was their choice, not his.

Mitsey looked up at him and raised her eyebrow.

"Oh! Sorry, Mitsey, I was miles away. Yes, of course, if you are happy with the locations, then go and run some exercises with the others and make sure you have the routines right. I want every one of those towers down and all the key locations set to blow before the main push begins. I expect your people to coordinate with Beth to ensure none of our people are anywhere near your blast zones."

"Yes, boss. You can rely on us," Mitsey promised. "Will we get the stealth armour and rifles we discussed by lunchtime tomorrow?"

"Yes, it's on my priority list. Dismissed."

Mitsey executed an elegant salute and left the war-room.

"You have a talent for inspiring people. That sapper squad is a terrific weapon for urban warfare," Beth said.

"They can disable weapons and machinery too, which means, with you and Glimmer in here, we can make surgically precise incursions almost anywhere. You pick the target; they bring it down within hours. I created the Chaos Squad for your use. It plays to the strengths of you and your war-room. If you could talk Beks into joining you in here, then it would add her expertise to the mix."

"Then, the plans are made. Nothing left but the waiting," Beth said.

Devon snorted. "Maybe for you. I've got over forty sets of armour and a load of equipment to craft before lunchtime tomorrow. With the steady flow of volunteers we're receiving, it may even be more by now. We'll aim to march for the city tomorrow evening." He sighed and ran his hands through his hair. "I might as well make a start on it all now."

Beth looked at him then a mischievous smirk crept across her face. "No questions, be here at eight this evening. I've got a surprise for you."

He went to ask a question, but Beth held her hand up and shook her head. He shrugged and made his way out of the war-room.

Devon pondered his latest design of camouflaged armour while waiting for the room selector to bring the hub door around. It had initially been Pip's idea, but he planned to take that idea a lot further. Positioned correctly, runic markings could guide light around the wearer, while others could cause the armour's surface colour to alter to match the background. If done well enough, it would render the person wearing the armour virtually invisible without sapping their mana reserves, or, with a little applied power, they'd become undetectable.

He walked across the hub to his favourite designer bench, relaxed into it, and then got busy.

****_****

"Put this on," Izzy said.

Devon had been expecting Beth, but instead, his beautiful elf had been waiting for him in the war-room. She was wearing an exquisite purple gown, and she had a smart dress uniform draped neatly over her outstretched arm.

"That looks fancy. Is this one of your designs?"

Izzy beamed her best smile. "Oo! You guessed. You like?"

Devon laughed. "Let me put it on first, impatient elf."

Izzy couldn't stop smiling as she excitedly watched him dress in her creation. She was starting to share Devon's passion for designing.

Once he had dressed in the black outfit and Izzy had spent a minute straightening every seam, he examined his new costume. The jacket was stylishly cut, burgeoning at the shoulders and tapering tightly down past his bum. The trousers had a more conservative, straight cut but were tailored perfectly. Unusually, he had dress shoes and socks instead of his army-style boots. The jacket had a wide belt and showy, golden buttons with his logo of the scales of justice embossed on each. To finish it all off, there was a mithril version of the Wayfarer's scales pinned to his lapel with the word 'Commander' inscribed in black.

"You like?" Izzy repeated excitedly.

"It's lovely, Izz. Very smart indeed. What's the occasion?"

Izzy walked over to him, glanced at his elbow, and then twitched her head.

Devon managed to work out the hint and held out his elbow, and Izzy slipped her arm through.

She looked at him proudly. "I love you. Does there need to be another reason?"

He shook his head. "I love you too, but I know you're up to something."

"Just walk, smartarse."

"Picking up new words from the natives, elf?"

For the first time in her life, Izzy was truly happy. The troubles weren't over. The battle for Triana was yet to take place, but none of that mattered to her anymore. Being with him, her lover, and her god, felt right. She now believed that she had been destined to end up here, and she knew which golden-eyed goddess to give thanks to for that.

****_****

When Izzy and Devon emerged from the gateway to his realm, there was a cacophony of applause and cheers. Devon looked around, startled by the sudden noise and saw the 'Hex', as people now called it, awash with people clapping and whooping. Everyone was looking directly at him.

"And here he is, our saviour and greatest ally, the Wayfarer, Reaper, and lord of souls, DEVON!" boomed an amplified voice.

Devon was looking around, trying to find the source of the voice. It sounded a lot like Sintra, but he couldn't see her anywhere amongst the crowd. Then he spotted her on the upper steps of the temple.

Izzy was already guiding him forcefully toward the steps, and Devon thought it churlish to resist. Madi and Sintra were still working on providing entertainment for the city, and maybe this was their inaugural event – whatever it was, a celebration would do everyone good.

When Devon finally got to the steps, he turned to the many faces looking up at him. He noticed a clear area at the front, and his Shadow troops lined up within the space. They were all wearing dress uniforms like his, and all looked extremely smart and proud. They all stood at ease and smiled up at him.

"Did you organise all this?" he asked Sintra in amazement.

"Madi and I wanted to do something special for you, and young Beks suggested a party. So here we are, my lord," she replied.

"There's cake too," Izzy whispered in his ear. She grinned when he shuddered at the sensation of her lips, touching his earlobe.

"We thought perhaps you might like to formally welcome your soldiers to the ranks of the Shadow Elite by giving them this insignia,"

Madi said. "It's traditional to pin it on their lapel, then shake their hand and say a few encouraging words." She showed him a box of badges.

"I'll nip in the temple and change. I want my badge too," Izzy said, her voice eager. After the campaign, the badge would become a historical memento, and she intended it to be the first keepsake of her new life.

"Would you like to say a few words to your people, my lord?" Sintra asked.

"Urgh! Okay."

Sintra offered him a strange fat stick with a ball at the end that was attached to a string. He refused it and instead cleared his throat to use his 'divine voice.'

"Ladies and gentlemen, males, females, and creatures of indeterminate gender." His voice was commanding and strong. It was magically enhanced to engage any audience and positively influence their attitude toward him. He was a god; he had skills. "Thank you for taking the time to gather here tonight. Winning your freedom was just the first step of our journey together. Now we must all work as one community, not only to keep ourselves free but to make our liberty count."

An uproarious cheer thundered from the crowd.

"First, I would like to pay tribute to the brave individuals who have volunteered to join the ranks of the Shadow Elite. A force dedicated to the fight, not only for your freedom but for the freedom of everyone who needs them. Their lifelong commitment is to put down those who seek to subjugate and oppress – a fight which we will begin tomorrow evening in Triana. I want you all to show your appreciation as I call each soldier up and welcome them. Then afterwards, I believe there will be cake." He grinned, and the crowd went wild. Apparently, cake ranked right up there alongside freedom in their estimation.

His new army had a name, a dress uniform, and an insignia. By tomorrow, they would have the most advanced armour and equipment his talents could create. He was a very proud god. It was impressive how everyone had joined together to organise and assemble everything that he saw before him. In all, he welcomed fifty-two soldiers to his new army. He was glad to see that the unicorn medics had swollen in number to twelve now and that the ranks included a wide variety of creatures, all keen to represent their species.

Devon called each volunteer up by name and welcomed them with a few encouraging words based on some helpful notes added to each soldier's profile, fed into his mind by Abi. One after another, each creature would walk proudly back down the steps to loud applause, sporting their new Shadow Elite insignia with immense pride. Pip, Grace, and Mitsey received special badges as they were now promoted to sergeants, while Lorn's was different to everyone's because Devon had made her the army's captain. He would still fight alongside her, but now they had an official chain of command. In effect, Lorn now commanded the entire army, answering to him alone.

Once the ceremony finished, Madi whispered a few things in Devon's ear, and he nodded with a smile. He held his hands up for quiet and, eventually, the uproar died back to a subdued murmur of excited voices.

"My friends, I welcome you all to your new home. Until now, we have just known the area in Earth realm as 'the settlement', but now we shall consolidate everything. I would like to name this new city spanning two worlds, Sanctuary. That is what that name should mean to all of us. Soon, we will join a third realm to the name, and our Sanctuary and the freedom it represents will span multiple worlds. Those that seek to steal it from us will perish, as will those that seek to corrupt it from within. THIS IS OUR SANCTUARY, AND HERE; WE ARE STRONG!"

The uproar nearly deafened him. Every person here felt strongly about preserving the freedom they had dreamt of, and tonight that emotion peaked.

When the noise dimmed a little and people began to settle, Devon continued. "Enjoy your night. Eat, drink, and celebrate."

Madi passed him a tankard of something, and he looked at her suspiciously. Gods couldn't get drunk on mortal liquor, so he felt confident he could drink whatever this amber liquid was, but he was still hesitant. She nodded to the tankard and then to the crowd, and he got the message.

"Let us drink our first toast together. Raise your glasses and drink; TO FREEDOM!" and Devon raised the tankard high.

A sea of arms raised from within the crowd, and the loud response nearly bowled him over. "TO FREEDOM!"

Gradually, the cheers lost cohesion and turned back into a general hubbub, and Devon was able to relax a little.

The night was joyous and stretched all through the small hours until dawn. Not needing much sleep, he outlasted just about everyone, but eventually, Gwen and Izzy dragged him off to bed. There, the night became even more perfect.

Chapter 27

Triana or bust

Devon and Beth had spent the last few hours going back over the Triana attack plans. They had discussed things several times and reached a strategy they both agreed upon. Beth had live images coming in from the city, and she'd be communicating via mental link to the five teams once they all split up. There would be three attack squads, a squad of snipers now known as the Eagle Squad, and the Chaos Squad.

Now he stood in front of Haven and looked proudly at his troops. They were all dressed in their new armour and equipped with all the gear he had lovingly crafted for them. Every soldier had a coloured armband depicting their squad designation. They stood to attention in tight rows, arranged neatly in their groups. The strange thing about that was, he hadn't asked them to do it. They had organised themselves. Even Izzy had joined the ranks. However, she was grinning at him in high amusement.

Devon felt a nudge against his waist. He looked down and saw Jet, resplendent in her shadow-cat form. She even had a black ribbon around her neck with a troop insignia dangling from it like a medal. "Hello, gorgeous. I was hoping you'd be joining us. You're looking smart."

Jet grinned at him and pushed her chest forward proudly. She had good reason to despise the fairy queen too and would fight by her master's side. No one would harm him unless they got through her first, and she wasn't about to let that happen.

Devon straightened to his full height and addressed the small army. "You make me very proud," he said with a loud voice. "I know that, for some of you, the induction process has been a little hasty. However, there is a bitch-queen and a city swarming with her minions that all desperately need to die. Tonight, we all make our mark in the history books." Devon paused to wait for the cheer that rang out to die down. "I will not judge you tonight. Work together, discover what you can do, learn from each other, and use your strengths. Most importantly, do not target anyone who is not hostile. This is not the time to settle grudges. If you have doubts, take prisoners."

He looked at the faces gazing at him. Some looked excited, while others looked nervous, but everyone looked proud to be there. "Lorn, you are blue squad leader. Your team have the task of securing the slave pens and the slums. Remove hostiles, free everyone, then escort them out of the city and into the forest. There, volunteers will take over and lead them safely back through the waygate."

"Yes, sir," Lorn responded.

"Grace, you lead the orange squad. Your task is to secure the residential areas. Again, clear out all hostiles and, like Lorn, free all servants and slaves and escort them to safety. Anyone who uses a slave as a hostage dies. Understood?"

"Yes, sir," Grace said, her diminutive stature belying the authority she carried within his army.

"Pip, you have Eagle Squad. Do you and your snipers know your target watchpoints?"

"Yes, sir."

"Mitsey, you have Chaos Squad. You know your targets, follow Lorn in and then get busy."

"Yes, sir."

"My squad will secure the trade district in the north and then move south to the palace gates to secure a rendezvous point. Once we're all back together, we go into the palace as a full group. I want you all to fight hard, but don't take silly risks. I did not recruit you as sacrifices. Stay alive, understood?"

"Sir, yes, sir," every one of them shouted at the same time.

Devon smiled broadly. "Well, you certainly scare me, now go and scare them. We leave in five minutes." *Wow!* he thought to himself. *They're just too good at the shouty bits.*

As dusk lengthened the shadows, they marched through the waygate then onward toward the city's western wall. Behind the wall were the slums where the slave pens and arena were. While Lorn's team had business in the slums, Devon planned to march his team clockwise around the circular outer wall to the northern part of town. There he would start clearing the trade district while heading south toward the centre. The city's inner wall surrounded the palace with its gardens and five towers that lurked underneath the accursed mana-restriction dome.

He remembered the first time he had been there. Back then, he'd been overconfident and marched on the palace alone. He had paid dearly for his arrogance. Now, freeing the subjugated faie was the task of his forces. His focus was purely on revenge. He had to get past this need for retribution and finally move on with his life. He had other things to do now.

He held his arm up, and the five squads stopped about one-hundred feet from the city's outer wall. The sound of the final footfall of each person landing at the same time amazed him. Even their marching was way too good.

Fortunately, the outer wall was just a barrier. There was no walkway on top for archers to fire down from or guards left to patrol its perimeter. The inner walls were different. They were wide and fortified heavily. "Grace, if you would be so kind. Make us a door."

Grace smiled, then stepped forward. After a second, her brow furrowed in concentration, both arms reached out in front of her, and she cupped her hands together, which immediately began to glow with a swirling silver light. When the light became too intense to look at, she broke her hands apart and thrust them forwards, palms outstretched. A bright pulse of silver light shot forward and struck the wall. The stone instantly surrendered; first, it glowed white-hot, then melted into slag, and flowed apart. Seconds later, there was a gap in the wall, ten feet wide, from top to bottom. Cooling stone could be heard plinking and cracking in a puddle on the ground.

Most of the troops just looked at Grace in amazement. The power they had just witnessed was beyond anything they had ever seen. In the few moments that it had taken the young mage to cast her spell, she had gained the respect of everyone there.

Grace looked back at Devon and winked. She knew how good she'd become in such a short time, wielding magic as if she'd been doing it for years. Devon grinned. There'd be no living with her ego now. He focused back on the task at hand and led his group through the gap.

<Listen up, everyone. Mental communication only, as of now. No one speaks. Beth, you with us?>

<Right here,> Beth thought. <Follow the road to your left, Devon. Grace, you need to head anticlockwise to the southern side. Lorn, you are heading a short way clockwise. You cannot miss the pens. They are huge. If anyone has something important to say, state your name first, then keep the message short. No chatter. Good luck.>

<Devon; orange squad, follow me in. Blue, follow Pip and Mitsey in. Pip, get your snipers in position first. I need the main roads secured.>

They filed into the city. Some troops knew the streets only too well because they'd been slaves here only a few days previously. Izzy led Devon's purple squad around toward the trade district. Everyone stayed vigilant, but the streets were utterly empty here. After a few minutes, he heard fighting taking place behind and to the right of him, which meant that Lorn had met resistance. They continued around the slums until they met a broad road leading to the centre. Following the wall, they noticed the buildings began to improve in quality as the streets became cleaner and better maintained. They were now on the outskirts of the wealthier, commercial area. Finally, they reached the northern entrance and met a small squad of elite orc guards who had been guarding the gate. By the time they realised they were under attack from within the city, it was too late for them. Six veteran soldiers lay dead in less than that many seconds and all with barely a sound. His people were good.

<Lorn; sixteen lightly armoured enemy soldiers down, no casualties. Watch out for the white wands they carry. They leech mana when they touch you and give you a very unpleasant jolt.>

Devon kept walking but reached out for the souls anyway. As Lorn had said, sixteen souls arrived along with the six from the purple squad's work. He was surprised to see how powerful the souls were, yet Lorn's squad had despatched them without anyone getting hurt.

<Devon; what species were the guards, Lorn? Did they have magic?>

<Lorn; elite orcs. They had a healer and a mage who cast chain and cage spells. We just targeted the mage, and the chains disappeared when he died.>

So, the queen still had casters. Interesting. Devon knew that the Earth realm was the only place where symbiots could be found, and the queen had destroyed any access to that over one-thousand, five-hundred years ago. It was a mystery to him how she managed to have magic users in her ranks still. Maybe she'd used some sort of enforced hibernation when the mages weren't required. He certainly hadn't been expecting to encounter spells from anyone but the queen herself. She had proved that she was still full of surprises, and he had to take care not to overestimate his chances. Jeffery had been right. His track record was poor thus far.

He sent scouts out to sweep each building from west to east while waiting with Jet, Izzy, Twilight, Eluna, and Djinn on the centre road, ready to sweep in should anyone encounter trouble. Twilight and Eluna were his squad's unicorn medics, and he was delighted to have them supporting his people. They were incredible healers and had empowerment spells to bolster morale and vitality. Unicorns were the most surgically attuned of all magical healers. They repaired wounds by magical manipulation akin to surgery but with powerful healing magic protecting their work and keeping their patient alive. They had detailed knowledge of their patients' anatomy, which assisted their talents considerably. It was almost miraculous what these beautiful creatures could do for the wounded. They also came with a vast library of focused healing spells. All his troops were under strict instructions to keep them safe. Devon had tasked Djinn with keeping these two under her watchful eye.

<Gwen; we've got some merchants and mercenary guards here. They have taken hostages.>

<Devon; we're on our way over. Hang tight.> Devon could see the targets with his shadow sight. It could see through objects and highlighted nearby hostiles. Knowing exactly where the enemy was meant they could weave through the back streets to get behind the group of hostage-takers.

<Gwen; the fairy in the centre is the leader. The others are the hired muscle.>

<Can you cage the leader, Izz? As soon as you land your spell, we can start on the thugs,> Devon thought to his group alone.

They had emerged into the street behind the small crowd that was facing off against Gwen and her team. The fairy was standing in the middle of a circle of seven heavyset orcs, each armed with a blunt weapon and one of the white mana-wands that Lorn had warned them about.

<Ffion; we've got another situation just up the road you're on. It's a stand-off for now.>

<Devon; noted. We won't be long, Ffi.>

Izzy's golden light-cage enclosed around the fairy and then chaos ensued. Four black cats emerged from the shadows in mid-leap, and immediately half the mercenaries were down and out of the fight. Dark flames erupted from the eyes, nose, and mouth of one, and a heartbeat later, black, mist-enshrouded chains wrapped mercilessly around another. Black ichor began oozing from the last thug's orifices as he choked and finally suffocated. Gwen or Sulkiss had hit the last one with a hex; it was a particularly nasty one.

After all the hostile targets were dead, everyone except Jet regained their standard forms. Devon admired the ice-statue that Djinn had created from the last mercenary. <How long does that trick take you?> he asked Djinn.

<Five seconds of channelling if they stand still for the first second. If you don't shatter him, then he'll defrost in five minutes,> Djinn replied, her voice a little proud.

Devon took a hammer from one of the dead orcs and hit the statue hard. Frigid shards of orc scattered the floor.

<Izz, close the box, please.>

Izzy gracefully extended her left arm with her fingers stretched wide. She concentrated for a second and then clenched her hand into a tight fist. Her light-cage shrank rapidly, squeezing the fairy tightly. The creature screamed as pain from the pressing cage bars coursed through his body. Then his cries ended abruptly as his skin couldn't withstand the growing pressure of the constricting bars. There was a wet explosive noise as gore fountained in every direction. Those wearing Devon's new armour stayed unblemished as the wet mess slid off them, but some of the slaves fared worse. Instead of looking horrified, they cheered and smiled widely.

"That'll teach that grasping bastard," one elf woman cheered.

"Take that, you sick, twisted pervert," a silthrine woman shouted. Her lizard-like features were grinning with joy.

Devon cast a 'divine truth' spell, and a golden cloud enveloped everyone in the street. Everyone's aura stayed golden, and so he knew that they'd removed all the enemies.

"Lord Wayfarer, my god, you really came for us, just as the prophet, Tolomine, said you would," the silthrine lady said, falling to her knees and clasping her clawed fingers together.

Devon grinned at her, cupped her chin, and guided her back to her feet in his well-practised, gentle way. "Do you have a name, lady silthrine?"

"Oh! Uhm, my lord, my name is Brielle. Though it would be an honour if you would call me Bree."

"Well then, my lady Bree. Would you be so kind as to assemble as many slaves as you can find and walk westwards around the wall until you find a gap. People will escort you to Sanctuary and a brand-new life. Please don't head north as there is still danger there. The outer sections are safe for you now, though. When you're settled, come and find me. We can talk then."

Izzy smiled and shook her head. <I love the way you do that. It's a joy to watch.>

Devon returned the small wave that Bree gave him and watched her collect her fellow slaves and lead them away. <Hush, elf. She's a leader if ever I saw one.>

<Devon; we're on our way, Ffi.>

Devon and his squad were back in their travel forms and, flitting from shadow to shadow, heading north.

Ffi's situation was different. A fairy man and his four guards held blades to the throats of five scantily-clad fairy females. At least twenty more similarly dressed ladies from various species were bound and gagged and sitting on the street outside what could only be a brothel.

<Devon; pick your target and take that blade away from the victim first. Medics get ready. This could quickly go bad.>

<Darcia; sir, I've got a shot on two. Just say the word.>

Darcia was another silthrine lady, and she was now one of his best sharpshooters, second only to Pip. Not only that, but she was the silthrine they'd met in the forest when she and her sister had tried to rob them on the way to reopen the waygate. She'd brought nearly four-hundred silthrine through the gate two days ago, joining the army alongside her sister that same day.

Devon hadn't realised that she was in range. By his estimate, she must be over two-hundred yards away from this point. <Are you sure, Darcia? That's a long shot, even for you,> he thought directly to her.

<I've got two of them before they can blink, boss. Just say the word.>

<Devon; stand down, purple squad. Darcia, mark your targets. Izzy, cage one of the others, and I'll chain another. Gwen, use your whip to grab the arm of the one on the right. Don't miss, Darci.>

Darcia snorted at him across their link. The mere idea she'd miss her shots was ludicrous to her. Two red arrows pointing downward appeared over the two mercenaries on the left.

<Devon; all go when Izzy lands her cage.>

He saw Izzy's snow leopard begin to cast her spell and readied his 'soul chains'.

As soon as the golden cage appeared around the fairy in charge, two mercenaries dropped in quick succession, large holes blossoming through their skulls. Devon's chains wrapped tightly around another mercenary's torso, pulling his arms to his sides and forcing him to his knees.

Gwen's whip arced through the air and snapped around the last mercenary's wrist. She tugged, forcing the orc's arm away from the fairy woman's throat. The orc began to bloat, and thousands of angry insects started to pour from his open mouth and nose. The creature quickly asphyxiated and fell. Sulkiss let out a whoop of glee.

Izzy closed her fist, and both the leader and Gwen's targets exploded. This time, there were cheers mixed with shouts of disgust.

Devon cast his 'divine truth' spell again and was surprised when the aura of the fairy female the leader had been holding hostage went scarlet. Realising her deception had been uncovered, she drew a dagger and flew at Devon with alarming speed.

A shick sound was heard, and a heartbeat later, the flying fairy's forward momentum was reversed when Devon's staff in spear form pierced her torso, heart, and emerged through her spine.

The fairy woman standing next to her screamed. Everyone stayed rooted to the spot, shock and horror keeping them where they stood.

The squad freed the hostages after the captured enemies were dead, but the ex-slaves just looked lost and confused.

<Devon; more refugees coming round from the north side.>

<Beth; understood, ready and waiting.>

"Please settle down. You are safe and free now. Please make your way anticlockwise around the wall where you will be met and shown to Sanctuary, your new home," Izzy said.

The brothel slaves looked at Izzy and then at Devon.

"Come on, girls," a shapely fairy with long blonde hair said. "Looks like we just became self-employed."

Devon laughed. "We have plenty of space in our trade district. I'm sure you can find premises there once you get settled. No one's going to judge."

"Mmm! I like you. Can I keep you?" another pretty fairy purred at Devon.

"You'll need to go through me and the elf first, butterfly," Gwen growled fiercely.

"Sorry, but I am very spoken for," Devon said.

The fairy sniffed and followed the others off to the west.

Purple squad methodically searched each business and residence and freed over two-hundred slaves. Nearly fifty more fairy slavers and a group of very aggressive dwarves met their demise while trying to flee. Sadly for them, they ran straight into Darcia's path and were dropped before they even knew they were in peril.

Not one slave died during their work, and once done, they made their way toward the palace gates up the slope to the south.

<Devon; trade district clear, heading south to clear rendezvous point.>

Chapter 28

Orc soup

Dark flames roared around the ogres' blistering legs, burning them with a sinister fire. A dripping ball of ichor arced into the centre of the remaining twelve hulking creatures. Devon had ordered the fast-strike soldiers to hang back because the monsters' heavy armour meant their attacks would barely penetrate. Instead, the enemies were under attack from more magic than the outer city had seen for centuries. The whole area was now saturated in magical energy from the waygate, and their magic could be used with impunity.

Devon had also called forward all their snipers now that the city was mostly under their control. Arrows flew into the fray while Darcia and the other sharpshooters shot explosive rounds from their custom-built rifles. The unicorns had energised everyone in range with empowerment spells, and they were all protected by a thick, golden dome cast by Izzy.

One of the ogres opened its mouth and shrieked like a boiling kettle. Steam poured from every extremity until it burst in a shower of boiled ogre pieces. Gwen had hexed the unsuspecting creature, and over the space of thirty seconds, it had cooked from the inside.

Silence fell as the last ogre succumbed to a fireball, large enough to engulf the ogre's entire torso – a gift from one of their pyromancers.

<Devon; main palace gate guards cleared; the gate is down. Tell Glimmer her guild's explosives worked a little too well. Ten feet of the wall from either side went with the gates and flew halfway across the palace lawns.>

<Beth; Devon, you've got guards heading your way on the walls, coming from both sides.>

<Devon; purple squad and Eagles, watch the walls. Take out anything that moves. Everyone else secure this area. We're digging in.>

Darcia began casting a spell. Devon watched in amazement as she shimmered then vanished. Seconds later, other sharpshooters and bowyers did the same.

Some guards dared to pop their heads above the nearby wall's parapet. There was a faint pffft sound, and the top of the furthest guard's head turned to paste, and he collapsed. Two more shots and his comrades joined him. *Hell's teeth, Darcia is good,* Devon thought. Regardless of his feelings about guns, he couldn't argue with the results. Every creature that stupidly showed itself on the wall met its doom with explosive bullets or arrows. Devon imagined what a group of sharpshooters and bowyers could achieve before the front-line forces even got close enough to engage.

Devon had lost track of the souls that had answered his calls because he had stopped counting at fifty. Every squad had been doing their jobs with lethal efficiency.

<Devon; the rendezvous is secure. Blue, orange, and Chaos report in.>

<Grace; the residences are all clear and with minimal resistance. On our way to meet up with you. Five minutes. One wounded and healed.>

<Lorn; on our way back through the waygate. Four-hundred and seventy freed and escorted through the gate. Pens cleared. Ten minutes out. Two down, not out. A guard hid among the slaves and then ambushed our bowyers. One of our medics stayed back at base with them.>

<Mitsey; last targets being prepared, with no resistance so far. Ten minutes 'til we can join you.>

<Devon; Ffion, take two others and head toward the palace's front door. Darcia, keep an eye on them. Check the windows for anything that moves, but don't go in. Any sign of trouble, flash back here. Understood?>

<Yes, sir!>

Two large black cats and something else set off at a sprint. The shadow warriors and shadow knights in his army all seemed to have the same cat form that he had. As for Ffi, she could take any shape she chose. He had only seen Izzy's travel form on a couple of occasions. She turned into the softest, most fluffy snow leopard he had ever seen. Everything she did was beautiful.

<Aww! Thank you, my lord,> she thought to him with affection.

Devon kept forgetting that she often read his thoughts.

<Beth; looks like they're assembling a force inside the palace. Forty-seven heavily armoured ogres. I've managed to get mimseys inside the building.>

He smiled. Beth's little flying eye creatures were a creation of genius. Her genius. They were proving their worth now as having invisible eyes inside the palace was invaluable. The relationship he and Beth had nurtured was a happy compromise akin to brother and sister now. They were there for each other, neither needing anything more intimate than a reassuring hug now and then. They both enjoyed time together, and the stress between them had evaporated. At least he thought so.

<Devon; Ffi, can you see anything?>

<Ffi; they're moving toward the front doors. We're coming back to you now.>

<Devon; no. Change of plan. Hide, let them pass you, then use your bows. Shoot once, then flash to another place out of reach. Harry them from multiple angles. Aim for anything not covered with armour. Stay out of reach. No risks.>

<Ffi; understood, sir.>

Amber moved forward a step to stand next to Jet, just in front and to the left of Devon. The dwarf was his squad's Wayfarer knight. She was a surly hulk in her heavy armour, but she was a vivacious, young dwarf with the friendliest demeanour out of it. As a knight, she fought with a reinforced, mana-empowered shield and a vicious war-axe that she had insisted on helping him design. She saw her place as right beside him, acting as his vanguard. Devon glanced at her and raised his eyebrow. Amber nodded and made ready. Her shield began to shimmer, and her axe took on a bright golden glow.

Jet nuzzled his leg as she took up position on his other side. <We be ready,> she sent to him with determined thoughts of camaraderie and protection.

Devon drew Wrath and began channelling mana into it. The mana-blades emerged from both tips to form a polearm of pure magical power. Dark flames started to swirl around Wrath's shaft. Djinn emerged from him and floated off toward the incoming force, and Sulkiss leapt into the air and expanded to about ten feet long as he began to circle.

The city's inner walls housed the queen's palace. The clearance of the city's districts had taken a little over eight hours, and dawn was still a long way away yet. The only natural light came from a gibbous moon. The surrounding gardens contained neatly trimmed lawns which formed a ring around the shimmering white walls of the building. Regularly spaced globes of bright white light mounted on metal poles illuminated the whole area. They revealed the gaudily painted windows that managed to contrast everything, creating a jarring effect on the eyes. A white marble path led through the garden straight up to some white marble steps. At the top of the steps were the palace's large, white double doors. Those doors had just been flung open and were now vomiting out a horde of the most humungous ogres Devon had ever seen.

<Devon; confirmed, over forty enormous ogres. Blue and orange, get here fast. Use your flight forms. We're going to need help with these monsters. Purple, hit them with all you have.>

He heard Darcia's gun start sounding off. This time, the explosions that the rounds delivered were more prominent and a lot more devastating. Arrows with specialised incendiary-filled tips buzzed across the palace lawn and found their marks. Flames erupted from the frontmost ogres, who charged on without hesitation.

An enormous light-infused fireball hurtled out of the sky and shattered in a massive flash of lava-like substance. The flames rose higher, the lava sticking to flesh and armour. Devon and Gwen sent black balls of darkness into the charging behemoths. Gwen's contained a stinking ichor that leached vitality from everything it touched. Devon's was a ball of concentrated darkness that engulfed every one of the ogres, burning them mercilessly. Black fire roared up from the floor, causing yet more damage. He could see arrows flitting in from three separate angles behind the beasts. The projectiles did minor damage, but each found its target and caused pain and annoyance. Balls of potions rained down on the ogres' heads, delivered like bombs by Sulkiss.

<Devon; Jinx, forget the bow, let's have you here with us.> Jinx was a shadow-knight, and her armour and attack style was a lot more robust than that of his shadow warriors.

More spells pummelled the ogres as they approached, and by the time they got within striking range, there was less than half their number remaining. All were a lot weaker than they had been when they started. Golden light enshrouded Devon's troops, and moments later, a white mist, originating from Twilight, joined the golden light in protecting the fighters.

Devon's staff sliced cleanly through an outstretched leg, and one ogre tumbled. He wrapped a nearby ogre with his soul chains, taking him out of the fight too. A vast war-axe swung at him, and he pumped mana into his jump. He somersaulted and brought his staff around hard. His attacker's head lolled sideways as his mana-blade almost wholly severed it.

Gwen flung several corrosive potion-balls into the confusion of ogres, then she flashed into her shadow-wraith form. She shifted to ethereal and flowed through the mess of bodies, then, seeing a target, she added corporeal mass to her state and placed a claw on the face of a busy ogre. The hex bit into flesh and sank below the skin. A witch's mark from Gwen meant certain doom, so she moved on.

The witch passed through the other combatants and out the other side of the skirmish. She moved some distance away from the battle then reverted to her standard form. Sulkiss landed on his hind legs on her shoulder, where he spent most of his time now. The dragon roared a silent roar, and foul miasma erupted from his jaws. Dark gas flowed over the ogres and clung to every hostile combatant. Then Gwen felt a massive impact and left the ground, ribs shattered, lungs torn, and she flew over ten feet to land in a crumpled heap. A huge mace had hit her hard in the side. She coughed twice then lost consciousness as her heart stopped.

Gwen's agony acted like a beacon to Twilight, who immediately absorbed half of it. With a thought, a white flash erupted from her, and a heartbeat later, she had transported herself to Gwen's side. An orb of protection instantly surrounded her, deflecting the charging ogre as it rushed in for the kill. Soft, pale-skinned hands pressed on Gwen's wounds. The medic used her deep knowledge of anatomy to carefully shape her magical energy, which travelled into the witch's battered body. The mana-flow delicately guided ribs to knit back together and ruptured organs to heal. Satisfied the repairs had gone well, Twilight restarted Gwen's heart while absorbing her remaining pain. She gritted her teeth as the agony the witch had been suffering bit deeply into her own core. Gwen had to get back into the fight, and the unicorn would willingly shoulder her burden of suffering for now. She channelled mana into a healing spell and then added some invigoration magic before releasing it into her patient. *There,* Twilight thought with satisfaction, *you're all better.*

Twilight took a moment for herself now she'd completed Gwen's healing. She cast a 'self-preservation' spell and began to glow red as her magic extracted the pain that she'd absorbed from the witch. The magic forced the pain essence into a soothing silver mist which seeped back into the unicorn, restoring some of her mana-wyrm's depleted vitality as it did so.

When Gwen opened her eyes, all she saw was a flash of brilliant white light as Twilight flashed across to Jinx, her next patient. The witch carefully tested her torso and found that her wounds were healed and the pain was gone. The only evidence of the massive trauma she'd experienced was the mess it had made of her armour. She got up, called Sulkiss to her, and went to work, hexing the ogre that she was sure had hit her.

Devon was relieved to see Grace and her troops sprinting up the road toward the gate. That relief died when he heard what Beth had to report.

<Beth; you've got more problems incoming. Two forces are approaching around the sides of the palace, from either side. Devon, there are over a hundred orcs in each group, almost everything the queen has left. Soon you're going to become massively outnumbered. Both forces will reach you in under four minutes. There is also a band of twelve ogres sneaking behind you through the back streets. They will probably get to you in a little over five minutes.>

<Lorn; rendezvous in less than two minutes, sir.>

<Devon; everyone, into their flight form and up onto the wall's ramparts. No exceptions. Snipers take out those lights. Orcs don't see well in the dark. We attack them from cover at range. We can't win this on the ground. Orange takes the anticlockwise wall; blue takes the clockwise wall. My team split up. Break engagement and move now.>

There were only three ogres left, and they were already in a very sorry state. Devon set about dicing them as they clumsily tried to strike him. He had cast 'dark time', which slowed everything around him. All the ogres could see were searing, black flames rising to engulf them and a shadowy blur that dissected them, a piece at a time. All three were dead in less than twenty seconds.

An enormous, black wyvern made from the smoky shadows rose up from the ogre-flavoured carnage, holding a shadow-cat delicately in its talons. The building's windows shook when it roared a challenge toward the palace then flapped off lazily to join Grace and the others on the wall. All around, there was the popping of the white globes as they exploded.

When Devon landed, he deposited Jet gently down on the wall's walkway. It was the first time that he'd transported her while in his flight form, and his companion seemed to have enjoyed the experience. She carried him most of the time. It was nice to return the favour for once.

Grace came to him and gave her report. "It was a mess in the residences, sir. There were no guards or nobles around. I think they fled, but there were hundreds of refugees just milling about. Most of them looked half-starved and desperate. We tried to guide them back to the western wall, but some just followed us back into the city."

"Good to know, thanks, Grace." Devon pondered the problem.

<Devon; Beth, get a message to Sintra and anyone else that isn't busy. Get them through the gate and rounding up refugees. I need those people guided back through the waygate and looked after. There are a lot of explosions coming, and I don't want innocents hurt. Everyone should help, no exceptions. Okay?>

<Beth; got it, Devon. I'll make it happen.>

<Devon; troops, ready yourselves. Don't hold back. Throw rocks at them if you have nothing else. You have my permission to be as creative as you are able. I want every one of them flattened. Understood?>

Shouts of "Yes, sir" rang out from the walls. They now numbered less than forty fighters and eleven medics, but their god fought by their side, and they would not fail him.

The two regiments of orcs charged into view. They looked momentarily flummoxed when they didn't see a battle going on at the gate. However, the queen hadn't recruited these creatures for their mental aptitude, and they just ran on anyway. Initially, they ignored the gore that had started to splash amongst them as exploding bullets and arrows found homes. Still, they couldn't miss the vast balls of fire, ichor, darkness, electricity, and frost that began to rain down upon them. Orc after orc perished under the onslaught of sculpted magical energy. Thousands of insects fell upon the army in a frenzy while large, jagged rocks pelted them from the sky.

The two orc regiments met at the gate. By now, they had realised that their enemy had taken to the walls. Unfortunately for them, while they had a few healers, they had no archers or offensive casters. His ranged attackers had long since targeted the healers, and so their race had finished before it had even begun. The lights were gone now, so it was almost dark. The orcs' weak eyes couldn't make out any targets even if they could strike back.

Devon noticed Grace was spinning her clenched fists in a barrelling motion. She then unclasped her hands and pushed a blue cloud toward the ground where the enemy now stood. Devon followed the magic's trajectory and saw that any earth it fell upon instantly turned into a deep, sucking swamp. Screams rang out as the few orcs that had managed to leap for the solid edges of the quagmire were pulled back in as their comrades tried to use them to climb out.

Grace was back to rolling her fists again. This time in the other direction. When the subsequent brown cloud hit the ground, the soil immediately returned to its original solid state. That left over seventy of the orc survivors buried well past their waists in solid earth. The onslaught of other spells hadn't let up, and the orcs began to perish at an alarming rate.

Grace was now rotating her hands, palms flat down in a horizontally circular motion. Red mist emerged from the gestures, and the orcs began to bake as the earth heated to extreme temperatures. Terrified yells of agony cut short as the creatures' insides expanded well past their skins ability to contain them. There was a series of highly unpleasant, wet, popping sounds as an army of orcs became soup. Silence descended on the scene as Devon's forces took in the reality of what had just occurred.

Devon didn't know what to think when Grace grinned up at him expectantly. "Bloody hell, Grace! That went well past creative. Well done, little star. You are now officially awesome."

Grace beamed at him proudly. "Thank you, Devon. I like that you like."

<Beth; those ogres are incoming. Your sharpshooters have already downed two; nope, make that four. No, never mind. It appears you've noticed them – all clear. The palace has some token guards remaining, but you've just wiped out almost all the queen's remaining troops. Congratulations, the city is yours.>

<Devon; are you soldiers ready for the final push?>

<Yes, sir.>

Chapter 29
Payback

Most of the magical lanterns that usually flooded the royal residence with light were now hanging broken from the walls. Now only a few shone, casting shadows as they feebly penetrated the purveying darkness.

Devon and his troops were flagging after a long, stressful night of liberation and combat. He reached down and took up the twelve-inch, white rod with which the fairy guard had just poked him. The effect, as soon as it had touched his skin, was alarming. His nerves had all fired at once, and his muscles spasmed, trying to force him to his knees. Unfortunately for the fairy, the pain was merely a passing annoyance to him. The wand was probably a slaver's toy that the fairies had weaponised, but he tucked it in his belt, just in case. He'd told his troops to grab as many of the wands as they could and to use them against the enemy if they got the chance. See how they liked it. While some of the fairies seemed intent on taking lives, others looked as if they were just going through the motions under duress. He would prefer to find out if any of them had lives that might be salvaged rather than wasted. People often behaved differently when not driven by a tyrant.

They had spent over an hour clearing out the ground floor and had freed over five-hundred slaves forced into hard labour within the palace.

Everyone looked on in disgust at the sheer opulence that surrounded them in every hall or corridor. Devon couldn't argue with their displeasure. He felt it too. The wealth invested in these ornaments and objet d'art could feed and clothe thousands. He had decided to send most of it into the mana-forge for recycling. After that, he would be able to create valuable items for the city from the materials. He had banned his troops from taking anything. Instead, he'd asked Mitsey's Chaos Squad, who had completed their initial tasks, to go through the place, hoovering up everything. He was also considering creating a museum. Even if it was uncomfortable for them, people needed to remember their darker times.

They climbed the marble stairs and despatched almost all soldiers in a small squad of fairy guards. Two had surrendered and found themselves tied up with all the other captives, sitting in the richly decorated reception hall by the double front doors. A few more small groups of guards met them and regretted it, causing Devon to wonder why the queen was sending them out in such small numbers. In the end, they had killed over fifty fairies and captured twenty-nine. Devon noted that all the enemies so far had been male. He knew female orcs and ogres existed, fairies too, but where could they all be hiding?

Nerves tingled through him as he felt the moment he'd been anticipating approaching. It was time to get this done and move on.

Finally, Izzy brought them to the throne room. All four guards on the door surrendered and were marched to the hall with the others. Devon had expected these guards to fight to the death for their queen, but that hadn't happened. He remembered something Fate had said about never trusting fairies. There was quite a sizeable number of enemies tied up in the hall. Was that the trick? How was that a trick? Could they be cursed to explode as Djinn had been? Just to be safe, he sent his dark warriors back to the entrance and told them and the troops he had already stationed there to strip every one of the guards naked, then tie them up again. No armour made them vulnerable, and they wouldn't last long in a fight.

This was it. This was the moment Devon had been anticipating with increasing fervour. He stood in front of the double doors and reinforced his emotions. The queen's mind trickery couldn't be allowed to influence him as it had done last time. The fairy was a specialist in illusion and mind control, and he had no defence against that.

<My lord, you have me, this time,> Lorn thought. Like Izzy, Lorn regularly monitored her god's inner dialogue. It was how she knew him so well after such a short time.

Devon snorted. <My brain is as busy as the library these days, with just as many visitors. Yes, Lorn, I have you, and for that, I am incredibly thankful. Look after me, Ms Kingsley. You may end up saving me tonight.>

Lorn and Jinx grabbed the handles to the double doors and looked back expectantly at Devon. Jet, Amber, and Fern flanked him with Izzy and Gwen next to them. He nodded, and they opened them up fully. They stood on either side and saluting as he passed. Devon allowed himself an inner smile. *They even nailed the salute.*

As soon as his feet crossed the threshold of the throne room, an angry, high-pitched buzzing began to torment his brain. Agony washed through him, and he groaned as he sank to his knees. He wondered why he bothered to live at all. All his plans seemed so futile now. The fairy queen was lovely, and all he wanted to do was ruin her happiness. He was a useless, unpopular failure who everyone despised. It would be better for everyone if he just ended his stupid, pointless life right here, right now. Devon could just make out several faint voices on the edge of his consciousness, but the painful buzzing that filled his head drowned them out. Misery consumed him. Tears flowed down his cheeks as he reached for his daggers and sent mana into them. He needed the sharpest blades so that he could cut his head off cleanly. That would be best for everyone.

<DEVON!>

The word appeared in his head but quickly became obscured by the angry buzzing that consumed his thoughts. He tried to think about who the voice belonged to but failed. The noise made it impossible to think about anything other than how wretched he felt. He noticed other members of his army dropping to the floor, hands clutching their heads in agony just as he had. Now his hands were busy; they crossed the mana-blades and pushed toward his neck. He applied as much force as he could to make sure his demise was quick.

<NO! DEVON! STOP BEING AN IDIOT AND LISTEN TO ME, YOU DUMBASS!>

He remembered that voice and the abuse that used to come with it. He puzzled over why his head hadn't been cut off. He tried again and again until he felt strong hands grab his wrists and pull.

<DEVON! LISTEN TO ME! THINK ABOUT LORN. LET HER IN. THINK! ABOUT! LORN!> The words flashed in neon pink and came with a sense of panic.

Why won't this buzzing stop? Lorn? Why Lorn? Devon felt an overwhelming urge to try and kill himself again. Then he winced as he was slapped hard on the forehead. The hand remained as the shock of the slap distracted him momentarily. The buzzing instantly stopped, and his thoughts cleared like a thick fog lifting. *What the…? Why am I kneeling?*

<DEVON!> Izzy screamed in his mind.

<Shhhhh! Why are you shouting, Izz?> he replied.

<Oh, for mercy's sake! You bloody idiot. No particular reason,> Izzy thought in exasperation. <I was just curious why you were kneeling on the floor crying while trying to cut your head off using mana-blades that cannot hurt you,> Izzy replied, sarcasm dripping from her thoughts.

Devon looked down at his hands. Just as Izzy had said, he was holding his daggers. When had he drawn and empowered those?

<Lorn; Devon, someone attacked you with a mental blast. It caused you to despair, and you tried to end your life. I don't know where the attack came from, but I am blocking it.>

Devon picked himself up off the floor and noticed other members of his force doing the same. He sheathed his blades and wiped the tears from his face. He was thankful that his troops all had mana-blades. Magical power couldn't hurt its source. <Devon; it was the queen. She is a powerful neuromancer like you, Lorn. Thank you so much.>

<Beth; what's going on?>

<Gwen; the queen just hit us with some very unpleasant mind magic. Lorn saved the day.> The witch grinned across at Lorn.

<Devon; we're going to end this now, Beth. Form up, everyone. Let's do this.>

He took a deep breath and stepped into the throne room.

This wasn't the first time Devon had stepped into this room. It still smelled of sweat disguised by strong perfumes that made his nose wince. This time there were even more fairy nobles crammed in. He estimated there to be almost five-hundred of them in here. So many that they outnumbered the serving slaves, who looked broken in will and spirit, which made his blood boil. The queen sat on her throne, grinning at Devon. Beside her was Entwaine, a thin and shrivelled-looking fairy. Devon had no idea how he had managed to survive for so long. He was still wearing tattered brown robes and a strange cap that sat flat upon his head and had wings that hung down past his ears. He had been whispering in the queen's ear, but when he spied Devon, he turned to glare hatefully at him with piercing red eyes.

The queen was as beautiful as she had always been, perhaps even more so somehow. Ageless because she was a demigoddess and vain beyond comprehension. Her long golden hair shone in the light of the chandeliers, and her deep blue eyes sparkled. Her face and full figure perfectly formed a stereotypical male ideal of good looks. Fairies weren't shapeshifters, but they could change their appearance over time, like many species of faie. Their appearance gradually altered to how the individual perceived themselves to be. When faced with so many beautiful creatures who adopt the same features, each one instantly became average and without character. The queen's beauty went beyond fairy ability, though. Her radiance felt magical somehow.

<Devon; I want the area behind those curtains secure. Orange, take the crowd on either side. Check for guards lurking among them too. Blue, you go behind the curtains, secure every exit in the room. My team, stay with me and watch for trouble behind us. Izzy, can you deal with Entwaine, please?>

As he'd ordered, the orange and blue squads marched forward and got to work on their assigned tasks. Quite soon, bound guards were led back through the curtains and marched away to be stripped and rebound in the entrance hall. Entwaine shrieked in rage when a golden cage appeared around him and shrank until he was forced into an angry crouch.

"My, my, aren't we thorough, lord Reaper. Have you come to punish me again? I did so enjoy the last time you visited," the queen said. Her regal tones conveyed all the sarcasm that she intended they should.

<Lorn; Devon, she is reaching out to your mind again with a great deal more power this time. I am blocking her, but she's really powerful. I don't think she realises that you are not being influenced.>

"Why, Triana, how thoroughly unpleasant to see you. I must say you've been in my thoughts a lot over the last week. So much that I just had to come and visit. I am very sorry about the mess we made in your city. As I intend to flatten it soon, I didn't think it mattered. You won't need all your guards and slaves now, either."

<Devon; Mitsey, blow the charges.>

"Yes, I had noticed a lot of debris in my garden. I will make you clean it all up with your tongue when I own you again."

There was a series of colossal explosions, and the whole building began to shake as small traces of dust fell from the ceiling.

"Oh, dear! There goes the rest of your palace and your precious dome too. How sad." He grinned wickedly at the queen.

Rage crossed the queen's face. Her forehead creased as she concentrated hard.

<Lorn; Devon, the energy she is using to try and take your mind is becoming too much for me. Will you permit Grace to distract her and break her focus?> Lorn asked.

<Grace, do it.> The battle was over, and so Devon dropped Beth's telepathy protocol. If Lorn needed help, then she should have it. Fast.

Grace stepped toward the queen. She clasped her hands together, and then, after a few seconds, she melted the marble dais the queen's throne perched upon. The throne dropped as the platform became liquid then toppled over as it hit the new level of the molten floor. The motion tipped the queen forward onto the scorching hot marble.

Triana screeched and clutched at her face, stumbling back to her feet. She swept her hands around and froze the floor. Instantly cooled, molten marble shattered and spat shrapnel everywhere. She rounded on

Grace and stalked toward her, hands outstretched as if she intended to strangle her. She had long, pointed fingernails that looked more like claws. "You little bitch, I will tear your eyes out and feed them to my dogs."

Grace stood her ground and gazed placidly at the queen, unafraid.

Devon cast his 'soul chains' spell and thick, black chains enshrouded the queen. The chains contracted and forced Triana into a kneeling position. The mist that exuded from the chains began to syphon away the fairy's mana quickly.

The queen screamed in frustration. "Your pathetic little tricks won't stop me from ripping her heart out, Reaper."

Meanwhile, Entwaine rocked around in his cage, shrieking in pain. As he touched the bars, they shocked him, causing him to sway the other way. Instead of learning and remaining still, he continued to inflict pain on himself. Everyone ignored him, though. Their focus was firmly on their queen.

"I punish anyone who threatens those loyal to my name, Triana. Besides, she is far more powerful than you could ever be. Now, you mangy piece of filth. Let's get down to business, shall we? You are hereby charged with mass racial crimes, genocide, genocide by proxy, fraud, infringement of rules pertaining to a divine duel, and destruction and theft of Pantheon resources. I am authorised to remove your soul and take possession of your realm upon your demise. While I will take your soul, I have promised your death to another."

The queen glared at him. Her face had already started to puff up after receiving some quite severe burns on Grace's molten marble. "I can destroy you, you puny little god. You shall bow before me. Release me, and we'll fight."

<I have placed a mental lock on her, Devon. She cannot fight with her mind powers. Shall I unlock her mind if you are to duel?> Lorn asked.

<Oh no! No, no, no! Leave her just the way she is. Last time, she cheated and had her minion, Entwaine, stun me while she reamed my mind. This is payback. You've been beyond brilliant, as always. Thank you so much for your help, Lorn. Remind me to make you something extra special. Anything you choose.>

<Oo! Cool! Thanks.>

Devon released the chains and allowed the queen to get to her feet and regain her composure. She had no mana, was without her defences, and Lorn had locked her inside her own head.

"By the way, Triana, your daughter asked me to say hello. You sacrificed her life to turn her into a living bomb, and she wishes to thank you for that personally. It was to her I promised your death. Say hello, Djinn."

Djinn floated forward until she was facing Triana. Her misty substance began to form into a likeness of April. "Hello, mother. I have waited a lifetime for this. It is time you learnt what real abuse feels like." The magical entity dissolved and reformed around Triana. Her essence oozed into the fairy queen's skin, who immediately began to moan a low guttural noise like the growl of a frightened animal.

The queen seemed to be concentrating hard, trying to fight off her new attacker. "What are you doing? April? We can talk this through. Stop this, please." Her growl rose in pitch steadily until it became a full-blown scream that seemed to come straight from her soul. Her body shook and spasmed, her concentration gone.

"Aww! I thought you'd be happy for your daughter. She has become what she always wanted to be – your nemesis," Devon taunted. "She's a lovely creature now. We go everywhere together and really enjoy each other's company," he teased. He could see that Djinn had hooked her essence into every nerve in her mother's body and was playing them like a harp.

The queen's burnt face contorted and went puce. She swayed back and forth. "When I defeat you, Reaper," she spat the last syllable, "I am going to grind you into the ground and burn you for eternity. I will have my guards use your head as a latrine. I might even piss on you myself."

Devon smiled. "Your guards are dead, and you will be joining them soon. Maybe you should worry about your daughter first. She's much more dangerous to you than I am."

The queen's brow furrowed as she tried to hit him with a mental burst of power that would have sent him reeling if she'd been able to. First, she realised that he'd drained her mana-wyrm dry, then she realised she could not access her skills either. During all that, she was being wrecked by the constant pain Djinn was forcing upon her.

"YOU BASTARD, WHAT HAVE YOU DONE TO ME?" Her scream raked at everyone's ears. The realisation of her predicament was now hitting her hard.

"There are thousands who would have me keep you alive and make you suffer in the most painful ways imaginable. I suspect my troops are wishing I would let them make a start on you right now. However, as the Wayfarer, I will not let them tarnish their souls on a piece of excrement like you, Triana. Your people can live on if they wish to do so. You will die. Djinn, please finish it."

The queen's face became desperate and terrified. She clasped her hands together and fell to her knees. "No, no, no, please, lord Wayfarer, spare me. I repent for the things I have done. I will make it right, I promise. I beg you for clemency. Just give me a chance, please. All I ask is you spare my life. I can change."

Devon smirked. Triana had switched from calling him Reaper now that she understood how powerless she was. She also knew that, as the Wayfarer, he was obliged to listen to her appeal. He cast his 'divine truth' spell, and the golden cloud descended from the ceiling. It enshrouded everyone in the room. He noticed a great many red auras among the nobles. Triana's was a deep scarlet colour that darkened further as he watched.

"Oh, Triana. It seems that your promises to change your ways have failed to reach your soul. I deny your appeal for clemency."

<Kill everyone in this room with a red aura. Leave the queen for Djinn,> he thought to his soldiers who quickly set about their macabre orders without signs of emotion or objection. Screams rang out as those that had been marked for execution realised their fate.

Izzy closed her outstretched hand into a fist, and the golden cage that encased Entwaine shrank further. It began to squeeze him hard on all sides, causing him to scream in agony. Izzy squeezed her fist tighter, and the shrivelled elf finally burst. Very little gore spattered around, though. It was almost as if he had dried out over the years.

A figure from the crowd of nobles ran at Devon, screaming in rage. His aura was dark red, and he brandished a bejewelled dagger.

Devon reacted fast, reaching for his polearm, but Gwen responded first. There was a loud crack as black mana strands from her whip encircled the fairy nobleman's neck. Devon's attacker froze, and his mouth was forced open by the foulest black ichor that oozed out. Unable to breathe, the fairy fell to his knees and asphyxiated slowly, eventually toppling to the floor dead. Devon shuddered. It was a nasty way to die.

Sulkiss launched himself into the air with a roar, expanding as he rose. Soon he was ten feet long and circling above the nobles' heads, watching every one of them with his bright red eyes. Devon smiled. It was good to see the old dragon enjoying his new role.

Djinn changed her torturing tactics and began to finish her work. The queen's body began to tremble as her daughter pushed tendrils into every organ within her mother's body. Once each one found its target, the queen's screams rose in volume, increasing fear and panic dripping from her cries. Her high-pitched wails of anguish were chilling, eventually becoming painful to the ear. Her face contorted and pulled taut as all her muscles contracted at once. Agony violated every cell in her body, leaving each one wrecked.

Everyone watched with morbid fascination as Djinn made her victim feel the demise of every part of herself in agonising detail. Tears flowed down the queen's face as her voice became raspy, her throat muscles torn by the strain of her screams. She shook and spasmed as the remaining parts of her insides were destroyed by the creature her daughter had become. The queen's screams died away once her life finally left her. Djinn emerged from the corpse and moved over to hover next to Devon.

<Thank you, Devon, your debt to me is paid. I shall willingly stay with you and fight for your cause.>

Devon gave her a small smile. <I hope it gave you the closure you craved.>

<Not at all, but I never expected it would. Revenge has such a bitter taste. Time and my new life with you may help. Maybe I can begin to make amends for the evil things my mother did to others. I have already discarded the shell of misery I occupied, which will be enough for now.>

Chapter 30

Family

Even though Djinn had just killed her mother, Triana was a demigoddess. Devon knew that her body would soon begin to repair itself, just as his had done when the accursed human aspect of him had perished. With that firmly in his mind, Devon acted quickly and began channelling mana out toward the queen's soul. Initially, it resisted his attempts to summon it, so he sent more mana into the twitching corpse. With his Reaper's sight, he watched his target as it vibrated and struggled against the inexorable pull of his magical power. Yet more mana flowed from his arm. He now had every mana-channel open, each at maximum capacity. Although Brack was getting tired, he kept the power coming like the star he was. The torrent flung itself into her chest, grabbed her spirit, and shook without mercy. Triana's soul finally gave in and fled from her wrecked body, then floated over to Devon. The shadowy self-image was twisted and highly disfigured by the evil it had done in the past. Every soul carried the scars of its deeds. The queen's soul glared at him unrepentantly.

He watched the souls of other dead creatures come to him with a vague but tired interest. His entire spirit ached, but it was over. They had destroyed Triana and the evil she represented. He wanted to laugh, cry, cheer, and sleep all at the same time.

He bundled her putrid black shadow up into a tight ball and stashed it away safely, then watched with detachment as several of his soldiers walked over and kicked the dead queen's body, their grief and hatred overflowing finally. He didn't blame them or feel the need to chastise them for their actions. Devon walked over to the corpse and, like his troops, kicked it hard. It didn't make him feel better. So, he did it again and spat. Even that didn't give him the sense of closure that he craved.

<It's over. The fairy queen is dead. Spread the word. Her realm is ours, and it will soon become part of Sanctuary.>

Devon felt the change inside him as the queen's realm changed its allegiance and bowed to him. He experienced an infusion of power as hundreds of his people rejoiced and gave thanks. It was their happiness and the new freedom they possessed that would give him the closure he needed.

He turned and looked at the remaining nobles. "All that swear loyalty to us may leave here alive. Those that don't; won't. If you choose to live, you can join us in Sanctuary as equals. Any rank, wealth, or privilege you may have enjoyed is now completely meaningless. We expect you to contribute to the overall good just like everyone else. Understood?" The nobles looked terrified, but every one of them sank to their knees and made the oath. "Anyone who wants to join our army can come and see me in a few days. Spread the word. Now make your way over to the west wall where my people will guide you to your new homes."

The fairies trooped out of the room. Devon checked to ensure all the prone figures that remained were genuinely dead and found no less than three fairies were faking it. He killed them in short order and added their souls to his collection.

That was it, all done. The queen was dead, and his revenge realised. So why did he feel like crying? A dainty arm wrapped around his waist, and he looked down to see Izzy gazing up at him with her glowing azure eyes. His mood instantly lifted.

"My wonderful idiot," she said with a smile. "Just so we are clear, I officially resign from the army, as of now."

Devon grinned back at her thankfully. Her insults had almost become terms of endearment now. With those few words, she'd lifted his melancholy. "That's a relief. It saves me firing you."

Izzy smiled up at him. Sympathy crossed her face when she saw how tired he appeared. "You poor thing. I think you have earned some rest, relaxation, and unashamed pampering. Gwen and I will organise some volunteers. Let us take you home, lord Wayfarer." Izzy squeezed him tightly again so that he understood there would be no argument on the matter.

<Devon; creatures of Sanctuary, I am proud of each and every one of you. You have my heartfelt thanks for this victory. On this auspicious day, we begin a new chapter in our history. There may be much left to do in this realm, but we have cleansed the evil here. You all played crucial roles in the queen's downfall and the demise of all who stayed loyal to her.

I want everyone to go back through the waygate, unwind, and get some rest. What is left here will still be here when we return to sweep up tomorrow. Now is a time for celebration. Dismissed, everyone.>

Jet nuzzled him affectionately. Her warm, consoling thoughts washed over him. <We forever be proud to fight with you.>

She was always just what he needed when he was down. Devon scratched his wonderful companion's head in thanks. Like everyone, she had fought hard for this ending. He put his arm around Izzy, and they walked.

****_****

Gwen stood back and watched the god she loved with such passion embrace Izzy. Even though she had talked with Izzy about it, there was still pain there when she saw him in someone else's arms. Tiredness pulled at her, and she realised that her depression was more to do with her physical state than anything else. Devon was hers. Anyone who challenged that would die by her hand. She would share him with Izzy as long as the elf played fair. Otherwise… She didn't want to consider the 'otherwise' option. It was a dark place even for her.

<I can still read your thoughts, Gwen,> Izzy thought to her. She sent warmth and friendship with the words. There was great concern for her friend in there too.

Gwen snapped out of her darkest reverie. Izzy was her friend. The only one who could see the darkness inside her and so truly understood what she had become. That made her feel relieved, suspicious, and fearful all at once. She needed Izzy as much as Izzy needed her. One of them needed to stay by Devon's side and keep him safe. Gwen had made a pact with Jet, and they both planned to guard him well. He got hurt far too easily and needed looking after.

Jet sent Gwen thoughts of warm agreement and camaraderie. She was grateful for such a powerful ally and would proudly carry her anywhere alongside her master.

She looked back at Devon and Izzy. She was pondering what it all meant. Gwen was a novice in matters of the heart. She just knew that she wanted him so much it made her insides sting sometimes.

Izzy turned to Gwen and outstretched her free arm toward her. <Come, silly witch. He needs us now. We are allies, not enemies. You, Jet, and I. Take my hand and join us.>

Gwen didn't need to consider the elf's words. She hastened over and joined them. Devon gave her a smile that made her shiver with happiness, and Izzy took her hand. They walked through the wrecked palace toward the front entrance. When they finally got outside the building, there were two extremely long lines of soldiers and refugees on either side of the path. As the four of them made their way toward the ruins of the palace gate, applause, whistles, and cheers rang out. Tears and exclamations of utter relief escaped unchecked from over a thousand individuals. At that moment, the four of them realised just how elated the creatures of this realm must be. Their bane and the terror she induced had finally perished. Life, for them, could now begin.

****_****

Devon lay there in his bed and thought. It had been nearly two whole days of resting for him and his troops since they had taken Triana, and he wondered what he should occupy himself with next. Abi had brokered the fairy queen's soul, Entwaine's, and some other named nobles for which the Pantheon had offered bounties. Now Haven had plenty of points again. He'd even managed to repay some of the favours owed to his mentors. Yet, there was still so much more left to do.

Devon rarely slept these days and often got some of his best work done while everyone else lay sleeping, but he didn't want to leave Gwen on her own. She was currently experiencing one of her rare moments of peace as she lay asleep, curled up next to him. Her slow breathing soothed his thoughts. These days his witch only ever slept in her room when he wasn't in his. Devon knew that she suffered from brutal nightmares, but she never shared the details with him nor revealed anything about her past. The only solution he had come up with to calm her night terrors was to cuddle her when she started thrashing about madly. With his assistance, she usually recovered quickly enough to awake, remembering nothing in the morning.

Now that Devon knew the villagers better, he realised that almost everyone had experienced some form of unpleasant trauma or abuse sometime in their life. Earth realm had become an oppressive place populated by two categories of human: the perpetrators and the victims. His thoughts must now turn to this world and fixing the global mess that was turning everything toxic. But where to start? He would need to quiz his mentors for guidance.

His conscious drifting was suddenly interrupted by Beth.

<Devon! You'd better come to the war-room, right now.>

****_****

The war-room buzzed with activity. Electronic components, cables, and hardware lay strewn across the table that had risen from the floor. Office chairs haphazardly surrounded the chaos as gnomes, goblins, elves, and humans bustled about. Beth and Beks had their heads together with Glimmer, who sat on the edge of the table so that she could maintain eye contact.

They'd hit the motherlode recently during one of their hacking sessions. They had managed to obtain access to an information storage resource that belonged to Hextaine Corporation, and Beth's technomancy had allowed the team to waltz right through their security systems.

Once inside, they found that nothing was encrypted or protected. The vast quantity of data they had found was in a secure corporate data sector that nobody thought might fall into enemy hands. They'd gotten careless and been caught out by a nerd rebel with some serious magical skills and payback in the forefront of her mind. Beth had been trying to get into Hextaine Corp's key information servers since she'd been in her teens.

Over seventy-five years ago, the Hextaine Corp had taken the world hostage when the vicious C25 virus had decimated populations. As millions perished, the world's economy went into free-fall. Hextaine formed an amalgamation of some of the largest corporations and rode roughshod over governments with their mercenaries. Now governments only existed as figureheads for the corporate machinations behind them. For Hextaine, slavery was a means to an end, and they had no morals when acquiring workers. The only authority that anybody recognised these days came from the owner of the biggest gun, and Hextaine owned virtually all the guns. At least, they had done until now. Some of Glimmer's projects would make their plasma weapons look like peashooters.

As far as Beth was concerned, Hextaine was the primary enemy. The fairy queen that Devon had wanted dead so badly was just a distraction for her. Since then, Devon had asked her to find targets in Earth realm, and she would damn well find them for him.

"The facial recognition software is ready and online, mistress. Shall I start the analysis?"

"Yes, please, Abi. The image feed is there waiting for you," Beth replied. One of the primary causes for her joy was a personnel file on every employee within Hextaine. Not only that, but it had an indexed three-dimensional image repository that visually identified each person and linked them to their file. With some clever design and a hefty dose of magic, the new vision implants she was working on would be capable of recognising and identifying Hextaine's employees after just one glance. Devon would be thrilled when she presented her latest creation to him. Making him happy motivated her more than she dared admit to herself.

"Mistress, my master appears in this database, linked by marriage to one of Hextaine's six leaders. He is identified as 'ex-husband' to Jennifer Bryant. Cross-referencing files now. Outputting to display."

Beth looked at the display in wonder. Her original suspicions that Devon was part of Hextaine were indeed unfounded, and here was the proof; but he had been married to one of the six leaders of that evil corporation, and they had – "Oh shit!"

<Devon! You'd better come to the war-room, right now,> Beth thought. <You need to see this.>

<On my way. Two minutes,> Devon replied.

While she waited for him, she let her mind drift to somewhere it often went, the god she had once hit across the head with a metal pipe – her darkest moment in recent months. Devon had so rapidly become a massive part of their lives. He had raised them all to become something more than any of them could ever have imagined. The man she had initially assumed was an enemy had empowered them and let them make their own way. He had brought so many people together, and they all became stronger under his guidance. Every time she thought about him, she got itchy, and her stomach tingled. Beth fought the feelings tooth and nail, but they never left her. They'd agreed to be good friends, and that would do for the time being.

Devon rushed into the war-room and headed straight for Beth. His eye caught the rotating display that hovered above the table and skidded on the slippery floor as he went rigid in shock. "CHLOE! Chloe, my little girl? But, but how? I'd forgotten her. How could I have forgotten my precious girl? Is she alive? Where is she? If you've found her, I can go and get her, right? She could come here. Where is she, Beth? Where's my Chloe?" He sank to his knees, his brain stuttering and belching memories from Earth realm back into place for the first time since his reawakening.

<Can we get a medic to the war-room, please? Devon's brain is about to pop. You'd better get here fast,> Beks thought across the combat group bond.

"Beks! Not helpful!" Beth protested, looking at Devon with concern. His eyes were flicking in random directions and were unnaturally wide. He had started to look manic.

"Look at him. I'm not wrong," Beks said.

"Devon, please! Just calm down and listen," Beth said, trying to keep her voice relaxed and using downward-facing palm motions in an attempt to soothe his turmoil. "We have found her, and yes, she is alive." Beth hesitated and bit her bottom lip in uncertainty. It didn't matter how she worded this next bit; he was going to lose the plot.

Glimmer jumped into a standing position on the table and turned to face Devon. Her big golden-brown eyes were damp and full of worry. "Boss, I'm afraid we have some bad news."

The end.

From the author

Thank you so much for reading my first book. I hope that you enjoyed the experience and that you would like to read more. Devon and his ragtag band of refugees will be back in the next book in the Reaper saga – 'The Wayfarer's Daughter'.

Visit my website (dougalreed.com) for news, artwork, extracts and more. You can also sign up for my news mailer there.

All comments would be appreciated but please, keep them constructive. I will strive to improve as I go, and with your comments, I will understand how.

You can find me on :

- Website - dougalreed.com
- Facebook – dougalreed
- Twitter – dougalreed
- Instagram - dougalreed

Stay well.

Dougal

Printed in Great Britain
by Amazon

62511935R00153